SISTER TO THE FAE

FOOL'S GOLD

D. H. Irving

WingSpan Press

Published in the United States and the United Kingdom by WingSpan Press, Livermore, CA

The WingSpan name, logo and colophon are the trademarks of WingSpan Publishing.

ISBN 978-1-59594-604-1 (pbk.)
ISBN 978-1-59594-665-2 (hardcover)
ISBN 978-1-59594-924-0 (ebk.)

First edition 2017

Printed in the United States of America

www.wingspanpress.com

Library of Congress Control Number 2017932458

1 2 3 4 5 6 7 8 9 10

To my girls, who have never read a single thing that I've written, and because of that will never see this.

Chapter One

I've never really considered myself a hero in the classical sense...
...or in any sense, to be perfectly honest.

Physically, I'm probably the last person that you'd think of when the discussion turns to noble deeds and unwavering courage. Where your average hero is tall, muscular and usually sporting a cartoonishly chiseled jawline, I'm of average height, average build, and have what my partner affectionately refers to as a "butt chin". My hair, short cropped, dark brown and messily tousled with more gel than I'd every openly admit, is about as far as you can get from the image of some romance novel beefcake with his long blonde locks blowing majestically around him. *My* hair wouldn't move in a frigging hurricane, let alone in some unseen theatrical breeze.

Mentally, while I understand and even appreciate that things like bravery and valor have their place in our world, I like to stay as far away from there as humanly possible. Don't get me wrong; I'm not exactly a coward, really, I've just learned that life isn't some late night movie or storybook fantasy. Fights may look cool or seem badass on television, but in real life getting punched in the face hurts.

A *lot.*

You could argue that courage is its own reward, or point out that it's always the gallant knight who rescues the princess and saves the day, and you'd be right. I myself can't help but notice that the hero usually has to climb over a pile of discarded bones and bleached skulls in order to do it. If being more cautious than courageous keeps me from becoming one of the skeletons that Fabio struts triumphantly past during his post-damsel banging victory lap? I'm kind of okay with that.

The point is, I'm no hero. So naturally, when the higher-ups at work decided to throw an award ceremony in my honor, I immediately felt like the world's biggest fraud.

The feeling began roughly six months ago, when I was the victim of a violent mugging, and has persisted since. While I have no memory of the robbery that landed me in the hospital, I do vividly recall waking up there with a killer migraine and pretty much nothing else. After giving my statement to the police, I was quickly discharged due to my lacking of anything that even remotely resembled health insurance, and sent to recover in the privacy of my own home.

Which I did, until the goblins burned it down.

I know now from both my ongoing training and the never ending stream of books that my partner constantly nags me to actually read and "not just look at the pictures", that the creatures who torched my apartment were indeed, goblins. At the time however, I thought that I was either going insane, or at the very least, hallucinating my way through a haze of some really good hospital drugs. Unfortunately, the police and fire officials who listened to my explanation as to why the apartment building had gone up in a raging inferno leaving dozens homeless, decided that the "raving lunatic" angle was a bit more plausible and tossed my ass into an asylum.

Believe it or not, being committed to a mental health facility actually turned out to be the highpoint of that day, because this is where I met my current employers, the lovely ladies of the F.P.I.

The Department of Fae Propinquity and Inquiry is a little known, but incredibly sexy government agency tasked with keeping an eye on the fairy world that occasionally bleeds over into our own. Yes, I realize how that sounds, and if you would have told me six months ago that fairies were real I would have forced a polite smile while casually checking your forehead for the telltale signs of tinfoil hat poisoning.

But it's true; goblins are real. So are imps, leprechauns and a million other mythical creatures that love to dance between their world and ours while stirring up all sorts of trouble along the way. According to my partner Raegan, there is a long and comprehensive explanation as to how all of this started; but it's boring as hell and I wasn't paying attention well enough at the time to grab a lot of the finer details.

But I did get the gist, which is almost as good and saves us all a ton of time.

Basically our world and the fairy world used to be the same place, then some epic-yet-surprisingly-tedious disaster struck and we were nearly torn in two. Now instead of one whole world we sort of over-lap, with little chunks of the fairy realm clinging to ours like a sticker that you can't quite scrape off.

The Fae were yanked to one half, and we humans were pulled to the other, but because we all used to be in the same place and fairies are pretty much winged horn-balls, there were creatures of mixed blood that didn't belong on either side. The majority of these poor bastards died almost instantly, literally ripped in two...I think. Again, I wasn't paying as much attention as I should have been. This stuff might sound exciting now, but when its being read to you in a teacher's monotone out of a book that looks like it should be chewing on Bruce Campbell's hand? Not so much.

Those that weren't torn in half or whatever, ended up on our side. But without fairies to mate with, their bloodlines became more and more human with every passing generation. Eventually the gifts and abilities usually associated with having Fae blood became little more than a recessive gene and a weakened reminder of the past.

Fast-forward a few hundred generations and occasionally a kid will still be born with some of their senses attuned to the fairy world. Whenever this happens, the FPI sweeps in and works with the family to ensure that their child is taught to fine tune and even consciously use their abilities. Those born with the sense of sight are raised as "Seers", and have pretty much won the genetic lottery as it is the rarest of all gifts. These kids are treated like royalty and promptly whisked away for a life of pampering, ass-kissing, and whatever the hell bonbons are.

Those born with any of the other senses are raised as Keepers of the Knowledge or "Keepers" for short, and sent to work as a Seer's companion. Although their talents are still usually pretty impressive, their primary role is to focus on the lore and history of the Fae. After a time-honored bonding ritual, the Seers and Keepers join together in harmony so that between the two of them they can work as one whole functioning person.

Keepers with the gift of hearing are in the greatest demand, as Seer's can usually only see into the fairy world and I assume that lip-reading is difficult if the creature you're dealing with doesn't have lips. Despite their differences, there are two things that Seers and Keepers always have in common: They are always incredibly, unfairly beautiful – a gift given by their fairy blood; and they are always, with absolutely no exceptions, female.

Until me.

It seems that the complimentary bump to my head that came free with my mugging jarred something loose in a way that they still can't quite explain. While I'm extremely male (*ladies*), without so much as a drop of fairy blood in my veins, I now have all six senses fully attuned to the fairy world at all times.

And I don't even have to concentrate.

This has earned me a place within the agency, and the ire of some of the more talented Seers who resent both my ability and the fact that I almost always pee standing up. Sadly, while I excel in raw, albeit unexplained talent, I lack any sort of actual training. The fairy world is a vast and in most cases, confusing place, and without the knowledge to go along with my ability I was seen as more of a danger than asset, so they paired me with a Keeper of my very own. At the time I had hoped that the bonding ritual would involve massage oils and dimly lit candles, but instead I ended up with something that I hadn't had since childhood: A family.

It turns out that exchanging energies and linking spirits and all of that hippy new-age crystal stuff is more of a fraternal practice than sexual one, which is good because just thinking about Raegan in that way is more than enough to give me an epic case of the dry heaves.

Not that she isn't drop dead gorgeous. Petite and fair-skinned with fiery red hair and emerald green eyes, she's beautiful enough to turn heads no matter where she goes. It's just now that we've bonded, I see her as more of a sister than anything else, which is probably for the best as there are no "urges" to distract us.

Seriously, none. We tried kissing once and both of us wanted to puke, so that crap's right off the table.

Paired, ritualistically bound and sent on our very first assignment, we ended up keeping a nice sized chunk of New York from exploding and stopped a crazy fairy from punching her way through the barrier that separates our worlds. It's a long story, but in the end we saved the day and were met with a Hero's welcome, which as I stated earlier, was super awkward.

And all of this was during my first week on the job.

So how do you top that? Well sadly, you don't. After the excitement died down and the congratulatory store bought cakes were eaten, my days at the Agency were spent less on killer fairies and more on training. Given my abilities, most of the Seer classes were a breeze; but the books and the studying and the Keeper testing?

Nightmares.

To make matters worse, Raegan takes all of this academic stuff super seriously and constantly grills me on whatever information that she thinks I should have learned in class. She carries around flash cards and *everything*. Just like that, my fast paced and exciting days in the FPI ended and I was restricted to training exercises and the tedium of book learning.

My only reprieve is the occasional case where I'm needed to eyeball some particularly hard to see pixie, and…

…my monthly liaison meeting with the leprechauns.

Despite what the cartoons or cheesy horror movies would have you believe, leprechauns actually look more like something out of the Lord of the Rings than some poorly drawn college mascot. Around four foot tall and thickly built, their bald heads shine in stark contrast to the long red beards that obscure their barrel-like chests. They're rude, crude and surprisingly perverted; not to mention quick to anger and even quicker to take revenge. Each and every one of them is a liar, a braggart and a cheat, and best of all, they've accepted me as one of their own.

Originally in an effort to teach my fellow Seer and self-appointed rival, McKenna Wallace, a lesson in manners and decorum, they stripped her of her title as "Liaison to the Leprechaun Council" and gave it to me, along with all of her clothing.

Like I said, "surprisingly perverted".

Luckily this proved to be only a temporary position and ended well before I had to act in any official capacity. Once the leprechauns felt that she had truly learned her lesson, they returned McKenna's title and position and I was subsequently demoted to "Relations Manager". This meant that instead of the quarterly meetings with the council members of the Seelie Court in which Agent Wallace spoke on behalf of the Agency and all of humanity, I was to report directly to the leprechauns themselves on the last Friday of every month to assist with the crucial tasks of drunken debauchery and poker.

Which is where I was headed now.

The drive to the pub in Boston that the leprechauns called home was a bit of a haul from depths of New York City, but I didn't mind. It felt good to get out from beneath the pile of musty text books and besides, I rarely ever get to drive. That duty usually falls to my Keeper who loves nothing more than to pinball her way down the express lane at speeds usually reserved for stunt pilots or space craft re-entering the atmosphere. Still, for all of her hairpin turns and Dukes of Hazzard style ramp jumping, she's actually a much better driver than I am and always seems reluctant to relinquish the keys.

Darby's Authentic Irish Pub was named after its owner Darby

O'Neill who had passed away a few years back. While I never had the honor of meeting him, over the last few months I've developed something of a friendly familiarity with his son Connor who had inherited not only his father's tavern, but his debt to the leprechauns who occasionally inhabited it. If the obligation was in any way a burden or a curse to Connor, he never let on. In fact, I suspected that he actually enjoyed it on some level.

Loose gravel crunched and popped under the tire of the company issued sedan as I pulled off the main road and into the pub's parking lot. Despite it being late afternoon on a Friday, the lot was mostly empty, save for a few familiar vehicles that may or may not have moved since my last visit. Coming to a stop close to the front entrance, I pulled the keys from the ignition and looked over the seat into the back of car.

My bounty was still there, safe and sound.

Like most Fae, leprechauns have an inherent weakness for milk; a weakness that I now seemed to share. Whatever it was that gave me my ability to interact with the fairy world also passed on, to a thankfully much lesser extent, a few of their flaws. Iron is a death sentence to most Fae, with even the briefest touch causing blisters, burns, and untold pain. To me, it's a mild irritant that causes a bumpy, itchy rash akin to poison ivy. While it doesn't really *hurt* me, I now go out of my way to avoid touching it lest I suffer from an extremely noticeable case of "yuck fingers".

Milk on the other hand, is nothing short of amazing. Cool, crisp and refreshing, it tastes sweeter, goes down smoother and gets them drunker than the finest tequila; a fact that was no longer lost on me, or the large metal canister that I had secured safely in the back seat.

Stepping out of the car with a quick stretch and brisk rub of my driving-numbed ass, I opened the rear door and carefully retrieved the milk churn from a makeshift container of now melted ice. Sloshing with a hollow splash of creamy white, I resisted the urge to sneak a quick sip, knowing full well that the boys would take insult if I started without them.

Fresh this morning from the seedy underbelly of the raw dairy black market, something that I swear to god actually exists, it cost more than you'd believe someone would ever be willing to pay for milk. My dealer, a young woman with dreadlocks and no apparent self-awareness in regards to her rather impressive display of armpit hair, assured me that it was one hundred percent organic, grass fed raw cow's milk, and I believed her. If you're going to buy illegal milk from a farming themed black market, the barefoot stoner chick in a sleeveless Phish t-shirt is rarely, if ever going to steer you wrong.

Heavier than I remember it being due to the metal churn and not my ridiculously weak girly arms, I had to heft the container of milk to near chest level as I penguin-walked it to the entrance of the pub. Awkwardly trapping it between my body and the outside wall as I fumbled with the doorknob, I wedged my heel in the crack of the door and pulled it open, half-spinning inside.

The pub looked exactly as it always did. Darker than the late afternoon that drooped lazily outside, but light enough to easily see once your eyes adjusted, the smell of stale beer and deep-fried every-thing washed over me in a disgusting-yet-delicious wafting of warm air. The pub was nearly empty save the hunched over forms of a few regulars and the bartender who now eyed me with an almost unper-ceivable arch of his brow.

"Mister Talik." He said with a nod of greeting, the unmistakable hint of an Irish accent lilting his words.

"Heya Conner." I nodded back, letting the door close behind me as I readjusted my grip on the can. "How goes?"

"Fair ta middlin'." He shrugged, polishing a mug with an old rag. That was always his answer, and almost always the extent of our conversations. Tall and thin with a pair of thick red mutton chops that crept out from under the sides of an old tweed cap, Conner was more a listener than a talker; a trait that I suspected came with his years of tending bar. Cocking his head to one side as I stepped further in, he eyed the milk churn with a hint of interest before offering me a rare second voice.

"Bit early this month, aren't ya?" He asked with the forced non-chalance of a man who already knew the answer.

I shifted the milk and glanced at my wrist to the watch that I wasn't wearing.

"Am I?" I asked, pausing in step. Conner wasn't exactly the chatty type, and the additional dialogue was throwing me off.

"Aye. A bit." He answered, nodding with the back of his head to the clock on the wall behind him.

"Huh. Damn thing must be fast." I frowned, still staring at my bare wrist. "Everything okay?" I asked suspiciously as I looked back to him. I may not be the sharpest knife on the Christmas tree, but I'm clever enough to know that when a quiet man goes out of his way to talk, you should probably listen.

Especially if he's in the employ of all-powerful creatures prone to mischief.

"Everything's fine." He assured. "Our mutual friends just told me that if ya were to show up early, I was to let ya know that they'll most likely still be settin' up for your meetin', and that you'd probably want to make a bit of a ruckus when ya popped in."

"The boys said that?" There was a playful warning to his tone, but it was still a warning.

"Aye. Somethin' about the dangers of how certain folks tend to react to bein' startled." He answered with the faintest hint of a smile.

I let that sink in.

"That's probably good advice." I admitted after a moment of imagined horror and chaos. "I'll do that. Thanks Conner."

Focusing my eyes on the door labeled "Office" at the back of the bar, I resumed my walk only to have the unusually chatty bartender call out behind me.

"Oh, and Mister Talik?"

"Yeah?" I asked, looking over my shoulder.

"That's a lovely shirt."

I let out a sharp bark of laughter and kept walking. If you were going to play poker with leprechauns, you needed two things; a thick skin and a sense of humor. Loud, obnoxious and bawdy by nature, I had been cheated a hundred times, told a thousand lies and insulted more times than I could count; so today I was going to have a bit of fun at *their* expense.

The door to the office was just that; a door and nothing else. Recessed into the back wall, there was no knob, no hinges, and no visible way of opening it. The patrons either assumed that it was a joke and part of the décor, like the dusty head of the horned rabbit adorning the wall of the men's room, or that it was magnetically sealed and could only be opened by Conner from behind the bar. All sorts of rumors surrounded it, but I was one of the few that knew the truth: The door was a portal to the fairy realm; or at least a small pocket of it.

With the separation of our worlds being anything but neat, little blobs of the fairy realm still occasionally bled over into ours, which frequently explained things like ghosts, haunted houses, or that one basement from your childhood that they couldn't pay you to go down into. Spots where the realms were still intertwined, especially large spaces, are pretty rare; so they're coveted by the Fae and often used as a bridge into our world.

Standing in front of the door, I carefully set down the canister of milk and fully unbuttoned my over-shirt. The cereal box leprechaun emblazoned on the t-shirt beneath it stared happily up at me in mid-frolic as he protected the marshmallow bits of sugar that those pesky kids were always after.

Okay, so it wasn't the most subtle or clever of digs, but in my defense, they absolutely *hated* him.

Reaching under the shirt that was going to probably be torn off in a half-scale fist fight at some point tonight, I groped around for the coin that I now wore around my neck as a charm. Feeling the cold metal disc brush my fingertips, I pulled it from beneath the fabric and held it up in the sparse light of the bar.

Pure gold in design, it slid smoothly along the gold chain that somehow supported it, affixed by fairy magic in a manner that I couldn't discern. The surface of the coin was practically flawless, marred only by two small dents in its surface.

It was my key.

Leprechaun coins are a funny thing, and by funny I mean "absolutely disgusting". You see, if you ever get your hands on a true coin, one of the few boons given as favor by the small Fae, they are obligated to grant you a single wish, which, because they're a bunch of miserable bastards, they hate doing. It saps them of their juice for a short while, and as they've described it, leaves them feeling like they have the world's worst hangover. So, in order to dissuade those who would seek them out for wishes and riches, they came up with an "alternate" version of the coin which they would not only freely distribute when asked, but more than likely leave somewhere for someone they disliked to miraculously "find". While the coin seems to be of the purest, finest gold in every way, it holds a sinister secret: You can melt it, craft it, polish it, or even give it as a gift; but the moment that you tried to spend it, use it as a form of payment, or bring it to your lips in a wish activating kiss, it reverts to its true form.

Which we won't get into except to say that it is probably the very worst thing that you'd ever want to put in your mouth, and I'm gagging a little bit just thinking of it.

The coin that I now held in my hand had once been one of those and the dents in its surface were from a test of the metal's authenticity. The leprechauns, so amused by my verification of the coin, had used their infinite magic to alter its true and ick-filled nature and repurposed it into what it now was; my passport into their pocket of fairy space.

Leaning forward I touched the coin to the door's flat surface. There was a soft cracking sound as the barrier was broken and the door swung open. Tucking the necklace back beneath my shirt, I picked up the milk and headed in as the portal slowly closed behind me. A few wooden steps brought me down into the store room where the mystical and wonderful items of the fairy realm such as "extra napkins" and "toilet cleaner" were shelved. Moving past these exotic items and to the double red doors that only appeared to those who had properly entered, I remembered Conner's words and took a deep breath.

"Alright you redheaded little smurfs, Daddy's coming for your

LUCKY CHARMS!" I yelled out, opening the doors with my back as I spun in.

The room, if you could call it a room, was draped in its usual darkness. Of course, being of pure Fae space it only felt like a room. In reality, the only walls that I could see were lit just well enough to show the myriad of paintings that hung from them. Actual, discernable things like corners and dimensions were hidden by the impossible blackness that obscured everything around me, making the place seem more like an endless warehouse than the cozy poker parlor I had come to know and love.

Normally, there would be a single unadorned light bulb hanging from some unseen ceiling as it illuminated the poker table and the five chairs stationed around it representing our official monthly "meeting".

Tonight was different.

A light still shone in the near darkness, but the card table, tacky paintings and four jolly occupants were missing. Instead, under the much paler, more somber light of the globe of magical energy floating above them, was a small gathering of Fae and fairy-folk that I didn't recognize.

And they were all staring at me.

"Uh. Hi." I said awkwardly, suddenly hyper aware of the fact that I was wearing what some might consider an offensive novelty t-shirt. The silence hung heavy in the darkness, lingering with the faint echo of unspoken words.

"John Talik." A woman's voice called in greeting. It was soft, sensual and laced with sultry undertones that made my heart dance in my chest. "What convenient timing." There was a knowing amusement in her words. "We were just discussing you."

Setting down the heavy canister of milk with a slowness born of caution, I took a couple of hesitant steps forward and brought myself closer to the group. Their backlit silhouettes slowly parted, bending and blending back into the shadows as I drew near.

The woman who had spoken was tall and beautiful, the delicate features of her face peeking from beneath the silver hood of the gossamer robes that draped her frame, outlining every perfect curve. Well over six foot tall and built like the default blueprint for all things Nordic, she stood poised amongst two smaller groups like a mediator separating factions. To her right stood all four of my boys; the small group of leprechauns that I had come to call my friends.

And they looked *pissed*.

Seething beneath their fancy red coats and well pressed matching pants, they glowered in embarrassment, the points of the elaborate caps that they now wore quivering with barely contained anger. With faces as red as the beards that hung from them, they stared daggers into me from the darkness and mouthed silent curses in my direction that I really didn't want to try and understand.

To the mediator's left were three figures that I hadn't seen before my grand entrance, two of which could only be described as "elves". Lithe, haughty, and obviously disgusted by my presence, the tips of their slender, pointy ears peeked through long blonde hair so pale that it was in danger of being mislabeled as white. Slightly taller than the man that stood between them, the remaining stranger was both familiar to me, yet utterly bizarre at the same time.

He was a leprechaun. Sort of. Dressed completely in black, he had all the makings of a classic Disney villain. Buttons and intricate patterns of gold laced his clothing, and he smiled triumphantly at me through a thick, but neatly sculpted beard as dark as the fabric that he wore. Running a well-manicured hand through his head of full, raven black hair, he turned to the woman that separated him from his red clad cousins and bowed slightly.

"As you can clearly see, the human's outlandish arrival only serves to further illustrate my point." He said smoothly, his voice driven velvet by the slime that all but dripped from it.

"I believe that they could say the same." The tall woman smiled, nodding elegantly to the group of leprechauns at her right. Quirking her head as she stared at me, the woman never took so much as a single step, but in an instant she was before me, her hand cupping my chin in a soft, supple grasp as she sought my eyes with her own. I was lost, swallowed in a vision of beauty so profound that my heart began to ache in her presence.

"And they would not be wrong, would they?" She whispered seductively as she studied my face.

I was helpless to do anything but stare and pray that I wasn't drooling on her shoes.

"Surely you would not side with them!" The dark leprechaun objected, his voice threaded with anger and disbelief.

"I take no sides Fenrus." She responded, instantly back in her original position between the two groups as if she had never moved. There was an underlying warning to her tone and the small man caught it as quickly as I had.

"Of course, Milady." He said, offering a quick bow in way of apology. "I did not mean to suggest–"

"This one's thread is not for our eyes, that alone warrants consideration." The woman mused. "The current arrangement shall stand."

The dark leprechaun now called Fenrus forced a tight lipped grimace of acceptance that spoke of anything but. His companions exchanged worried glances as the smaller man stepped back into their group, his ire filled gaze turning to me.

"Thank you, your Ladyship." Seamus, the leader of *my* leprechauns said with a humble bow, his deep voice breaking the agitated silence. "As always, you are as fair as you are wise."

"And *you* would be wise to get that one a time piece, Seamus." She said sternly, but with what I swore was the barest hint of delight. "These meetings are not for the Kind. Even one as unique as this." She added with a glance in my direction.

"Of course, of course. A thousand apologies." He admonished, obviously embarrassed. "We'll be havin' a word with the lad in private." I caught his eye as he spoke, his inflection like that of a parent waiting for other adults to leave the room so that they could beat their child behind closed doors.

Which really sucked for me.

"Well then." The woman said with a pleased sigh, her voice once again melodic and wonderful. "Court is adjourned. Good day."

14

Chapter Two

When a fairy disappears or crosses back into their world from our own, it never looks anything like the way that it does in the movies or popular fiction. There's no flash of smoke or explosion of glitter and sparkles; they're just *gone*.

The large female Fae was the first to leave, casually blinking out of existence with the sudden nothingness of a poorly spliced film. One moment she was standing before us, tall, exotic and beautiful, and the next she was simply not there. Fenrus and his two elven companions, obviously in disagreement with whatever had been decided, quickly followed. The darkness that obscured the room swallowed them in the space between heartbeats, the outline of where they stood still burned into my vision in a haze of grey.

With the meeting disbanded and its participants departed, I suddenly found myself alone with four rather annoyed looking leprechauns.

Seamus, Beircheart, Padraig and Michail were nearly identical in size and shape, to the point where most would probably have difficulty in telling them apart. Barrel chested and stocky, their solid, thickly muscled build made up for any lack of height that would otherwise allow for them to be mistaken as children. With their bald heads and long red beards, a source of pride among their kind, they looked infinitely more menacing than any drawing or cartoon could possibly depict.

And they were all staring at *me*.

"Seamus…" I started to apologize. Seamus was the eldest among the four and unquestionably their leader, if they actually had such a thing. Hard green eyes the color of cut grass narrowed as the small man held up one hand in silence and stalked towards me.

"Did you…" He growled, his fingers clenching into heavy, calloused fists. "…see the look on his face when ya came screamin' in like a feckin' banshee?" He asked jovially, his tone shifting to humorous heights before ending in a long, mirth-filled laugh. "Looked like he just got a mouthful of his own coin!"

I shook my head, let out a sigh of relief and unclenched my ass.

While I didn't think for even a second that any of them would ever do anything to hurt me, those occasional unexpected reminders that my friends were all-powerful, all-knowing Fae with godlike abilities tended to set my butt to "pucker".

Cursing into a chuckle under my breath, I turned to retrieve the milk churn and was thankful to see the familiar card table and tacky wall decorations now in place as I spun back to face them. Walking towards the group, I stepped onto the dark platform that marked the poker room and sat the container beside the too-small, fairy-sized chair that had been designated as mine. The seat had once belonged to Fergus, a leprechaun who had gotten into a bit of trouble and had come to me for help.

Sort of.

While I had never actually met Fergus, he had taken to visiting me between dreams and bouts of forced unconsciousness. Murdered by a woman that he had once hoped to help, it was his death that had led me here and to the group of leprechauns that had quickly become my friends. It was his influence that had guided me, and I strongly suspect, encouraged his brothers to readily accept me into the fold.

"So…what was that all about?" I asked, easily straddling the small chair as I slid up to the table. "And what's the deal with Hans Gruber's littler brother? He looked familiar." I had the feeling that I had seen the darkly dressed Fae before, but I couldn't quite scratch the itch at the back of my brain that would tell me where.

"Noticed that one, didja?" Beircheart asked sourly as he joined me at the poker table. While I hadn't seen him, or any of the others actually change, their clothing was no longer the fancy and overelaborate dress of the Seelie Court. Their ornate coats had been exchanged for rough spun tunics and comfortable pants the color of scrubbed rust and their bald heads gleamed in the overhead light, now devoid of the silly caps that they only minutes before wore.

"Kind of hard to miss the guy dressed like a photo negative of Santa Claus." I shrugged. "I take it he's the bad guy in tonight's film?"

The smallest of the four, Michail, snorted disdainfully. "His name is Fenrus." He grumbled. "Fergus' ne're-do-well brother."

"To Fergus!" Padraig toasted, hefting high a stone mug as it materialized in his hand.

"TO FERGUS!" The rest of us echoed, each lifting our own magically appearing drinks in response. The fact that the milk churn that I had brought was missing and that I was now holding an old, intricately carved stone mug full of frothy white liquid barely even registered as something that should faze me.

Fergus might be gone, but his legacy would never be. In the few months that I had been coming to these "meetings", I had drank to his memory a hundred times, and would likely do so a hundred times more. Leprechauns are big on toasting – be it to the memory of a departed friend, friendship itself, or anything else that they may deem toast worthy in the whim of a fleeting moment.

"Fergus had a brother?" I asked, taking a long pull from my mug. The milk was as amazing as I had hoped and I felt my mood lighten considerably as I began to relax.

"Aye." Seamus confirmed, wiping his bearded mouth on the back of his sleeve. "But don' let that fact sway ya, lad." He shook a finger in slow emphasis. "He ain't one of us."

"No matter how badly he wants ta be." Padraig said dryly,

producing a deck of well-worn playing cards and sliding them across the table to Michail.

"So he's *not* a leprechaun?" I questioned through another sip of the milk, which was quite frankly, amazing. Those hippy chicks really know their stuff.

"Oh, he's of tha blood sure enough." Seamus admitted reluctantly. "But that one's… different." He added as he glanced meaningfully between the others.

"He's got a darkness about him. Sets our skin ta prickle." Padraig explained.

"Likes ta play in things that best be left alone." Beircheart added, drawing a round of mumbled agreements.

"Takes pride in consortin' with all sorts of *unsavories*." Michail grunted. There was unspoken contempt stressed in the last word.

"More unsavory than *you* little bastards?" I questioned in disbelief.

The leprechauns laughed in open amusement, Padraig going as far as to toast the dig with a nod of his head and the raising of his mug.

"Aye. Much." Seamus nodded after a swig of his drink. "We're bastards one an' all, that's fair enough. But him? That one is…" He trailed off as if searching for a word that he really didn't want to find.

"Evil?" I supplied over the rim of my cup.

Seamus seemed to consider my words for a long moment before finally shaking his head no.

"Would be a lot easier if it were just a matter of him bein' evil." He sighed. "Evil ain't a hard concept. Evil we can understand." Murmurs of agreement were drown by the gulping of milk as the leprechauns sat in a rare, thoughtful silence.

"Aye. But it's worse than evil, now ain't it?" Padraig looked around the table, only to be greeted by frowns as he spoke. "We've known it fer a while now, but none of us wanna say it, so we keep it quiet for Fergus."

"To Fergus." There was no joy in the toast and they lifted their drinks much slower, physically labored by their thoughts.

"What's worse than *evil*?" I asked nervously.

Now, I can't stress enough how little attention I pay in my classes. No matter how cool the subject matter might seem, the ancient books and old crumbly scrolls that the lessons come from have this way of turning everything into a set of stereo instructions read by Ferris Bueller's teacher. That being said, from the small amount of accidentally gleaned knowledge that I did acquire, I knew that if the most potent Fae in existence called something "worse than evil", chances are that it had to be pretty bad.

My butt resumed its earlier state of clenching.

"Fenrus is…" Padraig chewed on the word. Struggling with it, he glanced to Seamus for help.

"Ambitious." Seamus swore, causing each of the men to turn their heads and spit.

Which given the amount of milk that they were pounding, was really, really gross.

"Ambitious." I echoed, unsure if the theatrics were real or the setup of some elaborate hoax that I wasn't in on. Once again the leprechauns turned their heads to one side and spat, and once again it was really, really nasty.

"It just ain't *natural*." Padraig explained, his voice breathy and strained with disbelief.

Leprechauns are lazy, which is great news for everybody because humanity on a whole would be boned if they weren't. Their natural sloth is what keeps the rest of us from being at the center of their constant mischief. Nearly immortal, a breath from omnipotent and brimming with magical abilities, the only thing keeping them "in check" is the fact that they don't usually stop goofing off long enough to really focus on anything.

"Okay. So he's amb-motivated." I amended in fear of inspiring more milk loogies. "What's his deal?" I asked. "Oh! And who was that big chick?" The memory of Amazonian hotness came sashaying back to my forethoughts as I asked.

"Ohhh." Beircheart drawled. "Took notice of her as well, did you?" There was an implied naughtiness to his tone.

"*That* my boy, was the Norn." Seamus explained, an undeniable respect shining in his eyes.

Something sparked the faintest of lights at the back of my brain. I had heard the term before, but was unsure as to where. The memory fluttered at the edge of recall, trailing snippets of half-thought just out of reach.

"Um, books and what-not right?" I asked with uncertainty. "Hangs out in libraries?"

"She watches over the threads of fate as they're woven into the very canvas of life." Padraig said in a hushed, reverent tone.

"Yeah, I have no idea what that means." I said.

Beircheart laughed over the edge of his drink. "Well ya might want to start payin' attention." His lewd grin accentuated by a lecherous waggle of his brows. "'Cause now she's got them eyes on *you*."

"On me? Why?" I choked. Even for a shameless attention whore such as myself, I knew that the spotlight was no place to be when it came to the Fae, no matter how hot they were.

"That langer Fenrus figured ya out and went snitchin' straight to her skirt." Michail chuffed.

"I'm guessin' that he expected the meeting to go a bit differently." Padraig said. "Her decision can't be sittin' too well with him."

"Aye. That sneaky bastage will find a way around the rulin', sure enough." Seamus agreed. "Keep an eye out for that one lad. He'll be comin' for ya, more sooner than later I wager." The warning came so nonchalantly that it took me a minute to realize that he wasn't joking.

"Wait, you're serious?" I panicked. "Fenrus is coming after me? What for? I mean, what in the *hell* did I ever do to him?"

"It ain't what ya did, it's what yer keepin' him from doin'." Padraig said, flickering a gaze to Seamus as if waiting for permission.

"Okay guys, you know how much I hate the cryptic fairy shit." I complained. I was used to the teasing, and normally it wouldn't even faze me – but if a pissed off miniature Johnny Cash impersonator was gunning for me, I'd like to at least know why.

Seamus gave a tired smile and nodded in agreement. "Aye. I

suppose it is." He sighed. "Go on Paddy. We've had our fun fer long enough. Let tha boy in on the joke."

"Ya sure now?" Came the hesitant reply.

"Aye." He confirmed.

Looking between us for a few seconds, Padraig finally shrugged and motioned towards my seat. "Fenrus wants tha chair yer sittin' in."

I frowned. "That's it? Hell, let him have it." I said, standing. The seat was way too small for me anyway.

"Not the actual chair ya idjit." Michail grumbled with a roll of his eyes.

"He wants the spot that Fergus left open. The spot yer *sitting in*?" Padraig added when I continued to look on in confusion.

"He wants Fergus' coin." Beircheart clarified with a chuckle.

Fergus' coin.

There are three types of coin associated with leprechauns; the unmentionable "poop coin" that they just *love* to hand out like the world's nastiest candy, a boon coin that grants the owner a single, unfettered wish…

…and the fabled soul coin that contains the leprechaun's essence and the very source of their ungodly power.

When Fergus was murdered, he had managed to send his coin away before it could be taken from him and used for evil. Until now I was under the impression that it had been lost, but if Fenrus wanted it, it meant that the boys had either found it, or even more likely, had it all along.

"You found it?" I asked skeptically.

"Round aboutly speakin'." Seamus said uneasily as he scratched at the back of his neck.

"So you do have it. I *knew* it." I said, his discomfort confirming my suspicions. "Are you going to give it to him?"

"No." The four leprechauns said in perfect, almost practiced unison.

"Why not?" I frowned. If giving the pint-sized Sheriff of Nottingham the coin kept him from coming after me, I was all for it.

"Firstly, it ain't ours ta give." Seamus started, shaking a single finger in explanation. "When one of us passes, all that we are goes back to all that we come from. When the time is right, and our peace has been made, the coin goes where it should go. It ain't up to any of us to say otherwise." His voice was hushed with respect. "And secondly…"

"Not one of us likes the uppity prick." Michail interrupted. This brought about a fresh chorus of agreement laced with rude comments, most of which were centered around Fenrus' hair.

"Make no mistake; he's got plans, that one." Beircheart said to no one in particular as he cut the deck of cards that Michail offered him. "Dark plans."

"Aye, well, there's no secret to which side of the court that fancy bastard takes a shinin' to, now is there?" Padraig said under his breath, drawing more murmurs of consent.

I looked around the table, still not following the conversation as well as I'd like to. Accepted as I was, I was still an outsider, so much of what they said went unspoken beyond a knowing look or a grunt of acknowledgment.

"So what does any of this have to do with me?" I asked, uncertain.

Seamus put a meaty hand on the back of mine and patted gently. The gesture was warm with untold patience.

"Ya met Fergus." He paused in thought. "Or at the very least, ya met a shade of him. Ya know better than most the things that he dabbled in and the things that he chose to do." Seamus's eyes looked infinitely sad at even mentioning it:

Blood magic.

Blood magic was the last resort of any "good" Fae. Wild, unpredictable and often coming at a steep price, it was frowned upon by all but the darkest of fairies. Fergus had used it, not to harm another, but to keep his own coin from falling into the hands of someone who had intended on using it to bring pain and misery upon the world. The fact that he knew how to cast it was a stain on his name; the fact that he actually did…

"That's not fair." I said a bit too defensively, a part of me wanting to protect the departed leprechaun's reputation. "He was trying to do what was right."

Seamus smiled softly. "No one here would dare argue that. In the end, Fergus set his wrongs right, true as true. But blood magic is unpredictable. Raw. There's a reason we don't dabble in them things, and there's a reason that his coin didn't pass on as cleanly as it should have."

"But now you have it." I pointed out again, but the statement was starting to sound like a question.

"Not *exactly*, as it were." Seamus hesitated. "Ya see, when Fergus sent that piece of himself away, and used blood magic to do it, things got, ahh..."

"Muddled." Beircheart supplied.

"Confused." Padraig offered.

"Fecked right up." Michail said bluntly, finally dealing the cards.

Seamus snapped his fingers and pointed to Michail, the grumpy leprechaun's vulgarity apparently summing up the situation with the most accuracy.

"So where is it?" I asked suspiciously, a dark feeling creeping over me.

Padraig forced a nonchalant shrug. "It weren't exactly a clean passin', per se."

"Per se." Beircheart agreed. "With tha blood and the chaos and all, it kinda got stuck."

"Stuck where?" The looming darkness grew by leaps and bounds. If they thought that I was going on some silly trek for a missing coin, then they-

"In yer head." Michail shrugged. "Ante up." He said, gesturing to the middle of the poker table.

"What?!" I yelped, standing so quickly that the small chair in which I sat flew behind me, tipping to the unseen floor.

"Calm down." Seamus frowned, a hand going protectively to his stone mug of milk.

"Calm down?!" I parroted. "Are you telling me that I have a god-damn *poop coin* stuck in my head?" I squealed a little too girlishly.

That absolutely slayed them.

Table pounding laughter, rousing squeaks of "that would explain a lot, shite-fer-brains", and even more laughter was followed by a solid five minutes of amusement and teasing at my expense before they could finally focus on anything with enough seriousness to form an explanation.

"No ya doorknob." Seamus finally chuckled, throwing in a good natured insult to soften my annoyed and impatient glare. "We're tellin' you that the one true coin of Crann Bethadh which bears more than a passin' resemblance to them scars you wear on the back of yer pipe slappers, is rattlin' around in that ugly melon of yours like a pingin in a soup can."

I looked at the back of my hands where the two faint, round scars still lingered. They had been impaled by a blood-letting device that would have allowed a true portal to open between our worlds, had I been of fairy parentage. Since I hadn't, the bad guy's plan had been thwarted, I had been healed, and other than a dull ache whenever it rained, I was no worse for wear. I ran a finger over one of the scars, tracing the tree-like imprint that the thickened tissue had naturally formed.

Then it hit me; the round spot on my x-rays from my stay at the hospital; my new and unexplained abilities - I *didn't* have Fae blood. My thoughts raced to an insult that I had heard a half dozen times from the leprechauns.

Piggybank.

"Jesus Christ." I said numbly, sinking down into the small chair that had been inexplicably righted and returned to its original place.

"I get that a lot." Beircheart said thoughtfully as he stroked his chin. "Think it's the beard."

The others laughed their approval and began picking up their cards from the table's surface. With their big joke out of the bag, the conversation was over in their eyes and any weight of burden that they might have had was lifted.

"How...how do I get it out?" I asked helplessly, giving each of them a slow, imploring look.

"Huh?" Padraig blinked up in confusion and tilted his head to one side. "What do ya mean?"

"What do you mean, "What do ya mean?"!" I said in a bad parody of an Irish accent. "How do I get the goddamn *coin* that I have stuck in my goddamn *brain, out*?" I clarified, stressing what I felt were the key words.

The leprechauns looked up from their cards in an exchange of perplexed looks.

"Well why would ya want ta go ahead and do a fool thing like that?" Michail asked, the lack of understanding obvious on his face.

"Well I don't know *Mike*!" I snapped in exasperation, using a version of his name that the smaller man absolutely hated. "What if it gives me a tumor or cancer or like a stroke or something?"

"Ain't much up there ta damage." He responded dryly.

"Yer not in any danger lad." Seamus assured.

"Well now, that ain't exactly true, is it?" Padraig asked under his breath. Raising a single hairy eyebrow he glanced up from his cards and regarded Seamus evenly.

I touched my fingers to the top of my head and felt around.

"I don't get why yer even upset." Michail grumbled. "You've done nothin' but whine an' fuss about wantin' ta know what ya are since the day we met. We finally tell ya and now yer squeakin' like a wash girl with her tit in the ringer."

"Yeah, but…" I frowned. I had no argument ready.

"But what? Would ya really rather go back to the way ya were before yer noodle got all magic'd up?" He asked.

The grumpy little bastard had a point; normal life sucks. I've always hated characters in film or comic-books who get an amazing, life-altering ability, and then spend the next hour or twenty pages lamenting about how they just want to be "normal".

"No, but…" I wavered again, the words of rebuttal refusing to be born.

"Have we let harm come to ya before this?" Michail asked, throwing a gold coin into the center of the table.

"Oh, you mean besides the beatings and the scars and whole "nearly murdered at the hands of a deranged ex-fairy" thing?" I asked sarcastically.

"Aye. Besides all that." He confirmed.

I gave him a bitter look.

"Let me explain it like this." Seamus said pointing to where the ceiling should be. "I can tell ya what Connor up there is going to have for dinner tonight. I can tell ya why the fella at the end of the bar never wears two socks that match. Hell, if I wanted, I could tell ya who yer next president is gunna be." He smiled with genuine joy. "But you my boy? Nothin'." Seamus slashed at the air. "I can't tell what yer gunna say, what yer about ta do, or even what you're thinkin' right now."

"*If* he's thinkin' right now." Michail added under his breath.

"Point is Johnny, knowin' all that we know and seein' all that we see?" Seamus gave a weary sigh. "It's a lot less fun than you could ever imagine. There's no spice. No mystery. No surprises. Ever."

"Until now." Beircheart said.

"Aye. Until now." Seamus agreed. "Why do ya think we have ya come out here every month? Why do ya think we swap stories and insults and treat ya like yer one of our own?"

"Because Padraig has a thing for agents?" I quipped quietly, referencing the leprechaun's well-known affection for the tall, blonde McKenna. Padraig blushed from ear to ear and mumbled something about my mother as the others roared in enjoyment of his discomfort.

"Son, yer *new* to us." Seamus grinned, looking around the table for support. "This ain't ever happened before, and most likely will never happen again. We don't know how any of this is goin' ta play out, or how yer story ends." He clasped me on the shoulder. "We like that a whole lot."

The other leprechauns, with the exception of Michail echoed their agreement. Frowning, Beircheart gave a rough elbow to the smaller man's ribs causing him to look up.

"Oh aye." Michail started sarcastically. "A right breath of fresh air, you are." He rolled his eyes. "Now are we playin' cards, or are we gunna start brushin' each other's beards while we gossip about our girly parts?"

Chuckling despite myself, I grabbed a few gold coins that I had won from previous games from my pocket and threw one into the center of the table. Finishing the ante, we exchanged cards in amused silence, but a question still burned in the back of my mind.

"So does this mean I'm one of you now? That I'm a leprechaun?" I questioned awkwardly, my voice cracking slightly.

Beircheart snorted and crudely grabbed his crotch. "You *wish* you were swingin' some of this." Padraig laughed and threw a handful of peanuts at him.

"Sadly yer still human." Seamus said almost sympathetically. "Just uniquely so." He added as if trying to soften the blow.

I sat in silent thought for a few seconds as they examined their hands and bickered quietly amongst themselves.

"Having this in my head, it's not going to hurt me, right?" I asked quietly.

"Not a bit." Seamus started to laugh, but then he tilted his head to one side in thought. "Well, it shouldn't. I mean, it hasn't, yet." A slow grin split his face. "Huh. I don't really know." He looked extremely pleased by being able to say that.

"Aye. Yer head could just end up hatchin' like a big ol' egg." Michail noted.

"Or fall right off." Padraig chimed in.

"Or-" Beircheart started, but I cut him off.

"Okay! I get it. You don't know and that's tickling you." I shook my head. "Still. Why now? After all this time, why tell me now?"

They exchanged worried glances that slowly pooled to Seamus.

"Necessity." He darkened considerably. "We'd like ta tell ya that we're the only ones who know what you've got goin' on in that misshapen piggybank of yours, Johnny."

"Aye." Padraig nodded. "That Fenrus might be a dandy, but he's sharp. Worked things out on his own."

"Called that little meetin' ya stumbled in on." Seamus continued.

"With the Norn?" I asked. "Why?"

"Poofter was pleadin' his case. Tryin' ta lay claim on ya." Michail looked disgusted.

"Then you stumbled in with yer ruckus. Surprised the shite outta all of 'em." Beircheart chuckled.

"You set me up." I said. I sounded surprised, but I probably shouldn't have been.

"Well, we had hoped to." Padraig shrugged innocently. "Like Seamus said, yer somethin' of a wildcard. Unpredictable."

"But now tha Norn sees that too." Beircheart added with a knowing nod.

"Don't think that was lost on her either. She sees clearer than any of us, but never saw ya comin'." Padraig grinned and nudged Beircheart. "I wager that put a spark in her britches that ain't been there in a long while."

There was a long bout of laughter at my expense followed by speculation about which of us would be "the woman" if she took a more romantic interest at me. I let them have their fun, my thoughts refusing to drift away from the image of a coin stuck in the middle of my grey matter.

"So now what?" I asked when the silliness began to subside.

"So now we play cards." Padraig answered as if it should have been obvious.

"That's it?" It seemed like there should be something…more.

"That's enough, for now ain't it?" He replied.

"What about Fenrus?" Call me kooky, but the dark leprechaun trying to lay dibs on my brain had me a tad bit worried.

Michail made a contemptuous sound at the mention of their rival's name. "He won't act against the Norn's decision. He might be a nasty lil' peckerhead, but he ain't stupid. No force on either side of the court would ask her for her judgment then defy it."

"Well, not directly." Padraig countered.

"But if everybody knows what I have…" I wanted to say "in my head", but the words trailed as I poked at my temple again.

"I wouldn't worry too much about that. It ain't like Fenrus plans ta announce it to the world." Seamus assured me. "He'll play his hand close outta the fear that someone else is gunna go after what he thinks is his rightful claim."

"You'd be wise to do the same." Padraig warned.

"Aye." Seamus agreed. "Don't tell a soul that yer all sorted out now. The fewer that know what ya got goin' on upstairs, the better."

"That ain't no secret you want out. All *sorts* of beasties an' baddies might suddenly sit up an' start ta take notice." Beircheart said.

I looked blankly at the cards that I held in my hand. It made a sort of sense I guess. How Fergus was able to talk to me, use me to right his wrongs; he had been in my head this whole time. Literally.

"So Fergus," I hesitated. Looking up I expected a toast to his name, as per tradition. Instead I found only sorrowful looks.

"He's gone lad." Seamus patted my hand gently. "You did him a noble turn and he's moved on." He offered a sad smile.

"Yeah, right up until my head explodes." I half-joked.

"Or hatches." Michail reminded.

"Or hatches." I amended. "Great gift."

"Speaking of gifts." Beircheart grinned and hefted his mug of milk. "Not a bad job with this night's contribution me boy." He drained his glass, wiping his mouth on his sleeve as he burped. "Not bad at all."

"To Fergus!" Padraig lifted his own drink in a delayed toast as Beircheart scrambled to refill his mug.

"To Fergus!" We echoed. The silence that followed our words was only mildly disturbed by the sounds of greedy gulping and sighs of appreciation. The mood had lifted, the serious talk was done, and I felt a weight that I hadn't been aware of carrying lift from my shoulders as I sat down my stone cup.

"Now." Michail beamed, putting a strong hand on my shoulder, his grip slowly tightening. "Let's discuss that shirt of yers."

Chapter Three

The cool night air felt wonderful against my face.

Inhaling deeply, I closed my eyes in momentary appreciation as a gentle breeze wafted past, its invigorating caress chasing away a growing case of "the milk sweats" before they had time to fully take hold.

Refreshed and renewed, I allowed the door to the pub to close behind me as I lurched forward, leaning heavily against the worn wooden railing of the pub's walkway for support. Another soft gust of wind flapped at my torn t-shirt and chilled my bare skin, causing me to shiver against the unexpected cold as it assaulted my chest. Pulling myself up to my full height, I was forced to clutch my over-shirt with one hand in order to keep it closed as its buttons were no longer intact; vehemently removed during an altercation that led to the untimely demise of its sole occupant, Lucky the Leprechaun.

Torn clothing, blood at my lip and my left eye feeling a little heavier than it normally should, all and all it had been a great night. My pockets were full of gold, sort of; I had won more than my fair share at poker despite the tendency to cheat that my opponents were notorious for, and I had a belly full of some of the best milk that money could illegally buy from young women named Willow.

Fumbling for my keys, the sound of several gold coins hitting the planks of the wooden walkway at my feet caused me to frown. Blinking slowly, I tried in vain to trace their paths as they disappeared into the many cracks and shadows that would become their new home.

"Ya ain't in no condition ta drive." A firm, but friendly voice pointed out behind me. I hadn't seen Seamus leave the table, or follow me out, but I also knew that I didn't have to in order to have the leprechaun magically appear at my side.

"Imnagunna." I said clearly, eloquently even. "Just gunna sleep in the backseat for a liddlebit." I explained, motioning towards the rear of what I really hoped was my vehicle.

"Oh aye." Came the drawn out, sarcastic reply. "And what a lovely sight you'd be in the mornin'. This is a family establishment, ya lightweight. We don't need ya scarin' away the payin' customers." He chuckled. "I had Conner call ya a cab." As if summoned by magic instead of a phone, a yellow cab turned off the main road into the graveled parking lot of the pub.

"Wuddabout my car?" I frowned. I was tipsy and feeling pretty good, but even in my altered state I knew better than to lose a government vehicle. My boss was a beautiful, kind woman, but she also had a scary side to her that I never wanted to see again.

"Don't ya worry about it none Johnny m'boy." Seamus clapped me on the back. "We'll get'er back to ya before mornin', safe an' sound. Ya have my word." He added reassuringly when I gave him a long, dubious look.

I smiled. "You're a good man Seamus." I said. Placing a hand on his shoulder I looked him in the eyes. "And a good friend."

"And yer drunk." He said, returning the gesture.

"I don't care." Damn it, I was going to have a moment with him whether he wanted to or not. I loved the little bastard. "Thank you, Seamus. For everything." I slurred.

"It's been my genuine pleasure Lad." He said softly. "Now git ta gone." Grabbing me by my outstretched arm he swiftly spun me around and gave a gentle shove in the direction of the waiting cab.

The driver had pulled to a wary stop about thirty feet from the building and was waiting patiently for me to stagger across the parking lot for my ride. Throwing an unsteady hand into the air in a drunken wave of goodbye to the pub and its fairy owners, I lurched forward, stones crunching loudly underfoot as I stumbled.

Acknowledging the cabbie with a quick nod of my head, I opened the door to the backseat and was about to fall in when a man's voice called out from behind me.

"Agent Talik?"

Surprised not only by the voice, but the use of my official name, I leaned heavily on the open door and turned the upper half of my body in investigation.

"Huh?" I said smoothly, blinking into the darkness.

"Agent John Talik?"

A slender figure hobbled into view. The man was shorter than me by a few inches, but not due to any lack of physical height. He was hunched over, nearly ape-like as he balanced his weight on the metal arm-brace crutches that supported him and allowed him to move across the loose stone. He was thin, sickly so - whether that was an actual observation or an influence of the braces, I'm not sure, but he looked tired. Worn. He was older than me by a few years at least, his short brown hair thinning at the temples and peppered with grey. Clean shaven, he peered at me through a pair of thinly rimmed glasses as he slowed his approach.

"Can I help you?" I asked, confused.

I didn't know him, or at least, I didn't *think* that I knew him. Sometimes it's hard to tell given my well-established knack for paying attention and noting the finer details and all.

"Somnus." The stranger said, leaning on one brace as he extended a hand.

I raised my arm to accept the offered handshake, but as I did the wind picked up and a cloud of dust, probably stirred up by the taxi pelted my face, causing me to cough as I inhaled it.

"What was that?" I asked, blinking the fine sand and debris from my eyes as I rubbed at them with the back of my hand.

"Somnus!" He said a bit louder, and again I was pummeled by small particles of soft, powdery dirt.

"Nice to meet you Somnus." I said, roughly grabbing his hand in mine and shaking it as I tried to wipe the dirt from my eyes. "What can I do for you?"

With a startled look, Somnus slowly began to back away from me, nervously glancing around. Before I could stop him the crippled man pivoted on one pole with surprising agility and spun, teetering off as quickly as he had appeared.

"Well that was just *weird*." I coughed. Spitting some of the dust back into the parking lot I shrugged off the strange encounter and slid into the back of the awaiting cab.

"Where to pal?" The driver asked before I could even close the door. Still coughing, I gave him the address to the hotel that the agency used and retrieved my cellphone from my front pocket.

"I've driven by this place a thousand times." The cabbie confided, gesturing towards the pub. "First call I've ever gotten though." There was a hint of suspicion. "Any good?"

"Owner bites." I said, rubbing a sore spot on my forearm. The cab driver didn't respond, and I'm not sure if he took my words as an insult or as literally as I had intended them. Either way, let it be known that leprechauns fight dirty.

The glow from my phone lit up the car like a one man rave as I scrolled with a thumb that throbbed and felt way too big for my hand through my list of emergency contacts. I was sore, tipsy and tired, and there was only one person who could help. Stopping in the "R's", I looked at the name "Ronnie", my pet name for Raegan, gave a fond sigh and then tapped the number above it.

Robbie's Pizza.

Like all good places to eat, I had stumbled across this little slice of heaven, pun intended, completely by accident. Run by the legendary "Robbie T.", no last name provided, Robbie's Pizza offered the three things that made the restaurant second to none: Amazing pizza, insanely delicious garlic chicken wings, and most importantly of all...

...24 hour delivery.

The cabbie drove in silence as I ordered my pizza and wings, throwing in a couple of bottles of chocolate milk as an afterthought because hey, I wasn't driving. Besides, the pasteurized, over-the-counter stuff was pretty weak. The chocolate milk would taste incredible, but it packed about as much wallop as a couple of light beers.

With dinner and the next morning's breakfast ordered, I allowed myself to doze lightly as the taxi continued its dutiful route to the hotel, waking only as we pulled into the mostly full parking lot.

From the outside, the hotel wasn't exactly the Ritz. Basically a plaza of interconnected apartments that you could rent by the hour, the week, or longer provided that you had enough money and didn't mind the occasional dead hooker stinking up your room, the hotel seemed about as classy as anything you'd see on a low budget crime drama. Provided by the agency, it was stocked with emergency provisions, money and weapons; a low-key safe house of sorts made much more luxurious and comfortable by the fact that Agent Wallace often stayed here when on official business.

McKenna Wallace didn't slum, and because of that, the place was absolutely posh.

Despite the apartments surrounding it, the unassuming hotel room had been retrofitted with new carpeting and appliances, the walls had been sound proofed and lined with iron, and the agency's top of the line security system assured that no one could easily break in and help themselves to whatever they wanted during the days and weeks that the safe house went unused.

It had a small entryway that doubled as a living room, a modest kitchen complete with a table and chairs for two, and a surprisingly long hallway that would eventually lead to both a lavish bathroom and a master bedroom. Much larger within than seemingly possible from the outside, I had dubbed the apartment "Elsa's Castle", much to the rather disturbed looks and confused stares of my peers.

Whether their confusion came from the fact that I was a grown man naming things after an animated princess movie, or the realization that I had actually seen it enough times to make the reference, I would never know. Not that it mattered; the place was the ice queen's fortress of pampering hidden in plain sight, and tonight, she was all mine.

Tipping the taxicab driver with a few bucks and a gold coin that I assured him was real, I moved towards the apartment with a lot less of a stagger than I had expected. Jamming the specialized key into the lock I forced my way in the room, almost forgetting to deactivate the alarm system that would have a swat team of government officials here in a matter of minutes.

Alarm safely disabled, I kicked off my shoes and threw my keys onto the counter that separated the living room from the kitchen, watching in detached disappointment as they slid across the smooth granite top and disappeared with a clatter onto the kitchen floor. Dropping heavily into a decadently plush armchair that sat opposite of a large screen TV, I sighed in content and reached for the remote.

Just as I was about to change the channel to the cinematic masterpiece classic: "Busty Cop 6: The Boobening", as provided by the best in late-night Skinamax, three sharp knocks at the door notified me of the arrival of my half remembered pizza.

"Just a minute!" I called out as I fought to free myself from the depths of the impossibly cozy chair. Glancing at my bare wrist I noted that I still didn't have a watch and nodded my head, more than impressed by the fact that Robbie's delivery was even quicker than usual.

Three more knocks alerted me to the fact that I was on my knees staring at my naked arm, so I stood, and stumbled towards the sound.

"Just a minute, dammit." I said as I slammed a bit too hard into surface of the door.

Fumbling with the auto-locks that secured the room from the inside the moment that the door closed, I started to pull it open as my senses cleared, my mind and instincts screaming in the horror of sudden, helpless realization.

I didn't smell the garlic wings.

Robbie's chicken wings were the best in the city, and as per my standard request, they always tripled the amount of garlic that they normally used, which allowed my order to be detected from space.

"If you forgot the wings…" I warned, ripping open the door. I was usually a heavy tipper, but no wings meant not only no tip, but that some pimply faced youth was about to make a second trip.

Instead of the acne riddled teenager that I had come to expect, I was greeted by three circles of grey rising in a bull's-eye pattern from the hard rubber bottom of a metal crutch as it rushed towards my face, catching me right between the eyes. The world exploded in a burst of bright light as I staggered backwards, my attacker quickly closing the gap as a second blow hit me hard on the right side of my head, deafening me with the ringing of my own stinging ears. The room spun as I clumsily raised an arm to ward off a third strike as it came down to greet me, and before it connected I caught the briefest glimpse of my attacker, Somnus.

Arm stinging, head swimming and no garlic wings in sight, the fourth and final blow of the crutch pushed me over the edge and into the arms of the awaiting darkness.

Chapter Four

If you've never been knocked unconscious, let me be the first to tell you that it sucks.

When the good guy gets knocked out on television, he usually awakens hours later, fully aware of his surroundings, rested, and ready to fight. In real life, if you're out cold for a few hours chances are that when you wake up, it's to a case of severe brain damage and the only thing that you're ready to fight is the chin strap on the unicorn-stickered helmet that you now have to wear.

Having been knocked out a few times in the past, I knew what to expect, so when I came to, instead of groggily glancing around and trying to figure out what in the hell had just happened, I played possum and let my senses gradually adjust to my surroundings.

I hurt everywhere, but the throbbing in my head from where I had been struck with the metal crutch took center stage, and it was all I could do to keep from crying out. My limbs tingled and my back felt stiff, probably due to the odd angle in which I was slouching. Hands tied behind me, I surmised that I was sitting in one of the high-backed chairs that belonged to the apartment's small dining area. I could hear my attacker as he moved through the cramped kitchen.

"I know that you're awake." Somnus said offhandedly, his tone almost conversational.

Well, shit.

"What the hell." I groaned more than I asked. Shifting in the chair I opened my eyes and felt a wave of nausea twist through my stomach. My attacker was about five feet away, his back to me as he rummaged through a black bag that he had set on the breakfast nook counter. One of the metal crutches was propped against the wooden cabinets beside him, fully freeing his right arm. The other was still attached and supporting his weight as he continued in his task.

"Sorry about the violence." He apologized, motioning towards the apartment's door without actually looking. "I usually attempt to avoid physical confrontation whenever I can, for the obvious reasons." He glanced over his shoulder to me. "But when you resisted the spell, I didn't know what else to do and I panicked."

Turning back to his bag, he continued to fiddle with whatever was inside, its contents and his hands blocked from my sight by his slight, bent frame.

"You robbing me?" I asked. My head was swimming and my hands, while numb from the angle and disuse felt as if they were wrapped in some sort of silk. The bonds were strong, but not tied particularly tight.

Somnus scoffed and turned his head long enough to give me a wry look. "Of *what?*"

Okay, that was actually fair. The apartment was opulent to the extreme, but aside from the TV and a few high end but bulky appliances, there really wasn't anything practical to steal.

He wasn't a thief, and beyond tying me up, I didn't appear to be in any dang-

My heart sank and my mouth went dry as my brain helpfully provided a worse-case scenario.

"Oh God. This isn't some kind of weird sex thing, is it?" I swallowed hard, dreading the answer.

"What?!" Somnus cried out indignantly. "No!" He turned again to look on me, his face a mask of disbelief and disgust. "What in the hell is wrong with you?"

I looked around woozily. "Then what's your deal Tiny Tim?" He stiffened at that, actually pausing in his work. "I'm guessing that if you wanted to kill me, you would have done it when I was unconscious."

"Why on earth would I want to kill you?" His voice was colder. I must have struck a nerve with the childish poke at his condition.

Casually shifting in my seat, I slowly flexed my arms behind me and tried to feel out my bindings. They were too soft to be rope, and felt more like a silken cloth or bed sheet. While they were definitely loosening, I could sense that they had been wound around my wrists several times before being pulled tight.

"Voices in your head, mother didn't hug you enough, that one weird uncle who hugged you a little too much." I provoked. "Take your pick." I wasn't sure what he was doing, but if I distracted him from it long enough, I might be able to work free of my bonds.

"There is no need to be vulgar." He chided stiffly. "And don't bother trying to untie yourself. Those ropes are woven from pure Ananasi silk. You can't escape them." He added with a knowing glance in my direction.

"So you know about the Fae." I said in surprise.

Somnus laughed derisively. "More than you could even begin to imagine."

"And you know who I am." Banter. Banter was good. I was able to turn one of my wrists more freely, and the pain between my shoulder blades lessened as the ropes began to give.

"Of course." He answered. "Everyone knows who you are, Agent Talik." Leaning heavily on his crutch, he turned to face me, his attention no longer on the dark bag he had lain upon the counter. "You're something of a celebrity, aren't you?" Somnus smiled.

His right hand was cupped, a scrap of bright blue cloth flowing over its edges as he took a hobbled step forward. He was holding something small, but its shape was too obscured by the piece of fabric to make out what it was.

"Well, I don't like to brag." I said coolly, trying not to show my panic. I was running out of time and there didn't seem to be a knot.

"Don't be modest." He said in an almost friendly fashion. "You're the first male ever reported to have the gift. That's something to be proud of." He shook his head. "And not only do you have it, but I've seen your scores, you test off the charts." Somnus crouched, bringing him eye level with me. "You're also the first man to hold the title of Seer." He looked at me with admiration. "It is an *honor* to finally meet you, John."

He was close, but just at the edge of striking distance.

"I'm getting a real "Misery" vibe here, Somnus." I confided. The sincerity in which he spoke was adding a level of creepiness that I couldn't easily express.

Tilting his head in confusion, Somnus pulled himself up by his crutch and slowly backed a few feet further away.

"Somnus?" He asked with an inquisitive turn of his head.

"That's your name isn't it?" The man had fingers like my grandmother, how in the hell were the ropes still this tight?

"It's Latin." He said warily, as if expecting a trick. "It means sleep."

"Yeah. Just had a nap, thanks." I said bitterly.

Somnus frowned. "I said that I was sorry about that." He shook his head, perplexed. "I'm not really sure what went wrong there."

"No sweat." I shrugged. "How about you just untie me and we'll call it even?"

He laughed lightly. "I'm afraid I can't do that." He apologized. "Do you know what this is?" Somnus stretched his arm towards me and pulled back the blue cloth that was obscuring the object he held. Beneath the soft fabric was a small mechanical spider about the size of a child's fist. Gleaming silver, every joint had been meticulously detailed, giving it a very real and life-like quality despite its metallic composition. An expertly carved gem made up its abdomen, the deep red of the stone eerily familiar, and I felt my mouth go dry.

I really didn't like where this was going.

"You raided Dracula's jewelry box?" I quipped, my voice cracking slightly.

"It's called a latrodenzian." Somnus explained. "You see, the stone isn't really an actual *jewel*, but a piece of-"

"Latrodectus." I said in numb realization. "From an Ananasi."

The Ananasi were giant, powerful Fae on par with leprechauns and nymphs in terms of bang-for-your-buck magical ability. Like a centaur designed by Wes Craven, they had the lower half of a giant spider and the upper body and head of a hobgoblin; a creature that looked human enough to give you nightmares, if you squinted. Like leprechauns the Ananasi were nearly godlike in ability, but thankfully, like my boys, they were also held in check by nature.

While the giant spider Fae were arguably less friendly and more likely to eat you, their magic was finite, a little bit being consumed each time that they exerted it. Because of this, they had the tendency to hoard their power, out of fear of losing it and growing weak. Solitary by nature, the only way that an Ananasi could possibly "recharge" their dwindling supplies would be by consuming the life gem – a blood red, glowing tumor in the shape of an hourglass that adorns their foreheads – of another spider Fae.

This of course turns them into paranoid, suspicious and distrustful shut-ins, which makes them less-than-fun to deal with.

I had watched as an Ananasi was murdered a few months ago, its latrodectus ripped from its skull, and the creature that did it was an absolute *monster*. If another of the gigantic spider fairies had fallen, I didn't even want to think about what was out there that could have taken it out.

"Very good." Somnus nodded, impressed. "Excellent job Agent Talik. Gold star." He said with the genuine demeanor of a school teacher.

"Fueled by a piece of latrodectus, a latrodenzian acts as a siphon of sorts, allowing one person to literally feed off the life essence of another." He explained. "Everything that person has experienced, knows, or essentially *is*, can be accessed and utilized by the controlling party." His eyes fell to me hungrily. "Every single thought, dream, or ability."

Uh-oh.

"And I didn't get you anything." I tried to sound confident, but I couldn't take my eyes from the mechanical creature in his hand.

Somnus smiled, my obvious discomfort bolstering his confidence. "Because of the materials needed to create them, the latrodenzian are exceedingly rare, and quite fragile." He said as he admired the metal spider resting in his palm. "I've had to use them sparingly, as not to arouse suspicion." He looked up at me. "But when I heard of you, of your abilities…" Something dark danced behind his eyes. "Let's just say that the time for discretion is over."

The latrodenzian twitched.

"Ahh, it's ready!" Somnus let out a breath of relief. "I was starting to get worried that it was a dud. That would have really been embarrassing." He confided with a small chuckle. "Shall we begin?"

Gently lowering the small mechanical spider to the floor a few feet from where I helplessly sat, Somnus crouched beside it and whispered a single word.

"Vita."

One of the spider's long, creepy legs slowly began to raise before dropping to the kitchen's polished wooden floor with a barely audible "tick". The latrodenzian's other limbs trembled as the creature came to life before my wide, now fear-filled eyes. Spinning in place, the mechanical spider skittered as it centered itself, rotating slowly until each one of its tiny red-gemmed eyes was pointed at me.

And then it lurched forward.

It only moved about a foot, but the speed at which it moved paired with its extremely realistic spider-like scuttle startled the hell out of me, and in a burst of pure fight or flight instinct, I leapt to my feet. The chair to which I was still tied now hung from my back like a poorly designed turtle shell as I scrambled backwards, slamming into the wall.

I looked down in amazement, then slowly up to my captor.

"You didn't tie my legs? *Really*?" I asked incredulously, noting only now that I could have stood this entire time.

The spider shivered and skittered forward again. Taken aback by my unexpected near-escape, Somnus stepped towards me as well, and cocked back his arm.

"SOMNUS!" he screamed, this time throwing a handful of that fine, powdery sand in my face. I turned my head just in time and avoided taking the majority of the blinding dirt in the eyes.

"JOHN TALIK!" I roared back with my own name, because if *that* was going to be a thing, I was going to win, damn it. Raising my foot I stepped forward and stomped the living ever-loving shit out of the small mechanical spider.

I felt it shatter underfoot with a satisfying crunch of glass and twisted silver.

"No!" Somnus yelled, extending a hand helplessly towards the world's scariest windup toy.

Now standing, I felt the ropes as they strained under the weight of the chair and gave a little shimmy, shaking them off. The chair fell, clattering loudly to kitchen floor. Looking down at it, and then behind me, I hoped that no one would notice the two little dents in the drywall.

Now free, I focused my attention on Somnus who began to slowly back up, his eyes expanding in alarm.

"Easy now Mister Glass." I said, slowly raising my hand. "Let's just take this nice and slow."

Somnus fumbled with the inside pocket of his jacket, and I unconsciously flinched as he pulled out a...

...small wooden wand.

"Really?" I asked, in disbelief, taking a step forward. "You're going to go all Harry Potter on me? Do those things even wor-"

"Vi!" he shouted, and from the end of his, and I can't believe I'm going to say this, *magic wand*, a small blue pellet of light shot out and hit me squarely in the chest.

I recoiled instinctively and slapped wildly at the impact with the closed-eye reflexes of a man fighting off a particularly large bumblebee. When no pain, agony, or stinging sensation followed, I froze in place, opening a single eye as I looked down. Beyond the tattered remains of my shirt and a few drops of dried blood from earlier, there was nothing.

"What was-" I started to ask, but Somnus steadied his arm and flicked his wand in rapid fire succession.

"Vi!" He cried out again. "Vi! Vi! Vi!" With every shout, a ball of crackling blue light erupted only to fizzle harmlessly against me wherever it struck, doing little more than filling my nose with a burning, electrical smell.

"Hey." I frowned in annoyance, brushing at my chest. "Cut it out." At that, the man's eyes went even wider as he was overcome with blind panic.

"Ignis!" he shrieked, flicking his wrist with renewed vigor.

"Okay. Now you're just *trying* to piss me-" A bright orange flame leapt from his wand, arcing towards me in a steady stream of fire that dripped and spattered trails of burning red beneath it.

My heart skipped a beat as I rolled to one side, my senses exploding with adrenaline and fear. The light show was one thing, but fire was a different game all together, and I felt the grip of pure uncontrollable terror clutch my heart.

When I was a teenager, my parents were killed in a house fire. I wasn't home when it started, but I had arrived just in time to smell the smoke, feel the heat of the flame, and watch the sky blaze intensely with the death of my family.

I gradually came to accept the loss. The pain lessened with time, and I thought that I had adapted to the tragedy quiet well. I never realized that I had a problem or phobia of any sort until a few months ago when a group of goblins burned down my apartment building with me inside, trapping me in an inferno of heat and dread. Since then, even the faintest whiff of unexplained smoke, or the hint of uncontrolled fire was enough to get my pulse racing.

This however, wasn't a tipped over candle or a bag of burnt popcorn, it was a goddamn flamethrower.

And Johnny don't do fire.

So there was no glib response or smartass comment as I closed the gap between us faster than I would have ever imagined I could move. There was only raw, primal, fear.

"Ig-" I struck the frail man harder than I have ever hit anyone in my life. My fist, strengthened by an explosion of fear and terror connected with Somnus' jaw like a sledgehammer and spun him with the symmetry of a top. There was no resistance as he hurdled backwards, never once even attempting to break his fall. Somnus collapsed in a heap of metal crutches and bony limbs as he crumpled to the floor like a rag doll and went perfectly still.

Spinning in place, I wrenched my head to the wall where the magical flame had hit in wide eyed dread and drew a panicked breath only when I was positive that there were no signs of growing flames. The wall was scorched and blackened where the magic had hit, but the fire hadn't spread.

"Jesus." I swore, my breath coming in heavy, sobbing gulps as my heart pounded against the inside of my chest. My entire body tingled with spent adrenaline and my legs felt suddenly wobbly and unsteady.

Turning back to my attacker's still unmoving form, I cautiously approached and prodded his lifeless body with my tip of my shoe.

There was no response.

"Hey." I said shakily. "Hey. Somnus." I called his out, but beyond the sound of faint, shallow breathing, he didn't stir.

I looked to my still balled fist and then back to the man that I had just knocked out with a single punch.

"HA!" I yelled in victory as I pointed down at his unmoving body in glorious triumph. "Not so goddamn tough *now* are we Captain…" Dawning comprehension crept in on a shadow of guilt as my habit of assigning clever-yet-biting nicknames died in my throat. "…97 pound crippled guy."

Maaaan.

Chapter Five

It usually takes me around four hours to drive from the agency to Boston. With light traffic, the right conditions, and a healthy disregard for the speed limit, I've made the trek in just over three. Raegan did it in two.

I had barely unlatched the last of the safety locks when the door burst open and my partner rushed in, gun drawn. Pizza crust in mouth, I spun to one side to avoid being bowled over and stepped back as she surveyed the room.

"Where is he?" Ronnie asked with the briefest of glances in my direction. Her finger was on the trigger of her agency issued weapon and she looked more than ready to shoot anything foolish enough to make anything that could even be perceived as a sudden move. The odd gun's wires and dials hummed and clicked with electronic impatience as the contents of its twin ammunition canisters sloshed with the force of her rapid aiming.

"Bathroom." I said through a mouth full of crust as I closed the door behind her with the back of my foot.

"Bathroom?" She asked raising a slender eyebrow as she lowered her weapon.

"Yup." I chewed. "Little bastard likes to play with fire, so I tied him to a chair and stuck him in the shower." I gestured with the pizza, mid-bite.

"The shower." Raegan repeated, somewhat confused. Satisfied that there was no threat of immediate attack she took in my calm demeanor with a frown and holstered her weapon, her eyes trailing towards the restroom.

"He's probably getting all pruney by now." I added in half-thought. Call me paranoid if you want, I'm okay with that. Because-

"Johnny doesn't do fire." My partner smiled knowingly, finishing my thought.

"Johnny doesn't do fire." I confirmed, the last word coming with an unexpected exhalation of air as she squeezed me in a relieved hug.

"Are you okay?" She asked. Looking up, her impossibly green eyes searched my face in worry as she gently touched the bruising at my cheek. Even as brotherly as I normally felt in her presence, I had to admit that she was stunning. A few inches shorter than me, long red hair tumbled around her in a waterfall of flame that framed the flawless pale skin of her face.

"Yeah. Just a little banged up, but nothing too bad." I reassured her while at the same time forgetting to mention that the split lip and puffy eye might have been acquired earlier at the hands of an angry leprechaun.

"What do we know about him?" She asked, stepping away and slipping back into secret agent mode. Anger touched the edge of her voice; a mama bear annoyed that someone had manhandled one of her cubs.

"Pretty much everything." I said. Holding up a square of brown leather, I wiggled it back and forth for her to see.

"You got his wallet?" A hint of amusement tugged at the corners of her mouth and threatened to strip away a large portion of her professional demeanor.

"Yup." I confirmed as I popped the last of the pizza crust into my mouth and handed it to her. "And he was nice enough to buy me dinner, too."

47

"Rupert Ambrose." Ronnie read, flipping open the wallet.

"Called himself Somnus." I added helpfully.

"That's Latin. It means sleep." She explained absently. "Ever see him before?" She asked looking up.

"He was outside of the pub last night, but before that, no." I shrugged.

"So what happened here?" She asked with a frown. Leaning against the small wall that separated the living room from the kitchen, she kept her eyes on the hallway to the bathroom as she listened.

"He must have followed me back here." I shrugged again. "When I answered the door he hit me with," *His medically necessary crutch.* "A length of pipe." I hesitated, not *exactly* lying. "Wham. Lights out."

Raegan glanced back at me, but she was too preoccupied to catch the artistic liberties that I was taking with my phrasing.

"When I came to, I was tied to a chair in the kitchen." I motioned behind her in hopes of further distraction.

Following my gesture, Ronnie pushed off the wall and stepped into the kitchen. I couldn't see her eyes but I knew that they were darting around, taking in every detail. Where my memory is selective at best, hers is what she calls "eidetic". If she concentrated hard enough, she could remember everything about anything, which really sucks if you screw up as often as I do.

It's hard to win an argument when your opponent has a playback button.

"Ugh." She grimaced, holding the back of her hand to her nose and mouth in dainty disgust. "It *reeks* in here." She moved towards the pizza box and the white foam container sitting beside it. "Robbie's? Really? After all of that, you still ordered pizza?"

"And garlic wings." I pointed out.

"Yeah. I noticed." She wrinkled her delicate nose. "From the parking lot."

"He came after me with that." I gestured to the scrap of blue cloth on the counter that was now being used to cover the remains of the shattered latrodenzian. Cautiously pulling the cloth to one side, Raegan tilted her head and lifted a single mangled leg from the stomped remains of the mechanical arachnid.

"What was it?" Raegan asked. She was trying to sound unimpressed, but her voice wavered as she stared into the blue fabric.

"A little metal spider thing." I answered, the crackle of fear in my voice matching hers.

Using the leg that she now held between two fingers, Raegan dug through the rest of the broken parts, moving them this way and that as she inspected the corpse.

"Oh, he also had this." I said, suddenly remembering that the spider hadn't been the only threat. Reaching behind me I pulled both halves of the broken wand from my back pocket and handed them to her.

"What is-" She took the pieces from me and examined them in disbelief. "Is this a wand?"

"I know! *Weird* right?" I asked, looking for confirmation. I had seen a lot of strange things since taking this job, but magic wands were a new one for me.

"What happened to it?" She asked, lining up the broken ends.

"Our new buddy Rupert in there was using it to huck this glowing blue shit at me." I nodded to the bathroom. "After I took him out, I didn't know what to do with it, so I snapped it in half." I explained sheepishly, trying my best to sound apologetic. In hindsight I realize that breaking the wand probably wasn't the best or brightest move, but at the same time neither was getting turned into a rabbit by a fantasy novel villain.

"He was actually casting spells?" Ronnie asked in a mixture of astonishment and worry.

"I think so?" I shrugged. "I dunno. They didn't really do all that much until he decided to go all Fire Nation on me."

My partner frowned and tapped the two halves of the wand against each other in thought. "This is unusual, even for us." She paused and looked to me. "Magic users are *extremely* rare. Are you positive that he was human?"

I nodded. "Yeah. Well, I think so anyway." I frowned, plagued by sudden doubt. "Right up until the whole magic thing he seemed pretty normal."

"How did you manage to beat him?"

I gave her a humorless chuckle. "Gandalf decided to add some pyrotechnics to his light show and I kind of lost it." I admitted. The heat of the remembered flame caused my stomach to flutter. "The rest is kind of a blur." Okay, so it was another white lie, but how in the hell do you look someone in the eye and tell them that you just cold-cocked the supreme leader of the Make-a-Wish Foundation?

I knew that she'd see the crutches and all of his frail glory in a matter of minutes, but goddamn it, I was going to hold onto my manliness for as long as I could.

"Why do you only have one sock on?" Ronnie asked, looking down at my feet.

"I, uh." I stammered, looking down as well. Admittedly, it's possible that my choice of gag was a little childish and petty, but c'mon – he threw *fire*.

"Let's have a talk with Mister Ambrose, shall we?" Raegan moved past me and out of the kitchen before I was able to explain my state of quasi-bare footedness. Chuckling to myself, I gave quick chase and followed her to the hallway.

"He's gone." She said, coming out of the small bathroom just as quickly as she had entered.

"What?" I asked in disbelief. "Did you check the shower?" Pushing past her I dutifully ignored the dry look just as hard as she threw it.

The bathroom was empty.

"What's this?" Raegan asked, reaching into the bottom of the shower. Standing, she held up a soggy length of silken rope and examined it.

"That's the rope that he tied me up with." I explained. "I used it on him, except *I* remembered to tie his feet." I said proudly. Unlike my attacker, I had tied Somnus' bindings painfully tight, almost to the point of cruel. It's not that I did it out of simple vengeance, but because this guy was throwing magic and mechanical spiders at me. I didn't know what else he had up his sleeves, and to be honest, I didn't want to find out.

"This isn't rope." Raegan breathed in stunned recognition. "It's-"

"Ananasi silk." I nodded. "Yeah, he also knows about fairies." I thought back to the encounter and the nonchalant way that the man had spoken. "And us."

My partner slowly shook her head in thought as she handed me the soggy rope and retrieved her cell phone from the inside pocket of her suit coat. "This isn't good." She said through the tops of her eyes as she rapidly tapped the screen. "I'll have someone run the name right away. If this guy is in the know, and a magic user, then he's got to show up on a record somewhere."

"You thinking inside job?" I asked warily. The last "inside job" to rock the agency almost ended in the destruction of the city and the painful death of yours truly, so I wasn't too keen on going down that road again.

Since that fateful day, security had been stepped up considerably. Every agent, no matter their status or perceived loyalty had been run through extensive background checks and new badges, identification and biometrics were installed and put into place. So far the precautions had turned up no further threats, but the Fae were old, insanely intelligent and infinitely resourceful.

Ronnie considered my words as the phone rang faintly against her ear before gently shaking her head side to side. "No. But I still want to rule it out. He could be a relative of someone in the know. Someone's cousin, brother or father." She explained. "But I'm not taking any chances. Not with this."

I nodded in understanding. Fool us once, shame on you. Fool us twice and the Assistant Director of the FPI puts on her scary face.

And *nobody* wanted that.

"Good morning Kimmie." Raegan said into the phone. "It's Agent Conno-" Her last name hung on her lips as she rolled her eyes in my direction. "Yes, he's right here." She sighed. "He's fine, thank you. Listen, I need you to run a search on the name Rupert Ambrose. A full search. Yes, *that* kind of full search."

I couldn't make out the words on the other end, but the tone had changed with the abruptness of a perky bubble bursting. A full search indicated a possible breach, and as Kimmie was the personal secretary to the aforementioned scary-faced Assistant Director, she would be at ground zero in the event of any explosion.

"Agent Talik and I are on our way in and will brief Assistant Director Blair the moment that we arrive." Raegan's voice softened. "No, I'm sure it's nothing, we just want to be sure. Thank you Kimmie." Hanging up the phone and returning it to her pocket, Ronnie pushed gently past me and moved back towards the kitchen.

I followed, dripping Ananasi silk in one hand, missing sock in the other and watched as she gently gathered the remains of the thoroughly stepped on spider. Wrapping it in the blue cloth that it had been presented to me in, Raegan turned to me, her eyes somber.

"I want to get these to Jonas for analysis." She explained. "If Fae magic or design held this thing together, there's no telling how long it will stay in our realm now that you've," She looked down at the parcel. "Expertly disabled it." She was already writing the report in her head and wording it in such a way that I wouldn't come off as a spider stomping sissy. As much as I hated paperwork, Ronnie seemed to love it, and in turn I loved her for loving it.

"What about Alistair?" I suggested.

Alistair Yashar had become something of a friend since our last encounter. Cursed to live pretty much forever by the King of the Fae for the crime of diddling his wife, Alistair was an expert in anything even remotely fairy related and owned an antique shop that specialized in all things magical. We had used him in the past when we needed help identifying fairy items, and as much as Raegan didn't trust him, I felt that he was a pretty okay guy.

Besides, his shop was pretty neat *and* he let me touch things.

Ronnie set her jaw stubbornly and pursed her lips. "Alistair would probably know more about this than Jonas, especially if it is a Fae artifact." She said begrudgingly.

I danced excitedly in place.

"But I don't like that you're getting so chummy with him." She narrowed her eyes. "He's dangerous."

"Oh come on." I sighed. "Alistair is cool."

"It always feels like he's up to something." She grumbled, chewing the inside of her lip.

"He's like a bajillion years old, of course he's up to something." I chuckled. "But he's one of the good guys, I promise."

"And if you're wrong?" She asked quietly. It wasn't a fair question, but it was the reason behind her distrust.

Ronnie was the most gifted Keeper in the agency, and I wasn't her first Seer. That honor had fallen to a woman named Lucy who had been murdered by one of the Tainted; a Fae that had been ripped from the fairy realm and made human. The process had driven the poor creature insane, and Lucy had been one of her first victims. At the time, Raegan had suspected Alistair's involvement, and even though he had since been cleared of any wrongdoings, her feelings about him were still peppered with that initial distrust.

I put a hand on her shoulder. "I know how you feel about him, but he's on our side. I swear. But If I'm wrong and he turns out to be an evil prick?" I smiled gently. "I have a secret weapon."

Ronnie brightened a bit and tried to shake off whatever sadness she was allowing to creep in. "What's that?" She asked.

"You." I said playfully waggling my brows.

That brought a genuine look of joy to her face.

"Okay, enough with the Hallmark moments." I said, pulling her towards me with the hand that had been resting on her shoulder and using the momentum to push past her. "Let's get moving."

Snatching my keys off the counter top, I gave the rest of the garlic wings a once over, but thought better of it. My car already had a funky sour milk smell to it; if I added the scent of Robbie's vampire repellent to the mix, it might make for an uncomfortably long ride.

Besides, they were already cold.

"What do you think you're doing?" Ronnie asked, as I dangled the keys at her meaningfully and headed towards the door.

"Driving." I said confidently. She loved to drive, usually drove, and if I didn't put my foot down once in a while, would always drive.

"I'm driving." She said. She was smiling now, and I could see that she wasn't even entertaining the thought of me trying to play Alpha Male.

"You always drive." I challenged, putting a bit of bass into my voice as I opened the door for her.

"Yeah, well, my car isn't upside down." She said pleasantly, as if pointing out something as harmless as an untied shoelace.

I froze in place as I realized how something like that could have happened.

"Or on the roof." She added, pushing past me in triumph.

I bowed my head and took a deep breath. "Hey, why don't you drive?" I suggested in defeat as I closed the door behind me and moved to catch up to her.

Goddamn leprechauns.

Chapter Six

Chewie dropped us out of hyperspace just outside of the city's old shipping and warehouse district, and I felt the engine rumble in exhausted thanks. More industrial than commercial, most of the buildings were either boarded up, or in the early stages of permanent storage. Aside from the occasional dock worker or wayward forklift, the entire area seemed almost abandoned.

Yashar Imports and Antiquities was an old wooden-faced storefront wedged tightly between two worn brick buildings that stood stoically in their never ending duty of holding the small shop up. To the average, untrained eye, the store might have seemed out of place, but not suspiciously so; the remnants of a time long past. But to *my* untrained-yet-magically-imbued eye, I could see that every door and window was adorned with a softly glowing symbol hovering inches above the surface of any actual wood.

Fairy wards.

Alistair Yashar dealt in rare artifacts and oddities, most of which just happened to be Fae in nature. Questionably obtained or not, these things tended to attract a certain amount of attention, and Alistair's normal client base wasn't the sort that you would want popping in unexpectedly. I wasn't actually sure of what the glowing symbols really did, but since I had never seen even the hint of a fairy in the area, I assumed that they worked pretty well.

Putting the car in park in front of the store, Raegan let the black sedan die with a merciful turn of the key before looking to me with a resigned sigh.

"Just try to be careful if you pick something up." She warned in a defeated voice. Raegan had learned long ago that telling me *not* to touch anything was an exercise in futility. It wasn't that I wanted to disobey, or that I'd do so out of defiance; I just have the attention span of a sugared-up eight year old and shiny things tended to catch my eye.

"I always am." I lied as I adjusted my over shirt in an attempt to pass for presentable. My shirt and pants were spattered with dried blood and pizza sauce, my face was cut and showing the early signs of bruising, and I was only wearing one sock.

But other than that, I looked damn good.

In the past I had always tried my best to appear halfway decent whenever I planned on visiting Alistair. It wasn't because I wanted to impress him, but because he was one of those "naturally handsome" guys who never had to work out, but still had those weird stomach muscles that served no other purpose than to make me feel inferior. On a good day he made me feel ugly; today I could just hope that I seemed like I had a nice personality.

Taking the lead I moved up the old wooden steps to the shop and pushed through the door without hesitation. I had been in the shop dozens of times now, and knew that the magical protections guarding the place didn't seem to apply to me. While Raegan couldn't see them, she could sense magical energy powering them, and that made her nervous. She followed a few steps behind me, cautiously looking upward as the old tin bell clanged loudly, announcing our arrival.

The shop was old and cluttered, but lovingly maintained. Intersecting rows of tall, high backed wooden shelves stocked with all sorts of ancient and unusual items lined the aisles giving the place an almost maze-like quality. Wooden statues, small dolls, and countless other artifacts were arranged in such a way as to give the impression that the store was more than likely cursed, or at the very least, extremely haunted. It was the kind of quaint and quiet place that Edgar Allan Poe might go antiquing, if he were still alive.

"Honey I'm hoooome." I called out, drawing an exaggerated eye roll from my partner as we picked our way through the looming rows of strange items.

"Johnathan!" A man's voice greeted from the back of the store. "How'd it go with Willow? She take good care of you?" He asked slyly.

I looked over my shoulder as Raegan arched a slender eyebrow and pursed her lips in disapproval.

"That is definitely not what it sounds like." I said a bit too quickly.

"So Alistair didn't give you the name of someone who illegally sells raw milk on the dairy black market?" She asked shrewdly.

I blinked.

"Oh." I said with a baffled expression as we exited the aisle. "Then, yeah. It's exactly what it sounds like."

The store's display counter and register took up most of the back wall, and was lined with bottles and bowls of pungent items that I couldn't easily identify. Alistair stood behind the register in a white button up shirt, held firmly in place by a pair of old fashioned suspenders. Amber colored eyes made more vibrant by the darkness of his skin widened in amusement, only to narrow slightly as Raegan stepped out of the aisle behind me and into view.

"And Agent Connolly." He amended politely, dipping his head in a greeting to my partner.

"Alistair." She said evenly, returning the gesture with a slight nod.

"Wow. You look like shit." Alistair said sympathetically as he brought his gaze back to me and motioned to my face. "Official FPI business then?"

"Yeah, sorry man." I apologized. I liked Alistair and felt kind of bad that I had no way of warning him that I wasn't alone before we arrived. I didn't want to ruin the trust that the two of us had built, but at the same time if I told him that we were coming, Ronnie would have probably added to my already impressive collection of bruises.

I hated being forced to take sides and the awkwardness that the situation brought by doing so. Thankfully Alistair took it in stride and didn't seem to be the least bit offended or upset.

"No problem at all." He smiled pleasantly. "Always glad to help out the agency whenever I can." He added, laying it on thick for Raegan's benefit. "What can I do for you?"

My partner stepped up to the counter and removed the bundle of soft blue fabric from her coat pocket. Setting it down gently, she unfurled the cloth and looked up at the shopkeeper. "Have you ever seen one of these before?" She asked, her eyes flickering to the space just above his head.

Besides being beautiful, smart, and having the natural skills of a NASCAR driver, Raegan could "read colors", as she called it. I didn't fully grasp the concept of auras, but I knew that if Alistair were to lie to her, she'd know immediately.

"Hmmm." He hummed in thought as he rooted through the remains. "It depends." Holding up a mangled twist of silver, he extended the leg and looked at me. "What was it, exactly?"

"A creepy little robot spider." I answered.

"And I'm guessing that this was your handiwork?" He asked with amusement as he held up another chunk of the crumpled metal.

"Tragic river dancing accident." I explained. Alistair forced a chuckle, but I could tell that he was disappointed. He collected the strange and unusual and generally liked those type of items to be in one piece, or at the very least, not horribly stomped on.

"Have you ever seen this man?" Raegan asked, setting my attacker's license on the counter.

Alistair glanced down at it. "Rupert Ambrose." He read the name and shrugged. "No. Sorry. I mean the last name sounds familiar, but I've never seen him before." He clarified. "He's definitely not affiliated with any of the normal markets." Alistair held up the piece of spider that he had been examining. "I take it that this was his?"

"He called it a latrodenzian." I supplied.

The shop keeper's eyes lit up in recognition and Raegan and I exchanged quick glances. She hadn't missed it either and was now casually skimming his aura with a bit more scrutiny.

"You know what this is, don't you?" She asked eagerly.

Alistair gave a hesitant nod. "I think so." He admitted. "I've never seen one in person, but yeah. Give me a minute." Pushing through the beaded curtain that separated the shop from the main storeroom, he disappeared into the back in pursuit of whatever half-memory he was chasing.

Ronnie was like a cat getting ready to pounce. Eyes vibrant, she shifted her weight from heel to heel as she watched and waited for Alistair's return. I chuckled softly as I leaned against the counter and dragged my hand lazily through a bowl of dried, petrified nuggets beside the register. They were small and round and smelled strongly of cinnamon and that sharp peppery scent that burns the back of your nose.

"Admit it." I said. "You love this place."

My partner stopped bouncing and frowned at me, folding her arms beneath her chest. "No I don't." She denied with a grumpy sort of guilt.

"Yes you do." I teased, gesturing around the store with a handful of the sharply scented balls. "All of it. The statues, the books, the freaky little odds and ends." I let the dried potpourri trickle from my fingers and back into the bowl like a fossilized waterfall. "You just want to run through the aisles touching everything, like a kid in a toy store."

"Stop playing with that." She scolded.

I let the last of the pellets roll off my fingertips and wrinkled my nose. "Smells like Grandma's house." I said, making a face.

"Your Grandmother kept bowls of petrified Gnome testicles in her home?" Ronnie asked sweetly.

I froze in place. "What?" I asked, my hand still hovering above the container.

My partner smiled slightly and nodded meaningfully to the bowl that I had been idly digging through seconds before. "GAAAH!" I yelped. "What in the hell is *wrong* with you people?" I demanded as I played Lady Macbeth on the front of my pants.

Raegan laughed softly and brought a slender hand to her lips in an attempt to hide her amusement. "Relax." She said, her eyes twinkling brightly with mischief. "It's just a bowl of allspice."

I gave her shocked look.

"But *you* didn't know that, so stop touching stuff." She smirked as Alistair reappeared with a small stack of ancient looking books.

Spreading them out on the counter top, he picked through the dusty old tomes before pinpointing the one that he had been searching for. Raegan crowded close, leaning heavily on the glass and standing on her tip toes in attempt to get a better view. Thumbing through a few of the yellowed pages, the shopkeeper stopped on a passage in a language that I couldn't even begin to comprehend.

"Here we go." He announced. "Latrodenzian."

I glanced at the book, or more aptly, the small, hand drawn illustration of the mechanical spider and nodded. "Yeah, that's it." I confirmed.

Alistair angled the book so that Raegan could view the page without climbing further over the counter, and the two read in silence as I lamely looked on. The older the book, the more likely it was to be written in some language that no one had ever heard of, which would give me zero hopes of even trying to decipher. Shaking his head, Alistair whistled low and looked up at me, his golden eyes serious.

"These things are bad news." He informed me.

I chuffed in agreement. "Tell me about it. *You* didn't see the frigging thing come to life." The memory of the spider skittering towards me would have top billing in my nightmares for weeks to come.

"No." He corrected. "I mean, if someone is coming after you with one of these, they're not playing around." He explained. "And they really know what they're doing."

"What does it do, exactly?" Raegan asked, looking up from the book.

"When attached to the host, it induces a dreamlike sleep. The victim is rendered unconscious, but left otherwise unharmed." Alistair explained.

"That doesn't sound so bad." I said. "It's sort of like an eight-legged Ambien."

"Once unconscious, all thoughts, memories, and *abilities* of the host can be transferred to another." He said with emphasis. "Through this." Alistair pushed the book in my direction and stabbed his finger below an illustration of a heavily jeweled tiara.

"A pretty-pretty princess crown?" I asked, unimpressed.

"Each latrodenzian can be controlled by a single matching gem. This crown allows the wearer to link with up to eight of them at a time." He said gravely.

Raegan gave a groan of understanding. "If he were to incapacitate the right people, he'd be unstoppable."

"Unstoppable how?" I shifted uncomfortably. It was all fun and games until Ronnie got worried.

"Imagine the training of an MMA fighter, mixed with the strength of an Ogre." Alistair said. "Or the knowledge of a Norn paired with the untapped power of a nymph. These things work on humans and Fae alike. Think Alexander the Great, Charlemagne or Genghis Khan. You might have destroyed one, but if this man has a crown, he could have seven more of them."

Silence filled the store, loudly magnifying my nervous swallow as I absorbed Alistair's words. If one spider was enough to ruin my night, seven of them all twitching to life in my direction would be enough to ensure that I never slept again. I thought back to the small kitchen and my almost sex-crime thorough searching of Somnus. He had a small black bag with him, but beyond the latrodenzian it had been empty.

"I searched him pretty well." I said, my voice cracking from disuse and not fear. "That was the only one that he had." I tried to sound hopeful, but Alistair was already shaking his head.

"These things are extremely rare and valuable." He said. "I doubt that he anticipated you being able to defeat him, so he wouldn't have needed to bring more than one with him."

"Yeah, well, he didn't seem that strong to me." I said, bristling with insult.

Raegan grinned at my posturing. "Maybe not physically." Her smile deepened tellingly and my heart sank. Did she know that he was-

"But he was a magic user." She said, turning to Alistair just in time to miss my relieved sigh. "Actual spells. And he used this." She finished, handing him the broken wand.

"Really?" Alistair sounded impressed as he took the wand. "Wait. You're saying that he was a true magic user?" Something clicked, you could almost hear it. "Hang on, hang on," He echoed. Searching through the small pile of books once again, he snagged one and began to flip through it, his head moving side to side as he quickly read.

"Aha!" He exclaimed. "Ambrose." He brightened, his finger hovering triumphantly over a dense block of words that I knew in my heart I'd never, ever willingly read.

No longer content to scale the glass display case like her own personal Everest, Raegan ducked under the flip top divider and joined Alistair behind the counter.

"Shit." She swore under her breath, and I beamed with pride.

Ronnie had only recently taken up the habit of reflexive swearing, but she was coming along nicely. It might have been due to our bonding; the ritual that effectively made us siblings and adapt each other's traits, but I liked to think that it was a completely natural effect and due to nothing more than my bad influence. Still, she did it with enough rarity that any joy that I was receiving from her corruption was overshadowed by the fact that I knew that this was not going to be good.

"The Order of Emyrs." She said, looking up at me expectantly.

"The Chef from Boston?" I asked, shattering that expectation.

"Merlin." Alistair said flatly. There was no love lost in his speaking of the name.

"Wait. Like the wizard? From knight and castle times?" I asked, my heart beginning to pound with excitement. "THAT GUY WAS FRICKIN' MERLIN?!" I was awestruck and let down at the same time. From the fantasy novels and bad Sci-Fi movies of my youth, I knew that Merlin was the original spell-chucking badass, but I never would have expected him to be wearing arm braces or have a glass jaw.

Still, look at me baby, I took out frickin' *Merlin*.

"No." Raegan shook her head, a soft tumble of red hair dashing my dreams. "The Order of Emyrs are a secret society of men who claim to be the direct descendants of Myrddin Ambrosius."

I stared blankly.

"Merlin." She sighed. "The Order devotes their lives to the study of the elements, magic, and the Fae." She finished with an awkward glance to Alistair.

"So what's Merlin's tie to the Fae?" I asked. "Was he banging the Queen too?" I teased.

Alistair stared at me in unamused silence as Ronnie quickly waved her hands beside him in a motion for me to stop.

"Are you *serious*?" My jaw hit the floor. "Man. I have got to meet this chick." I said mostly to myself.

Ronnie cleared her throat and put a steadying hand on Alistair's arm. "Merlin was said to have been close with the Queen of the Fae." She said diplomatically. "In return for his companionship, he was allowed to take the magic that he had learned at her side into our world. The Order of Emyrs are-"

"Delusional children for the most part." Alistair interrupted. The annoyance that he had been radiating was gone, replaced by an unimpressed roll of his eyes as he spoke. "Black robes, a few old relics and the occasional book well above their reading level, sure." He explained. "But they're harmless. I've yet to see even one among them with even the smallest amount of actual magical ability.

"I have." I pointed out, a cold tendril of fear touching my spine as I remembered the flames.

"Could they have made the latrodenzian?" Raegan asked.

Alistair thought for a moment and then shook his head. "I highly doubt it. The magic required is overwhelming and well beyond anything that humans could ever be capable of. I cringe to think of what harnessing that much raw energy and power would do to his body if he tried."

Uh oh.

"Plus," Alistair continued.

"He would have had to kill an Ananasi." Raegan finished the thought.

I had seen the guy in action. It would take more than a lightshow and a little fire to take down an Ananasi. If he couldn't beat me, then he wouldn't stand a chance against the monstrous spider Fae.

"So either this guy went toe to toe with one of the most badass fairies around, or what? He was the highest bidder on Evil EBay?" I asked.

Alistair thought about it for a second and shrugged. "I'll make a few calls. Some of the, ahem, *people* that I do business with might have heard something useful. It's a longshot, but it would be impossible to move something like this without turning at least a few heads."

"Thank you." Raegan said sincerely, gently touching his arm.

The shop keeper smiled softly down at her. "Like I said, I'm always happy to help." He offered her a playful wink. "Besides, whenever you two get wind of something, all Hell tends to break loose. It'll be a nice change of pace."

Raegan grinned and ducked under the counter, moving to my side. "C'mon." She said. "The Assistant Director is going to want a full report, and we have a ton of research to do."

Alistair gave me an urgent look and gestured with his head to the room behind him, recovering with a natural grace before my partner could notice.

"Uh. Yeah." I stalled. "You go ahead. I'll catch up in a second."

Ronnie stopped in her tracks and looked at me, her eyes narrowing in suspicion. Any second now those piercing green eyes would be flickering to the top of my head, and I'd be in a whole lot of trouble.

"Someone has to pay the man for the milk." I sighed. "Or do you not mind being a witness to the transaction?" I asked, knowing her usually stringent following of anything even remotely resembling a rule.

She frowned disapprovingly and shot Alistair a withering look. "Make it quick." She ordered, shaking her head in a tumble of judgmental red as she pushed past me. Stepping back into the maze of shelves and demonically possessed bric-a-brac, she disappeared in hurried condemnation.

I stepped closer to Alistair, and we waited a full breath after the door chimes clanged my partner's exit before we spoke.

"I want you to know, this wasn't easy to get." He said quietly, as if Raegan could still hear us. Reaching under the counter, he produced a small, clear tube of a creamy brown liquid.

I could feel myself smiling stupidly. "This is it?" I asked, taking it from him with the eagerness of a child on his birthday. "It doesn't look like very much." I pointed out as I tugged on the vial's cork.

"Stop!" Alistair cried, covering my hands with his own and preventing me from opening it. I stared at our entwined hands for a moment and then looked up at him.

"This stuff does work." I said dreamily.

Alistair snorted a laugh and slowly released my hands. "Not in here. Eros." He swore, I think. The word sounded Latin and he was old, so I'm pretty sure it was naughty.

"Sorry." I said sheepishly, tightening the stopper.

"Just be careful, okay? The smallest *dab*, and not a drop more." He let out a small sigh as if second guessing his giving of the gift. "You really have no idea what you're messing with."

"But it *works*." I said, looking for confirmation.

Alistair laughed a bit easier. "Oh yeah." He grinned lecherously. "It works."

Grabbing the blue cloth that contained the broken pieces of the latrodenzian, I unfurled the fabric and deposited them on the counter. Carefully wrapping the glass vial, I placed it carefully into my pocket and flashed Alistair a naughty grin.

"You rock man." I said, holding out my closed fist.

"I know." He grinned back, bumping his knuckles against mine. "Seriously, just be careful with it alright?"

"Careful is my middle name." I said suavely. It's not. It's actually Andrew, but that didn't sound as cool in this context and would have ruined the moment.

"How much do I owe you?" I asked.

Alistair held up his hands palms flat towards me.

"You let me keep what's left of your little friend here, and we'll call it even." He offered.

"Done." I accepted.

Glancing towards the exit, I gave Alistair one last nod of thanks and turned, heading towards the door. The rows of scary shelving swallowed me in an instant and the last thing that I heard before stepping out of the shop was Alistair asking himself a single question with a rueful chuckle.

"What have I done?"

Chapter Seven

"Heya Sis."

Raegan looked over her shoulder at me and smiled. The sudden motion caused a wave of red hair to crash around her as if she were auditioning for her own personal shampoo commercial.

She had insisted that I get a shower and a couple of hours sleep before our debriefing, and as much as I had fought her on it, as usual, she was right. The shower had washed away the dried blood and grime of the day, but had taken with it whatever reserves of energy I had keeping me on my feet. I was asleep before my head hit the pillow and the pure, dreamless rest of my power napping had left me questioning how I would have been able to function had I not listened to her.

No longer forced to squat in the parody of a hotel room that was the "emergency housing unit", my new apartment was only a five minute walk from the agency's main building, separated by a small but peaceful, bench-lined park. Sure, it was still provided by the FPI, but it was far more generously furnished than anything that I would have ever done on my own. Plus, it came without the threat of soviet-era kitchen appliances or arsonist goblins.

Which was nice.

A shower, shave and fresh suit had left me feeling like a new man. Company standard issue black on black styled in a way that made my clothing scream "I totally work for a secret government agency", I always felt like James Bond whenever I got dressed. Still, where I might have looked *damn* good, Raegan looked downright amazing.

Like me, she had cleaned up and changed her clothing, although I highly doubted that sleep ever entered into the equation. Dressed in a formfitting version of my own outfit that hugged and accentuated every feminine curve, there was no doubt that she'd turn the head of any guy out there who wanted a bloody nose, because stop looking at my sister like that, pal.

"You look better." Raegan said with motherly relief. Turning to fully face me, she handed me several thick folders which I took without question as she reached up to straighten my tie.

"How long have you been here?" I asked, looking at the lettering on the door that read "Office of the Assistant Director". We had agreed to meet here in an effort to save time, and even though I knew that I was a few minutes early, I still felt a twinge of guilt for making her wait.

"Not long." She lied, the crushed shoulder of her suit from where she had been leaning against the wall, silently tattling out the truth. "How are you feeling?" She asked, taking the small stack of files from me as she stepped back.

"Like a million bucks that just got its ass kicked by David Copperfield." I admitted.

"Oh it's not *that* bad, you big baby." She teased. "I doubt that anyone is even going to notice." Placing one slender hand on the door knob, she looked to me and took a small breath. "Ready?"

I nodded my response and followed as she opened the door and stepped into the small waiting area that skirted the edge of the Assistant Director's office.

Apart from a few comfortable looking cloth chairs and a table strewn with old Time magazines in various stages of ripping decay, the reception area was largely empty. The receptionist herself sat at the forefront of the room, perched behind a small oval shaped desk. Like every other woman who graced the agency, she was hauntingly beautiful, a fact made only more noticeable by the large smile that illuminated her face as we entered.

"Agent Connolly." She greeted. "Agent Tal-OH MY GOD! What happened to your face?" The secretary's eyes widened in surprise as she stood, all but leaping from her desk as she moved to my side for a closer inspection.

"No one is even going to notice, eh?" I said under my breath, earning me a roll of emerald eyes.

"Is the Assistant Director in, Kimmie?" Raegan asked. Her voice was even and professional, but laced with just enough annoyance at the receptionist's doting that it would be impossible to miss.

"Yeah, sure." Kimmie responded without looking as she slowly touched my face. "Oooh, does it hurt?" She asked, her eyes heavy with concern. "You poor baby."

Okay, the annoyance was *nearly* impossible to miss.

"Naw." I bluffed. "Although it probably would have killed a lesser man." I started to flirt, only to be cut off as Ronnie coughed loudly and deliberately cleared her throat.

"Kimmie?" She asked pointedly, her voice firmer, strengthened by her irritation.

Straightening immediately, the receptionist smoothed her skirt in an embarrassed fashion and stepped away from me, properly addressing my partner.

"I mean, yes. Yes Agent Connolly. Miss Blair is in and she is expecting you. You may go right in." She said respectfully, the professional demeanor of a full time personal assistant slipping back into place.

"Thank you." Raegan said with a sigh. Sharing some of the irritation that had been directed at the receptionist with me, she placed the small stack of folders that she had been carrying into the "In box" on Kimmie's desk and nodded meaningfully to the closed office door before stepping towards it.

"Thanks Kimmie." I whispered, hurrying to keep up. With a

meaningful wink to the now blushing secretary, I followed my partner into the Assistant Director's office, and gently closed the heavy wood door behind me.

Gloria Blair was a striking woman in what I would assume to be her early fifties. I've never been good at guessing a woman's age, and the job was made all the more difficult by the Fae blood coursing through her veins. Like myself and the receptionist Kimmie, she was one of the rare few brunettes swimming in the sea of blonde and red that seemed to make up the majority of the Agency's staff. Eyes the color of cold steel were cast downward, scouring a page from the apparently never ending pile of paperwork that peppered her desk in small clusters. Two evidence bags leaned heavily against a tower of reports, their contents obscured, but still familiar through their plastic coverings; the length of Ananasi silk and a wallet, now devoid of pizza money and an overly generous tip.

In her prime, the Assistant Director was said to have been one of the highest ranked Keepers ever to work for the agency. Now she ran it. Although her title was "Assistant Director", as far as I could tell she the senior-most management at our office, so I'm not exactly sure as to who she was supposed to be an assistant *to*. All cases, assignments and debriefings were coordinated through her, and there had never been so much of a whisper about anyone "higher up" on the managerial food chain. In fact, in my first few weeks here, I often joked that her first name really was "Assistant-Director" and that as a child she had been taken in and raised by a roving pack of wild bureaucrats.

"Agent Connolly. Agent Talik." She greeted without looking up from her writing. "Please have a seat." She added, motioning with the top of her pen to the twin leather chairs positioned in front of the desk.

I waited until Raegan sat before doing so myself. Assistant Director Blair had never showed me anything but patience and kindness, but in her office I always felt as if I were on the edge of a scolding. It was high school all over again, and even though I hadn't done anything wrong, it was always a good idea to be on your best behavior in the Principals' office.

"Agent Connolly." She said closing the file that she had been making notes on. "I just finished going over your report. Excellent job, as always." Raegan nodded in modest acknowledgement of the praise, but a barely contained smile twitched at the corners of her mouth.

"When in the hell did you have time to write a report?" I whispered in awe.

The Assistant Director sat back in her chair and looked up at us for the first time. Although her manner was that of a strict professional, I could always catch the briefest gleam of amusement in her eyes whenever we spoke. Now those eyes were searching my face and narrowing with fret.

"How are you feeling?" She asked with honest concern.

"Um, better?" I fought for my words, thrown by her worry. "I mean good. It's a lot worse than it looks." I recovered awkwardly.

"Good. I'm relieved to hear that." She nodded. "And excellent job turning the tables on your assailant." Holding up the evidence bag containing the wallet that I had recovered, I thought I could see that tiny twinkle of humor in her eye.

"Yeah, well," I puffed up braggingly. "I didn't want it to have to get rough, but, hey. I had to do wha-"

"Now please explain to me exactly how he managed to escape your custody." She ordered. My breath caught in my throat and I coughed as I tried to swallow and breathe at the same time.

"I...he...there..." I stammered.

"As stated in my reports, the attacker was a magic user." Raegan explained. She followed rules that I wasn't even aware I was breaking and took orders without question like a seasoned solider; but there was a protective, almost defensive edge on her words as she came to my rescue.

The Assistant Director nodded in acceptance of the fact and looked down at the folder in front of her. Opening it to an ear-marked page, she read briefly before looking up. "True, but you also state that Agent Talik had him tied with Ananasi Silk." She gestured to the bag containing the rope. "And had locked him in..." She tilted her head to one side and looked at me for clarification.

"The shower?"

"He had fire." I said sheepishly.

Her eyes flashed with sympathy and understanding, but in an instant it was gone, quickly replaced by her managerial responsibilities.

"As you undoubtedly remember from your classes," There was a heavy twist of knowing sarcasm at the mention of my schooling. "The Ananasi Silk would have negated any of his abilities, natural or magical, and left him paralyzed, making escape impossible." She explained. "Yet Agent Connolly reports that you were able to free yourself from it as well. How?"

"He didn't tie it that tight?" I answered without confidence as I looked to Raegan for help.

Instead of coming to my defense, my Keeper frowned and turned in her chair to face me. "But he wouldn't have had to." She said. "It's *Ananasi Silk*."

"Oooh!" I said, pretending to understand.

Raegan's frown deepened and she flickered her gaze above my head. Rolling her eyes, she took a breath to say something, but the Assistant Director spoke first.

"Regardless of how, I'm just glad that you're safe." She smiled at me before giving a troubled sigh and standing. Lifting a thin red folder from the top of the filing cabinet beside her desk, she handed it to my Keeper and looked her directly in the eyes.

"Because I'm going to need both of you on this case, immediately."

Raegan and I exchanged worried glances as the Assistant Director silently moved across the room and stood facing the award strewn wall, her hands clasped behind her back.

Skimming the file that she now held, I watched as Raegan's eyes narrowed and then widened. She began to flip faster and faster through the report, until I was certain that there was no way that she could actually be reading it.

"Is this accurate?" She asked in a small voice, the color draining from her face.

"I'm afraid so." Assistant Director Blair answered. Lifting one delicate hand, she lightly touched the glass surface of one of the many foil stamped certificates that hung on the office wall.

"What is it?" I asked.

"An employee file." Raegan said, turning to me with a look of shock. "John, he's one of *us*."

"*That guy* is an agent?" I asked in skeptically. Standing I shook my head. This didn't make any goddamn sense. "Wait, wait, wait." I waved my hands in front of me. "I thought that I was the only guy batting for Team Estrogen."

"The only agent, yes." The Assistant Director answered, still facing the wall. "But you are far from being the only male employed by the agency."

"I don't understand." I admitted.

"He's a teacher at the academy." Raegan explained. She held up a piece of paper containing a bad photocopy of an ID Badge.

"The academy?"

"The Weis Institute of Cosmetology." The Assistant Director sighed again, tapping the glass of the diploma that she had been studying.

"I got my ass kicked by a *beautician*?!" Man, if word of this ever got out, I'd never live it down.

The tension in the room wavered as Raegan laughed softly. "It's the cover identity for our youth training facility. It's the perfect explanation for any nearby locals who may question why our girls are, ah…"

I could see that she was looking for a way to say "really attractive" without sounding vain.

"Yeah yeah, fairy blood, I get it. You're all super models." It was my turn to roll my eyes as I took the folder from her and flipped through it. "So Somnus is a teacher at Hogwarts for hot chicks?"

Assistant Director Blair turned at the waist and shot me a puzzled look. "Somnus?"

"Yeah, that's what he calls himself. Kept shouting it at me." I explained offhandedly as I flipped through the information on the school.

"Somnus is Latin. It means-" She began, but Raegan waved her off.

"So how did he get past all of your background checks and what not?" I asked.

"That's just it." Raegan said, moving to my side. Turning to the last page of the folder, she pointed to the results of the vetting process. "He's clean."

"Agent Connolly is correct." The Assistant Director confirmed as she faced us. "Before last night, there were no incidents and nothing in his past to even remotely draw suspicion or indicate that he'd be of any threat. I spoke with the Headmistress at the school and she insists that he's been an exceptional, even model employee and was insulted that we would suggest anything to the contrary." She explained. "And, it gets worse."

"Let me guess." I said dryly. "No one has seen gimpy in a few weeks, right?"

"That's just it." She shook her head. "Everybody has seen him. In fact, he's there right now. They have no record of him leaving the campus, and apparently he was volunteering at a school "lock in" event during the time of your attack."

"Bullshit." I objected.

"There has to be some mistake." Raegan countered a bit more gently with an imploring look in my direction.

"I thought so as well." The Assistant Director admitted, graciously ignoring my outburst. "But I had Agents Wallace and Young verify. They confirm that he is not only there, but cooperating in every way. If anything, he seems as baffled by all of this as we are."

"McKenna and Lydia are already on site?" Raegan asked, raising a slender eyebrow.

Assistant Director Blair nodded. "Remember when I said that it gets worse? Two months ago, a student at the academy, Kara Saunders, went missing. We worked with local authorities, but she was never found." Stepping towards the desk, she retrieved another folder from one of the many piles and handed it to Raegan. "Yesterday morning, two more girls failed to report to class."

Raegan's eyes darted over the contents of the file. "They're all Seers, and wow." She said, handing me the file. "Look at their marks."

I skimmed the first few pages, but had no idea what I was looking at.

"They're at the top of their class." Ronnie explained quietly.

I flipped through a few more notes for good measure, before closing the folder. "So you think this guy is snatching kids?"

The Assistant Director shook her head "no" in frustration. "Neither of the girls attended the lock-in. Their beds were found slept in, but empty. There were no signs of struggle and their roommates each slept soundly through the night. There is no way that Professor Ambrose could have been involved."

"But I'm telling you," I slapped at the folder in my hand. "*That* is the guy who jumped me." I was getting frustrated. Coming after me was one thing, but going after kids? That was low.

Assistant Director Blair nodded her understanding. "Which is why you two leave immediately. This takes top priority over anything else that you may have been assigned. If those girls are in any danger, my four top agents are their best hope. Find the girls, find out Ambrose's connection to all of this, and put an end to it." Her emphasis on the word end had a cold, finality to it.

"Security-" Raegan began as we stood.

"Has already been informed of your arrival, and has offered their cooperation. Headmistress Merry has personally assured me that you will have full run of the campus and access to anything that you may need."

Taking my partner's lead, we turned in unison and moved towards the door, the gravity of the situation hastening our steps.

"One last thing." Assistant Director Blair called after us. I had beaten Raegan to the door by several steps and was already in position to open it. "Where is the latrodenzian?"

I felt my heart stop beating as I threw my Keeper a panicked glance.

"With Alistair Yashar." She said, turning to face our boss. As horrible of a liar as Ronnie was, I really could have used the mercy of a little white one right about now.

The Assistant Director raised a questioning eyebrow, her gaze moving past my partner and locking onto me like a steel grey tractor beam.

"Given the nature of the device, we thought it best to have an expert examine it for any residual traces of magic that might lead us back to its owner." Raegan explained, not exactly lying, but pretty much stretching the truth to its breaking point.

"Excellent." Assistant Director Blair said, accepting the answer and releasing me from her stony gaze. "I expect a full report on his findings on my desk when all of this done. And make sure that you get it to research and design as quickly as possible. I wager that Jonas is going to be chomping at the bit to get his hands on it." She sounded amused by the thought.

Spinning to leave once again, Ronnie narrowed her eyes at me. "Of course. That won't be a problem." She said heatedly.

"I should hope not." The Assistant Director replied, her eyes locking briefly with mine.

I smiled uncomfortably and opened the door. My partner stepping through, accidentally elbowed me painfully in the ribcage as she passed by.

"Oh, and Agent Connolly?" Assistant Director Blair called out once more.

Raegan swore under her breath and turned her head, forcing a smile.

"Yes Ma'am?"

"Max says hello."

The forced smile turned real with such speed and force, I thought that my Keeper's face was going to split in two. I waved an awkward goodbye to our boss and quickly moved through the reception area and into the main hallway in an effort to keep up.

Ronnie's face was a dangerous mixture of overjoyed and over-annoyed, so I decided to add a bit of fuel to the first fire in the hope that it would steal the flames from the second.

"Max?" I asked, finally catching up. It worked, and her grin widened into a mischievous smirk. "Who is this Max?" I prodded as we moved down the long, brightly lit corridor. "And what's with the sudden influx of dudes? I thought that I was the only eye candy that you ladies needed." I teased.

Raegan scoffed at that.

"Oh please. Have you ever *seen* Javier from maintenance?" She asked rhetorically, a bit of blush creeping to her cheeks.

I grumbled something incoherent under my breath.

Man, I hated Javier.

Young, buff, and naturally bronzed, he had one of those Latino accents that caused every woman in a fifty mile radius to spontaneously ovulate as their panties ignited with the heat of their lust. He was a flirt, a bit of a player, and worst of all…

…he was just *shitty* at his job.

I mean, I've changed hundreds of light bulbs in my day, so I know for a fact that in can be done in less than an hour, and never once while doing it did I ever feel the need to slowly peel off my t-shirt halfway through the process. If given the right audience, Javier would make plunging a toilet look like the filming of a Spanish soap opera, with unseen breezes and barely contained lip bites of passion.

And the ladies ate up every second of it.

"There's also Matt in Payroll, Greg from legal," She continued, pulling me from the darkness that was my all-consuming hatred for all things Javier.

"Okay, I get it. I'm not a beautiful or unique snowflake." I pretended to sulk.

Mostly.

"Oh hey. Thanks for covering for me back there." I pointed behind us in the direction of the now out of sight office.

The annoyance that I had been trying to thwart crept back into her eyes. "I wasn't covering for you." She said flatly. "When this is over, you're getting it back from Alistair."

"But."

My Keeper stopped in her tracks and slowly looked up at me. Jade fire danced dangerously behind her eyes like an agitated cat getting ready to strike. She might have been a good five inches and sixty something pounds smaller than me, but in that instant, my stomach and groin felt as if they were joining forces at the top of a rollercoaster.

"But?" She asked, daring me to press my point.

I held up my hands. "Okay, okay. Yeesh. I'll get it back. Settle down Beavis." The flames behind her eyes died down, but didn't quite extinguish as we resumed walking. After a few agonizing minutes of tense silence, I noticed that we weren't heading for the exit, but for the main bank of elevators that lead to the many other levels of the agency.

"Where are we going?" I asked, stepping into one of the lifts after Raegan.

"Research and Design." She responded, supplying the answer to my question and commanding the voice activation of the elevator in the same breath. "I want Doctor Peppar's take on the latrodenzian. Plus it wouldn't hurt to…" A pained look crossed her face.

"Check up on the old guy?" I supplied.

"He was closer to Caroline, to Agraveagh, than anyone." She explained, her voice soft with compassion. The elevator dinged our arrival and a moment later we stepped into the main hall of the Research and Design unit.

"Don't tell me that he blames himself." I said sympathetically. "She had everyone fooled, including Blair." If Agraveagh had managed to go undetected beneath the steely gaze of the Assistant Director, no one else would have had a prayer of flushing her out.

Raegan shrugged. "They spent years working together. I suspect on some level, they were actually friends." She breathed a small, sad sigh. "I'm told that he's taking her betrayal really hard."

A peal of laughter cut through our quiet conversation, bouncing off the sterile white tile of the surrounding walls and echoing past. Exchanging confused looks, we hurried our pace and rounded a corner before coming to rest in the door way to the primary research lab.

What we saw stopped us in our tracks.

Doctor Peppar was leaning heavily against a lab bench as he doubled over with what I would have to describe as, and please note that I'm pushing the definition of the word to its absolute limits, laughter.

A combination of snorting and wheezing ending in a high pitched whine that only certain breeds of specially trained dog could hear, his old body bobbed and shook with the effort of the world's weirdest cackle.

Standing beside him was a young woman in a white lab assistant's coat. She was about average height and build, with dark red shoulder length hair. Her face was emotionless and unreadable as she watched the Doctor laughing like a crotch kicked hyena on helium with a sort of clinical detachment. Normally, I would have considered her another beautiful addition to the FPI, but her lack of expression gave the skin on her face a smooth, almost doll-like quality that was starting to really wibb me out.

"Yeah." I agreed with Raegan, nodding to the pair. "He looks positively devastated."

As I spoke the two turned to us and with a friendly wave of greeting, I stepped into the room.

"Heya Doc!" I called out in a casual effort to show this new woman that I was no stranger to the Doctor or his lab.

Doctor Peppar straightened, a mirth-filled smile still spanning his lips as he turned and moved to greet us. The expressionless woman in white followed wordlessly, but kept herself at a silent, cautious distance.

"Agent Talik! And Agent Connolly!" He beamed. "How nice to see you both! How nice!"

I extended my hand, and had it crushed in an enthusiastic handshake. "We're not interrupting anything, are we?" I asked slyly with a playful nod to his lab partner.

"Yes, you are." The woman spoke in a cold monotone.

"No, no. Of course not. Of course not." Doctor Peppar said quickly, as if he hadn't heard her speak.

As I stepped back, Raegan took my place in front of the Doctor and offered him a gentle hug.

"How are you, Jonas?" She asked with quiet concern. Ronnie had never been a lab assistant, as that job came with risks that far outweighed any possible reward, but she had spent a lot of time prowling the facility's archives and over the years had developed a kind of a father/daughter relationship with the older man.

The Doctor smiled behind his thickly lensed glasses, each impossibly magnified crack and wrinkle of skin becoming a chasm of age. "Excellent, my dear, excellent. Thank you." He assured her. "Here, here. Let me introduce you to my new assistant. I've told her all about you two. All about you!" With a gentle arm around Raegan, he steered her to face his lab partner.

The woman didn't so much as twitch, she simply watched us with the detached interested of a scientist being introduced to two new white mice that she might later need to dissect.

"Agent Connolly, Agent Talik, this is Emma. Emma Addams." He introduced. "She's been filling in for you-know-who since she turned out to be a you-know-what." He whispered less than covertly past the back of his hand. "Emma was just telling me the most wonderful joke! You see these two protons collide because they're observing the bottomonium mason, and…" The Doctor trailed off into a torrent of delighted titters before waving his hands rapidly. "Oh, I can't tell it the way she does." He giggled. "Quite the cut-up this one. Quite the cut-up."

Raegan widened her eyes at me, and I struggled to keep a straight face.

"Emma," Doctor Peppar continued, unaware of the exchange. "This is our top Keeper, Agent Raegan Connolly. And *this* is-"

"Johnathan Andrew Talik." Emma cut in, stepping forward. "The only verifiable male Seer on record. Top marks in all six senses, despite only having a statistically average intelligence quotient. Current popular hypothesis is that you developed your abilities as a side-effect from head trauma and possibly irreversible brain damage."

"Um, just John is fine." I said awkwardly, offering her my hand.

Emma took it in a firm grip and shook it twice. "May I examine your brain?" She asked. Without waiting for my answer, she looked over her shoulder to the Doctor and asked again. "May I examine his brain?"

Doctor Peppar quickly slid forward and took Emma gently by the shoulders.

"Ah, no. No dear." He said with an apologetic look in my direction. "Touchy subject I'm afraid. Touchy subject." Leaning in, he conspired in a not-so quiet whisper. "Although, in the event of his passing, we do have first-"

"Hey!" I objected.

The Doctor lowered his head in shame.

"We'll discuss this more at a later time." He promised his assistant quietly through the side of his mouth.

"I liked it a lot better when they didn't talk." I said loudly to Raegan, who seemed to be enjoying the exchange a little too much.

Running a hand over the top of his head, Doctor Peppar smoothed down the shocks of white hair that jutted from the sides of his bald dome and adjusted his mammoth glasses.

"So what brings you to our little lab?" He asked pleasantly, their calling of "dibs" on my brain already forgotten. His eyes suddenly expanded behind his glasses, and for a moment I swore that I could see through his magnified pupils and into the cobwebby recesses of his skull. The goddamn *Hubble* didn't use lenses that thick. "Are you here to test the new field equipment?"

"Yes!" I said excitedly.

As dangerous and unpredictable as the lab was, it was also a tech-geek's wettest dream. Devices of every shape and size lined the endless field of countertops and workbenches, as they softly hummed and clicked with untold purpose. Doctor Peppar might be odd, but the man is a genius in that whole "I'm positive that he's going to try and make a Frankenstein's Monster out of spare parts, I'm not even kidding" kind of way. As dangerous as that may sound, it was always cool, and he always let me touch stuff.

"No." Raegan said with a stern look aimed directly at me. "Honestly, we were stopping by to check in on you." She explained. "But I can see that you're in excellent hands." She nodded to Emma who stared blankly back in response.

"Oh, I'm fine. I'm fine." The Doctor assured her with a dismissing wave of his hand.

"And I was wondering if I could ask a favor and borrow any

information that you may have on an artifact we came across." Raegan continued.

Like two dogs begging for the same cookie, Emma and the Doctor slid forward in rapt attention, their shoulders melding into one as they spoke in excited unison. "What artifact?!"

I took my place at Raegan's side, just in case one of them had to be tapped on the nose with a rolled up newspaper.

"It's called a Latrodenzian." She said hesitantly, taken aback by their sudden hunger.

"Where is it?" Emma asked eagerly.

"Is it with you? Oh my oh my oh my!" Doctor Peppar danced in place. "Miss Addams! Prep the dissection lab immediately!" Squealing in delight, the Doctor and his assistant spun away from each other and shot across the lab in opposite directions as we watched in stunned silence.

"We'll need to syphon off any residual command energies!" Emma exclaimed, ripping open a cabinet and tearing through its contents. "Electrostatic transducer?"

"Excellent idea! Excellent!" Doctor Peppar agreed. "It's in the cabinet with the-"

"No, you moved it when-" Emma corrected.

"Oh, heavens. You're right. Try the-"

"No no, that's the transd*uctor*, not-"

"Holy shit." I swore, turning to Ronnie in comprehending disbelief. "There's two of him."

Raegan looked at the chaotic exchange guiltily and cleared her throat. "Doctor, Emma. Jonas? Jonas!" She called out, trying to get their attention. "I'm sorry, but we don't have it with us." She explained remorsefully. With the sudden stop of someone hitting a switch, Doctor Peppar and Emma each hung their head and joined the other in a long, collective "aww" of disappointment.

"We just need whatever research notes or information that you'd be willing to share." She explained.

The Doctor's frail chest heaved with a dejected sigh. "Of course. Of course." He forced an unhappy little smile. "Emma, be a dear and retrieve the annotated copies from the lab archives for Agent Connolly."

Emma returned the sigh and sulked off, nodding her affirmation of the request with a soul crushing sadness usually reserved for commercials about rescued animals or starving children. When she was well out of sight, I leaned over to the still disappointed Doctor and gave him a playful poke in the ribs.

"Nice job there, Doc you old dog." I teased. "Still some fire left in the old Bunsen burner, eh?"

"Pardon?" He blinked up at me, adjusting his glasses. "Oh. OH!" His eyes tested the limits of his glass frames and he blushed in understanding.

"What is she? Twenty six? Twenty seven?" I prodded.

"Twenty-five actually." He corrected. Looking over his shoulder before he spoke, he leaned in lecherously and jabbed a boney old man elbow into my side. "But she has a verified Wechsler score of well over 160." He confided. "Well over, *if* you get my meaning."

I did not.

But I pretended as if I did anyway.

Raegan coughed loudly to remind us both that she was still there, and I grinned and waggled my eyebrows in response.

"You said something about field testing new equipment?" She asked, trying not to laugh.

"That's right!" Doctor Peppar snapped his fingers loudly. "Now where did I put that blasted…" He trailed off as he turned to dig through a nearby stack of boxes and equipment like a white haired badger excavating a den.

"You're bad." Ronnie chided as I took my place beside her.

"Hey, at least he isn't sulking." I pointed out.

"Aha!" The Doctor exclaimed with a triumphant cry.

In his arms was a large, bulky looking metal box that should have been far too heavy for the old man to lift, let alone carry with ease. Setting it down on the edge of a lab counter with a loud, weight-confirming thud, he peeled back the lid and beamed victoriously.

Exchanging worried glances, Ronnie and I inched forward and attempted to steal a cautious peek.

"Come along, come along." The Doctor urged us. Sharing a nervous look of apprehension, we stood hesitantly behind him as he gestured to the container's contents like a proud father.

"As you can see, I've made several modifications to your firearms." He explained, retrieving a sleeker, more futuristic version of our standard issue sidearm from the box.

Our current weapons were pretty cool, but looked like they had been cobbled together from spare parts and hastily assembled minutes before the start of a steampunk convention. Each handgun had the customary grip and barrel, but everything in between was a chaotic roadmap of wires and dials that needed to be perfectly calibrated and set before it could be fired.

As part of my training, I had spent some time on the FPI gun range, practicing with both normal weapons, and our FPI issued pistol which fired a polymer coated glob of liquid iron that did little more than sting and leave a nasty looking bruise on most humans.

For the Fae however, the effect was devastating.

The majority of fairies have a fatal allergy to iron, which can cause burns or even death if they are touched or wounded by it. The metal is so potent, possessing any form of it no matter how innocuous is considered a grave offense, and would get you immediately exiled from the fairy world.

Our weapons were big, unwieldy, and looked about as intimidating as a supersoaker.

But this? This was *awesome*.

Gunmetal black with veins of glowing red running across its surface, it looked like something that you'd see the bad guy in a sci-fi movie use to vaporize orphans. With no visible wires, dials, or containers of gooey resin and liquid metal sloshing around, it felt like the gun that a secret agent of my caliber needed.

No, *deserved*.

"We've managed to increase the tactile strength of the polymer, greatly reducing the amount needed to encapsulate each shot."

Doctor Peppar explained as I somehow managed to pull my attention away from my second amendment induced erection. "This gives us a lighter weight, increased accuracy, and a more fluid design."

"Oh man." I drooled, turning the gun over in my hands. "She's beautiful." I grinned up at the Doctor and nudged him teasingly. "It's not going to explode or make my hair fall out or anything, will it?"

"I, uh…" Doctor Peppar mumbled something under his breath and with a guilty half-smile took the weapon gingerly from my hands and set it back in the box. With a sigh of defeat he handed me a different weapon; a smaller, less bulky, yet still wire and dial inundated version of what we currently used. I stared at it blankly for a moment before comprehension set in.

"Dude. Not cool." I scolded, causing the Doctor to hang his head in shame.

Raegan reached into the box and pulled my gun's twin from the carefully cut packaging. Turning it over in her hands, she tested the weight, and held it at arm's length.

"You fixed the pull from the wet weight." She noted. "But where are the ammunition canisters?" She asked, examining the side of the gun.

"Gone! All gone." The Doctor beamed, happy to have a sudden change in the subject. "Like the other model," He looked to me and forced another apologetic smile. "We managed to reduce the amount of liquid needed per shot and incorporate them into a more standardized magazine." Removing a small metal rectangle from the box, he handed it to my partner.

"It loads in the bottom of the grip, and can be quickly exchanged for another should you find yourself in that sort of situation." He explained.

Ronnie nodded her approval and continued to examine the weapon, her eyes flashing over every detail. I could see her making mental notes, and as she adjusted one of the many dials, I suddenly felt out of place and rather stupid.

Raegan actually understood these things. Me? I just took it on face value that they'd do what was needed when they were needed.

"And what is the main function of this mechanical addition?" I asked, trying to sound intelligent as I pointed to a tangle of wires that disappeared into a glass bulb at the front of the gun.

"Ahh!" The Doctor grinned in appreciation of my newly discovered attention to detail. "That," He started, flipping a tiny switch. "Is what we like to call a "flashlight". It illuminates the darkness." He said, spreading his hands out before him with the showmanship of someone explaining the mysteries of the universe.

"Of course it is." I said with a dry look to Raegan, daring her to laugh. Taking a deep breath and avoiding my eyes, she renewed her focus on the gun in her hands.

A shuffling sound from the back of the room gave way to the returning Emma as she moved forward with slow, robotic grace. In her arms were several folders and a large white binder.

"Here you are my dear." Doctor Peppar said, taking the stack from his assistant. "As you asked, as you asked." He waited patiently as we exchanged our old weapons for the new and adjusted our shoulder holsters before offering the reports to my Keeper.

"Thank you." Raegan said to both of them. Doctor Peppar waved away the thanks, and Emma nodded in response, the gesture the closest thing to emotion that I had witnessed the woman using so far.

Thumbing through the stack, my Keeper exhaled loudly and frowned at me. "Looks like I've got a bit of reading to do." She said, double checking the files. "Which means…"

"I get to drive!" I said excitedly.

"You get to drive." She confirmed with a sigh of utter defeat. "Thank you Jonas." She said, looking up at the man fondly. "I'll take good care of these."

"Of course, of course." The Doctor dismissed any concern of worry with a wave of his hand.

"And it was nice to meet you Emma." Raegan said politely.

"You as well." Emma said distantly, her eyes focused on me. Or rather, my head.

"Yeah, well, later Doc." I said, briefly shaking the man's hand. "And great to meet you Wednesday." I smiled at the doctor's assistant.

"Make sure you give Lurch and Pugsly my love." I shot her with my finger guns and clicked my tongue, but elicited no response beyond the creepy, detached stare.

As we turned to the exit, I gave Ronnie one last alarmed look and rolled my eyes in Emma's direction, but it was completely missed as my dutiful Keeper was already skimming through the folders. Rounding the doorway, I heard a faint, but very enthusiastic change in the woman's voice as we moved just out of ear shot.

"I cannot *wait* to examine his brain."

Chapter Eight

"So it's just like, *stuck* in there?" Raegan tilted her head inquisitively as she stared at me from the passenger seat.

The long drive had been the perfect time for reflection, and to get her opinion on my newly discovered condition. I told her the entire story; from my run in with the comic book villain leprechaun Fenrus, to the boys finally cluing me in to how my abilities came to be.

To her credit, Raegan never once appeared to be shocked, or even really that surprised. If anything she seemed more intrigued, and a part of me wondered if she was tempted to get in line for "dibs" on my brain.

"It's not like the thing is all loose and just banging around." I said on the brink of being offended. I could see her making that connection as an explanation of why I had such a tendency to be, me.

"But it *is* in there." She pressed.

"Well, yeah." I conceded. "But I think it's more like my brain absorbed it or something. Like a vitamin." I added for clarification. "That's why it stopped showing up on the scans or x-rays."

Raegan nodded in slow acceptance, my words apparently filling in whatever remaining blanks she had been trying to work through.

"Wow." She breathed.

"Yeah." I agreed.

"I still can't believe you met a Norn." There was a hint of jealous resentment as she sighed, as if I had wasted an opportunity that she would have quite literally killed for.

"*I* still can't believe that the little bastards finally told me the truth." I snorted. "I was starting to really question whether or not they actually knew."

"And you believe them?"

"Yeah." I chuckled inwardly at the thought of this being another elaborate prank, but I knew that they had been honest with me. "I mean, I know that they can be little assholes and all, but they seemed pretty serious."

Raegan frowned, her face heavy with concern. "What about this Fenrus?"

"No idea." I shrugged. "But something tells me that Gimli and the Legolas twins aren't just going to take the Norn's decision laying down. I've seen way too many horror movies to write off the bad guy this early in the film." I joked, but there was no doubt in my mind that I'd be hearing from the dark leprechaun and his buddies a lot sooner than I'd want to.

"Who else have you told?"

"About the brain thing?" I asked. "No one. Seamus was pretty adamant about not telling a soul." I assured her. "He said that if word got out, I'd be ass deep in all sorts of baddies before I could even blink."

"But you just told me."

I turned to the passenger seat just long enough to give her a dumbfounded look.

"Well, yeah." I admitted. "But you're *you*." I explained, not really understanding why I had to. "If they didn't think that I was going to tell *you* about all of this, then they're going to have to start dropping that whole "all-knowing" thing from their resumes." I hadn't even considered not telling Ronnie about my condition and had just assumed that her inclusion was an unspoken understanding at the time.

"You don't count." I said with certainty.

Ronnie blushed crimson and looked down at the stack of folders in her lap as she flipped absently through the pages. I have no clue what I said, but I had the sudden feeling that it was somehow the right thing.

"Still." She finally spoke when she was done being weird. "Until I've had a chance to research this properly, and gods, where would I even *begin*?" She mused more to herself than me. "You have to keep this a secret. From everyone."

"Oh, yeah." I agreed. "Totally."

"I'm serious John." She said sternly, her eyes narrowing in motherly worry. "This is huge. You can't tell anyone. Not even Assistant Director Blair can know."

"Keep my big mouth shut, got it."

Raegan studied my face for a moment, and then let her gaze shift to the top of my head. Satisfied that I was sincere in my answer she smiled softly and resumed absently thumbing through her papers, her eyes barely skimming the pages.

"So where is this place anyway?" I asked after a few seconds of silence. "And where in the hell are we?"

I hadn't spent a lot of time in Pennsylvania, and what little knowledge that I did have of the state had been heavily influenced by a night of bar hopping and binge eating in Philadelphia. This vast expansion of endless countryside sprinkled with old-timey farms that we were now driving through was nothing like I remembered, and I was beginning to worry that we were lost.

"Is the cover for this place a beauty school or an organic hemp ranch?" I asked as we passed, I kid you not, a horse and buggy.

Raegan smiled, waved to the Amish couple and pointed past the windshield. "It's coming up on the right." She instructed. "And be nice. The school is isolated for a reason."

"I know, I know." I rolled my eyes. "Nobody can take the hotness that is your magical fairy blood." I said, wiggling my fingers sarcastically. "So you'd have to deal with teenage hormones and the occasional panty raid. Seriously, what's the worst that could happen?"

"You've heard of the witch trials, haven't you?" Raegan asked. "Being stoned to death or burned at the stake tends to ruin the whole college experience for most people. Turn here." She instructed. Her tone hadn't changed, but the intended weight of her words hit home.

Generally, as a rule, people suck. For every smart, kind, genuinely good person that you meet, there are at least a dozen selfish, stupid, easily scared morons who react violently when confronted with something that they don't have the mental capacity to understand. Pair that ignorance and fear with a school packed to the rafters with supernaturally beautiful women who hold weird midnight rituals and claim to talk to fairies and even in this day and age, bad things are bound to happen.

The road to the school itself was long and winding and stretched over a hill that almost completely blocked the university from sight. Ending at a security booth and manually operated gate that blocked any accidental access, the campus stretched out before us more like a well-guarded industrial complex than any institute.

Slowing to a stop, we were greeted by a female guard who as she stepped out of the small multi-windowed shack, clipboard in hand. She was cute, perky, and visibly armed. Approaching just to the edge of actual reach, she bent slightly at the waist and regarded my Keeper and I with a natural suspicion that overlapped her practiced smile.

"Identification please." She said firmly, but politely.

Removing my sunglasses, I slowly reached into the interior pocket of my suit jacket to retrieve my badge.

"Agents John Talik and Raegan Rachelle Connolly." I announced, stressing my partner's middle name. "We're with the FPI." I said, coolly flipping open my wallet and exposing the metal shield within.

No one ever mentions this, but the worst part about being a secret agent is the fact that you usually have to keep it a secret. The fact that I got to flash my badge in an official manner was sending the sugared up eight year old in me into geeky overdrive.

"Just a moment." The guard nodded before jotting something down. Returning to her booth, she stepped out of earshot as she presumably went about the task of verifying our credentials.

"Really?" Raegan looked at me flatly, obviously questioning the unprovoked use of her middle name.

"What?" I asked with feigned innocence.

"You're an ass." She was trying to look offended, but I could see the humor reflected in her eyes.

"I happen to think that Rachelle is a lovely name." I said, trying to sound sincere.

"Whatever *Andrew*." She chuckled.

"I think you mean," I put my sunglasses back on with a slow, dramatic flair as the guard stepped out of her booth. "Danger."

"Thank you Agents." She nodded as she crouched down next to the open car window, saving me from any rebuttal. "I was told to welcome you to the school and to inform you that the head of Campus Security is waiting for you over in the staff parking lot." She slid two visitor passes through the open window and pointed past the gate. "You're going to want to veer right when you come to the fork. After that, it's three lots up and across from the main building. You can't miss it."

"Thank you Officer. Your assistance and exemplary performance of duty will be fully noted in our report." I grinned roguishly, because that's what secret agents are supposed to do.

Now beaming ear to ear, the security guard stepped back into her shack and lifted the gate, allowing us to pass.

"Wow." Raegan said, shaking her head as we pulled away.

"What?" I said staring at the road in front of us, trying my damnedest not to smile.

"I think that you really *might* have brain damage." She laughed.

Following the guard's directions, I veered right at the fork in the road and passed a couple of lots before turning into a large parking area. Aside from a scattered cluster of cars, it was nearly empty.

"That must be security." Raegan observed as we pulled into a parking space. I followed her gaze across the lot just as a large white golf cart came to rest in front of the stairs that led up to the main entrance. The vehicle's driver offered a friendly wave and stepped out to greet us as we exited the car.

"Jesus Christ." I said in quiet blasphemy as I stared in awe at the head of campus security.

"Max!" Raegan squealed in happy surprise as she ran to meet her friend.

Heavily muscled and standing well over six and a half feet tall, the security guard towered over my sister, effortlessly hoisting her into an enthusiastic hug that scooped her from the ground. Long black hair tied in a neat ponytail mirrored the darkness of Max's eyes as they turned in my direction. Setting Raegan down gently the two walked side by side as I walked numbly towards them.

"John Talik," Ronnie called out mischievously as I drew near. "I'd like you to meet Maxine Stonebridge, *head* of Campus Security?" She both introduced and asked at the same time, grinning up inquisitively at her friend.

Max was a woman.

Attractive in the whole Amazonian, Xena Warrior Princess sort of way, Maxine Stonebridge looked a lot like how I would have envisioned a real life version of Wonder Woman, had Linda Carter ever overdosed on horse steroids.

"Call me Max." The woman offered, taking my hand in hers and crushing it into a meaty pulp. Her voice was surprisingly soft and undeniably feminine, even with the sound of my blood rushing through my ears. "And it's no big deal really." She added with a false modesty as she puffed out her already expansive, and probably somehow six-packed chest. "No one else wants the dirty jobs, am I right?" She grinned, releasing the mangled remains of my hand and slapping me heartily on the shoulder.

I watched in detached, painful silence as my right arm separated from my body and went skittering across the parking lot before coming to a rest under a nearby car.

"So this is your new Seer, eh?" Max asked, looking down at Raegan. "You didn't say that he was such a little stud muffin." She added in a booming whisper.

"So, how do you two ladies know each other?" I asked, as casually as I could with the wind knocked out of me.

"Me and Ray Ray?" Max grinned. "Oh we go way back." She explained, jerking a thumb behind her to the school. "We both used to go to school here when we were kids. 'Cept she graduated early, and I never left." She explained. "Used to tutor me back in the day. Real book worm this one." She added affectionately.

"Some things never change, eh Ray Ray?" I teased.

"What about you?" The giant woman asked, nudging me lightly with her fist and sending a shockwave of pins and needles through the haze of static numbness that was my arm. "Male Seer eh? You know, you're pretty much a legend around here."

"I am?" I asked weakly.

"Oh yeah. You got the girls all excited with the rumor that we're about to go co-ed." She teased.

Raegan laughed lightly at the thought and smiled up at her friend. "Sadly, Agent Talik's condition is rather unique."

"Oh." Max said with a bit of disappointment. "Oh." Her dark eyes widened suddenly. "So does that mean that you two, you know?" She asked, motioning awkwardly with her hands.

Raegan shook her head a little too quickly for my fragile ego. "We're *bonded*. Keeper and Seer, brother and sister." She explained, her eyes bright with humor as she slid me an entertained look.

"Oh yeah." Max nodded, a connecting memory drawing out the word. "I saw them pictures on the internet."

My mouth went dry and my heart climbed into my throat.

McKenna. I was going to have to kill her.

"For the record, I was tricked into-" I started to explain, but a sharp laugh and hearty slap on the back from the She-Hulk forced me to spit up my kidneys, which interrupted my words.

"Ha! From what I saw, you've got nothing to be ashamed of J.T! You rocked that dress!" Maxine assured me. "Great legs, and a real strong core too." Her voice dropped half an octave. "You work out a lot?"

"Well I try to stay in shape. You know, for the job." I managed to squeak out when I was finally able to get enough air to form the words.

"Don't I know it." Max sighed, glancing back at the school. "Welp, best get you two over to the Headmistress." She announced, swinging her arms in front of her and clapping her massive hands. "You know, before old Bloody Merry gets too scary." She whispered to my Keeper.

"Shit." Raegan swore under her breath. "She's *still* here?" The dread in her voice overpowered the incredulity, but not by much.

Max gave her an odd smile and tilted her head, obviously surprised by her words. "Shit yes she is!" She laughed, parroting my sister's vulgarity with child-like enthusiasm. "You know, rumor is that if you say Bloody Merry into a mirror at midnight, she'll appear in a cloud of black smoke and give you detention." She whispered to me, punching me lightly in the arm.

When I finally regained consciousness we followed Maxine across the parking lot and to the stairs of the main building.

"You know, I don't think that I've ever heard you cuss before." Max observed, turning her head to Raegan. "I kinda like it." She added, nodding her approval to me as we reached the main door.

The halls of the school were surprisingly warm and welcoming, a stark contrast from the building's cold, almost nondescript exterior. Lined with artwork, sculptures and inspirational posters, it was the kind of school setting that every kid only dreams of, but still secretly hopes actually exists somewhere outside of coming-of-age television dramas.

With no apparent time allotted for sight-seeing, the halls blurred by in a smear of polished wood and startled students as our guide lead us through the carpeted corridors of Xavier's School for Gifted Chicks at a blistering pace.

"It's right up here." Max said, pointing to a rapidly approaching doorway as we struggled to keep up with her long, powerful strides.

The administrator's office was eerily similar to what we had at the Agency in terms of setup and design, and for a moment I wondered if we had inadvertently walked through some sort of weird fairy portal. Stepping in behind Max, I allowed Raegan to slide through ahead of me before quietly closing the office door.

No receptionist graced the unoccupied desk at the front of the room, and Max strode by it without hesitation or thought. Knocking twice on a closed hardwood door, she was answered almost immediately by a muffled, but unmistakably impatient voice.

"Come in, come in."

Opening the door, Max held it in place with one large hand and motioned for us to step through. I followed my keeper hesitantly into the room, reflexively ducking under Max's arm despite the fact that I had a good foot or two of actual clearance. As we entered the school's Headmaster stood, as did the two agents seated before her.

Shoulder length, stark grey hair pulled into a tight bun, Headmistress Elizabeth Merry was a shapely, sharply dressed woman. In her matronly black dress with white collar, she might have once been considered beautiful in her youth, but years of ill-temper and refusing to smile had carved deep scowl lines into her face, giving her the look of someone who immediately wants to speak with the manager, no matter where she is.

Ronnie took the lead without slowing and nodded in passing acknowledgement to the other team of agents. McKenna Wallace, a tall, thin, statuesque blonde brought to life by the sheer will of every horny teenage boy in existence, responded in kind and to my amazement extended the gesture to encompass me as well.

Over the last few months, the leggy Seer had warmed up to me a bit. Her normally artic demeanor was now merely ice cold in my presence, which might not sound like much, but compared to when we first met, it was like being hugged by an armful of fuzzy bunnies.

Her Keeper Lydia on the other hand, had never been anything but affectionate to me.

Nearly half the size of her partner, the tiny agent fought for every inch of her four foot eleven frame, and let me tell you, it was a *good* fight. Where her height may have allowed her to be mistaken for a child, the hourglass curve of her hips and overly-generous swell of her incredible chest removed even the slightest chance of confusion. Her light green eyes sparkled as they met mine, crinkling with the humor of an almost unperceivable wink that caused my heart to skip half a beat.

Like Ronnie and I, McKenna and Lydia were bound by the rite of sisterhood. However, unlike us, the two of them were also tied together by actual blood. Night and day in attitude, demeanor, and contrasting, uh, *physical* attributes, I had staunchly refused to believe that they were cousins, a fact that I had actually forced my Keeper to pinky swear was true.

Their family reunions probably put the playboy mansion to shame.

"Hello Headmistress Merry." Raegan said in her official "on the job" voice, ripping my attention from the voluptuously naughty Lydia. Extending her hand, she continued her greeting. "I'm Agent Co-"

"I know who you are Miss Connolly." Came the stern reply as they shook. "I remember you quite well from your time here."

Raegan forced a strained smile and nodded, whispering a quiet "Of course you do" under her breath.

Headmistress Merry stepped around my partner, and offered me her hand. "And this must be Agent Talik, the legendary Male Seer that we've been hearing so much about." She said, obviously unimpressed.

"All good I hope." I said playfully as I took her hand in mine and offered her my most charming of dashing looks.

It was like thumb-wrestling with a snake.

The Headmistress's lips slit into what I'm assuming I was supposed to take as smile as she indicated to the two empty chairs in front of her desk.

"Please, sit."

Raegan took the chair to Lydia's right, leaving me thankfully on the end. That gave me a better chance of actually making it to the door if our host decided to rip off her face, exposing the lizard head that undoubtedly lay beneath.

We waited in patient silence like pupils called to the principal's office as the Headmistress rounded the large desk and slid into her chair.

"Let me start by thanking you for your assist-" Raegan started, only to be cut off once again.

"No Miss Connolly, let *me* start by informing you that I am not happy about this entire situation. I find it quite unnecessary to have four Federal Agents gallivanting around my school whilst throwing around unfounded accusations about my staff." Merry overstepped, taking command.

"With all due respect Miss Merry," My Keeper countered, trying to defuse the situation.

"Headmistress." The correction rang through the air like a fight bell as Raegan squeezed the word through her tightly clenched teeth, and I instinctively inched away.

"Headmistress Merry." She amended. "As unhappy as you may be, let's not forget that you have three missing children and the prime suspect in an attack on Agent Talik is a Professor at your school."

Headmistress Merry bristled and shifted in her chair in a show of offense.

"We have *one* missing girl and two who are simply unaccounted for at this time." She argued. "Do not misunderstand me Miss Connolly, Kara's disappearance is a tragedy that weighs heavy on each and every one of our hearts. That being said, local law enforcement found no evidence of a crime and suggested that the poor thing may have simply run away. Not all of the girls who come to us are cut out for this school." She added with an air of disdain. "As for Samantha and Gabrielle, they have been *missing* for less than twenty-four hours. Unlike which ever member of my staff foolishly alerted your agency, I have no doubt that they will soon be found.

"Have you contacted their parents?" Raegan inquired.

"No Agent Connolly, I have not." Came the crisp reply. "This is a *school*." Headmistress Merry reminded irritably. "While I can assure you that it isn't the practiced norm, it is hardly unusual for some of the older students to occasionally skip a class or leave the campus on some childish adventure."

"And did they ever occasionally skip a class or leave the campus with Professor Ambrose?" Raegan asked pointedly.

The Headmistress smiled like a hungry shark. "I can assure you that they have not." She said coldly. "Rupert has not only been at the school this entire time, but on camera. We have video, and well over a hundred students and faculty that can verify his presence. Ms. Stonebridge?" She prompted, gesturing to Maxine.

The hulking woman gave a halfhearted shrug of apology. "The little guy was locked in the gymnasium with everyone else, so he was on camera the entire night. I went over the tapes half a dozen times, myself."

"As you can see Agents, he never once left our sight." Headmistress Merry said victoriously. Her eyes narrowed slightly as she glanced to me before turning back to Raegan. "You say that Agent Talik was attacked." She leered. "Tell me, have you ever *met* Professor Ambrose?"

Uh oh.

Raegan looked to me in confusion, then back to Merry. "No?" She admitted uncertainly.

"I thought as much." The Headmistress confirmed with a cruel sort of satisfaction. "This is the most recent photograph of our staff." She handed Raegan a large glossy picture. "The Professor is the gentleman in the front row, furthest to the left, for obvious reasons." She all but purred.

Ronnie took the offered photograph. Searching the page, her eyes widened in comprehension as she turned to me, embarrassment tangled in rage streaking through the glare.

"Just for the record, the little crippled guy hit me first." I explained weakly. I could tell by the green fire dancing behind her angry stare that my selective omissions would not be forgotten, and I would pay for them later.

The Headmistress smiled smugly from her chair, any pretense of hiding her joy cast uncaringly aside. Raegan took a breath and composed herself before slowly returning the photograph to the desk's edge.

"As you are well aware, appearances can be deceiving." She pointed out. "Tell me, has Professor Ambrose ever spoken of involvement with the Brotherhood of Emrys?"

Lydia and McKenna exchanged alarmed looks and began

hurriedly whispering between themselves, the mere mention of the Brotherhood sparking some flame of alarmed conversation.

Headmistress Merry on the on the other hand, only laughed.

"Rupert? Our Rupert?" She asked mockingly. "The poor man can barely hold a pen; you can't honestly be suggesting that he has the tremendous levels of manual dexterity required for actual magic?"

Lydia prodded McKenna with a tiny elbow, and nodding in agreement the tall Seer cleared her throat, expertly bringing the room's attention to her as she spoke.

"Of course not Headmistress." She said respectfully. "But I'm sure that you can understand the Agency's interest in protecting both the school and its students. If this man is indeed affiliated with the Order of Merlin, or even remotely connected to the disappearances in anyway, then things may not be as they appear."

Headmistress Merry considered McKenna's words in silence for a moment before conceding.

"The loss of Kara has been difficult on us all. She was a talented Seer and a very promising student." She said with genuine fondness. "She reminded me a lot of you at that age, Miss Wallace."

McKenna was a teacher's pet. Go figure.

"All three girls have classes with the Professor." Lydia chimed in high pitched excitement as she piggybacked on the opening that her partner had forged.

"And I'm sure that their families would be especially appreciative of any extra attention that we give to this matter." McKenna added meaningfully.

Merry looked between the two and nodded once. "Very well." She sighed. "But I do not wish for this to become a witch hunt." The very air in the room seemed to change with those two words, and she looked to me of all people in warning. "Your fellow Agents have already spoken with Rupert and found nothing out of the ordinary. He has been extremely patient with this silliness, and is not to be bullied."

"You spoke with him?" Raegan asked, leaning forward as she addressed the other team.

"The moment that Assistant Director Blair called us." Lydia confirmed.

"And?"

"He seemed confused, but he was completely cooperative." Lydia turned to McKenna uncertainly and the tall blonde motioned for her to continue. "Still, there was something about him that felt *off.*"

McKenna shrugged contritely.

"I was speaking with the roommates of the missing girls at the time, and examining their dormitories." She explained. "There was nothing that indicated that they were planning to leave, and no obvious signs of a struggle."

"So only Lydia saw him?" Raegan asked rhetorically. "Is he still on campus?"

"Should be." Max cut in. The large woman had somehow managed to shrink into the background, to the point where I had almost forgotten that she was present. "He's probably in his classroom. Little guy practically lives there."

"You know, I wouldn't mind popping in on ol' Somnus. Maybe catch him off guard." I said quietly to Raegan.

"I want to see the tapes first." She asserted. "If they've been doctored, we should be able to tell. This way we'll have something solid to go on."

Max pushed off the wall and stood to her full height. "Sure. I think they're still queued up."

"I'd like to see them as well." McKenna announced as she stood. "Lydia can show Agent Talik to the Professor's classroom, and assist him there." She suggested. "Perhaps he can pick up on whatever she felt was off."

The normally frigid Agent Wallace offering to mix teams threw me for a loop. McKenna normally played her cards extremely close to her chest. If she was looking to share, it meant that she was probably getting the upper hand. Lydia was an amazing Keeper in her own right, but it was well known that Raegan was the best that the Agency had to offer.

I looked warily at the leggy blonde before shrugging and deferring the decision to my Keeper.

"It's okay." She said quietly, but not without her own hints of suspicion. "We can meet back here in an hour and exchange our findings." She suggested, turning to our host. "That is, if that's alright with you?"

Headmistress Merry gave a regal nod. "Of course." She said. "Despite what I'm sure you're all thinking, I too would like to get to the bottom of this mess." She waved dismissingly. "And I'm more than confident that the missing girls will have turned up by then."

The rest of us stood.

"Well then." Lydia chirped, happily. "After you, Agent Talik." She purred huskily, gesturing towards the door.

Raegan smiled as I walked past with a pleading look and held the door for my new pocket-sized Keeper. Brushing by just a little too close as she stepped past, the scent of her hair mingling with the brief, unexpected contact set my senses on fire, and I my heart thumped in my chest.

Exiting the office, we turned down a nearby hallway and I slowed my step to keep pace with my miniaturized counterpart.

Everything about Lydia screamed sex.

From the standard issue clothing that managed to show more bare skin than should have been possible, to the sway in her step that sent waves of gold rippling through her long blonde hair. Her gifts, both physical and magical, were the result of her nymph blood; blood that helped shape her into what could only be described as the diminutive, but undeniably personification of the female form. My ears burned as I caught an eyeful of glorious cleavage that caused several body parts to battle for my blood supply at the same time.

"So, uh, when you say that something was off," I started clumsily, my brain struggling to maintain any semblance of focus.

She slowed in step and her mouth contorted into a pretty little frown as she looked up at me. "It was the way that he stared at me." She explained. "It was just creepy. Like he was," She thought for a brief moment on the perfect word. "Hungry."

I laughed out loud.

"Yeah, well, I can absolutely understand that." The words left my mouth before I could stop them.

Lydia's demeanor changed in a heartbeat. "Oh, you can, can you?" She asked huskily, her eyes suddenly aflame.

"Um. Well. Yeah." I stammered. "I mean, it's just that aaah!"

With astounding speed and surprising strength the tiny blonde keeper grabbed me by my suit jacket and all but threw me into an alcove. Pulling me tightly to her, she crushed her lips to mine in deep, mind-numbing kiss. My resolve melted instantly and the world faded away as I let myself be devoured. Her tongue finding mine, we swirled together in a haze of lust and she moaned against me.

"Wait." I halfheartedly protested. "Someone might see us."

"I *know*." She growled, lifting her leg to my side and wrapping it around me. Grabbing my hands, she guided them to the sides of her massive chest, and even through the layers of fabric, I could feel the softness and warmth of her skin.

It was intoxicating.

"Go ahead." I laughed lightly. "No, I can't." Whimpering, I reluctantly pulled away, breaking the kiss. Lydia pouted sexily, but didn't back off.

"C'mon. You know that I want this." I pleaded.

"So I see." She purred, looking downward at the absence of space between us.

Keeping our relationship a secret was getting hard, no pun intended, and I'm amazed that we hadn't been busted or found out at least a half a dozen times by now. Lydia loved the risk. Anything that was taboo or even the slightest bit naughty turned her on to no end, and the fact that I had once rejected McKenna only seemed to further her desire.

Before she had blossomed, and apparently forgot to stop, Lydia was the chubby kid; the fat but funny friend that every tall, skinny, and impossibly beautiful woman seems to acquire. In Lydia's case, that hot chick was her cousin McKenna, and growing up, any boy that my now buxom beauty showed even the slightest interest in, McKenna took as her own.

Since I had managed, somehow, to resist the leggy Seer's photo-shopped-by-real-life charms, Lydia's conquest of me was the kind of victory that she had been dreaming of since childhood.

And I didn't mind the fact that she was using me one tiny bit.

My sister on the other hand, was a completely different story. She and Lydia were close, and I didn't want to come between that. As smart and as kindly as my sister was, she didn't have very many friends and often preferred the company of a book to actual people. Lydia was good for her, and her silly, perky naughtiness was the only thing outside of myself that seemed to bring Ronnie out of her shell.

So when Lydia and I started our own private *study sessions*, we both agreed that in the interest of our professional and personal relationships, we'd try to keep it as quiet for as long as we possibly could. Which again, was incredibly difficult given the fact that Lydia was something of an exhibitionist and the threat of getting caught only fueled her sex drive.

"But, missing girls. Creepy Professor." I insisted. My thoughts were coming slower and slower with every kiss.

"Fiiiiine." Lydia sulked, widening the gap between us a hair's breadth. Tilting her head, she patted the front of my jacket and looked up to me in confusion.

"What's this?" She asked, gently probing the pocket.

"Oh!" I remembered as some blood finally managed to trickle back into my brain. "So." I grinned. "Alistair managed to get his hands on-"

"Alistair?!" She cut me off excitedly. "Ohmygod. You actually got some?" Her eyes locked on my chest and she traced the outline of the vial with the tip of her perfectly manicured finger hungrily.

Fire rekindled, she kissed me with renewed vigor and tried to push me back into the alcove.

"Later." I laughed, trying to hold her at bay. "Later." I said more sternly. "I swear."

Pulling away with a ravenous smirk, her light green eyes captured my own and froze me in place. "I'm holding you to that." She promised, her hand dipping low between us as she gave me a meaningful squeeze.

Shoving off, she straightened her jacket and continued walking as if nothing had happened, each step accentuated with a bit more sway than needed, undoubtedly for my benefit.

"Goddamn." I swore under my breath. "That woman is going to end up killing me." I sighed happily, my pulse still racing as I moved to catch up.

"His classroom is up here." Lydia said as she pointed down the long hallway. "Is he the one who…" She slowed in step and looked up to the scrapes and bruises that marred the side of my face as she made the connection.

"Yeah yeah, laugh it up." I grumbled.

It was bad enough that Raegan now knew that I got my ass handed to me by Captain Crutch, my girlfriend teasing me about it was a blow to the ego that I had been praying to avoid.

"You poor thing." She said sincerely, without a hint of mocking in her tiny, squeaky little voice.

I sighed in relief and opened the classroom door, allowing her to step in. Brushing by me, I resisted the impulse to bury my nose in her hair as she moved past, her scent reigniting the flood of hormones that I had still battling within me.

The sound of chalk scraping against a blackboard pulled me from my urges, and with a frustrated sigh, I put on my game face and followed her in.

"Professor Ambrose?" Lydia called out, announcing our presence.

The classroom was surprisingly unremarkable, and contained pretty much the same standard make and model of granite topped desks that I remembered from my high school days. It seated around twenty students, and other than a few filing cabinets and a large desk, was largely unremarkable.

"Yes?"

The voice belonged to Somnus, but it had an odd, tinny echo to it that immediately brought my eyes to the creature at the front of the room absently scrawling class notes across the chalk board. Man shaped, or Rupert Ambrose shaped to be exact, it was a perfect duplicate of the man in every possible way…

…except color.

Slate grey and devoid of any hue, the creature looked more like a moving statue than it did a man. It made no threatening gestures and in all honesty, didn't seem to be paying us very much attention at all.

Drawing my weapon I stepped protectively in front of Lydia and took aim at the thing as it finished its notes.

"Go get Raegan and McKenna." I ordered, my hands shaking as adrenaline rocketed through my veins. "Now!" I said more forcefully as she stood there, paused in confusion.

"What's wrong?" She asked. Nervously backing up, she split her gaze between the greyscale version of the Professor and myself.

She couldn't see it. Shit.

"That's not Rupert Ambrose." I whispered.

Setting the chalk that it been holding into the metal tray at the base of the blackboard, the creature turned its head and regarded us for the first time. It looked exactly like Ambrose. Every facial feature and hair on its head right down to the metal arm braces that jutted from its lifeless grey skin, were identical to the man we were looking for.

"But he's the one that we-" Lydia argued.

"No." I said, releasing the gun's safety which caused the weapon to whirl to life. "I mean, that's not *human*."

Chapter Nine

"What is he?"

Lydia was backing towards the door as she asked, her own weapon now drawn. Even through her confusion, I could hear the intrigue in her voice, and knew that she wanted to stay.

Keepers, yeesh.

"I don't know." I admitted, my focus never wavering from the black and white version of Rupert Ambrose. "But you need to go and get the Raegan and McKenna, *now*." I pressed, leaving no room for argument.

"Be careful." She implored, and a second later her hurried footsteps echoed down the hallway as she ran to get the others.

Lydia running. Man. I wish I could have seen that.

"Don't fucking move." I growled, my finger twitching on my weapon's trigger as the creature took a small step forward, pulling me from the brief fantasy. Freezing in place, it raised his hands in a show of compliance, fear and alarm spanning its grey features.

"What is the meaning of this?" It asked in a frightened voice. The thing sounded exactly like Somnus, but its words vibrated with a hollow echo as if someone were playing back a recording.

"Drop the act Fifty Shades." I snapped. The rush of adrenaline was fading, and the buzz of energy that had come with it was slowly turning to annoyance. "What are you?" I demanded.

Eyes narrowing in thought, the creature turned its head as it regarded me. "Was bin ich?" It asked softly to itself. "Nein, nein. Was bist du?" It mumbled, clearly fascinated.

German. Once again, World War II themed video games saved the day. Take *that* out of touch political campaign ads and overzealous social justice warriors.

"Huh?" I grunted. The games might have allowed me to easily identify the language, but unless this guy was screaming for more ammo or telling the squad to hurry up, I wasn't going to be understanding very much.

"What are you?" The creature asked in English. Its voice was deeper and now wrapped in a thick German accent.

"Me? I'm about two seconds away from shooting you in the bean-bag. That's what I am." I threatened, dropping the barrel of the gun so that it was now pointed directly at the grey man's crotch. "I'm asking the questions here Gandalf. What are you, and where's Ambrose?"

Straightening its back, the creature stood to its full height. Keeping its distance, it slowly began to circle me, its odd grey eyes unblinking. I cautiously stepped backwards, widening the gap so that it couldn't get between me and the door, and as I did the creature began to change.

Arms still in the air in a non-threatening display, its torso thickened as its clothes melted, sinking into its body. Ambrose's face blurred and smeared into a barely human mask and the creature took a confident step forward.

"Last warning Dorothy." I cautioned, leveling the weapon at its chest. "One more step and you're going to see Oz in all of its Technicolor glory."

The arm brace that the creature had been leaning on suddenly shot out with an impossible quickness, knocking my weapon from my hand. Before I could react, the thing was on me, its flesh like a hard but malleable clay under my fingertips as we grappled.

108

It was still changing.

Shrinking in height but growing stockier by the second, it swung clumsily at my face. I ducked the attempt easily, the blow thrown off balance as the monster's arm brace thickened and retracted back into its body. Sliding to one side I used the momentum of my dodge to launch myself into the air and returned the punch. My knuckles connected with its still shifting jaw in a hard, satisfying smack of wet flesh.

The creature staggered backwards as it tried to recover, a perfect imprint of my fist indenting its face. Scanning the tangle of over-turned chairs and toppled desks, I located my gun at the same time as the creature, both of us diving for it in an effort to beat the other to the advantage.

We collided in a flurry of thrown punches, our combined effort causing the weapon to skid across the room where it tumbled even further out of reach. The thing was definitely strong, but we seemed pretty evenly matched. While I was growing more confident that it couldn't overpower me, I had no idea what other tricks it had in its arsenal. The thought of it suddenly biting into me with a dozen mouths, or its hands sprouting Wolverine inspired claws filled me with a panic.

With a fear strengthened shove, I separated myself from the thing's grasp. Rolling into a defensive crouch, I squared off against it as it mirrored my stance, each of us undoubtedly planning his next attack.

"FREEZE!"

My Keeper's voice hit the room in a fearsome roar, and like two quarreling children the creature and I immediately froze guiltily in place.

I grinned triumphantly and relaxed my stance, causally straight-ening my badly rumpled suit as I stood.

"Ha. You're in some deep shit now Dorian." I gloated. Spinning on one heel I turned to face my rescuers.

Reagan, Lydia and McKenna stood blocking the doorway, their weapons drawn and ready. Each wore an identical look of confusion and alarm as they glanced uncertainly between themselves.

"The Calvary has arrived." I said happily as I moved to join them.

All three guns turned towards my head.

"Um, Ronnie?" I squeaked as I raised my hands in the universal showing of "please don't shoot me".

"Don't move." Raegan snarled. "Either of you."

Either of us?

I looked over my shoulder at the creature who had taken a similar stance to my own. Hands raised in surrender, he looked just as puzzled as I was. Now dressed in a well-tailored suit and tie, the grey skinned man looked younger, healthier. In fact, he looked less like Somnus and more like...

"Oh come on!" I protested loudly, stretching my arm towards the creature and gesturing with one hand. It no longer looked anything like Rupert Ambrose because it now looked exactly like *me*.

"Ronnie." I implored, taking an instinctive step towards my sister. Her gun whined with an intimidating pulse of energy, and her hand shook as she prepared to fire.

"I'm warning you John."

There was no mistaking the threat in her voice or the intention burning behind her eyes, and once again I froze in place. A glance to McKenna told me that she was taking her direction from my Keeper, but unlike Raegan she looked far less hesitant to fire.

Lydia just looked terrified.

"McKenna. Find Max and let the Headmistress know that we're dealing with a doppelganger. I want this school on total lockdown. Nobody in, nobody out." Raegan commanded. Agent Wallace's eyes widened at her words, but she nodded her acquiesce.

"Lydia, watch the halls." She continued. "No one enters this room until we sort this out." She flashed her eyes to her still horrified counterpart. "No one, understand? I don't care who they are or what they say. If anyone tries to come in, shoot them."

It took longer for Lydia to nod her acceptance, but when she did both she and McKenna moved as one, expertly filing out of the room with purposed speed. Raegan glanced behind her and closed the door with her foot. Gesturing sharply with the gun she motioned for me to back up.

"C'mon Ronnie, this isn't funny." The doppelganger said in a hollowed out version of my own voice.

Man, I hope that I don't really sound like that. I winced inwardly.

"I'm not laughing." Raegan agreed, her eyes hard.

"Are you serious? You really can't tell the difference between me and Captain Monochrome here?" I asked, jerking a thumb towards my grey skinned double.

Raegan narrowed her eyes and looked between us. Before I could speak the doppelganger inched forward and pointed at me with his thumb, perfectly duplicating the motion that I had just performed.

"He's all grey." It explained. "No colors anywhere, just, grey."

The sneaky bastard.

"What? *You're* all grey!" I objected.

"Your *face* is all grey." It shot back.

"Your *mom's* face is all gr-"

"Enough!" Raegan bellowed, her voice surprisingly fierce. "Both of you just shut up until I figure this out."

If Ronnie truly hated anything in this world, it was not knowing the answer to something. She was quicker, smarter, and better read than anyone that I had ever met and little things like this that she had no possible way to prepare for, irritated her to no end.

"So just ask me something that only I would know." The doppelganger suggested and I found myself nodding in agreement with him.

"That's a good idea." I admitted.

Ronnie shook her head causing a shockwave of red curls to bounce around her. "That's not a good idea." She countered. "It's well known that doppelgangers are psionically gifted telepaths."

My evil twin and I stared blankly before slowly turning to each other and exchanging identically confused shrugs.

"For crying out loud." Ronnie grumbled under her breath. "It means that they can read minds!"

"Ooh." The doppelganger and I said in unison, nodding amongst ourselves in understanding as we caught on. It made a twisted sort of sense, really. If you were going to mimic someone, knowing exactly what the person that you were trying to fool expected you to say or do would be a tremendous advantage.

"Got it!" I said, snapping my fingers. "Ronnie, do your thing." I said through my teeth, pointing to the doppelganger with my head.

"What thing?" She asked suspiciously.

"Your *thing*." I insisted, trying not to give anything away. "You know, with your colors?" I stressed, deliberately looking towards her hair line like I had seen her do on countless occasions.

"Oh yeah!" The doppelganger said excitedly. "His aura! Nice call man." It complimented me, and for a second I found myself wanting to like the guy. "Read his aura!"

I wasn't sure as to why the creature was trying to help me, but I appreciated the praise nonetheless. Maybe he wasn't such a bad dude.

Raegan shook her head once more. "They can control that as well." She explained. "Doppelgangers are master mimics. Not even our best Seers can detect them."

"Well shit." The creature swore in my voice. "There has to be something you can do Ronnie." It said with a tired sigh.

"Stop calling her that." I grumbled.

"Drop the act Fifty Shades." It snapped back, and I watched in horror as the barrel of Raegan's gun slowly angled a bit more towards me.

"Hey!" I objected, ignoring the fact that I was about to get shot. "Get your own goddamn material Fritz!" It was bad enough that the thing was stealing my, well, my *everything*. But plagiarizing my adorably cheeky quips?

That was crossing a line.

"Don't call me Fritz, Hans." It retorted.

"Don't call me Hans, Schultz!" I countered angrily.

"Enough!" Raegan boomed with more force than her small frame should have been able to produce. The doppelganger and I fell silent, but I swear to God that it stuck its freaking tongue out at me.

"God damn it." Ronnie swore as she pinched the bridge of her nose between her finger and thumb. "One of you was bad enough." She muttered. "I should just shoot you both."

The doppelganger turned to me and smiled. It wasn't a look of humor or enjoyment, but one of victory, and it made my stomach twitch in a flurry of butterflies.

"That's it." The creature said slyly.

"What's it?" I asked suspiciously, but it was ignoring me as its focus locked on Raegan.

"Shoot us both." It grinned.

"What?" Raegan asked, her eyes softening.

"What?" I repeated incredulously.

"Ronnie." It continued, paying me no attention as it crept forward. "Shoot us *both*." It insisted.

"No Ronnie." I said quickly. "Absolutely *do not* shoot us both." I wasn't sure what the thing's plan was; maybe it was hoping to overpower her as she shot me first, but it didn't matter. Getting shot, even with our glorified paintballs, would knock a grown man on his ass. I was allergic to iron, and in that concentration who knows what it would do to me.

And if those weren't good enough reasons to avoid being blasted, it really frigging hurt.

The doppelganger leered at me as it inched towards her. Stretching out its hand, the creature continued to speak. "Think about it." It cooed. "A couple of weeks ago? Your place?"

I watched in horror as a light flipped on behind Raegan's eyes.

"Sci-fi night." She said in quiet understanding.

"Sci-fi night." The creature confirmed. "Kirk. Spock. Star Wars. Shoot us *both*." It told her, gently straining the last word.

"Oh for crying out loud!" I threw my hands in the air, no longer caring whether or not I won this little contest. I could accept that it was smarter - Hell, I could accept the fact that this grey skinned asshole was somehow a better me, *than* me – but mixing up the classics?

That was unforgiveable.

"It's Star *Trek*." I corrected. "Not Wars, Trek. Seriously, why does everyone mix the two of them up? They're not even part of the same univ-"

The classroom exploded in twin claps of thunder as two shots rang out in rapid succession, striking my double in the center of his chest. Propelled backwards like a puppet whose strings had been violently yanked, the creature's mouth opened in an inhuman scream of anguish as it fell. Tendrils of grey flesh erupted from its body in a hiss of oily smoke, lashing out violently as the doppelganger thrashed and flailed against the hard tiled floor. Recovering my weapon, I rushed to Raegan's side and pointed it at the still convulsing Fae.

It no longer looked like me.

Concentration broken by pain, the thing had melted back into what I assumed to be its true form; a man-shaped glob of glistening clay with vaguely humanoid features. The creature writhed in agony at our feet, its skin steaming and bubbling wherever the liquid iron had penetrated its flesh.

"Took you long enough." I grumbled gratefully to my partner. "What gave it away?" I asked, unable to take my eyes from the still convulsing doppelganger.

"It wasn't reading your mind." She answered, stealing the briefest of glances to assure herself that it was really me. "It was reading mine."

"And you thought sci-fi night was stupid."

"It is." She insisted, but I knew that every eye roll and bored sigh of endurance had been worth it.

"Yeah, well," We moved as one, stepping closer to the injured Fae as its spasms began to grow weaker. "Leonard Nimoy would have still been proud."

The creature's breath came in shallow, wheezing gasps. The fleshy tentacles that had whipped around its body now lay lifelessly beside it and were starting to melt at the edges.

It was dying.

"Hey." I called to it. "Hey. Where is he?" I asked prodding it lightly with my foot. "Where's Ambrose?"

The doppelganger turned its head towards us. Grey fluid pooled at the corners of its lipless mouth and drooled down its cheek in a river of monochrome blood.

"You are too late." It coughed, flecks of dark spittle spattering the air around us. "You, you vill never find him." The creature gurgled, its German accent returning as it labored for breath.

"Where is he?" Raegan insisted.

She looked as pained as the creature was, the guilt of pulling the trigger undoubtedly settling in. Ronnie loved the Fae and had dedicated her life to understanding them; killing one was like killing a small part of herself.

"Die Stadt. Die Stadt in der Mitte des labryinth." The doppelganger choked, the words leaving its throat in one long, final breath. The shape shifting fairy shivered and went still, its body blurring slightly as it died.

We stared in silence, and I touched it lightly with the tip of my shoe to ensure that its death wasn't some kind of elaborate ruse.

"Did it say labyrinth?" I asked quietly.

"Yeah." Raegan confirmed.

"That creepy muppet movie starring David Bowie's crotch?"

Ronnie looked away from the now melting corpse, ignoring the question. "It was speaking German." She explained. "Labyrinth literally means,"

SPLORCH.

In the space between words, the doppelganger's body tripled in size like a swiftly inflating balloon and popped in a splash of thick grey, runny goo that coated the classroom and everyone in it.

"Maze." Raegan finished, the side of her face covered in yuck and slowly dripping with the creature's remains.

The door to the classroom burst open and with gun drawn Lydia rushed in. Her eyes went wide as she scanned the room, and I could hear the gasp of surprise as it caught in her throat.

Her weapon fell numbly from her fingers as she ran towards me, leaping into my arms with a muffled cry. Covering my mouth with hers in a deep, trembling kiss, I could feel the fear shaking throughout her tiny form as I held her.

Raegan coughed quietly and raised an eyebrow when I glanced in her direction.

Lydia held herself tightly to me, breaking our embrace only

115

seconds before McKenna burst into the room, the hulking Maxine fast on her heels.

"Is everyone alright?" She questioned, uncharacteristically frantic. Her eyes moved to her Keeper first before finally falling to my sister and me.

"You guys okay?" Max asked, echoing her concern. "We heard whatever that was from down the- ugh!" She recoiled, clamping a mammoth hand over her nose. "What in the hell is that *smell?!*"

Chapter Ten

"And you're positive that it was a doppelganger?" Headmistress Merry's voice was an unsteady, taken-aback combination of disbelief and real, actual fear.

Seconds after Max had secured the classroom, we were rushed back to the school's main office and thrust before a rather alarmed looking Headmistress.

McKenna had been out of the room during the explosion, and Lydia, even after throwing herself into my arms, was largely untouched. Raegan and I on the other hand, were a mess.

Still drenched in the smelly and now drying grey goo that was Rupert Ambrose's doppelganger, Maxine had managed to provide us with a couple of small wash cloths and a bright yellow tube of moist towelettes. They were the kind that were usually reserved for cleaning bathrooms, not faces, but given the stench that wafted from our clothing, neither of us gave it a second thought as we tore into the container.

As she had been closer to the remains at the time of their unexpected popping, Ronnie had taken the brunt of the slimy blast to her chest, face and arms. Now, in the safety of the closed office, she paused in the task of removing a chunk of sticky grey flesh from the depths of her cleavage and looked up at the Head Mistress with hard, serious eyes.

"Quite." She answered curtly, clenching her jaw to hold back what I assumed was the torrent of less than lady-like words that she actually wanted to use.

Headmistress Merry bristled. Overwhelmed and exasperated, she took a deep breath and began pacing behind her desk in a spastic display of frustrated hand gestures and barely formed half words.

"Impossible." She insisted, wringing her hands. "How could a doppelganger have possibly gotten into the school?" She shot an accusing glance to Max who calmly shrugged it off.

"Don't look at me." The head of Campus Security said, raising her hand in front of her in defense. "I've said since day one that he was a creepy little dude." She glanced towards us. "All frail and sickly." She explained scrunching up her nose. "But he always sniffed out human." She finished, looking back to the Head Mistress.

"Sniffed out?" I asked, tipping my head to Raegan.

"She has the gifts of smell and touch." She answered quietly, flashing her eyes and a quick smile to Maxine.

"Troll blood." Max grinned proudly, flexing her massive arms. "I can scent a Fae a mile out. Last year we had a gremlin in the boiler room. Found the sneaky little runt before he even had a chance to touch a dial." Her black eyes gleamed with the memory of the encounter. "But what you guys are covered with?" She tilted back her head and inhaled deeply in our direction. "That ain't Ambrose. And whatever it was, it hasn't been on campus long. I would have picked up on it, especially if it smells like that."

Clamping one hand over her nose, Max offered an apologetic shrug but edged down the wall a bit, as if the extra couple of inches would somehow lessen our stink.

A thought hit me as I followed the large woman's scootching with a frown.

The Agency was warded out the wahzoo against the Fae, and that was to protect grown adults armed to the teeth. Even then, the last breach we had took an inside job and a bunch of disabled wards. How was an FPI funded school full of potential Agents not better guarded?

"Don't you guys have enchantments and junk in place to keep this stuff out?" I asked, not caring about the proper terminology.

"Ass loads." Max confirmed. "There's no way in hell that thing just strolled in."

"Mirrors." Lydia said quietly, looking up. It was the first time she had spoken since the classroom and she still seemed a bit shaken up by the encounter.

"Mirrors." Raegan echoed, her tone indicated that she was kicking herself for not having said it first.

"Mirrors." I parroted, not understanding but not wanting to advertise it.

"Doppelgangers can use them, sort of like portals. They can come and go through them as they please." Lydia explained as softly as her high-pitched voice would allow.

"Through mirrors?" I blinked in surprise.

"A number of Fae have that ability." Raegan said quietly. The reproachful look in her eyes told me that I should have probably known that.

"I knew that." I lied.

"Yeah, but all of the mirrors here are warded." Maxine considered her words as she spoke them "Unless someone snuck a normal one in." She deliberated. "But it would have to be huge."

"I'll bet you anything that ol' Somnus has one back at his place." I agreed.

"Classroom as well. We never checked the cabinets." Raegan said, looking to the other Keeper.

"That would explain why Ms. Stonebridge said he seemed to live there." Lydia nodded. "The doppelganger would have wanted to stay close to its portal."

"Could it have, you know. Pulled one of the girls through?" I asked uneasily. The thought of getting yanked through a mirror all Alice in Wonderland-like by a living wad of play-doh was weirding me out, and judging by the growing looks of horror on the faces of the other agents, I wasn't the only one.

Raegan and Lydia exchanged words quietly until they reached some sort of an agreement.

"I don't think so." Lydia said uncertainly, shaking her head.

"In order to do so, the creature would have had to expose itself to its victim." Raegan added.

"Ew." I grimaced.

"Not like that." Raegan chided. "In order to open the mirror to another, to a *human*, the doppelganger would have to revert to its true form."

"Even then pulling a non-Fae through this side of the mirror would destroy it and negate any of the surrounding Fae space." Lydia nodded. "If the creature had taken the girls through its mirror, it wouldn't have been able to return to the school for months. Maybe even years."

"What if there was more than one?" I asked.

There was another quick exchange of looks as the Keepers consorted, before once again shaking their heads in consensus.

"It's not impossible." Lydia said hesitantly. "They're usually solitary by nature, but there have been reports of them working in pairs to quell their hunger in the past."

"Hunger?" I asked, not liking that word.

"They eat children." Raegan said darkly.

"Of course they do." I sighing to the ceiling.

Raegan turned to the Headmistress. "Have any of Professor Ambrose's students made mention of odd behavior or requests?" She asked. "Perhaps noted any anomalies that we could attribute to the presence of the doppelganger? Anything that could give us an idea of exactly how long it has been at the school."

Merry shifted in her seat and looked towards Maxine who merely shrugged her shoulders. "One." The Headmistress said, with unmistakable annoyance. Pushing the intercom button at the edge of her desk, she leaned forward and spoke into the small silver box.

"Sharon, please send in Ms. Avalon."

Shifting in our seats, we turned to the wooden office door expectantly and watched as it slowly cracked open. An elderly secretary entered, followed closely by a shy, timid looking girl dressed in a school uniform.

"That will be all Sharon, thank you." The Headmistress nodded, waving away her assistant and leaving the girl alone to nervously fidget with her bracelet as she glanced around. Eyes downcast, it was painfully obvious that being brought to attention in a room full of adults was making the poor kid uncomfortable.

"Agents, this is Viviane Avalon. She shared a room with Kara, before her disappearance." Merry introduced.

We answered in a chorus of polite hellos that won us an awkward smile as the girl timidly brushed at the dirty blonde bangs that threatened to completely cover one eye.

"Like the other girls," The Headmistress paused, choosing her words carefully. "Viviane is a blossoming Seer of no small talent. She is doing quite well in her studies and has several classes with Professor Ambrose." She added meaningfully. "Viviane, please tell the Agents what you have told me."

"Yes Headmistress." Viviane said quickly. It was an automated response, no doubt due to the training the teen had been receiving at the school. The girl stood straight, shoulders back and took a deep breath, but as she realized that every eye in the room was on her, a wave of panic flashed across her face.

"Um." She hesitated, brushing at her bangs again, this time allowing the hair to fully cover her eye as she looked to the floor. "For the last few months, Professor Ambrose has been asking us what we know about the, um," Picking up her head slightly she glimpsed towards the Headmistress who motioned for her to continue. "The, um, Dark Path."

McKenna, Lydia and Raegan gasped audibly and exchanged rapid looks of alarm.

"He said it was for a project, and had some of us helping him in his research." The girl continued. "I'm not in trouble am I?" She asked, turning her nervous eyes to the Headmistress.

"The Dark Path?" I asked, leaning towards Raegan with a skeptical laugh. "What, is this guy? Some sort of Sith Lord or something?" I chuckled, but my laughter clung to the sides of my throat as I choked back the memory of the blue bursts of energy that Somnus had conjured.

"Oh Jesus Christ." I looked around the room. "He's *not* a Sith Lord, right? I mean, that's not really a thing, is it?" I was still tipped towards my Keeper but the question was directed towards the entire room.

Headmistress Merry forced a tight, humorless smile. "I assure you Mister Talik, it is not." She said with the patience of someone talking to a not-so-bright, clueless slacker. Which I guess, in her defense and all, fair cop.

"The Dark Path is a legend and nothing more." Merry continued as she resumed her slow pacing. "The blueprints for the original campus make reference to a series of emergency tunnels that once ran beneath our school. They were safely collapsed during renovations some time ago, and no longer exist. However," She added reluctantly. "Some of the older students learned of them and made up outlandish stories about an abandoned Unseelie barrow in order to frighten their younger, more gullible counterparts." Her lips turned upwards in a bitter look of disapproval. "The Dark Path is a rumor that has persisted since my own days of study, and I assure you, nothing else."

"Then why is she here?" I asked, pointing to Viviane. I gave the young Seer a reassuring smile, and it was shyly returned.

The Headmistress darkened. Pursing her lips in disdain she slowly approached the frightened girl.

"Ms. Avalon was found breaking into the Barry Mausoleum." She explained, moving behind Viviane, her fingers curling over the poor kid's shoulders as she gently grasped them. "She gave this story as excuse for her trespass. Of course, we initially dismissed it as fabrication, but now, in light of your more recent discoveries..." She trailed, moving out from behind the girl.

"Wait. You *dismissed* it?" I asked, shocked.

Merry forced that humorless, bitchy smile and flickered her eyes to the women sitting alongside me.

"Ms. Avalon is not the first student that we've caught breaking into the mausoleum, Mister Talik." She said with a meaningful glance down the row of chairs. Lydia and Raegan were swapping flushed glances, and even the prim and proper McKenna was beginning to look uneasy. "It is quite the popular hangout spot with some of the older students."

Max chuckled silently as I caught her eye and gave me a knowing look.

"Okay, what I am I missing?" I asked, looking around the room. I hate not being in on a joke. "What's the deal with this place?"

"It's just off the main campus." Max explained, pointing behind her with her thumb. "Staff and teachers rarely, if ever go there, so the kids will sneak off in order to drink, or smoke, or, um, you know." The huge, heavily muscled giant of a woman was actually starting to blush.

"Make out." Lydia said quietly, learning forward to catch my eye with the barest hint of a naughty smile.

I laughed and shook my head.

"Teenage hormones. Gotcha." I grinned. At first, I wasn't sure why they were all being so weird about it, then it hit me.

"Wait." I said, tilting my head suspiciously to one side. "I thought that this was an all girl's school?"

"It is." Lydia smoldered, playfully waggling her eyebrows.

"This school is so awesome." I blurted out numbly.

Headmistress Merry cleared her throat loudly and brought our attention back to her stern and disapproving stare. Like children caught passing notes in class we sat up straight and composed ourselves as proper adults should.

"Viviane." Raegan said, putting on her professional voice as she addressed the girl. "What made you think that the entrance to the Dark Path was in the Barry Mausoleum?"

Once again taking her cue to speak from the head of the school, Viviane shifted uneasily from foot to foot and spoke in a quiet voice. "I was returning books to the library for Professor Ambrose and tripped in the hall." She mumbled. Being forced to admit her lack of grace to a room full of adults, had to suck. "He must had forgotten to remove some of his papers, because they fell out. I didn't mean to, but when I saw what they were…" She looked down.

"You read them." Raegan asserted gently.

The fear of reprimand left Viviane's eyes as she searched Raegan's face. Finding something kindred there, she grinned sheepishly and looked to the floor in guilt. "I couldn't help it." She admitted.

"What did they say?" My Keeper prodded.

Viviane shuffled in place. "There were some drawings of a maze, and a bunch of notes about the old mausoleum. I couldn't read or understand everything, but I figured that if the Dark Path was real, maybe I could find something down there, you know, magical. Something that would help me find Kara." She explained, shyly meeting Raegan's eyes through a half-curtain of hair.

"A labyrinth." I said quietly to my Keeper.

"A fairytale, Mister Talik." Headmistress Merry corrected as if she were explaining something to a child.

I blinked slowly.

"You're really going to stand there, knowing what you know, and openly dismiss a goddamn fairytale?" I rebuked as I stood. "And it's *Agent* Talik, lady." I said, tapping my badge for emphasis. Or the place my badge would be if I actually wore one.

My jacket.

I tapped the front of my jacket.

But I think she got the point.

Meeting my stare with a defiant, almost challenging intensity, Headmistress Merry snorted in disdain and briefly broke eye contact as her gaze darted past me.

"Miss Stonebridge." She commanded before locking eyes with me once again.

Maxine pushed from the wall and stood to her full height with an apologetic sigh.

"After the other two went missing this morning, the Headmistress had me poke around, just to be safe." She reported, her words reinforcing Merry's glare. "I gave the place a solid onceover, J.T." Max said, trying to defuse the situation. "There were just some beer bottles, a bunch of cigarette butts and a few old porno mags."

"As you can see *Agent* Talik." The Headmistress said with strained patience. "I leave nothing to chance. Not even goddamn fairytales." She mocked, throwing my words back in my face.

"But I ain't no Seer." Maxine continued. Merry's eyes flashed in outrage as she looked to the hulking woman. "So I guess I could have missed something."

The Headmistress snarled and opened her mouth to speak, but anything that she wanted to say was apparently forgotten as Agent Wallace slowly and deliberately stood.

The leggy blonde hadn't spoken since our run in with the doppelganger and our return to the office. While I had assumed her to be sitting in her normal haughty silence, she had instead been processing the information, taking in every detail and waiting for the perfect moment to bring the attention of the room back to her, where it belonged.

"I won't." She said coolly. There was no boast in her voice, just clear, irrefutable fact. She turned to Maxine and issued a single order. "Show me."

Max's face fell. "Yeah, sure. I can take you." She agreed dejectedly. "Unless Agent Talik wants to go instead?" A sudden hope gleamed brightly in her dark eyes.

"Uh." I felt my face flush warm as I was put on the spot. Thankfully Raegan stood, inserting herself between us as she nodded in agreement.

"You can take us both." She offered. "A fresh set of eyes can't hurt."

Where Max looked a little disappointed at Raegan's offer to join us, Lydia seemed nothing short of relieved. Her eyes flashed a grateful "thank you" to my Keeper before settling on the much, much larger woman in what would have been a warning glare, had Maxine been looking down and noticed.

"If Ambrose is using the Latrodenzian on those girls, he'd have to make sure that they remained safe and secure." Raegan reasoned as she turned to me. "The maze would be the perfect place to hide them. Close by, so that he could come and go, but unreachable to anyone but him."

"If it's real." I pointed out.

"It's the only thing that fits." She countered.

McKenna approached and dipped her head to Raegan. "Let me go with you." She offered. "Agent Talik was able to quickly and easily spot the doppelganger, something that not even I can do without the proper time and focus." She continued quickly as my Keeper opened her mouth to object.

I shook my head and did a double take at the unexpected praise. Ronnie, apparently as shocked as I was, could only gape like a fish in reply.

"But before we investigate anything," Agent Wallace smiled, drawing pleasure from her ability to stun us into silence. "He should meet with the rest of the staff." She pivoted on one expensive heel and looked towards our host. "To ensure that everyone is exactly who they appear to be."

The head of the school said nothing, mutely indicating her agreement with a single nod of her head.

"Agreed." Raegan nodded. "Do you remember which books you returned to the library?" She asked, turning to Viviane and engaging the girl before she could fully shrink into the background.

"I kept a list in case Professor Ambrose needed me to retrieve one of them for him, but it's back in my room." Came the nervous reply. "I've been too scared to sleep there since Kara disappeared." She added meekly.

"I'll go with you." Lydia offered, giving her a friendly smile as she stood. "I'd love to see the old dorms again." The gesture was reassuring and I could see Viviane's body relaxing at the promise of company.

"See if there are any notes in his classroom as well. We need to see what he was reading." Raegan said quietly as Lydia moved past. The tiny blonde Keeper gave a subtle nod of agreement.

Agent Wallace watched the exchange with an air of approval before turning to our host.

"Headmistress Merry." She addressed the woman respectfully, but her tone was that of command. "If you could please gather your staff in one location for a head count, it would greatly assist Agent Talik with his observations." It might have been my imagination, but I swore that I heard a slight, corrective emphasis on my title.

The Headmistress bristled and puffed up a bit. This was a woman who was used to giving orders, not taking them.

"I will arrange an emergency staff meeting after hours." She said curtly. "I see no need to disrupt classes."

McKenna smiled. It was a slow, icy gesture that crept across her face like spreading frost, and I instinctively held my breath. Agent Wallace was stunning; tall, blonde and graceful, there were few things in this world that could ever hope to even slightly mar her beauty.

That smile was definitely one of them.

"No dear." She said sweetly. "I'm afraid that all studies are to be suspended immediately. The students are to return to their dormitories and stay there until further notice." Holding up a single slender finger to silence the Headmistress before she could protest, McKenna turned to Maxine. "No one is to leave this school or these grounds until we're certain there are no more threats."

The hulking head of security nodded in quick agreement, her forehead creasing and her black eyes serious as she spoke.

"I'll call down to the gate and have my best people on it. No one in or out." Max assured her. "As for the teachers, I'll send'em all to the gym. There's plenty of room and it'll be easy to see if anyone is missing, or if they try to sneak out. That okay?"

McKenna smiled in genuine gratitude. "That'll be perfect. Thank you."

"Give me half an hour." Max said as she quickly moved across the room and towards the office door. Raegan touched the big woman's elbow as she passed, pausing her in midstride.

"Agent Talik and I need to clean up." She said quietly. "I'll take him to the gymnasium and then meet you and Agent Wallace in your office."

Max looked down at her arm to where Raegan's hand still lingered, and then over her shoulder to the clash of power between McKenna and the Headmistress. Bobbing her head in silent acknowledgement, she opened the heavy wooden door and exited, letting out a relieved breath as she escaped.

"I will not allow this." Headmistress Merry announced, quivering with insult. "This is my school. You have no right to give orders here."

"Fortunately for us, your consent isn't required." McKenna cut the woman off, dismissing her with an elegant wave of her hand. "Lydia?"

Despite the girl dwarfing her by a good four inches, Lydia stood protectively by Viviane's side and took her cue from McKenna. Standing straight and adjusting her red framed glasses, the busty Keeper took a deep and magnificent breath before she began to speak.

"You had a known predator of children within the very halls of your school. Three students are missing, and you ignored both warnings and testimony from a key witness." She started, motioning with her head to Vivian. "Page 27, section C, Paragraph 14 of the Agency Charter Agreement for this school states that in the event of suspected Fae corruption or influence on any staff member or student body, that the F.P.I. has full jurisdictional control of the grounds and all governing bodies until the safety and well-being of all parties can be fully ensured." She recited smartly.

Call me biased, but the reciting of agency legalese in Lydia's tiny, high-pitched cartoon voice was incredibly sexy.

"This is *my* school." Merry fumed.

"It was your school." Agent Wallace corrected. Then as to indicate that she was finished with the conversation as only she could, McKenna simply turned and walked towards the open doorway, arching a finger as she passed in a gesture for us to follow.

"Show me your room sweetie?" Lydia asked, guiding a stunned Viviane gently by the hand to the exit.

Wow. I mouthed to Raegan, trying my damnedest to keep a straight face as my Keeper and I quickly filed in behind them as they left.

Ronnie somehow managed to keep a straight face, but her eyes sparkled with humor and surprise.

"I will be taking this up with your superior immediately!" Headmistress Merry sputtered from behind us, and as my hand grasped the door handle to pull it closed, I could hear her angrily fumbling for her desk phone.

"Oh! Tell her I said Hi!" I said cheerily before I could stop myself.

Raegan gave me a sharp jolt to the ribs. I winced and grabbed my side as we stepped through the reception office and emptied into the hall. Lydia and Viviane were moving steadily out of sight, the voluptuous Keeper's voice squeaking in the distance like an adorable balloon with a perky little leak.

McKenna had lingered only long enough to inform Raegan that she would meet her in the main security office before leaving us abruptly alone.

"Man. I would give anything to hear that call." I chuckled as I followed my sister down the school's pristine halls.

"She's about to have her ass chewed off sideways." Raegan swore with a small chuff of laughter.

"Bah." I waved off the idea. "She's the Assistant Director, she's got to be used to it by now." I reasoned. "It comes with the job."

"I was referring to the Headmistress." She countered, grinning up at me and I involuntarily winced.

Assistant Director Blair had always been kind to me, and other than the occasional professional irritation at something going awry, I had never seen the woman come even close to losing her temper.

And something instinctively told me that I never wanted to.

We walked for a while, slowing only as we came to the bottom of the wide staircase that lead to the gymnasium. Raegan seems purposely hesitant, but before I could inquire as to why, she cleared her throat and glanced up at me.

"So." She said meaningfully, meeting my eyes. There was something there that I couldn't quite place.

"So." I replied suspiciously.

"Now that we're alone?" She beamed up at me in question.

"Yeah?"

"When exactly were you going to tell me about you and Lydia?" She asked, narrowing her eyes into angry slits.

Chapter Eleven

Other than Raegan and myself, the girl's locker room was empty. With no boys attending the school, there were no other real options, and even though Ronnie assured me that it was perfectly okay, it still felt *weird*.

The lady's room was one of those forbidden places that every guy knew existed, but never got to actually see; like the changing rooms at Victoria's Secret or the Playboy Mansion. I felt like any second I would be busted for Porky's themed hijinks and dragged by the ear back to the principal's office.

Stripped to our underclothes, we washed in front of a large mirrored sink in silence, each of us careful not to look at anything but our own bodies lest we glimpse something that could send us running for the nearest Vomitorium. The dry, weird smelling soap and the scratchy brown paper towels didn't exactly provide the cleaning power that we so desperately needed, but they helped to alleviate the worst of our combined stink.

Risking an eyeful of sisterly skin and the wave of nausea that would undoubtedly follow, I looked up into the mirror and through it caught Ronnie's eye. The conversation had turned to my secret relationship with Lydia well before we had ever reached the gym, and upon hearing the details she had gone uncharacteristically quiet. Other than a quick phone call to Maxine asking her to retrieve our emergency clothing from the car, we hadn't spoken.

The silence was making me uncomfortable, and the longer it progressed, the more I needed to know that the air between us was clear.

"You're not mad at me, right?" I asked her reflection. I actually felt guiltier for her finding out about Lydia and I the way that she had, than I did for withholding the information.

She shrugged slightly and looked down. "I'm a little hurt." She admitted before looking up through the tops of her eyes. "You know that you can tell me anything, right? Anything."

My heart sank. I could feel the injury in her words.

"Of course." I tried to smile. "It's just that…" I sighed, trying to find the right words to explain the situation without risking further wounds.

"Oh my God." She said, physically turning to face me. "It was Lydia's idea to keep it quiet, wasn't it?" She accused.

"No no no!" I said quickly. "Well, kind of." I corrected. "But it's not like that!"

Raegan gave me a long, hard, skeptical look and shifted her weight to one side as she put a hand on her bare hip.

"It wasn't you that she was worried about." I explained, looking away as I seriously considered scrubbing my eyes with the coarse, sandy soap. "She didn't want McKenna to find out." I clarified through the safety of the mirror.

"Plus, you know, we work together. She didn't think that the Assistant Director would approve." I added lamely.

To my relief Raegan crooked a smile and began scrubbing at her neck. "Well you're probably out of luck there." She teased. "She doesn't miss very much."

I knew that she was joking, but my heart still skipped a beat. The thought of being called into that particular meeting filled me with a sense of pending doom.

"So, how long?" Ronnie asked, reaching for the stack of paper towels and soaking one in the running water.

"About a month and a half." I said sheepishly. "Remember that day I got lost on the way to the library and you didn't see me for like two hours?

Raegan looked up from scrubbing her face and frowned. "You lied to me?"

"What? Oh, no. I totally got lost. That place is frickin' huge." I admitted. "But I might have left out the fact that I ran into Lydia and she offered to take me there." I offered the mirror weakly. "We started talking and, well."

My Keeper paused in mid-rinse, the dark paper towel still covering the lower half of her face.

"Look. I know you two are close." I started contritely.

"Not as close as she was with Javier." She snorted under her breath contemptuously.

I bit my tongue and fought off a series of eye twitches and neck convulsions brought on by the mere mention of the hunky janitor's name. Man, I *really* hated Javier.

My sister chuckled into her paper towel at the sight of my one-eyed sputtering and crushed it around her mouth in an effort to hide her laughter.

"Sorry." She snickered, the mood finally starting to lift.

"Ronnie, I really don't want to come between you guys." I said with sincerity, acknowledging the possibility. "If you want me to stop seeing her…" I let the implication of my words hang meaningfully. To my relief, my sister's reflection shook its head back and forth in a tumble of red curls.

"No. It's okay." She promised. "I get it, I really do."

I glanced up and smiled through the mirror.

"And I'm happy for you." She added. "Lydia deserves to have a nice guy in her life, for a change." She smirked.

"Aww shucks." I said lamely, ignoring the Javier throwback and bumping her awkwardly with my shoulder.

"It's just going to be a bit awkward." She continued with a heavy-hearted sigh.

"What? Working together?" I asked, tilting my head in question.

"No." She hesitated. "Having the talk."

It was my turn to snort.

"I'm pretty sure that we're well past the need for the talk, *Mom*." I groaned, rolling my eyes like a teenage girl.

"Ew. No." She gagged, punching me in the arm. "Don't be gross."

"Then what do you mean?" I asked, confused.

Raegan sighed again and shrugged one shoulder. "She's just, a *really* good friend." Her voice was sad, almost remorseful. "And I don't want my threatening to beat her squeaky little ass all the way back to Titsberg if she breaks your heart to jeopardize that." She said with a teasing look, but a serious, almost scary undertone of warning lingered behind her eyes.

Focusing on getting clean with renewed vigor, I said nothing as I pumped the soap dispenser and ran my hands under the water, the threat of sisterly vengeance still hanging heavily in the air.

Apparently, dead Fae are a whole lot easier to see than living, because Ronnie was having no difficulty wiping away the last few remaining splotches of liquid Doppelganger. Where I looked as if I had been rolling around in grey mud for the last hour, she was virtually untouched; her pale, milky skin flawless in the dim florescent light, its supple softness causing my stomach to churn.

"You guys still in here?"

Max's voice called to us from the depths of the locker room, cutting through the uncomfortable silence as the large woman quickly approached.

"Back here." Raegan called out as she rinsed her hands for the last time and shut off the faucets in front of her

"Oh man. Nice glutes!" The giantess complimented as she rounded a stack of lockers and came into view.

It was then that I was reminded of how mostly naked I truly was.

Initially it had been pretty awkward, but with absolutely no sexual interest dancing on either side of the fence, undressing in front of my sister had been like, well, undressing in front of my sister; embarrassing, but tolerable.

In fact, in a conscious effort to avoid seeing Ronnie's lack of clothing, I had all but forgotten about my own. Until right now.

"That's Batman, right?" Maxine asked, referring to my formfitting, yet totally superhero themed boxer briefs.

Frozen in mid-scrub, I watched through the mirror as Raegan stole a quick peek of confirmation and repressed a giggle.

"Thank you Max." She said sweetly, taking two large plastic covered bundles from the much larger woman. "You're a life saver."

Setting one of the packages on the edge of the sink between us, my Keeper stuck her tongue out teasingly before taking the head of security gently by the hand.

"Let's give Agent Talik time to finish cleaning up. You can fill me in on the rest of the staff as I get dressed." Raegan said, leading Maxine further into the locker room as she spoke.

"Yeah. Okay." Max agreed, turning in body but still staring at me as she was pulled away. "You sure he won't need any help with anything?" She asked softly.

"He'll be fine." Raegan reassured her as they rounded a stack of lockers and stepped out of sight.

We had checked all of the changing room's mirrors for the proper wards and protections before we had even thought about cleaning up, but at the moment, I wished that we hadn't. Staring at my mortified reflection, I silently prayed that another doppelganger would appear and pull me through.

When it didn't, I took a deep, disappointed breath and reached for the bundle of clothing.

Chapter Twelve

"Are you sure that you don't want me to stick around?" Raegan asked, her eyes darting through the small crowd of teachers and staff that had gathered in the gymnasium.

"Naw." I assured her. "I've got this."

The premise was simple enough; I would watch the crowd for a while to see if I could pick up on any obvious threats, and if that didn't work, I'd have them line up single file.

Then, I'd just sort of look at them, I guessed.

The girls were largely convinced that the doppelganger had been working alone, so this was basically just a formality. It was a task that required no real knowledge and with my talents, I could do it pretty quickly. Even I could handle staring at people and looking for anything weird, or so I thought.

As the numbers began to swell easily into the fifties, the thought of addressing a crowd much larger than I had anticipated was daunting.

"Good luck." Raegan chuckled. Looking up at Maxine she gestured to the exit with her head, indicating that she was ready to go.

The massive security guard grunted in acknowledgement and took a step towards the gymnasium's large double doors.

"Hey, Ronnie?" I called after them before they had a chance to move very far away.

"Yeah?" She asked, looking over her shoulder in confusion.

"Go easy on her, please?" I begged. "For me?"

My sister's lips parted in a surprisingly evil smile, and saying nothing more, she turned and exited the gym.

Poor Lydia. I thought guiltily. I have always hated emotionally tense or awkward situations, to the point where I couldn't even watch the many television comedies that seemed to rely on it in lieu of a plot. There was just something truly unsettling about being stuck in that moment of right before resolution that had always made my skin crawl.

Still, as awkward conversations go, Lydia had it a lot better than I did. Where she and Raegan would probably cry and hug and then go out for those weird green face masks with the cucumber eyes, or whatever it is that women do after they've shared a tender moment, I had to deal with McKenna.

On a good day you'd get frostbite if you stayed in her shadow for too long. On a bad day? I shivered involuntarily at the thought and refocused my attention on the gymnasium and to those who had gathered there in an attempt to forget about my looming fate.

The teachers and staff had separated into a myriad of smaller groups, each whispering and droning with a hushed, nervous chatter that filled the room like the buzz from a hive of suspicious bees. Occasionally a head would pop up, prairie dog style, and necks would crane in my direction for a better look, but so far no one had dared to approach, or offer anything but a curt acknowledgement of my presence.

I let them stew for a few minutes. Not because my keen mind told me that the longer that I kept them in the dark, the more helpful they'd be as they sought answers, but because I really, really hated speaking to any sort of crowd.

Especially if they were all women.

Resigning myself to my Agency-appointed duties, the room's buzz deepened and all eyes turned to me as I moved towards the open bleachers and climbed a few of the hard metal steps.

"If I can have everyone's attention please." I said politely from my makeshift soapbox.

A few of the heads stayed turned in my direction, but the majority of them quickly peeked back down as the flurry of whispered conversation grew in intensity.

"Excuse me, ladies." I said in a louder voice, making sure to add a bit of bass to it in an effort to give it that official tone.

The crowd pressed in closer and the chatter immediately died, leaving a suddenly stark, empty silence in its wake.

"My name is Agent John Talik." I announced. Before I could continue the conversation crashed back into place like a returning tide.

"Who is this guy? One voice asked, apparently not impressed by my professional and purposefully manly speaking voice.

"Does anyone know what this is about?" Asked another.

"Max said that there would be coffee and cookies, but I don't see coffee *or* cookies." Said another still.

"Hey!" I shouted, surprising even myself. Reaching into my jacket pocket I pulled out my badge and held it high over my head. "As I was saying." I started again. "My name is John Talik. I am an Agent with the FPI. As you may be aware, we are here to investigate the disappearance of several students from your school."

They stared up at me in rapt silence. Before I could lose their attention again, I pulled the picture of Professor Ambrose that I had snagged from his file from my pocket and held it up for all to see.

"Does anyone here know the whereabouts of this man?" I asked, showcasing the photo.

A fresh wave of surprise and murmurs rippled through the crowd as fifty-something sets of narrowed eyes squinted up at me.

"Oh my God, that's Professor Ambrose!"

"Is he missing too?"

"They don't think that he had anything to do with it, do they? He wouldn't hurt a fly!"

"Has anyone even seen a snack table?"

"Ladies, please." I said loudly, once again struggling to maintain control. "Has anyone seen Professor Ambrose, or do any of you know where he might be at this time?"

"Have you tried his classroom?"

"Or the library."

"Did he take the girls?"

"You can't possibly believe that Rupert is involved!"

It was starting to get loud again. Cracks appeared in the small groups and factions were split as the women began to argue. Speculation fed gossip and gossip fed resentment as they began to bicker amongst themselves. I could feel any hope of regaining their attention slipping.

"There was a doppelganger in the school." I announced as loudly as I could without screaming.

You could have heard a pin drop as every person in attendance stopped in mid-argument and turned to face me in stunned, horrified silence.

"Now that I finally have your attention," I scolded. "I need all of you to focus. Please, look around. Is there anyone missing besides Professor Ambrose? Is there anyone else that you think should be here, but is not?"

The crowd widened, the space between them doubling, sometimes tripling in distance as they eyed one another with suspicion and distrust. There were still small pockets of chatter, but it was much more managed and at times even helpful as they scrutinized each other and tried to determine if anyone else wasn't there.

"Where's Mildred?" Someone asked loudly.

"I'm here!" A panicked hand shot up in fear of being marked absent. This went on for thirty seconds before a certain level of trust was regained and they began to crush back in together, each and everyone one of them looking up at me in expectant silence.

"So no one is missing? Everyone is here and accounted for?" I confirmed. "Good. If you would all now please form a single file line, starting at me, we can get through this next part quickly and get you back to your classrooms." I instructed, pointing with both index fingers to where I wanted the line to be.

Slowly and unsurely, they began to comply and the makings of a line began to form. One of the staff, an angry looking woman in her late sixties pushed her way to the front of the line and regarded me with a sour sort of self-importance.

"We demand to know what this is about." She said firmly.

I smiled as politely as I could. "We're trying to make certain that the doppelganger was working alone, and that everyone here is who they claim to be." I said over the head of the woman in front of me, addressing the line of teachers so that everyone could hear my answer.

"Just by looking at us?" Someone asked dubiously.

"That's the plan." I answered.

Four or five teachers back, a thin woman in a floral print house-dress raised her hand and spoke in a kind, motherly voice.

"Excuse me, Agent, ah," She faltered.

"Talik." I supplied.

"Pardon my asking, but shouldn't you have a female Agent with you? You know, someone with the gift? Like a Seer?" She asked soft-ly, as if she shouldn't be saying that word to a stranger.

"Actually, I am a Seer." I explained. The looks of surprise were actually kind of satisfying and I felt myself starting to relax as my stage fright finally began to fade.

Greta Grumpinstuffle in front of me let out a contemptuous little snort and preened as the crowd focused on her. "Men can't be Seers." She challenged.

"I had me one of them special surgeries." I whispered behind the back of my hand. "Don't know who the donor was, but the damn thing looks like a baby elephant's trunk." I confided as she gasped in offense and held a hand to her chest. "You're good to go dear. Thank you for your time." I said loudly, looking to the next woman in line and motioning for her to step forward.

The woman just stood there, staring up at me in shock.

"Next?" I said with just a touch of impatience when she didn't move. Gracelessly forced from the front of line by the approach of the next person trying to take her spot, the mortified woman stammered and sputtered before finally stumbling away.

"Are the students in any danger?" The next in line asked me ner-vously. Her sincere concern for the children over her own wellbeing was touching and I found myself wishing that I had a teacher like her in my life as a kid.

"They're fine." I assured. "This is just a formality. We have ev-erything under control." I promised, before indicating to my left.

"You're all set." With a quick nod of thanks she followed the path of the first woman who was still lingering nearby, now watching my every move.

"You're fine, you're fine, and you're fine." I said in rapid succession, quickly whittling down the line.

"So are there going to be cookies or not?" A short woman with a mane of unruly curls and dark framed glasses asked as she glanced around, presumably in search of the snacks that she had been promised.

"Next." I said dryly.

Clutching her purse, her body slumped in profound disappointment. Dejected, she followed her peers into the cookie-less void of discontent to my left.

"I've heard of you." A sultry voice informed me as it drew closer.

I turned my head so quickly, my neck nearly snapped.

Working in the "Land of the Insanely Hot", it had taken me a while to get used to the influence that Fae blood has on the human body. Flawless skin, perfect hair and proportions that would make a Barbie Doll cry foul were the constant norm. Every single day was like taking a stroll through a never ending beauty pageant.

Now, while I am always on my best behavior, do my best to keep it professional, and made strides to become the personification of "Perfect Gentleman" on the outside, I am technically still a guy. So occasionally, when confronted by a particularly attractive member of the opposite sex, my brain will totally and completely stop working.

In this case, it packed up its shit and went home for the day.

The woman was nothing short of a Goddess. Tall and athletic, but exceptionally curvy, she moved with a swaying, feline grace. Smoldering, dark brown eyes watched me with a sexy sort of amusement as I faltered and stammered like an idiot.

"Uh, hi." I said numbly as I managed to suavely channel my inner awkward teen.

"Hello." She said coyly. Her lips were full and inviting, and tinted with the barest brushing of deep red in a perfect contrast to her rich ebony skin.

"So, uh, how's it going?" I asked lamely, my brain fighting to refocus.

She laughed lightly and the sound was like the chiming of bells against angel wings.

"I'm fine, thank you." She smiled. "They say that you fought a Redcap, and won." She turned her head slightly to one side and slowly looked me up and down. "Is that true?"

Now between you and me, calling my little run in with the Redcap "a fight" was beyond generous. The truth was, it had kicked the living shit out of me. The damn thing had broken both of my wrists, impaled my hands and left me with two large, round scars that started to ache whenever it was about to rain.

But if you thought for second that I was going to tell *her* any of that, then you don't know your boy Johnny.

"Well," I swaggered, puffing up a bit. "I don't like to brag."

The air between us grew noticeably warmer as she brought one delicate hand to the nape of her neck in apparent appreciation. Obviously impressed by my heroic deeds, and maybe even a little turned on, I gave her a little smile and stood up a bit straighter, flexing under my suit.

"So, have you been teaching here long?" I asked, my voice dropping a few octaves.

Before she could answer the gymnasium doors thundered open, cracking a whip through the air and driving a wedge between the sexy teacher and my inappropriate flirting.

An older girl in her mid-teens took a deep breath as most of the room turned towards her, and lowering her head she moved with determination across the polished wood floor with a hurried gait. One of the teachers towards the back of the line intercepted the girl, addressing her by name.

"What is it Emily?" She asked apprehensively when she noticed the red flush of the girl's face.

Emily, with her long legs and gangly arms went crimson as every set of eyes in attendance fell upon her. The epitome of awkward teen, she looked horrified to be at the center of attention, but at the same time resolute in her duty to complete whatever task she had been given.

"Headmistress Merry sent me to get him." Her voice shook as she pointed to me with a long, pale finger.

"What's up kiddo?" I asked. I gave the poor girl my friendliest grin in an attempt to put her at ease.

"Something happened." Emily swallowed hard, her eyes that of a startled deer. "In one of the dorm rooms."

"What? What happened?" I asked, moving down the bleacher steps, a sense of dread sweeping over me

"Someone got hurt." She choked.

I closed the gap between us in an instant.

"Hurt? Who got hurt? What happened?" I was trying to keep calm for her sake, but failing miserably.

My quick approach and rapid fire questions caught the girl off guard and she locked up, freezing in place at the sudden confrontation. Her large eyes glistened wet and she seemed like she was fighting back a flood of tears. "I don't know! I think it was one of you." She stammered. "One of the Agents."

Ronnie.

I scanned the long row of women that stretched before me. Leaning out of line and craning their necks for a better view of our conversation, I saw nothing out of the ordinary as I searched. No colorless flesh or empty eyes and not a drop of grey amongst them.

"You're all good." I announced. "Go back to your classrooms and stay there. Someone will be around to fill you in." I ordered much more harshly than I had intended.

Looking to the anxious teen, I forced myself to remain as calm as I possibly could.

"Take me there. Now." I instructed.

Having resisted the urges of fight or flight from the moment that she had stepped through the gymnasium doors, Emily took the order with a breath of relief. Spinning on her heels, her long, bird-like legs lent to impressive speed and it took everything that I had just to keep up as we rushed from the room.

We sprinted through the halls. The long rows of lockers punctu-ated by classroom doors passed in a hurried blur as we ran across the school and down the large, multi-windowed corridor that separated the teaching facility from student housing. Turning sharply, Emily threw herself at a heavy metal door, forcing it open as we rushed into a cramped staircase. Taking the steps two and three at a time, we swiftly climbed to the third floor.

Winded, I struggled to keep up as she burst out of the stairwell into another hallway, her large flat feet slapping loudly at the tile as she slowed.

"Down here." She pointed, stopping to catch her breath.

Following her arm I could see the end of the hallway and the small crowd that had gathered there. Several heads had snapped in my direction before returning nervously to the two figures at the group's center.

"What's going on?" I called out as I quickly approached.

Headmistress Merry was standing protectively over a student, gently rubbing her back and shoulders in surprising gesture of moth-erly comfort. The girl was on her knees, her head in her hands as she cried, whatever had happen shaking her to the core.

"Where are the others?" The Headmistress asked. She seemed concerned, even frightened as she looked past me to the hallway and the distant figure of the nervous-yet-curious Emily.

Glancing around, I scanned the faces of those gathered in hopes of gleaning some context of the situation from them. Following sev-eral sets of guilty eyes to the doorway in front of us, I pushed past them, and with my heart in my throat, stepped into the room.

Lydia lay on the floor of the small dormitory, her tiny, crumpled form curled on one side amidst an open heart-shaped box of scattered chocolate. Falling to my knees beside her, my mind raced as I pan-icked, checking her for wounds or any signs of injury.

She was still breathing. Her breath came in short, relaxed, heavy inhales that caused her side to rise and fall as if she were asleep. Unsure of what to do, I placed my hand tenderly on her shoulder and gently began to shake her.

"Hey." I said softly. "Hey baby, it's time to wake up." I whispered. Lydia's body rocked with the motion, but she didn't stir.

The room swirled around me. I wanted to cry, to scream, to laugh in relief that she was alive. Every feeling that I had twisted inside of me and bubbled with a darkness that threatened to erupt to the surface in an explosion of pure rage.

"What. Happened." It wasn't a question; it was a demand, and it left my throat in a throaty growl of raw emotion as I looked up at the woman that I had felt enter the room behind me.

Headmistress Merry swallowed hard, and there was a fear in her eyes that nearly disarmed me. She seemed somehow smaller and more frail than I had remembered.

"There was a-" She started to answer, but her words were jostled loose and lost to a startled yelp as McKenna burst past her and rushed into the room.

The tall blonde threw herself to the floor beside me and picked up her cousin's head, cradling it in her lap. Her eyes were wide with fear as they sought mine for explanation, giving her a vulnerability that I had only seen once before; a sight that only fueled my growing anger.

Raegan entered as I slowly stood, and quickly joined McKenna on the dorm room floor as they examined our fallen friend. Fast on their heels, Max stopped in the doorway, and came to a halt at the Headmistress's side. With a quiet "whoa" of surprise, she looked around the room.

"You have exactly two fucking seconds to tell me what happened here." I snarled. Taking a step forward, I felt my hands clench into fists as I moved towards Merry.

"Hey. Easy J.T." Max gently warned as she stepped in front of the much smaller woman and put out a staying hand.

"John, look." Raegan's voice broke through the fog of fury that was enveloping me, and at the sound of my name, I turned towards her. With her head still cradled protectively in McKenna's lap, Raegan gently brushed aside a handful of soft honey-blonde hair and revealed the nape of Lydia's neck.

Something silver glinted against her skin, and in the heat of the moment, it took me a moment to realize what it was. The Headmistress forgotten, I joined them and once again slowly knelt at Lydia's side.

"God damn it." I swore quietly. As serious as the situation was, I couldn't help but feel a small amount of relief as the tiny, mechanical spider came fully into view. The latrodenzian were meant to incapacitate, not kill.

McKenna looked frantically between us, my change in demeanor filling her eyes with hope as she spoke.

"You know what this is?" She asked in a small voice.

"It's a latrodenzian." I sighed, gently touching the back of Lydia's neck where the device had burrowed into her skin. I felt exhausted, the gambit of emotions that I had run in the span of seconds was leaving me both mentally and physically fatigued.

McKenna looked at me, not fully understanding. "Is she going to be okay?" The raw worry in her words broke my heart.

Raegan swallowed hard, choking back her own feelings and nodded, wiping at one eye with the back of her curled index finger. "Yes." She said. "Yes. I believe so." She sniffed, her voice growing more firm with certainty. "It isn't harmful, exactly."

I looked to the doorway and the sea of curious faces staring back at me. Behind the Headmistress, in the almost unperceivable gap between her and the protective Maxine, I caught a familiar eye.

"Hey." I said gently, forcing a smile. "It's okay. Come here." I held out my hand in beckoning.

Uncertain if I was talking to her, Headmistress Merry shifted her weight to take a step forward, allowing just enough space for the young woman that I had noticed behind her to squeeze cautiously through.

"It's Viviane, right?" I asked softly, my hand still outstretched.

The crowd parted, giving the girl plenty of room. Eyes still wet with tears, and her skin flushed from crying, the student that we had met back at the office nodded once as she approached.

"Can you tell me what happened?" I kept my tone gentle and overly friendly, afraid that if I moved too quickly or spoke with too much force that she would break down once again.

With a sharp, shuddering breath Viviane nodded and spoke, her voice cracking as she shook with fear.

"I was looking for my notes." Fresh tears welled at the bottom of her eyes. "She asked if she could have one." Viviane explained, pointing to the chocolates that lay smashed and scattered around us.

Nymph blood.

With the exception of myself, every member of the FPI could trace their lineage back to a human and Fae pairing that started their bloodline. Lydia, like McKenna was of Nymph ancestry, which lent to certain physical characteristics and appetites; the mildest among them being a weakness for all things chocolate.

"When she opened it, that *thing* came out." Viviane explained, tears slowly streaming her cheeks. "It started to come after me, but she pushed me out of the way."

Stepping into the room, Maxine pulled the girl to her side and rubbed her shoulder in a reassuring half-hug.

"Where did you get the chocolate?" Raegan asked, looking up from her examination of the creature embedded in Lydia's neck.

"It was a gift from Professor Ambrose." She sniffed. "But I don't like chocolate, so I never opened it."

"Viviane." Raegan said, drawing the girl's attention when it wandered to Lydia's limp body. "Do you know if any of the other girls were given chocolates?"

She nodded slowly, her focus still centered on the unconscious Keeper. "Sam and Gabby." She sniffed. "He gave them to us before the lock in."

"The missing girls." I said, understanding the connection Raegan had already drawn.

"Was there anybody else?" Ronnie pressed.

"I don't think so." Viviane shook her head and pointed to Lydia, still cradled in McKenna's lap. "Is she going to be alright?"

"She better be." McKenna answered, her eyes narrowing as they locked onto Headmistress Merry.

"We gotta find this guy, Ronnie." I said to my sister as she stood. "Like, yesterday."

She nodded in agreement. "Max was just about to take us to the mausoleum when…"She let her words die as she cast a guilty look to McKenna and Lydia.

"I'll rip the place to the ground if I have to." The muscular security guard promised. Her black eyes serious with the need to help.

Raegan smiled a soft thanks before moving to Viviane. "Do you still have the list of books that Professor Ambrose was reading?"

The girl pointed to an open notepad beside McKenna that Lydia must have been holding when she fell. Raegan moved to the tablet and picked it up before giving it a quick once over.

"One of these might help." She said, looking at me through the tops of her eyes. "I need to make a quick stop at the library before we go."

"Not alone you're not." I informed her. We had three missing students and my girlfriend was lying unconscious at my feet. If something happened to Ronnie, I'd come unglued.

Despite the situation at hand, Raegan looked please and I could tell that she understood what I was thinking without my speaking the words.

"I can show you." Viviane offered, gesturing to the notepad. "It'll go faster." The kid was trying to be brave, steeling herself against her own fears and it wasn't lost on my Keeper.

Turning to McKenna, Ronnie's eyes softened and she bowed her head, taking a breath to speak.

"We can-"

"Go." McKenna ordered. "I'm not leaving her side." Then the normally icy blonde Seer did something that I had only seen once, and hoped never to see again.

She started to cry.

"Just find him." She pleaded. Wiping at her eyes, she lowered her head and brushed a bit of hair from Lydia's face. "Please."

"We will." Raegan vowed.

And for just a moment, I felt pity for him when we did.

Chapter Thirteen

The trip to the library passed without incident.

With Viviane's help, Raegan was able to locate almost all of the books listed on the notepad with surprising speed and only one or two minor exceptions. Between them they had expertly whittled the massive pile down to a single, tattered, leather-bound tome bulging at the middle with loose scraps of paper and hastily scanned photocopies. Any notes that Somnus himself might have taken may have been long gone, but Raegan was confident that she could reconstruct his research with the materials that they had managed to cobble together.

Not exactly the bookish types, Max and I had spent the majority of our time perched protectively above them as they worked, from the vantage of the massive library's well-polished balcony. From there we had all of the entrances covered, and would be able to easily spot anyone foolish enough to attempt to sneak through the seemingly endless aisles and rows of books housed below.

No one was.

Because the students and staff had been restricted to their living quarters, there were no interruptions to be had and the girls were able to focus on their work with undisturbed efficiency. Eventually Raegan signaled that their fast paced research had come to its end and Max and I left our watchful posts to rejoin them on the first floor. Still, as we descended the staircase I couldn't help but feel a twinge of remorse in leaving; the moment of peace that our quiet vigil provided had been a nice little distraction from the madness surrounding us.

And it was only bound to get worse.

With McKenna refusing to leave Lydia's side, and Max dutifully at ours, it was pretty much group consensus that Viviane should accompany us for the duration of our creepy graveyard tour. She was still technically a target, and while I had dismissed the teachers as threats en masse, none of us were exactly comfortable with letting the girl out of our sight. There was a good chance that the mausoleum was going to be a bust, and no one wanted to come back to face the aftermath of another attack; especially one that we could have prevented.

The graveyard itself was just that - your average, run-of-the-mill boneyard.

Old, well taken care of, and encompassed by wrought iron fences and towering gates, it had that sort of quiet charm that one would look for when scouting out that perfect place to be brutally murdered by Dracula and his minions. Crammed tightly into the compact seating of the Maxmobile, we followed a densely packed, winding dirt road through a forest of tombstones and old monuments, before finally coming to a standstill in front of a house-sized grey marble building.

"Huh. So *this* is where we're going to die." I mused as the security cart's electric motor whirred to a soft stop.

Ducking under the roof, I stepped out of the vehicle and peered up at the Barry Mausoleum. Large white columns sprouting from the floor of a concrete slab stretched above us like the bones of a long dead giant before disappearing into the over-hanging roof that protected the modest entryway. The place had a certain finality to it, and I found myself reluctant to be the first to approach.

"Home sweet home." Max grinned as she rounded the cart, pausing at my side.

Blinking in surprise, I looked back and forth between the Max-sized building and the Max-sized Max before making the connection.

"You don't really live here, do you?" I asked uncertainly.

Maxine laughed loudly.

It was an honest, happy, and surprisingly feminine sound filled with humorous appreciation; appreciation she showed by punching me lightly on the shoulder.

"Naw." She grinned as I staggered forward, thrown off balance by the force of the blow. "I've got a little place just off campus." She chuckled. "Full gym, waterfall showers, and hey! You should totally come see it when we get all of this stuff sorted out. Maybe get a work-out in!" She offered excitedly.

My arm dangled uselessly from its shattered socket, and I held it with my free hand in order to prevent it from flopping around on damaged nerves. Unable to remember my own name through the pain of the good natured jab, let alone come up with an excuse that would prevent me from being dragged back to her Amazonian lair, I smiled weakly up at her and tried to speak.

"Don't let her fool you." Raegan said as she stepped out of the cart. "This is like her second home. When we were training to be Keepers, Max spent more time here than she did in class." She teased.

Catching her eye, I shot her a look of desperate thanks for the impromptu subject change before latching onto the offered re-steering of the conversation.

"You're a Keeper?" I asked in honest surprise.

"Flunked out." Maxine shrugged. "My sense of smell might rank off the charts, but I never got a taste for all that nerdy stuff like Ray Ray." She motioned to where Raegan was standing but lowered her head to me. "I'm more of a hands on kind of gal, if you know what I mean." She whispered, ending the sentence with in husky tones. "I like to get dirty."

"There's a small window in the back." Viviane said, quietly reminding everyone that she was still with us. "The metal covering pulls up." She added shyly when we turned to face her. "That's how everyone gets in."

Craning her head to the side of the building, Raegan pursed her lips in thought as she weighed her options.

"Max?" She questioned.

"On it." Maxine nodded, taking the inquiry as direction. Stomping forward, she headed straight for the massive metal door at the front of the building. It had been painted the same color as the surrounding marble in an effort to obscure the entrance and gave the front of the mausoleum a seamless stone look from the distance.

"You might want to stay back." The big woman cautioned, stretching one hand towards us in warning. Leaning back, she shifted her weight to one leg, lifted the other, and kicked. With a grunt of effort and the sound of a hammer striking steel, the metal door exploded inward.

Ripped from its hinges, it bounced against the interior flooring before disappearing inside the building, taking its entire frame and several large chunks of stone with it.

"I have *always* wanted to do that." Maxine announced with a satisfied sigh and a crack of her neck as the dust and debris settled in a brownish-grey cloud around her.

"Subtle." Raegan said dryly as she approached. "But I meant for you to use your keys." She clarified in a disapproving voice as she moved past the towering woman and into the crypt.

Maxine's face fell as she looked down at the large key ring affixed to her belt that she had forgotten in her excitement to become a human battering ram.

"Don't mind her." I whispered, carefully stepping in through the hole where the door once stood. "That was awesome."

Rock, dirt and debris littered the old, well-worn carpet that followed a square path around the interior of the crypt. Once red, the passage of time had stained it a murky shade of brown that did an incredible job of reminding you that you were standing in an actual building full of corpses.

Rows of name plaques lined the center of the vault, each housing a slab of marble that served as a doorway to the dead that lay just beyond it. Benches and statues dotted the short hallways, with each of the four corners containing a different, but similarly designed stone sarcophagus. I had no idea who occupied each of the places of honor, but I assumed since they were connected with the school, they wouldn't mind the sudden appearance of a badly crumpled metal door amongst them.

It was dark, and with the large chunks of broken marble, dangerously so. Iron braziers and sconces peppered the walls at even intervals, but offered no source of light as whatever they had housed had burned out a long time ago.

"Hang on." Maxine grunted as she fiddled with her belt. Removing a large black flashlight that could easily double as a Billy club, she gave it a twist and illuminated the darkness in front of us. Empty beer bottles, cigarette butts and more natural trash such as leaves and dirt were scattered to every corner, but there were thankfully no signs of life.

"Don't you guys find it just a little bit creepy that a school has its own personal cemetery?" I asked as we cautiously looked around.

"Most of the older institutions do." Raegan shrugged. "Yale, Harvard, Duke; they all have small burial sites either on campus or really close by."

"Yeah, well how many have old escape tunnels running through them?" I asked wryly.

"You have to remember; society wasn't exactly receptive to most things." She explained. "There were times in the not-so-distant past where simply having our gifts would have been seen as a form of sickness or curse. Witch burnings may not have been as prevalent as tourist towns like Salem would have you believe, but stoning, beatings or flat out murder? They were far from unheard of." Raegan gave a dry chuckle as she looked around. "Ironically enough, a cemetery would be the safest place to hide, if you were trying to escape death."

I thought about that for a moment, and tried to picture what it would have been like to be a Seer back in those days. Images of being tied to a large wooden pole and placed atop a bonfire danced before my eyes. I quickly shook my head to clear away the thoughts as I my pulse begin to quicken.

"Yeah, no." I shivered. "I don't do fire."

Stepping past me and into the left side of the hall Max paused and gave me a genuinely gentle nudge. "Another thing we have in common." She mumbled.

I flashed her a grin as she passed, and then looked over my shoulder at Viviane who was still lingering in the decimated doorway. "So Velma, what is it exactly that you were looking for in here?" I asked, the mystery behind the whole damn situation feeling just a little too Scooby Doo for my liking.

Viviane gave me a timid, but apologetic shrug.

"I'm not sure." She admitted. "I was just looking for anything out of the ordinary, I guess."

"Out of the ordinary in an above ground mass grave?" I raised a brow.

Raegan opened the book that she had taken from the library and scanned a few pages. How she could make anything out in the dim light was beyond me.

"There's a lot of details about the legend of the labyrinth, but as far as I can tell, only passing references to anything that would even suggest that this is the entrance." She looked back at the girl with a confused frown.

"There were more notes, I swear!" Viviane said quickly. "He must have went back for them."

Ronnie and I exchanged skeptical glances without speaking as we followed the main hall around the first corner, Maxine's flashlight illuminating the way.

"Well, if you came here, you had to have some sort of idea about what you were looking for." I surmised, glancing back. "What was it about his notes that lead you here?"

Viviane paused in thought. "Latin." She said in sudden remembrance. "Something about resting, or a place of rest."

"This whole place is a place of rest." Max said under her breath.

"There were also sketches of the mausoleum and like, angels. Or maybe they were demons." Viviane continued, trying to help.

153

"They're supposed to show the way to the Dark Path, but that's all that I can remember." She said apologetically.

"There could be a hidden switch or lever." Raegan mused as the beam from the flashlight hovered over a carving of an angel.

I snorted. "Yeah, well, I call "not it" on any frigging spider holes."

Ronnie stifled a giggle, but Viviane froze in place, fear washing over her features in a mild panic.

"Spider holes?" She asked in a petrified voice.

"Long story." I said grumpily, hoping that Raegan would catch the dirty look that I was throwing her way.

She didn't, because instead of paying attention to me, she seemed lost in a sudden thought.

"What if rest doesn't mean death?" She mused, moving swiftly to one of the iron benches that lined the wall. Nudging it firmly with her knee, she frowned and looked my way.

"It's bolted to the floor."

"Here, let me try." Max offered, handing me the heavy flashlight.

Gently ushering Raegan out of the way, she bent at the knee and grasped the bench in both large hands. Straining slightly she wiggled the seat back and forth to test the hold, but there was hardly any give.

"Wow. It's nailed down pretty good." She grunted in appreciation. Putting more of her back into it, Max tugged again, this time straining with effort as she lifted.

There was a loud cracking sound and the screech of metal on concrete as the bench in its entirety was ripped out of the floor. Pointing the flashlight's beam over the spot where the heavy iron seat once sat, I searched for any signs of a lever or switch, but saw nothing.

"Anything?" Max asked curiously as she peeked around the back of the black metal bench that she now held several feet off the floor.

"Just a huge hole in the cement and a few broken tiles Miss Walters." I said in astonishment.

Max sighed in disappointment and let the iron bench fall back onto the mausoleum floor which vibrated beneath my feet as a loud boom of impact echoed throughout the building. The walls themselves seemed to hum as the sound faded into the tinkle of falling stone and the settling of dust.

"Did you hear that?" Raegan asked, tilting her head.

"I think the dead heard that." I quipped, rubbing at still ringing ear with one finger.

"No, I heard it too." Viviane said, stepping closer to Raegan. "Like something falling, right?" She asked, looking to my sister.

"Like a huge metal bench?" I offered.

"Shush." Raegan scolded. Pursing her lips, she looked up to Max.

"Can you do that again?" She asked, gesturing to the now bent and twisted seat. "But harder?"

A smile split the big woman's face as she nodded, all too eager to be of assistance. I watched in awe as she leaned over, and with one freaking hand picked up the pile of warped iron and hefted it far above her head.

"Ready?" She asked, reaching up with her other hand, not for support but to steady the looming weight.

Raegan shook her head into a quick yes and we all took a few wary steps backward and put our fingers in our ears.

The bench hit the floor with the impact of a bus crash. Shards of broken wood, tile and concrete exploded around us as one of the thick iron legs buckled and bent under the force of the blow. This time, prepared for the thunderclap that followed, I was able to hear what my sister's ears hadn't missed the first time around; the unmistakable sound of cascading pebbles.

"Over here!" My Keeper said excitedly. Running several steps ahead of Max's flashlight beam, Raegan skidded to a stop at the base of one of the stone coffins that adorned each corner of the mausoleum.

"There." She pointed triumphantly.

Dust swirled in foggy patterns as Maxine focused the light onto the floor just past the end of Raegan's still outstretched finger. The tile beneath the marble tomb was cracked and several small chunks had fallen away, leaving two nearly invisible holes in the stone at its base.

"Nagel." I read from the sarcophagus' plaque as Maxine lifted the light to inspect the rest of the container. "That mean anything to you guys?" I asked hopefully.

Raegan shook her head no, her eyes never leaving the holes at the bottom of the coffin as she explored them with one slender finger.

"There's definitely something beneath this." She said, thinking out loud. I didn't need to see her face to know that the gears and wheels were spinning behind her eyes.

"Maybe it slides open?" Viviane offered quietly. "There could be a lever or something, like you said." She added uncertainly as we all looked her way.

Raegan stood, nodding in slow agreement, causing Viviane to hum with shy pride. "Everybody look around for anything that seems like it might-"

There was the sound of someone punching a slab of raw beef as Maxine hit the side of the massive stone sarcophagus with her shoulder in a low tackle. With an angry growl she started moving forward, her legs straining beneath her as she shoved.

The building shook.

All around us the stone screamed in a chorus of screeching metal and sliding rock as the muscular woman continued to push. Then, with a loud, dangerous sounding crack, the sarcophagus broke loose from its moorings and slid freely across the open floor. Ripping up the badly stained carpet in its path, it crashed against the far wall with surprising speed before rocking to a stop. Something metallic clinked softly behind us, and we turned just in time to see one of the wings fall off the carving of an angel that Ronnie had been inspecting before.

"Hey guys? I found the secret lever." I said helpfully as the angel's now ruined limb tumbled to the floor with a thud.

Unable to speak, Raegan and Viviane watched in silent, open mouthed wonder as Max slowly picked herself up from the floor. Having pushed the enormous sarcophagus away from her as it broke free, she had twisted herself backwards in an effort to avoid falling into the recesses of the deep hole that had been hidden beneath.

Dusting herself off as she stood, Max's face was a mixture of

surprise and barely contained pride. "I figured that might be quicker."
She explained casually. I could see that she was unsuccessfully fighting a grin as she shined her flashlight into the blackness at her feet.

Old stone steps disappeared into the darkness, partially obscured by the settling debris that still spun and swirled in the cool breeze emanating from the depths of the forgotten staircase. Snatching up a chunk of shattered tile, Raegan flicked her wrist and sent it careening into the abyss, the sound of it skipping and bouncing as it fell growing more and more distant with each passing second, until it eventually fell silent.

"That seem just a little too deep for an escape tunnel to you?" I asked, stressing the word "little" as I moved to the edge of the hole.

Raegan frowned in response and pulled her weapon from its holster. Taking her lead, I did the same and for the first time remembered that I had a handy-dandy flashlight attachment of my very own.

"Max, take Viviane back to the school." Ronnie ordered, switching on the light at the end of her gun. "Let Agent Wallace know what we found. If she asks wh-"

"No."

Viviane's voice was firmer than I would have ever expected and it echoed throughout the mausoleum with a stubbornness that defied argument. Shocked, the three of us turned to face her, trading surprised glances as we did.

"Please." She said, much softer. The confidence in her voice began to waver, and I could almost see the tremble in her words. "I just want to help." She pleaded.

Raegan softened noticeably. Stepping closer to the girl, she placed a comforting hand upon her slender shoulder. "I know that Kara was your friend." She said gently. "But this is dangerous. If something-"

"But I'm a Seer!" The girl argued, her eyes frantically searching Raegan's. When she found only resistance, she turned to me. "You guys need me." She insisted. "Tell her!"

I hesitated.

"Maybe another set of eyes isn't such a bad idea." I said to my Keeper in a quiet voice.

Yeah, I was having doubts.

The golden ticket crammed into my skull might allow me to see and hear things that the others couldn't, but it wasn't like I was without my share of personality flaws. If I missed something obvious because I was spacing out, or worse; I didn't realize that what I was seeing was *supposed* to be something obvious, I would never forgive myself.

"She's just a kid." Raegan argued, her eyes flickering to Viviane in fast apology.

"And you know that McKenna isn't going to leave Lydia's side." I argued. "Do you really want to take the time to figure out how many Seers you actually have working at the school? Or better yet, how long will it take you to convince one of them to help us?"

Her frown deepened as she considered my words. The ride back to the campus would only cost us about ten or fifteen minutes; trying to wrench McKenna away from her cousin's side would take a miracle. The school's staff, while well-versed in the Fae world from a teaching standpoint, couldn't exactly be the cream of the crop in terms of natural ability or talent, or they would already be in the field. Our best bet laid with the student body, or more specifically, with Viviane.

And Raegan knew it.

"Fine." She conceded in defeat. "But stay close to Max." She warned, poking a motherly finger in Viviane's direction. The girl nodded her rapid, unquestioning agreement, and shot me an appreciative look of thanks as soon as Raegan looked away.

That settled, we turned back to the stairwell, each of us shining our lights into the impossible darkness below as we exchanged uncertain glances.

Max threw back her head and inhaled deeply, her chest expanding impressively as her eyes closed in concentration.

"Yeah." She blew out her breath. "This is the way." She confirmed, opening her eyes. "I can smell Ambrose."

"Well then." Raegan didn't sound all that thrilled as she gestured to the staircase with her weapon. "Let's follow the dark and scary steps into the freshly vandalized grave, shall we?"

"Ladies first." I said sweeping into a gallant bow and motioning for them to go forward.

"Gee, how chivalrous." She said sarcastically before following Max down into the hole.

It was stifling.

Even though we had barely begun or descent, the walls seemed to grow tighter around us, and it felt like we were about to be buried alive at any moment. We walked in nervous silence, each footstep sending a small shower of dirt and crumbling stone tumbling ahead of us in an avalanche of stale, dusty air. The tunnel around us began to quickly transition from tile, to carved cobblestone, and the pressure behind my ears got more noticeable with every passing step.

"Probably around the hundred foot mark by now." Maxine said, her voice louder than it should have been despite her efforts to keep it low. "Good stonework though." She mused, one massive hand tracing the wall. "Almost no tool marks."

"The Crypt Keeper only pays for the best." I explained, my eyes following the stone that she had just brushed past, but noticing nothing. Viviane forced a small pity laugh, and I wasn't too proud to take it.

It was starting to get cooler. Not exactly cold, the stairwell was taking on the atmosphere of an old wine cellar, and although the walls were dry, everything felt as if it should be damp. The stairs were also changing, growing steeper and narrower, causing each of us to reach out to the surrounding stone for balance.

"Anyone else having a real hard time believing that Billy Bad-legs came down this way." I grumbled after nearly losing my step.

"Maybe he used magic." Raegan answered, but I could tell that she was thinking the same thing.

"Or maybe he tripped." I joked at first, but the more I thought about it, the more amazing the idea became. "Man, wouldn't *that* be a nice change of pace." I chuckled. "No confrontation, no fight, just Dr. House laying ass-over-teakettle at the bottom like a broken slinky."

"Head's up." Max whispered back to us, her voice rippling over the surface of the surrounding stone. Slowing to a careful stop, we pressed in closely behind her as she extinguished her flashlight. Following her signal, Raegan and I did the same and the darkness that we had kept at bay instantly consumed us.

At first, I didn't see anything at all. The black around us was absolute not only in its lack of light, but its silence, and the sound of our combined breathing rumbled like a herd of winded rhinos in my ears. Then, as my eyes began to adjust, I could see it; there, in the lower distance was the barest pinprick of light.

Moving as one, we skulked forward, the light growing in intensity with each nervous step. As we reached the bottom of the stairwell, I could clearly see the earthen walls and hard compact dirt floor of the short hallway as it was bathed in a dancing, purple light.

"What is it?" I dared to breathe in a ghost of a whisper as I stepped past Raegan and Viviane, taking my place beside Maxine.

Although the corridor was only faintly lit, it seemed as bright as daylight in contrast to the darkness of the cold stone steps. Barely twenty feet long, it ended in an archway that looked as if it had been modeled after some classic cartoon mouse hole. Cautiously, we approached club-like flashlight and guns in hand as we warily scouted the room that lay beyond.

Perfectly round and domed at the ceiling, the room was nearly empty save for a grisly statue of a winged woman at its center, and the now obvious source of the light that we had seen from the stairwell. Recessed channels had been dug at chest level into the walls that encircled the room. Filled with a shimmering liquid, the surface burned with an intense purple flame that gave off no heat, even when touched.

"Fairy fire." Raegan said from behind me, startling me and causing me to nearly drop my weapon.

"Don't *do* that!" I scolded, rolling my arms in a frustrated dance.

She winced a quick apology, but the smile at her lips made it smack of insincerity.

Exchanging nervous glances, the four of us slowly spread out and began to investigate the room. Max, unimpressed with her initial inspection of the purple flame followed Viviane to a break in the wall that outlined a closed doorway similar to the open one that we had entered through. With our eyes on the statue that made up the focal point of the room, my Keeper and I slowly approached, guns at the ready should the damn thing decide it needed to come to life.

Carved from what appeared to be a single piece of shiny, coal-black stone, the perfect visage of a harpy poised in mid-strike strained forward to greet us. Arms extended, its outstretched hands ended in razor tipped claws that made the silent screech frozen on its obsidian face all the more menacing. The carving's tongue, protracted and obscenely long, snaked from its mouth in a hideous sneer so realistic that I half expected the creature to blink.

"Well, this is embarrassing." I said quietly, drawing a serious, questioning look from Raegan. "I have this same exact statue in *my* scary torture dungeon." I said, my explanation earning me an exasperated groan.

"This isn't a door." Max called out to us from across the room as she slapped her palm against the closed archway. "It's solid." She clarified, slapping it again. "And at least a few feet thick." Putting her shoulder against the blocked doorway she grunted, but it didn't budge.

"Isn't this the same chick who attacked our car that one time?" I asked quietly, turning my attention back to my sister and the statue poised before us.

Raegan tilted her head slightly and pursed her lips. "I don't think this is a harpy, exactly. There are definite similarities, but something is off." She said quietly, her eyes vibrating in her head as they darted back and forth in study of the sculpture.

"I dunno." I mused, staring at the bird-woman's bare chest. "I never forget a pair of-" I could feel time stop as all three women turned towards me, waiting for me to finish my sentence.

"Wings." I coughed, gesturing to the large and obvious pair of avian appendages jutting out behind it.

Satisfied with my answer, Raegan brushed her fingers over an inscription carved at the statue's base. It was written in a language that

I had never seen, which in all honesty only *barely* ruled out English.

"I think it's Badhbh." Ronnie said after a moment of study.

I took a step back in alarm. "You mean the thing is full of bees?" I whimpered as I eyed the sculpture with renewed suspicion and fear.

"What? No." Raegan said, turning to me in confusion. "Not bee-hive, Badhbh." She clarified with as far as I could tell, absolutely no change in pronunciation. Frowning at my lack of response, she narrowed her eyes and spoke slowly. "One of the bean-sidhe."

I could tell by the way that she said it that this was something I was probably supposed to know.

"Ooooh." I nodded unconvincingly.

She scowled but let it slide.

"This isn't good." She frowned, putting one hand to her chin. "Badhbh was said to tell of conflict. She was an omen of battle, or of death." She crouched for a closer inspection of the inscription. "I think that this a warning."

"Really? The huge jet black statue of a demonic bird woman ready to attack is a warning?" I asked dryly.

"Can you read it?" Max asked, moving closer at the mention of battle and death.

Raegan rocked her head to one side in consideration. "It's Goidelic." She deliberated.

Only silence answered her.

Looking up she took an annoyed breath to explain, but Viviane spoke up, cutting her off. "That's old Irish, right?" She offered with the nervousness of a student with an unsure answer.

"Exactly." Raegan confirmed with a grin of approval that caused Viviane to glow with a relieved sort of pride. "It's not my strongest language." She mused, turning her focus back to the writing. "If Lydia were here, she-" Her eyes widened in alarm and she whipped a panicked gaze up to me.

"It's alright." I tried to smile. "What's it say?" I motioned for her continue and with a sad nod, she did.

"Red-mouthed. Badbs. Crying home." She read with a series of pauses that would make William Shatner proud. "Rain shared thrice."

Ronnie's forehead scrunched in concentration as she hovered her finger over the last word. "Potatoes?"

"Well, it's definitely Irish." I confirmed.

"Yeah. I can't make out the last word." She explained, standing with a frustrated sigh.

"What does it mean?" Viviane asked in reverence, kneeling to get a better look at the words herself.

"I haven't the foggiest." Ronnie pouted.

Max stepped forward and bent slightly at the waist, her black eyes narrowing as she inspected the harpy's open jaws.

"Look at the tongue." She said quietly. Putting her head almost completely into the creature's mouth, she sniffed at the carved rock.

"Oh, oh don't do that." I moaned. "Why would you do that? That's what people do right before the monster comes to life." I informed her as I began to back up. "Do you want to get your face bitten off? Because that's how you get your face bitten off."

Ignoring my warning, the heavily muscled security guard reached into the statue's mouth and scratched at its tongue. Stepping back, she brought her outstretched finger to her nose and sniffed at it daintily before giving a tentative lick.

"It's blood." She said in amazement, turning to Raegan.

"That's gross." I pointed out.

Covering her mouth with her hand, Viviane reflected my own disgust, but Ronnie's face was suddenly awash with understanding. "That's it!" She said as she excitedly slapped me on the shoulder.

"Why is everybody always hitting me?" I complained, rubbing at my arm. She wasn't even a fraction as strong as Max, she did manage to hit me in the same exact spot, and it was still tender from before.

"It's not drops of rain. It's blood!" Raegan continued, ignoring me. "We have to feed it three drops of blood!"

Blood.

The single word caused my hands to ache and I clenched and unclenched them into tight fists of painful memory before lifting my arms and holding them out to her with my fingers splayed. The perfect coin shaped scars at the center of each palm were hard to miss, even in the soft purple light of the fairy fire.

"I gave at the office, thanks." I said, excusing myself from the very notion of volunteering. If Johnny don't do no fire, then Johnny doubly didn't do no blood.

"I've got this." Max offered, stepping forward. Reaching towards the tip of one of the statue's clawed talons with her finger, she gingerly probed it before immediately pulling back her hand.

Blood was already welling at the tip.

"Wow. That thing is like wicked sharp." She blinked in surprise as she looked at her bleeding finger. With a nervous glance around the room, she took a steadying breath and nervously reached for the creature's mouth.

"Max." Raegan said softly, putting a small hand on the crook of the much larger woman's elbow.

"Relax Ray Ray." Maxine said anxiously. "What's the worst that could happen, right?" Squeezing her finger, she carefully placed three drops of blood on the creature's tongue and stepped backwards.

Popping her wounded digit into her mouth, she suckled softly. As she did the room grew impossibly still, and none of us dared to move. Seconds seemed to stretch into days as we waited with our breath held, and just when we thought that nothing was going to happen…

…nothing happened.

"Well that was anti-climactic." I frowned. "Guess we'll just have to break the shit out of it." I suggested, my thoughts flashing back to all of the skill and engineering that went into hiding the secret passageway above us, and how quickly it was disregarded in the face of Maxine's incredible strength.

Grinning her agreement, Max cracked her neck and stepped towards the statue, but Viviane's voice held the hulking woman in check.

"Agent Talik, look!" She said, pointing with an alarmed gasp.

I didn't have to follow her arm to know what she was pointing at; the doorway we had come through had closed. Staring past her and across the room to the now opened arch on the opposite side of the chamber, I lowered my head and slowly began to make my way towards it.

"Don't bother kid." I heard Maxine say from behind me as her large, meaty hands slapped at the hard stone. "It's as solid as the other one."

"But how did it get behind us?" Viviane asked, her voice a near panic.

"It didn't." Ronnie answered. "I think the room itself rotated." She guessed correctly, as usual.

"Wouldn't we have felt that?"

"Guys?" I said, coming to a stop at the now opened archway, too stunned to care that the term "guys" in no way applied to the rest of the group. "You might want to see this." I said in awe.

A vast underground cavern, far too big to possibly exist, especially given the short distance we had just descended, stretched before me as far as my eyes could see. Illuminated by no discernable source of light, a grey cloud of fog encompassed the vast roof of the cave, obscuring it from sight.

Standing in the archway, now once again at the top of a large, winding staircase, I stared out in wonder as the open air and jutting rock below gave birth to a seemingly endless, gigantic stone labyrinth.

Chapter Fourteen

The newly opened exit was almost flush with the jagged wall of naturally formed rock that gave the massive cavern stretching out before us its shape.

"There's no way we came down this far." I objected, looking upward for confirmation.

The roof of the cave was obscured by a swirling grey haze that reminded me of the morning fog after a heavy rain. While I couldn't determine any source of light, the cavern was extremely well lit and we could see the entirety of its impressive size without much difficulty.

"How is this possible?" I wondered out loud.

"Fae space." Raegan answered, her voice breathy with wonder. Squeezing into the doorway beside me, her eyes were awash with awe and brimming with happiness. "But I never dreamed that an area this large could exist in our world."

Viviane's hand crept to my shoulder and tightened in its grip as the girl stood on her tiptoes for a better view. "Is it safe?" She asked fearfully.

"Probably not." Max said dryly before nudging me gently on the back with the curve of her hand. Moving forward, I took a single step out of the archway to allow the much larger woman enough room to pass.

Standing atop a rust colored hill of densely packed dirt and rock that crunched beneath our feet like fresh snow, we surveyed our surroundings before taking a few tentative steps forward. Raising her hand to shield her eyes, Maxine squinted into the distance with a frown.

"What do you think?" She asked, looking over her shoulder to Raegan for instruction.

"It's all going to depend on what this place was used for." My Keeper answered with an apologetic shrug. Leaving the safety of the doorway she joined us on the small overlook. "It's an echo of the Fae Realm, and a strong one at that. I've never felt anything like this before. Time, space, even reality could have different properties here." She added with a glance towards the cavern's misty ceiling.

"Is that why it isn't dark?" Viviane asked in a small voice as she took a cautious step in our direction, gingerly testing the ground.

I gave her a reassuring smile as she approached. The room behind us might have held a certain amount of safety when compared to the alien landscape that surrounded us, but it also held a certain amount of scary blood drinking harpy statue. I doubted that anyone wanted to be left alone with that thing for very long.

"Weird, right?" I gestured to the fog swirling above us. "It's like being on Mars or something." I kicked at a reddish-brown rock and sent it skittering for emphasis.

Viviane smiled nervously.

"J.T. and I are going to scout ahead a bit." Max announced, motioning with her head towards the path. "You two should stay here." Turning from the group she took a couple of steps and then looked back at me expectantly. Raegan and I exchanged silent glances as I indicated to Viviane with my eyes.

"Let's see what we can find in our notes." The redheaded Keeper said brightly. Opening the book that she had been carrying with her, she engaged the girl who leaned in, eager to help.

Spinning on my heel, I turned and quickened my pace in an effort to catch up with Max. We walked to the edge of the hill, stopping just at the curve in the path where it began to descend.

"Think that's the labyrinth then?" Max asked, gesturing towards the structure.

I followed the faint outline of the trail past the end of her outstretched finger with my eyes. The path turned slightly before coming to an end at the base of a smooth, flat wall about a quarter-mile away. Even from where we stood, I could tell that the maze was enormous. Stretching across the opening of a natural narrowing in the cavern like a dam, its many paths and turns were merely hinted at as any further detail became obscured by both the distance and the cloudy grey haze that loomed around us.

"It's either that or they're opening a new mall." I offered with a shrug.

A startled cry from behind us ripped our attention away from the labyrinth wall and whirling in place, we scrambled for our weapons.

My gun was in my hand before I realized that I had actually drawn it. With my finger twitching against the curve of the trigger, I frantically darted my eyes in search for the cause of the alarm. Where I was locked in place, ready to dispense liquid justice on anything foolish enough to have attacked, Maxine was already stalking forward, the muscles in her neck straining against her skin as she brandished her flashlight like a club.

The scream had come from Viviane and the sound of her distress was still vibrating across the surrounding emptiness as we realized the source of the girl's anguish:

It was nothing.

Or more aptly, it was a whole lot of nothing where *something* should have been. The doorway that lead us into the cavern was gone.

Raegan was the first to reach the rocky wall, her hands cautiously probing the spot where the entrance had once been. Finding only loose stone, she widened her search before looking over her shoulder and shaking her head.

"I got this." Max growled as she stomped forward. Sliding the flashlight into the loop at her belt, she raised her arm and slammed the bottom of her immense fist against the face of the stony wall. Several more test thumps followed before the hulking woman stepped back with puzzled frown. "Or maybe not. That's pretty solid." She confirmed looking down to Raegan, her dark eyes apologetic.

"No calling for help either." I said, holding up my cellphone to show the lack of signal. Each of them retrieved their own phones and tested for connectivity, but I could tell after a few seconds of frustrated thumb movements that theirs were as useless as mine.

Shaking her head, Raegan moved beside me and squinted into the distance, her emerald eyes focused on the imposing stone maze.

"So now what?" I asked quietly.

"Now we go forward." She answered, her jaw clenched in determination.

"What about the kid?"

Viviane hovered close to Max, her eyes filled with fear and concern as she watched the larger woman continue to test-punch the rock wall. Raegan seemed to consider my words as she looked back and observed the two.

"Max?" She called out. Grabbing the woman's attention, she motioned to Viviane with her eyes and gave her a meaningful look.

Max nodded. "No worries. I'll keep her safe." She grunted.

I didn't doubt it for a second.

The winding path that lead to the labyrinth's entrance was littered with loose rock and small, easy-to-miss holes that threatened to snag the tip of your shoe as you passed over them. It was rough, but manageable, and aside from a few awkward stumbles and the occasional tumbling of kicked stone, we made it safely to the end.

"Man, how big is this place?" I asked, taking in the maze as it towered above us. The archway that marked the beginning of the labyrinth was easily fifteen feet in diameter, and set in a stone wall thirty feet high.

"There's no way to tell." Came Raegan's reply. "It could literally go on forever." Worry crept into her voice. "Without food or water…" She faltered, turning to me.

"Hey." I put on a confident smile. "I don't plan on being down here that long, do you?" I asked, trying to set her at ease.

"No." She replied, mimicking my false bravery with a shaky grin of her own. "I most certainly do not."

"Good. Because I totally have to pee." I announced, stepping through the large entryway. "So which way?" I asked, turning to face them, my arms outstretched to show that I was unharmed by walking in, a thought that only occurred to me after the fact.

Raegan came to the edge of the doorway and leaned in, looking left, then right, without actually entering. Both directions seemed to go on forever, curving at the edge of vision as they extended far out of the range of sight.

"The Right Hand Rule." She answered with certainty as she took a careful step forward, into the maze. "If you follow the right wall, you will always get through a maze." She explained as I gave her a puzzled look. "It might take a bit longer in the end, but you won't get lost."

"This." I beamed. "This is why I love you." Her confidence set my mind at ease and I felt the weight of uncertainty begin to lighten.

"At least that's how it *should* work." She shrugged, placing one hand on the wall and facing right. "Rules don't really apply here."

And just like that, the weight came crashing back.

The walls of the labyrinth towered over us, giving the space a closed-in feel that made the corridor itself seem small and cramped despite being at least ten feet wide. We hiked in uneasy silence, the echo of our footsteps only lending to the claustrophobic atmosphere.

Having the strongest gift of sight, I took the lead several steps in front of Raegan who was lost in concentration, her eyes focused on the pages of her book as she searched for any information that she might find about the maze. Viviane followed just behind her, the small girl's head twitching around in an alert, bird-like fashion, every odd sound or trampled on bit of debris seeming to set her further on edge. In the rear, Max trailed silently, her dark eyes never wavering as she watched over her newly appointed ward.

We weren't sure of what to expect, but I doubted that any one of us was foolish enough to think that this was going to be a simple hike.

"If I'm reading this correctly," Raegan spoke, breaking the silence. "There are going to be traps and challenges along the way. If we pass them, we'll be lead deeper into the maze and closer to the Keep at its center." She looked up briefly before turning the page. "If Ambrose brought the girls here, that's where he'd be keeping them."

"That's a lot of ifs." I pointed out with a quick look over my shoulder.

Ronnie shrugged a weak apology. "Ifs are all that we have to go on." I could hear the frustration in her voice as she bowed her head and resumed her book-burrowing. Rounding the first of many corners, our group continued to walk as I dutifully followed the rightmost wall to the point of occasionally leading us into several visible-from-a-distance dead ends.

You see, apart from the occasional brain teaser traced out on the back of a kid's menu with a crayon while waiting for drunken, 2am pancakes at Denny's, I knew precisely dick about the intricacies involved with solving a maze. Ronnie on the other hand was the smartest woman that I had ever known. If she gave me a job, I was going to do it until she said stop.

Or until one of us fell into a giant pit of pointy death.

"Whoa Nelly." I warned.

Throwing out my arm as a barrier, I caught my Keeper squarely in the chest like a mother playing human seat belt in a caravan that had just come to an abrupt stop. She had been walking with her head down, lost in her book, and blinked in confusion at the sudden interruption.

"Would you call that a trap, or a challenge?" I asked, pointing to the large hole that was blocking the path a scant few inches from her foot.

Raegan's eyes widened as she looked down. The realization of how close she had come to falling caused the color to drain from her already pale face, leaving it somehow, impossibly whiter.

The pit stretched a good ten feet in front of us, its edges jagged and rough with broken boards and loose rock. Long, cruelly sharpened spikes lined its bottom, stained black with dried blood and gore. Amongst the debris and fallen rock, several human shaped skeletons lay shattered, their bleached bones scattered about and picked clean. A rotting mass of still clothed flesh moldered in one corner, who or what it belonged to either too alien or too decayed to tell.

"Ugh." Viviane winced, covering her nose and mouth with her hand as the smell hit us.

Max moved forward and knelt at the pit's edge. Probing the soil with her hand, she broke off a small, thin piece of wood and held it up for examination. The chip had been painted the same color as the flooring of the labyrinth, and carefully carved to resemble the stone at our feet.

"Tiger trap." She announced, looking up, well, actually *over* to me, as her kneeling made us almost the same height. "The whole place is probably lousy with them." She muttered, flicking the chunk of disguised wood into the pit.

"Awesome." I sighed. "I was just thinking: Do you know what a place like this really needs? Tigers."

Viviane raised a finger to interject. "I think she meant-" She started with a confused look.

"Just let it go." Raegan instructed, gently placing a hand on the girl's wrist and lowering her arm.

"We should probably slow our pace a bit." Max frowned. Standing to her full height, she surveyed the pit one last time before motioning to the small strip of flooring that skirted past it. "We don't know how many more of these things are out there, and from the looks of it, they're going to be pretty hard to spot."

"We'll just have to be more careful." Raegan nodded gravely, motioning to the ledge that lined the pit. "But maybe Max should join you up front." She suggested to me. "I'll walk with Viviane."

Max and I exchanged glances. "It's probably not a bad idea." The big woman shrugged her agreement as she moved towards the wall.

"Her sense of smell is a thousand times better than mine or even yours." Raegan continued as we carefully picked our way around the gaping hole in the floor of the maze. "And even in this space, you can still probably see and hear things that we might not be able to." She reasoned, taking my hand as I helped her from the ledge. "Between the two of you, we just might stand a chance."

"Relax J.T." Maxine grinned. "I'm pretty quick." She assured me, offering me her hand as I cleared the last leg of the hole. "I'll probably catch you before you fall."

I smiled my thanks as she took the lead. "Wait." I paused. "Did she say probably?" I asked in a little voice as Raegan and Viviane giggled past.

And so we walked; the grey of the walls and floors blending with the obscuring haze of magical fog that clouded the ceiling of the cavern. Paired with the dusty brown stone at our feet, and the bleak repetition of the labyrinth around us, it felt as if we were draped in a shroud of hopelessness, despair, and worst of all for me, boredom.

Oh sure, we were searching for a real life wizard in a magical maze hidden in a pocket of leftover fairy space that had been ripped from their world and forgotten by time, but goddamn it , did it have to be so frigging tedious?

If the scenery didn't change, and fast, I was going to break. Just like my ribs.

"Hang on." Max said, mom-arming me as I had done to Raegan, but with a more considerable amount of force. The rest of the group froze in place without question, probably out of fear of stepping on the lungs that I had spat out the second my steroid filled airbag deployed against my chest.

Approaching the wall, the large woman dropped to one knee and retrieved what appeared to be a foot long white stick of some sort from the edge of the corridor floor.

"It's a bone." She said, turning to me and holding it up for show.

"Chicken?" I asked with false hope, knowing full well that it was too large and too thick to belong to any kind of bird.

Standing, Max examined the bone, turning it over in her hands before holding it to her nose and giving a dainty sniff. Immediately her eyes widened in disgust and she let out a surprised yelp before dropping it and jumping back as if she had been burned.

"What is it?" Viviane asked, her voice quivering with a knowing dread.

"Human?" I guessed.

"Worse." Maxine spat, dragging her hands the length of her security uniform in an attempt to get them clean again. "Goat." The undeniable revulsion and honest-to-God loathing that she lent to the word did nothing to explain her reaction.

Confused, I turned to my Keeper for clarification while keeping half an eye on the still disgusted giantess.

"And a goat bone is worse than a people bone, because why?" I asked slowly, still trying to process whatever it was that I had missed.

"Because goats are mangy, disease covered little monsters." Max growled. Jaw clenched, she lowered her head and stalked forward, purposely and viciously kicking the bone into the wall as she passed it.

I watched in bewilderment as she stomped on, resuming the walk only when Raegan and Viviane pressed onward in an effort to keep our group together.

"She get bit at the petting zoo as a kid?" I said quietly to Raegan as I lingered, my eyes never leaving the still rampaging Max as she Godzilla'd her way across the maze.

"Troll blood." She answered. Her tone was serious, but cracking with humor, and there was no hiding the amusement on her face.

"Ahh." I said genuinely for once, because I actually understood. "So I'm guessing that the Three Billy Goats Gruff wasn't exactly a beloved bedtime story in the Stonebridge household."

Behind us, I heard Viviane stifle a giggle.

"Guys! Guys!" Max's voice rumbled throughout the corridor and all but flattened us. "Hey guys! Up here! You've *really* got to see this." She called out excitedly.

The anger that had darkened her normally jovial nature barely a minute ago was gone so quickly that I almost doubted that it had ever been there. Arms waving, she motioned for us to hurry up as she danced impatiently at the turn in the maze.

"You're not going to believe this." She grinned happily as we caught up.

Unsure as to what could cause the sudden and drastic change in her mood, we warily rounded the corner to join her, and then gasped in collective surprise.

"You've got to be kidding." I stared in disbelief.

The new passage widened considerably, easily doubling in size before coming to an abrupt, yet definite end in the form of a gigantic, solid gold gate. Blocking the path like the doors to Heaven itself, it was at least twenty feet across and shimmered and sparkled in the not-exactly-sun light, filling the hall with a warm, soothing glow.

"What is it?" I asked as we slowed our approach, each of us lost in our very own cloud of personal awe.

"It's a gate." Raegan answered breathlessly, her pale skin taking on an almost healthy sheen in reflection of the golden light.

I gave her a long, dry look, but let it slide. Whatever spell the gate's majesty had cast over me was broken by her words, and I moved in for a closer inspection.

Twin doors set in a thick framework of stone loomed over us, and made any hopes of climbing them impossible. Beautiful and ornate, they closed at the center, and I got the distinct impression that they opened outward even though I could see no hinges or devices on which they'd swing on. Sealed with an almost comically large padlock that seemed to be molded from the same metal as the rest of the barrier, I gave the gate a test jiggle and frowned at the result.

There was no give. The damn thing it didn't so much as shake.

"Is that real gold?" Viviane asked, chewing on her bottom lip. Her eyes were wide and glimmering with wonder.

"I think so." I confirmed, not really knowing for sure.

"You could always bite it to check." Raegan suggested impishly.

I ignored her, for obvious reasons.

"Could be a trap." Max pointed out casually before wrapping a hand around one of the many bars that lined the door. Shaking it with a strength that I could never dream to muster, I watched her arms as they bulged through the fabric of her shirt, but the gate didn't budge.

175

"So you shake the piss out of it?" I asked incredulously.

The tall security guard smiled, and then shrugged playfully. "Best way to find out who laid the trap, is to spring it, right?" She asked slyly.

"No. No it isn't." I countered fearfully. "Who told you that?"

"I don't think it's a trap." Viviane said quietly. Moving closer she bent at the waist like a dancer as she examined the door plate just below the lock. "I think that's a sign." She said uncertainly, turning her head towards Raegan.

Handing over the book that she had been carrying to Viviane, my Keeper stepped forward, and knelt, her fingers lightly tracing the flat piece of metal.

"She's right." She said in surprise, looking up at us.

"Can you read it?" I asked, astonished that Raegan had missed, well, anything. To me the sign appeared to be nothing more than an ornate square of gold, carved with odd squiggles and designs; a door plate to save on wear and tear from the lock. If that was an actual language, it might contain a clue to what we were dealing with.

"I think so, yes." Ronnie said, her fingers tracing the faint impressions. "It's hard to follow, but I think it is a form of basic Fae; a common language spoken between the different races." She shook her head slowly and chewed her bottom lip. "I can't believe I missed this." She lamented before turning her gaze to Viviane. "Good eye." She praised with a soft smirk.

The girl blushed crimson and looked bashfully at the ground, glowing, if possible, more brightly than the gate at my Keeper's words.

"What's it say?" I prodded.

Renewing her focus, her lips moved as she silently traced odd patterns between the words as if attempting to track the flight of a bumble bee.

"Hmmm." She hummed before tucking a lock of hair behind one ear. "The good news is I think that we're on the right path." She frowned, her eyes never straying from the writing.

"And the bad news?" I asked, praying that there wasn't going to be any bad news.

Raegan cringed slightly before slowly looking up at me.

"Apparently the key to the gate is guarded by something called the Pharoo'zah."

"Of course it is." I sighed. I had no idea what a Pharoo'zah was, but I had a feeling that it wasn't going to be something I'd want to cuddle with.

Ignoring my moaning, Raegan turned her attention to the lock, tracing the edge of the keyhole with her finger.

"Damn it." She swore under her breath.

"I'm not going to like this am I?" I asked, already knowing the answer.

"Feel." She instructed, taking my hand in hers. Retracing the key-hole with my finger, she looked up expectantly, but I felt nothing beyond the cold metal.

"It's magical." She explained when I failed to sense what she had. "We're not going to be able to pick the lock. Only the exact key will open it." She lamented, and I could almost feel her disappointment.

Ronnie loved picking locks, and carried a set on her just about everywhere that she went. It was a harmless, interesting hobby, and it gave her a chance to focus on something logical whenever her studies into the Fae got a little too bizarre and she needed a breather.

She had gotten good at it too. So good in fact, that calling it a "hobby" was nearly along the line of suggesting that a chess grand-master was merely playing a board game with friends whenever they had a match.

"This is ridiculous." I complained. "And who in the hell builds this shit?" Yeah, it was the wrong crowd to whine in front of, but I was annoyed. "Do they just have some sort of mythical Home Depot down here or something? Where do you even find magical locks and giant frigging gold doors?" I grumbled.

Standing, Raegan gave me a patient smile and walked towards Viviane, motioning for the book. Not knowing what else to do, I followed.

"I think I saw something that mentioned the Pharoo'zah in here earlier." Ronnie mused, flipping through the pages as Viviane and I crowded in, reading over her shoulder.

As we did, I watched out of the corner of my eye as Max tested the gate once more. Backing up a couple of feet, she stepped forward and slammed her shoulder forcefully into one of the metal doors. There was a loud, weird vibrating sound, but the barrier remained unscathed.

"Wow. That's pretty solid." She admitted, sheepishly rubbing her arm when she drew our attention.

"You should get a running start." I teased in response to her efforts before looking back down at the passage that Raegan was trying to read. "Seriously though," I sighed again. "Why is it always this Dungeons and Dragons bullshit? Can't they just get an alarm system or a guard dog or something?" I asked rhetorically.

There was another ringing of metal followed by a quiet "hmm" of introspective thought as Maxine bounced off the door for a second time.

"Here it is." Raegan said, tapping at the page. I couldn't read the inscription, but I didn't really need to as the picture itself used up its metaphorical thousand words in what could only be described as a litany of terrified swearing.

Roughly ten feet tall when shown next to the comparison outline of what I feared to be your average, ordinary human; the Pharoo'zah looked like someone had used some mad scientist's lab to crossbreed a Venus flytrap with Velociraptor. Countless razor sharp teeth protruded from each one of the four mouths that the creature shared amongst its twin heads. Anyone luckily enough to avoid being ripped apart and devoured, still had a heavy, club-like spiked tail and foot long claws to contend with.

"I think that might trump a guard dog." My Keeper said apologetically.

"Are you serious?" I asked, throwing my hands into the air. "What is that?" I lamented pointing at the picture.

"It gets worse." Ronnie said in a small voice.

"Worse? How could that possibly get worse?" I demanded.

"It's venomous." She continued.

"Of *course* it is." I said, waving my hands in front of me. "Why wouldn't it be?"

"On your left." Maxine said, interrupting just long enough to steer my sister to one side.

Raegan shrugged one shoulder and glanced back down at the book. "Well, if you think about it, it really is the perfect pred-"

Even though she was well out of Max's path, the speed in which the large woman passed us was enough to startle Raegan, and force her flinching into my arms.

With a grunt of effort and an enthusiastic battle cry, Maxine launched herself into the air before slamming shoulder first into the golden gate. There was an explosion of stone and a long, high-pitched whine of twisting metal as the left side of the gate broke free from its frame and bent inward in a shower of rock, dust and debris.

"Holy shit." Viviane swore in astonishment before looking back at us, her mouth open in an expression of stunned shock.

While the golden door and padlock were still technically intact, they were now swinging freely from the right side of the gate. Whatever magic that protected the doorway and its lock apparently didn't extend more than a couple of feet into the stone, which was crumbling and falling from the decimated archway in large chunks.

Seemingly unharmed beyond a few small cuts and scrapes, a dusty, dirt covered Maxine slowly stood, brushing at her clothing as she coughed.

"You okay?" I asked as I slowly approached.

"Yeah." She confirmed, looking over to me with an embarrassed grin. "I didn't think that would really work." She chuckled. "Wow."

"Well it did. Holy shit Max." I pointed out, parroting Viviane's perfect choice of words.

Maxine looked over her shoulder to the now opened gate. The magic was already beginning to fade, the golden metal flickering and sputtering like a dying candle. "You know, I've heard of these Fae pockets before, but I've never really been in one." She said, turning back to me. "I feel good J.T., real good. Stronger even." She said, flexing her massive arms in an attempt to explain.

I had to admit; she did look, well, *bigger*. Her clothes, which were already close-fitting across the arms now drew tight against her skin, straining at her chest. Diamonds of open space between each shirt button gave generous peeks of the lace bra that lay beneath. It might have been a trick of the maze, or some byproduct of the fairy world, but she really did seem stronger.

I felt fingers pawing for my arm and glanced down to find Raegan, numbly pointing towards the now ruined gate.

"Good news." I grinned. "Max got the door open."

"But, but," Raegan stammered, her finger blindly tapping the passage that she had been reading. "What about the key?"

"You mean the key that's being guarded by a walking Sarlac pit? Yeah, no thanks." I chuckled sarcastically.

"But you can't open the gate without the key." She insisted. Looking down at her book Raegan's eyes scanned the open page in an effort to make some sort of sense out of our non-conventional solution to the puzzle.

"We don't need a key, we've got a Max." I assured her as I gestured to where the giantess stood, still brushing the dust from her clothes.

Turning away before she could repeat her argument, I made my way towards Maxine and the newly renovated doorway. The left side of the gate hung limply by its center, still attached to the padlock that held it in place. The damaged door's golden hue had faded into a lifeless metallic grey that still occasionally shimmered and sparked with its dying light.

"Between you and me?" I said quietly, pausing at Max's side. "That was the sexiest thing I've ever seen." I confided before moving past, carefully picking my way over the rubble and chunks of shattered stone.

Blushing a deep crimson, Maxine rubbed the back of her neck sheepishly and opened her mouth to speak but her words were lost to the embarrassed smile spreading across her face.

"Regulators, mount up." I called behind me, snapping each of them out of their individual bouts of shock and awe. "We don't know how long this light will last." I explained as they moved forward in clumsy silence. "And I wanna see what else Max can break before it gets dark."

Laughing at my own joke, I started down the newly opened corridor with a smile. I was suddenly feeling a bit more optimistic than I had when we started.

Who knew that solving a labyrinth would be this easy?

Chapter Fifteen

W e walked in silence, Max and I sharing the lead as we plodded on at a steady, but cautious pace. The threat of falling into a pit full of spikes was still fresh in my mind, and despite the generous width of the pathway, we had taken to walking closely alongside the corridor's towering walls.

"I think it's this place." Max spoke softly, addressing no one in particular with her words.

While I never considered myself to be a chatterbox, the reflective quiet in which our group had been walking was slowly driving me insane, so I welcomed the conversation.

"What's that?" I asked, looking up at the much larger woman. Although we were all but hugging the wall, we were still basically walking side by side, which put me at about chest level to Max. Sweat dampened her clothes which were already clinging to her body, revealing a startling amount of surprisingly soft looking flesh.

Well, until she flexed that is.

"This place." She repeated, drawing up one arm in a sleeve-splitting show of bulging muscle. "I think that's why I feel stronger. More, ungh!" She pumped her arm with the gesture, and for the first time in my life, I honestly feared the very real possibility of death by Snusnu. "Ya know what I mean?" She prompted, smiling down to me.

"Not really." I admitted. "I don't feel any different. Maybe a little tired, but that's about it." It was true. Whatever effect this place had over Maxine had skipped me completely. If anything, I felt sore from walking, and more than a little bored.

My mind was wandering to food, and the thought of how amazing a nice, overstuffed roast beef sub would taste, when Raegan joined the conversation from behind us.

"She's not wrong." My sister said, the normal musical lilt of her voice edged with worry.

I paused and the group slowed to a stop.

"So she really is getting stronger?" I asked, turning to face my Keeper. "Is it the labyrinth?"

"It's hard to explain." Raegan frowned, searching for the words.

"It's our blood." Viviane said quietly. "This place calls to it." She explained using the creepiest frigging words possible.

Eyes widening, I looked to Ronnie in alarm, only to find my sister nodding in agreement at the girl's words.

"She's right." She said as if the Kool-Aid was only now starting to kick in. "The magical energy here is overwhelming. I've never felt anything like this." She said in amazement, her eyes filling with the realization of that truth.

"Um. Should I be getting worried?" I asked, already worried.

"No." She said reassuringly. "It's nothing bad. This place is just *infinitely* stronger than any pocket of Fae space I've ever heard of. Even the Ananasi Lair didn't feel like this."

"It's nothing bad J.T." Max grinned. "I just feel, well, good. Real good. Sharper and more focused." She bent her arm and slowly curled her fingers into a fist, her knuckles cracking and popping with strength. "And man, I can smell everything!" Tipping her head back, she closed her eyes and inhaled deeply in emphasis. "Or at least I could, if you two didn't still reek of doppelganger." She grumbled, letting out her breath. Opening one eye, she tilted her head to the side and looked down at me. "And candy?"

I coughed uncomfortably, ignoring the look of confusion coming from Maxine and turned to my Keeper.

"What about you?" I asked in an attempt to refocus on the subject. "You going to Hulk out on me too?"

"I'm fine." She said bashfully. "My talents are less visible."

I suddenly realized that I had no idea what type of fairy blood coursed through my sister's veins. I mean, I had always assumed from her fiery temper, red hair and green eyes that she had more than a drop of leprechaun bouncing around in there, but it had never really occurred to me to actually ask.

Out of nowhere, a horrifying thought struck me like a bolt of lightning, and I felt my stomach turn.

"Oh god." I groaned. A queasy, uncomfortable feeling was washing over me and the room began to spin. "It's not nymph, is it?" I whimpered. "Tell me that it isn't nymph!"

I had experienced firsthand what nymphs were capable of when they were feeling "sharp and focused". My current girlfriend aside, I had once returned a missing acorn of incredible value to a grove of the naked, nubile vixens and in return they had thanked me.

I mean, *really* thanked me. Several times. To the point where upon departing from the naughty appreciation party, I pulled a stubborn leaf from a tangle in my hair, only to find it incredibly painful to pluck.

If Ronnie was going to start feeling her oats, I was going to start throwing mine up.

"Actually," She trailed in a husky whisper as she moved towards me, each step accentuated by a noticeable bounce of her hips. Pursing her lips, she licked them with a slow, deliberant consideration before speaking.

I felt the blood drain from my face as my heart simply stopped beating.

"No." She grinned before losing her composure. Cracking herself up to no end, she leaned against me, slapping my chest as she was overcome by laughter.

"Don't do that!" I shrieked. Pushing her away as she snorted herself silly, I looked to the other women who seemed way too amused by my discomfort for my liking.

"You're sick, you know that?" I muttered angrily. "Like, there's seriously something wrong with you."

Ronnie wiped at her eye with the back of her hand as she finished chuckling, her face split by a wide, mirthful smile. "Siren."

I frowned and tilted my head. Other than her ragged breathing and ebbing laughter, there was nothing. "I don't hear-" I started, only to be cut off by my Keeper.

"No." She rolled her eyes. "Not siren, *Siren.*" She clarified, stressing the word.

I knew her teaching voice when I heard it, and quickly nodded at the double meaning as I thought back to our many lessons. "Oh! Like mermaids and what not, right? Like in the Odyssey?" I asked in relief.

When it came to Ronnie, anything had to be better than nymph.

"It means that she can sing." Max offered helpfully. "That girl's got a set of pipes on her like no one I've ever known." She added proudly.

"You sing?" I asked as we slowly resumed our walk.

There had always been something to her voice that I couldn't place, but I had always chalked it up to the remains of a fading accent. A sense of guilt mixed with shame swept over me as I realized how little I really knew about the woman that I considered blood. Hell, more than blood; family.

"Not really." Raegan blushed, scolding Max with her eyes. "I mean I do, but-"

"Don't let her fool you J.T." The large woman grinned unabashedly as we picked up the pace. "Angels wish that they could sound that good."

"Well this I gotta hear." I teased. "C'mon *Ray Ray*, belt us out a few bars." Okay, maybe it wasn't nice to put her on the spot like that, but after that little wiggle and lip lick nightmare, I owed her some payback.

Nudging me in the back, I could hear the humor in her voice, but there was also hesitation. "This probably isn't the best place for it." She explained.

"Why not?" I pressed. "Closed in walls, smells like a bathroom – hell; I bet the acoustics in this place are amazing." There was no way that I was going to let her off the hook that easily, especially after tormenting me the way that she had.

"Maybe she's right J.T." Max said, her tone uncharacteristically serious. "I mean, here? Feeling like this?" She flexed her arm and slapped at her massive bicep. "I bet I could throw a truck. But her? I dunno. What if she gets humming too loud and like melts our brains or something?"

I couldn't help but feel that that was an excellent point.

"Hey, new rule everybody." I said quickly. "No singing."

Another nudge from behind acknowledged the teasing, and I grinned despite the possible threat of brain meltage.

"What about you Vivs?" I asked, barely glancing over my shoulder as we walked.

"Huh?" The girl squeaked, caught off guard by my question.

"Well, Ronnie is rocking the pipes, and Max apparently sucked up a butt load of gamma radiation." I looked up at the muscular security guard, hoping that she wouldn't punch me in the arm in appreciation of the joke and smiled. "So what's your super power?"

Viviane shrugged and absently kicked at a stone laying in her path. "I'm not really sure." She admitted. "The blood skipped my mother, and my father wasn't enlightened, so we really didn't talk that much about it."

"Enlightened?" I questioned, looking back.

"Sometimes the gift will pass entire generations." Raegan explained. "It's not uncommon for males marrying into the blood to be kept in the dark until the need to include them arises."

"Like when your kid starts bench pressing the family car?" I asked, drawing a chuff of appreciation from Max.

"It's usually a little more subtle than that, but yes." Raegan smirked.

"Actually, my grandmother was supposed to be really good with animals." Viviane said quietly. "They said that she could even talk with them."

"I'm not sure that's a super power." I chuckled, glancing back at her. "I think that's just what old people do. But hey, if you get the sudden urge to drive eight miles with your turn signal on, play bingo or bake the hell out of some cookies, let me know. I'm starting to get hungry."

Viviane picked up her head at the teasing and smiled prettily. It had to be hard for a kid to be stuck in a group of adults for this long, so I was doing my best to treat her like a peer. Which, given my maturity level and the fact that she was probably more prepared for this than I was, wasn't hard.

As we continued onward, I made a conscious effort to keep a steady stream of conversation flowing; I asked a thousand questions, told every joke that I knew, and did anything that I could to distract from the reality of our situation. The maze was grey and bleak, and aside from our soft chatter, deadly silent. It was the kind of atmosphere that could easily wear away at any cheeriness or optimism that we were holding onto, and the last thing that any of us needed was to focus on the fact that we were, for all intent and purpose, hopelessly lost.

"Whoa." Maxine whispered under her breath as the wall to our left widened and yawned into the entrance of a large, open room. Following her gaze, I felt the same rush of excitement and awe overtake me as I leaned back to speak with my Keeper without taking my eyes off what I saw.

"Hey Ronnie? I know that we're following your whole 'right wall' thing and all, but," I pointed to the chamber. Raegan gasped from behind me, and I felt her hand close against my shoulder. Veering left, the maze at our feet narrowed into a cobblestone path that cut its way through the lush, soft looking grass of a small, meticulously maintained park.

While the room itself was barely the size of the school's gymnasium, the sudden change in scenery and the lack of confining walls made it seem like a sprawling countryside. Elaborately carved benches circled the edge of the walkway, framing a large, multi-tiered fountain that sparkled and bubbled at the center of the oasis. Water, clear, clean and crisp, danced and glittered brightly in the light which seemed to intensify until it was shining like a spotlight into the room.

"Man, I don't even care that this is obviously just a big ol' trap." I said numbly. Upon seeing the promise of rest, my legs began to burn with want.

"That might be fresh water in the fountain." Max said, her voice suddenly deep with longing.

"There's benches." Viviane chimed in. "Maybe we could sit? Just for a couple of minutes?" She asked hopefully.

Like children begging to stop at a passing McDonalds, we slowly turned to Raegan, each of us ready to promise the world, or throw a tantrum until she gave in.

Ronnie looked just as captivated as we were, but there was a hardness behind her eyes; a distrust borne of knowledge that spurred her to protest. I could see the word no forming on her lips, but then, unexpectedly, she softened and mumbled something quietly beneath her breath.

"What was that?" I asked leaning in.

"I have to tinkle." She repeated with strained embarrassment.

"Oh." I said, turning red myself.

"Yeah, me too." Max echoed. "And there are plenty of flower bushes in there." She added, craning her neck as she surveyed the room without stepping in.

"So let's check out the park and make sure it's safe." I said. "That way we can all get caught in this blatant-ass trap and get ticketed for public urination."

Walking closely together, we followed the smooth cobblestone path as we combed the gardens for any threats or signs of danger, but found none. The floral scent of roses and other flowers filled the air, and the light above us beat down like a warm midday sun, giving the illusion that we were above ground. We found two other entrances to the small park, each leading back into the grey confines of the labyrinth, but no signs of life beyond the bevy of bushes and topiaries dotting the area. Marking the opening that we had come through with the jacket to my suit, we determined the area to be safe enough for a potty break, and each separated to our own private clump of bushes.

I was the first to finish, because as a guy my plumbing is pretty straight forward and doesn't contain the mysteries of the universe, which is nice because it saves us a bit of time. Moving to one of the benches in front of the fountain, I stared at the ground in front of me and waited for the group to reform so that I didn't seem like some sort of weirdo with a bathroom fetish as I peeped around.

The sound of footfalls on stone alerted me to the return of Viviane, who cleared her throat in polite announcement her presence.

"How you holding up?" I asked as I straightened and leaned back against the wooden seat.

"I'm okay." She said softly. Sitting at the opposite end of the bench, she glanced around in wonder. "It's pretty, isn't it?"

"Sure." I shrugged. "But I don't think it's the center of labyrinth, do you?"

"No." Viviane shook her head. "The book mentioned a Keep that leads further into the earth. This looks more like,"

"A garden?" I supplied.

"Yeah." She agreed. "Plus, the center of the labyrinth is supposed to be guarded, but there's nothing here." She added, looking around as if to verify her own words.

"Guarded by what?"

"Traditionally, it's a minotaur." Raegan's voice answered as both she and Maxine rejoined the group.

"Like, a big cow monster?" I asked, standing at their approach.

"Something like that." She chuckled. "It has the body of a man, but the head and horns of a bull."

"So a big cow monster." I reiterated dryly. "Well, if it shows up, that's all you kid." I said, looking to Viviane. "We'll put them old lady powers to work."

The girl's eyes went wide before she realized that I was teasing. Sticking her tongue out in reply, she smiled bashfully and stood as well.

"Hell, I ain't scared." Max said dismissively. Bending at the waist, she leaned over the fountain and put her mouth in front of one of the dancing streams. "Ahh. A good fight sounds like fun, right J.T.?" She asked, turning her head and grinning through a mouthful of water.

"I take it that the fountain is clean enough to drink from, Groot?" I chuckled.

Smacking her lips in appreciation, Max wiped her mouth on her sleeve and stepped back. Looking around, her eyes focused on my jacket-marker at the base of the entrance we had come through and she let out a tired sigh. "So, where do we go from here?"

"Back to following the right wall?" I asked, looking to Raegan.

"Your guess is as good as mine." She shrugged half-heartedly. "I'm not even sure that's a valid tactic here."

"Hey, it got us this far didn't it?" I pointed out.

Raegan shook her head as she looked at the surrounding garden. "I'm not so sure." She admitted. "I have a feeling that the labyrinth is leading us exactly where it wants us to go."

"You think that the *maze* wants us here?" I asked, gesturing to the fountain. "Why?"

"I have no idea." She frowned. "I feel like I'm missing something; like this whole place is just some sort of elaborate -"

"Trap?" An unfamiliar female voice supplied. There was an air of amusement to the tone that immediately set my hair on end. Pushing Raegan and Viviane behind us, Maxine and I stood side by side as we spun to face the source of the interruption.

Walking towards us, arm in arm as if they were merely enjoying a leisurely stroll, were a man and a women dressed in out of place, old fashioned court attire. The woman wore a long, free flowing dress of electric blue that hugged her tightly around the waist and accentuated her generous neckline. Her hair was long and curled and bounced with each elaborate step, sending shockwaves of pure white to dance against her pale neck and shoulders. With her high cheekbones and flawless skin, she was attractive by any measure of the word, but her eyes held an instability; an almost manic eagerness that made her seem more dangerous than beautiful.

The man was dressed in a similar style, but wore a crushed velvet tunic and comically baggy pantaloons the same vibrant color as his partner's gown. Like her, his hair was stark white, but quaffed into a Prince Charming-esque parody that framed his eerily handsome face.

They slowed in their approach and made no move to attack, seemingly content to observe us with interested but polite smiles.

"Yeah. We already thought of that." I said conversationally. "But Raegan really had to pee." I explained, jerking my thumb behind me.

"How odd." The woman said, turning her head to the man beside her.

"It tries to speak." The man replied with amusement.

And then they shimmered.

Like a butchered splicing of frames between scenes in a movie, their bodies twitched and jerked, giving them a creepy ghost-like quality that made my knees go weak. Beside me Maxine froze in place, her arms taut and unmoving. I could see out of the corner of my eye that the girls had done the same, and taking their lead, I too went still.

Stepping from their flickering stance, the two approached, their crystal blue eyes oddly enough, the same shade as mine.

"Could this be it?" The man asked curiously, giving me a once over.

"It is with her." The woman pointed out, her eyes moving between each of the women in my group.

"He said it was."

"He did."

"So is it?"

"It must be."

The woman stepped uncomfortably close, her face inches from my own as she searched my eyes in wonder, tiny crackles of electricity sparking behind her own.

"It's not remarkable." The male said with a certain amount of disappointment, as if noting that the weather was beginning to turn.

"But not *un*." The woman said with an appreciative grin. Reaching up with a pale hand, she gently stroked the side of my face. Her touch was impossibly soft, like the smoothest silk, and her fingertips vibrated against my skin.

"Uh, hi." I said awkwardly.

Caught off guard by my speaking, the couple in blue jumped backwards, obviously startled. Maxine, who had been standing as still as I was, also flinched and pulled away from their retreat.

"What the?!" Max growled in surprise. Balling her hands into softball sized fists, she looked around uncertainly, slowly moving back until she stood protectively in front of Viviane.

"Quicklings!" Raegan whispered in astonishment from behind me.

Recovering from their own shock, the couple turned and frowned in stereo, the woman giving my sister a look of utmost disapproval.

"How rude." She sniffed.

"Such vulgarity." The man agreed. Shimmering and flickering in place once again, I turned my head only to see the world slow to a stop around me, and immediately understood. The others weren't freezing in place out of fear or caution; they were literally freezing in place as time came to a standstill.

Turning back to the strange couple, I put one hand on the butt of the weapon at my shoulder and raised the other in a warning for them to stay back.

"What are you?" I asked as menacingly as my shaking voice would allow.

"It still moves." The man said in amazement, turning to the woman beside him.

"It does." The woman cooed, her own shock melting into a curious delight.

"Like us?" The man asked.

The woman considered this for a moment before shaking her head. "Not like us." She replied. Hands up in a sign that she meant no harm, the woman approached, this time more carefully. Peering up at me she slowly stood on her tiptoes until we were once again eye to eye.

"But not *unlike* us." She said quietly.

"Blood?" The man asked, tilting his head. Following his partner's lead, he moved forward and stuck his nose to my ear, almost touching it as he sniffed.

"Hey. Back off big man, that might work with the chicks, but not with me." I frowned, stepping backward and slapping at my ear.

Blinking in confusion, the strange man stepped back and brought a hand protectively to his nose. "Not blood." He said, his voice muffled and nasal.

"John?" Raegan said my name nervously as she fought for my attention. I felt her fingers brush my shoulder. "What's happening?"

"It's okay." I reassured her. "I think." I added apprehensively.

This time I felt the difference in the air as the couple shimmered and Raegan again went still. It felt more purposeful, as if the others were an annoyance or distraction.

Stepping away out of fear of bumping into them and having them shatter like glass, I was approached once more by the woman in blue, who now moved around me like a vulture circling its next meal.

"Something else?" She asked, looking to her partner as she dragged a hand lightly across the small of my back.

"Something else." He nodded in confirmation.

"Oh! Cousin!" She said from behind me. Even though I could freely move, I instinctively held still.

"Hmm." The man hummed. "Perhaps." The word came out darkened, as if it troubled him.

"Oh, *cousin*." She purred. Her soft, vibrating touch lingered over my ass as she breathed the word. Heart in throat, I leapt forward and spun to face her, cradling my backside in each hand.

Amused by my response, the woman laughed in delight as Raegan, Viviane and Max all turned to me, their eyes widening in disbelief.

"How are you doing that?" Raegan asked fearfully.

"Doing what?" I squeaked, still holding firmly onto my rump.

She didn't answer. Time had already slowed to a crawl for her, leaving in her place a redheaded statue that stared at me in confusion and distrust.

"Sister." The man said sternly, gliding past me to intercept the woman who had already resumed her game of stalking me.

"Brother?" She paused, a look of worry flittering across her delicate features.

"We hunt kin."

The woman gasped and brought a hand to her mouth in horror. "We don't."

"We do." The man insisted.

"But he sent us."

"He knew."

She gasped again. "He didn't."

"He did." He replied firmly.

We stood in silence as they stared at me, their eyes scanning my every inch as I stood there awkwardly and tried to make some sense of their conversation. Finally the woman sighed and shook her head, breaking the quiet.

"That will not do." She scowled.

"Not at all." Came the firm agreement.

"We are many things." She started.

"But not this." He finished.

"Well, not to kin." She grinned, her eyes wandering mischievously past me before settling on my frozen companions.

"Or to cousin." He added.

"Agreed." Meeting my eyes for the briefest of seconds, the woman smiled and gently touched my cheek. Turning her head, she looked up at her brother and nodded once.

The man tilted his head before gasping in false surprise and understanding. "He will be upset." He warned, clucking his tongue in mock chiding.

"*We* are upset." She said dangerously.

"Aww, he upset us." The man said in a pouty voice, taking her chin in his hand.

The woman closed her eyes at his touch and nuzzled his fingers.

Motioning towards where Raegan and the others stood motionless with a wave of her hand, she gave a weary sigh.

"What of *her*?" She asked.

"She belongs to him." The man soothed.

Opening her eyes with a knowing smile, the woman turned her head and considered his response.

"Let her do this?"

"If she can." He confirmed, stroking her cheek.

"Then we are finished." She said happily. Spinning to his side, she looped her arm through his and turned her gaze towards the far exit. Moving in sync, the flickering couple began to walk, their reason for being here apparently now drawing to conclusion.

"Wait a minute." I called after them. They turned to me in startled surprise, as if they had forgotten that I was still there. "What do you mean, she is his? Who are you talking about?"

There was no way to tell who they were speaking about, or really, what they were speaking about, but icy fingers trailed my spine in a feeling of dread nonetheless. I stole a glance to where my friends stood motionless, and quickly ruled out Raegan's participation in anything that could even possibly involve betrayal.

Which only left Viviane and Max.

Tilting their heads towards each other, the Quicklings exchanged curious, yet amused looks of incomprehension. It took me a moment, but I finally realized that they didn't seem to understand me.

"Um, he sent her?" I said awkwardly as I tried to match their way of speaking.

Confusion turned to understanding as the woman squeezed her brother's arm tightly, pawing at his shoulder in amazement. "It doesn't know!" She breathed scandalously.

"It doesn't know." The man echoed, his voice laden with intrigue. "Curious." He moved forward in a blur before I could react, once again forgetting any notion of personal space as he stood in front of me, searching my eyes.

"And curiouser." His sister echoed, instantly at his side.

"How do I find Ambrose?" I asked, once again drawing nothing but blank, bemused stares from the two. "Damn it." I muttered. "How does it," I pointed at my chest. "Find him?"

Stepping away from me, their faces brightened considerably as they traded fascinated looks.

"It is brave." The woman said, impressed.

"It is cousin." The man snorted, puffing up with pride.

"It will not matter." She said, worriedly pulling at her companion's arm.

"No. Not to that." He agreed sadly.

"That is merciless."

"It will end there."

"Oh! It mustn't!" The woman pleaded.

"It will." The man said firmly. "Unless." He added with a mischievousness of his own.

"Oh. Unless!" His sister repeated knowingly. "Should we?"

"We should."

"He will be cross." She warned in a sing-song voice, drawing out the last word.

"*We* are cross." He reminded her.

"Um. Hi." I said, slowly raising my hand and wiggling my fingers in greeting. "Remember me?" I asked, wondering how they had already forgotten that I was still there. I was trying to follow their conversation, but listening to them speak was like watching two hummingbirds fight over a feeder.

Stepping forward, the woman met my gaze and took a steadying breath. "The entrance, is not." She spoke slowly and deliberately as if speaking with a child.

I blinked. It was the first time either of them had addressed me directly, and the unexplainable oddness of it was overwhelming. I got the distinct impression that communicating outside of themselves was a rare occurrence, and while I was honored by the gesture, I had absolutely no clue what she meant by that.

"I don't – it doesn't understand." I explained, correcting myself.

"To, but not through." The man said in an almost pained voice, before looking to his sister for affirmation that he had spoken correctly.

She nodded her approval.

"Past but not far." The woman continued, her words coming easier.

"Vines are not vines."

"Such pretty vines." She sighed happily.

"Oh! They are." The man agreed, as if only now realizing it.

"Okay. So, go to the entrance, but don't go through it. Gotcha." I reiterated, only to draw blank looks from the strange siblings. "I think." I added uncertainly. "What entrance are you talking about, specifically?" I asked, trying to follow, but my words were lost on them. I dragged my hand down my face, pressing hard with my fingertips in frustration. "I don't -" I sighed, correcting myself once again. "It doesn't understand."

"It doesn't understand." The woman echoed in a tired voice.

"A pity, that." The man frowned.

"For we tire?" She asked.

"We do." He nodded.

"And now we leave?"

"Now we've left." He announced, taking her arm in his.

Resuming their stroll without another word, I stood dumbfounded as they flickered and jumped like a film reel beginning to break. Moving towards the closest exit, they quickly disappeared around the corner before I was struck by the sense to follow.

"Goddamnit." I swore under my breath. "Wait!" I called out, chasing after them.

But they were already gone.

Only the empty maze, spanning endlessly in each direction greeted me.

"Well, shit!" I shouted in frustration. The strange couple had not only disappeared, but they had taken with them my best chance at finding Somnus and saving Lydia. I could feel the rage growing inside me, and the thought of her laying there helpless only fueled it.

"John?" Raegan's voice called out from behind me, trembling with uncertainty and concern.

Taking a deep breath, I forced my anger back inside its little bottle and turned to see Raegan, Viviane and Max still standing together, now exchanging worried, suspicious looks.

Forcing a smile, I slowly shook my head from side to side and walked back towards my group. It was subtle, but Maxine gave a lazy stretch and slowly moved forward, positioning herself at Raegan's side. She was trying to look relaxed, but her muscles were tightly coiled and she seemed to tense at my approach. Viviane hung back, her eyes quivering and nervous as if she were about to cry.

"Are they gone?" Raegan asked, looking past me to the exit.

"The Bobbsey Twins?" I followed her gaze over my shoulder. "Yeah. As soon as they turned the corner, they vanished." I grumbled.

"How'd you do that?" Max asked suspiciously as I approached, her voice gruff.

"Do what?" I frowned, looking up.

"You moved as fast as they did." Viviane explained quietly. "It was amazing."

"Yeah, well this place is just full of secrets, isn't it?" I snapped in annoyance. Okay, so it was a bit snarky, but the Quicklings, or whatever they called themselves, recognized one of those two, and I doubted that was a good thing. Until I knew who I could trust, there was no goddamn way that I was going to let my guard down.

Viviane gave me a confused look before glancing to Raegan for explanation, but I was already moving.

"You got a sec?" I asked, taking Raegan by the elbow. She looked startled but nodded and didn't resist as I lead her away.

I hated playing the whisper game in front of the other two, but right now, Ronnie was the only one that I could trust, and the last thing that I wanted to do was tip my hand.

"We've got a problem." I said quietly.

"The Quicklings?" She asked looking around.

I shook my head no, drawing her attention back to me. "No. They were actually pretty helpful. I think." I added in afterthought.

"I'm not following." She frowned.

"They were sent for me."

Raegan's eyes widened. "By who?" She asked in a harsh whisper.

"Ambrose, possibly. I'm not a hundred percent sure." I admitted. "But they recognized one of those two." I said, glancing over to where Max and Viviane were doing their best to listen without making it seem as if they were eavesdropping.

"What?" Raegan scoffed too loudly. "Are you sure?" She asked, her voice tipping with skepticism. "How could you know that?"

"They told me." I explained. "Well, they told each other, really. Like I said, they weren't exactly easy to follow."

"Who?"

"The Quic- the albino twins from the Matrix." I said, pointing in frustration to the exit.

"When?" She asked, suspiciously folding her arms.

"Just now." I said, growing exasperated at having to explain the obvious.

"John." Raegan said my name as if calming a crazy person. "They were here for all of seven seconds."

"What?" I paled.

"They blurred in, the three of you buzzed around, and then they were gone." She explained slowly, not understanding my confusion. "That's why Viviane said you move like them."

"No." I shook my head. "They didn't move fast, you guys slowed down." I explained. "I thought that they hit you with some kind of freeze ray or something at first."

A light shone behind her eyes, and I could see her piecing it all together. "That explains why you weren't affected!" She said in relief. "They must project a localized pocket of magical energy that slows the world around them."

"Whatever." I waved irritably.

"Your condition," She hesitated, trying to find the right word. "It must protect you from magic. That's why Ambrose wasn't able to affect you!" Her face awash with understanding and amazement, Raegan began to talk to herself, ticking off points on the ends of her fingers as if she were doing mathematical equations.

"Yeah. Wonderful. You're super smart." I said hurriedly, interrupting her inner monologue nerd-fest. "Ronnie, we can't trust them."

"The Quicklings?" She asked, distracted by her thoughts.

"No, and I don't think that they like being called that." I added, thinking back to their reaction to her use of the word. "I mean Max and Viviane." I said quietly. "I'm almost positive that one of them is working for whoever is behind all of this."

Raegan quickly shook her head. "I don't believe it." She said emphatically. "It's not possible. I've known Max for years John. I trust her with my life. And Viviane?"

"I know." I agreed. "Ninety-six pound teenage girls aren't exactly the industry standard for your average Bond villain. But I know what I saw. They definitely recognized one of them."

"And you just believed them?" She asked skeptically.

"Yeah." I sighed. "Like I said, it wasn't what they said, but how they said it. You had to be there. Well, you know, be there and not be all frozen." I amended.

Raegan frowned in thought, but didn't look convinced.

"Are you telling me that you haven't wondered how a doppelganger got into the school undetected?" I asked, pressing the point. "Or how Viviane just happened to share a room with the first missing girl, and get the same candy as the other two, but was never attacked herself?"

She shifted her weight and sighed. I could tell that those thoughts, or at least similar ones had crossed her mind. Slowly nodding in agreement she sighed and looked up to me, her eyes brimming with sadness.

"So what do we do?" She asked.

"Nothing." I said quietly, looking over to the others. "Right now, we do nothing. We march on like good soldiers. Like nothing happened. But we keep an eye on them. And if one of them decides to go all Lando on us? We drop'em." I said darkly.

Glancing back over to the two, I secretly prayed that the mole would turn out to be Viviane; not because I had any reason to suspect the girl, but because I doubted the ammo that we carried would do anything more than really piss off Max.

"I don't suppose your new friends told you the way through

the maze?" Raegan asked grouchily. The specter of having a traitor among us was already beginning to sour her mood.

"Sadly, no." I shook my head. "But I think you're right." I acknowledged, drawing a raised eyebrow from my sister. "I don't think that it really matters. Something tells me that we're expected, so eventually we're going to wind up wherever it is we're supposed to be."

Raegan nodded her head. "I've suspected that for a while now. Technically, we should still be in the first few rings of the maze, but-"

"It feels like we're miles deep." I finished for her.

"Exactly." She agreed.

"Oh. Yeah. One more thing." I said, suddenly remembering the Quickling's parting words. "If and when we find the center of the maze? Let's not go in through the front door, or main entrance, or whatever they have closing it off."

"Why not?"

"I honestly have no clue." I confessed. "But Heckle and Jeckle made it seem like ringing the doorbell would be a really bad idea.

"And you trust them?" She asked dubiously.

"Right now, other than you, I don't trust anyone." I shrugged, not really knowing what to make of the strange couple. "But if they wanted to hurt us, we wouldn't have been able to stop them. Plus, they seemed pretty pissed about being sent after me. Especially since one of them was already here." I said with a subtle gesture towards Viviane and Max.

"Right." Raegan said firmly. "So we play it by ear."

"For now." I nodded before turning to where Max and Viviane stood waiting. They were growing uneasy and restless and I actually felt a pang of guilt for having to exclude them from the conversation. Still, if one or both of them weren't who they were supposed to be, it was the smartest move I could make.

Silently praying that I was wrong, Ronnie and I approached the two, and swinging my arms I put on my biggest smile.

"Okay Ramblers, let's get rambling." I said, snapping my fingers into a fist that I capped with the opposite hand.

Max stretched and rolled her massive shoulders. I could see the thick muscle rippling under her steadily growing tighter shirt as she turned to face me, shifting her weight to her back leg as she did.

"What was that all about?" She asked, her eyes narrowed in suspicion.

"I think I know how to get to the center." I explained.

Max raised an eyebrow and gave Viviane a sideways glance.

"That so."

"Frick and Frack." I lied, gesturing towards the exit that the pair of Fae had taken. "I think they told me the way."

"Why would they do that?" Viviane asked softly. Moving to Maxine's side, she darted her gaze to the larger woman, nervously gauging her response.

"That's exactly what we were discussing." I twitched a finger between myself and Raegan. "It could be a trap."

Max grunted in acknowledgement, but I wasn't sure that she was buying any of it. "What do you think Ray Ray?" She asked Raegan while keeping her eyes firmly fixed on me.

"I think that they didn't attack us." Ronnie answered in a strong, clear voice. "And if they wanted to hurt us, we wouldn't have been able to stop them, right?" Even though they were my words, they still somehow managed to feel reassuring coming from her mouth. "I say we follow John." She said firmly, leaving no room for dispute.

Scratching her chin in thought, Maxine looked down at Viviane and shrugged. "Well, we've come this far." She considered. "It's not like we can just give up and head back."

"But how did Agent Talik match their speed?" Viviane asked worriedly.

"I honestly have no clue." I admitted.

"I do." Max said, stepping forward.

I swallowed hard as the giantess loomed over me, blotting out the light provided by the mist swirling above our heads.

"You were worried about us," She said in a low, solemn voice. "But now you found your super power!" Smacking me happily on the arm, Maxine laughed, clearly relaxing as my teeth clacked and clattered in my head.

Rocked to one side by her normal jovial mood returning in one bone crushing slap of comradery, I couldn't help but smile as the large woman turned back to the fountain for one last drink.

"Just one thing Max." I said, letting a bit of seriousness creep into my voice.

"Yeah?" She asked, narrowing her eyes as she bent over the steady stream of cool water.

"When we get to wherever it is we're going?" I paused for effect, noting her quick glances to the other women before breaking into a toothy grin. "Let *me* do the knocking, okay?"

Chapter Sixteen

W e gave up on the whole "following the right wall" thing the moment that we were able to confirm that the Labyrinth was indeed shifting. Stumbling upon a dead end, we had turned around only to find that the way we had come had disappeared, replaced by a similar but entirely different section of maze.

With the illusion of choice shattered, we plodded on in the hope that whatever was guiding us would soon lead us to the center, or at the very least, another garden in which to rest.

"That's not fair." Raegan said, throwing her pencil at the wall of yet another abruptly ending passage in frustration. Unlike the rest of us, she still had faith that the maze could be navigated logically and had been mapping our path as best she could.

"You say that so often." I purred in a bad attempt at a British accent. "I wonder what your basis for comparison is."

Angry, vibrant green fire danced behind Ronnie's eyes as she slowly turned her withering gaze to me. "What did you just say?" She asked dangerously, daring me to repeat myself.

I'm stupid, but I'm not that stupid.

"It was, um, a Labyrinth reference." I explained sheepishly. "You know, the movie?"

Clenching her hands into tiny, yet surprisingly intimidating looking fists, Raegan bit back her retort and pushed past me, her head bowed in determination. Ears burning, I rubbed the back of my neck to brush away the prickles of discomfort and glanced over to Viviane who gave me a sympathetic smile.

"Maybe she's not a fan of the classics." She offered.

"It's not *that* old." I grumbled.

"Did you ever watch it on a VCR?"

"Yeah."

"Then it's old." She smirked before moving to catch up with the others. Left alone at the back of the pack, I decided that now would be an excellent opportunity to enjoy a rare bit of quiet time.

Over the next twenty minutes we made our way across muddy swamps, scorching deserts and even a frozen wasteland, all within the boundaries of the maze's looming walls and sharp-angled turns. Cold, wet and frustrated, we trudged on in miserable silence. So weary were we, that not even the returning heat or occasional sprout of green stretching across the stone at our feet could spur more than a grunt of acknowledgement from any single one of us.

The small shoots of undergrowth began to gradually thicken and grow until the labyrinth floor was eventually carpeted in a sea of lush green leaves that muffled our steps as they consumed the stone beneath. Plants of every shape and size climbed the walls around us, surrounding us in a veritable forest of thick vegetation and brightly colored flowers whose fragrance hung on the wind like an expensive perfume.

"Gah!" I flinched, swatting at my ear as something buzzed by close enough to give me goose bumps. Resisting the urge to do the "Is there a bee on me?" slap dance that comes neatly bundled with any close encounter of the insect kind, I instead stopped in my tracks and followed the blur of motion as it came to a rest on the petals of an oversized rose.

Hearing my manly call of alarm, the others had slowed in their tired plodding long enough to look back, stopping only as they followed my gaze to the patch of flowers trickling the Labyrinth wall.

Small fairies darted between the blossoms like humming birds, or more fittingly, like really shapely butterflies. Hovering on delicate, shimmering wings, were what appeared to be tiny, completely naked women.

The trek forgotten, our group stood in silent wonder and watched as the creatures went about their business, paying us absolutely no mind.

"Finally." I said happily, drawing a quirked eyebrow from my sister. "A real fairy." I smiled. "I finally get to see a real fairy."

"Actually, they're Pixies." Ronnie corrected. Matching my smile, she moved to my side and quietly observed as the creature that had buzzed me darted back and forth between two brightly colored flowers.

"Whatever they are," I grinned, reaching towards it. "*This* is what a fairy is supposed to look like."

"Watch it." She cautioned. There was enough warning in her voice that I stopped and pulled back my hand. "They bite."

There was a twinkle of mischief in her eyes, and I wasn't sure if she was kidding or not, but I decided that the "look, no touch" rule should apply here nonetheless.

"Thanks for the warning Hoggle." I chuffed. The pixie that I had been reaching for turned to me as if noticing me for the first time and gentle pushed off the flower in approach. "They look harmless enough." I said, smiling at the little woman as she darted closer, her face glowing with curiosity.

"They are for the most part." Raegan admitted. "Think of them as bees. As long as you don't bother them, they shouldn't bother you."

"Bees?" I questioned, turning my head to face her without taking my eyes off the small woman hovering in front of me.

"Mhmm." She hummed. She was trying to play the part of the disinterested scholar, but I could see that she was just as fascinated by the tiny creatures as I was.

"Are you telling me that doll-sized naked chicks are the *bees* of the Fairy Realm?" I asked incredulously.

"It's actually a pretty fair comparison." She shrugged. "They're integral to the pollination process, and like bees, they can be broken down into workers, drones, and even a Queen."

"Are they smart?" I asked, extending a finger as a perch for the small fairy to land on.

Tilting its head to one side in a very human expression of puzzlement, the creature looked to my hand and then to my eyes before cautiously inching closer.

"Just the Queen." Viviane said from behind me. "I think she's the only one of them that can actually speak." She added, leaning in. Her eyes were focused on pixie, but like Raegan she wore an expression inspired more by academic captivation than my childish wonder.

"That's what I've read too." Raegan nodded. "Although like the others, she is still very primal and just as likely to attack-" She trailed, smacking my hand. "If you keep poking at them."

Startled by the sudden movement, the pixie at my finger lurched backwards and zoomed away, quickly disappearing into the protective mesh of green leaves at the labyrinth wall.

"Huh. They're all girls." I noted, rubbing the back of my hand like a scolded child.

"Oh, you're just noticing that?" My Keeper teased.

"Well, no. I mean, yes, but no." I tried to explain. "It's just, if they're all female, how do they, you know." Talking with my hands I crudely jabbed my finger into the hole of my opposite fist as a stunning visual aid. "Make little, littler fairies?"

"Oh, hey! I know this!" Max said excitedly. The large woman had been watching with a polite disinterest, her body only half turned towards the cluster of pixies which were either too small or too common to hold her attention. But now that the conversation had turned to sex...

"The boy ones are like super rare." She continued, moving closer to the group and looming over us. "And they don't have wings, so they can't leave the nest."

"Hive." Raegan and Viviane said in stereo.

"Whatever." Max shrugged. "Either way, they're taken away and kept safe until they're old enough to tend to the Queen." Stressing the word 'tend' as she made eye contact with me, Maxine arched her eyebrows suggestively and mimicked my earlier hand signals enthusiastically.

I laughed, but couldn't help but notice that her finger gestures were just a little bit stronger and, well, *bigger* than mine.

"So the women are in charge and the men are used for sex." I said with mock indignation. "That seems to be a reoccurring theme." I pointed out, my thoughts wandering back to the nymph grove and the horrifyingly awesome way that those Fae repopulated their numbers.

Raegan looked as if she were going to object, but then shrugged a shoulder in acceptance of my statement. "Most Fae do tend to live in Matriarchal societies." She agreed. "Probably due to the fact that they're proven to be more nurturing, logical and far less prone to violence and war." She added impishly, biting the tip of her tongue in humor.

"Yeah." I scoffed. "Right up until somebody breaks a nail or shows up in the same outfit."

Instead of good-natured laughter, three sets of extremely una-mused eyes reminded me that this was probably not the best crowd for even the most innocent of sexist jokes.

"Wow, would you look at the time!" I exclaimed, glancing to my bare wrist. "Well, we should uh, probably keep moving." I suggested as I began to awkwardly pick my way through them. "Excuse me. Just going to step over here and, oh sorry, two left feet. Heh."

With our humor reserves apparently exhausted, we resumed our tired journey, walking until even the wonder of the pixie fairies faded into the flowery jungle around us. Becoming more of a nuisance than anything else, for the most part they left us alone, content to flit about in the normalcy of their daily routine. But every so often one would fly too close and the buzz of their insect-like wings would earn them a reflexive swat.

"Ooh, sorry Tink." I cringed in apology as I brushed at my ear and unthinkingly sent one of the tiny fairies staggering. It let out a tiny, almost comical "Eep!" before fluttering away, its flight pattern a bit more erratic and dazed than it had been before.

"So what are we looking for?" Max asked, glancing back over her shoulder. She had once again taken the lead and was paused in the act of stepping over a large log that beyond adding to the ambience, had absolutely no reason for being there.

Raegan and I exchanged quick glances.

"You said that the Quicklings told you the way, right?" The large woman asked suspiciously. "So, what is it that we're looking for out here?"

"They didn't say, exactly." I replied lamely, unsure of what to say without letting on that I knew more than what I was sharing.

Luckily for me, Ronnie was much faster on her feet.

"What he means is: we have more of a general theory than direction." She explained with a sideways glance that told me that she had this. "In order for Ambrose to use the girls, he'd have to keep them safe. Keep them close to him."

"So how do we know where he is?" Max asked, finishing her climb over the fallen tree trunk. She still wore an air of suspicion, but it was quickly dissipating.

"The latrodenzian are like transmitters." Raegan continued. "They draw energy from their victims and transfer it to a host. In order to work properly, they'd have to be aligned with a natural focal point; a place that could properly channel that power. The center of the labyrinth would be the logical location."

I knew that she was just covering for me, but her words made perfect sense.

"So that's why he came after me at the safe house instead of just sending me a gift basket full of spiders." I realized.

"Exactly." Raegan nodded, looking to her feet as she walked. "He would have needed to incapacitate you away from the agency, or some place that he could have easily retrieved your body."

A prickle of fear at the thought of falling victim to Somnus' attack struck me unexpectedly, but not nearly as hard as the memory of Lydia laying lifelessly on the floor, her blonde head cradled in McKenna's lap. A sudden heaviness tugged at the bottom of my throat, and looking away I pretended to take great interest in the labyrinth wall.

"But they're okay?" Viviane asked in a worried voice. "I mean Kara, and the others?"

Raegan nodded again. "They should be fine." She assured the girl, but her eyes flickered in sympathy towards me. "The latrodenzian induces a sort of stasis; a dream-like state. Eventually they'll lose the need to eat or drink or even breathe, but they're still alive and connected to whoever wears the crown. If something were to happen to them, it would be a massive jolt to his system. It could even kill him."

"The crown?" Viviane asked. Not understanding, she turned to me to see if she was alone in her confusion.

I set my jaw and tried to put on a smile, but the Quickling's words still rang fresh in my ears. As much as I liked the kid, I couldn't trust her any more than I could trust Max. One or maybe even both of them had something to do with this and if it was her, I didn't want to tip my hand.

Then again, if it *was* her, she'd already know about the crown.

"Our boy Somnus likes to feel pretty." I said, tapping at my forehead. "The spiders are controlled by a jeweled headpiece. It might make him look like a Disney Princess, but as long as he wears it, he can tap into them. Use 'em like batteries." I tried to maintain my normal levity, but as I pictured Lydia's life slowly being drained away, the humor faded from my voice.

Arm braces and gimpy legs be damned, that bastard was going to pay for this.

"And you guys are sure that he's down here?" Max asked, absently slapping at a pixie with a swipe of her large hand. The small creature dodged the half-hearted blow easily, and hovered just out of reach. Sticking out its tongue, the fairy placed her hands on her tiny little hips in what I thought was a very Tinkerbelle-like fashion…if Tinkerbelle was a nudist who was prone to giving the finger.

"It makes sense." Raegan shrugged, tucking a stray lock of hair behind her ear as she walked. "And if there is indeed a Keep at the center of the maze, it would be the perfect place for him to set up shop."

Max shrugged in acknowledgement of my Keeper's reasoning, but said nothing.

"Why is it so freaking hot?" I asked brushing away another curious pixie, this time purposefully missing any actual contact by several feet. The little creature seemed to notice my intent and chirped happily, blowing a little kiss in thanks. "And is it me, or is it actually starting to get darker?"

Raegan frowned and slowed her step as she looked up.

"It's the fog." She said, staring up into the haze swirling lazily above us. Completely obscuring the rocky roof of the cavern, it looked like the late afternoon sky, to the point where I had forgotten that we were actually deep beneath the earth.

"I've been watching it for a while." Raegan continued, slowly resuming her normal pace. "Whatever magic they have in place to generate light must have some sort of artificial nocturnal cycle as well."

I didn't like the sound of that one bit.

"Yeah, well, real or not." I started, glancing to the ceiling. "I for one don't want to be wandering around this place at night."

"Me either." Viviane swallowed.

Max grunted from ahead of us in what I took to be agreement. "Could be all sorts of nasty things lurking around here in the dark." She said, looking up.

Viviane and I exchanged nervous glances.

"Is it me, or did she sound almost excited?" I asked quietly, only half-joking.

"I think we still have some time before it gets dark." Raegan chuckled, but then shrugged in thought. "Not that time has any sort of meaning here. Have you guys checked your phones?" She asked nonchalantly.

As the group slowed to a stop, I fished my cellphone from my now badly rumpled jacket pocket and ran a thumb over its surface.

"That can't be right." I frowned.

"What?" Max asked, looking up from her own device.

"According to this, we've only been here about twenty minutes." I explained, holding up my phone for them to see.

"Huh." The large woman said, looking at hers in surprise. "Mine says fifteen."

"Mine too." Viviane confirmed, placing her phone beside Max's.

"Okay, so that's weird." I acknowledged. Slowly shuffling forward with the rest of the group I looked over to my sister who was purposely keeping stride at my side.

"Not weird. Bad." Raegan corrected.

"Why bad?" I started to ask, but then I realized what she meant. "Crap. If we've only been here a few minutes…"

"Then it could be several days before anyone up there even notices that we're missing." Raegan finished, looking up at the ceiling.

"Hey!" Max called out in a harsh whisper from in front of us. "There's something happening up here."

At first it was barely noticeable, but the jungle setting surrounding us was beginning to recede, and patches of stone wall were visible beneath the blanket of green. The corridor was also growing wider, and while it allowed us more space in which to move around, the sudden expansion after walking the closed-in tunnels for so long was almost strange and left me feeling unexpectedly exposed.

"Are we shrinking or are the walls getting taller?" Viviane asked nervously.

Gradually sloping upwards, the labyrinth walls were indeed growing, lengthening and expanding until they leveled out, stopping only when they collided with the sides of an enormous wooden wall.

"I think it's a door." Max said quietly as she slid her hand along the barrier. "Like the kind they would have on an old castle or something." She added in amazement.

"You think this is the Keep?" I asked with a sidelong glance to Raegan.

"It might be." She responded. There was an underlying relief in her voice that was hard to miss.

We approached cautiously, the impressive wooden gates stretching far above us, making it impossible to know what was housed behind them. Recessed in the stone wall of the maze and capped at the end by large pillars, they appeared to open inward at the center.

"Welcome to Jurassic Park." I said in disbelief.

Max knocked twice on the wood, the blows making almost no sound. "Oh man. There's no way I'm breaking this bad boy down." She said throwing a sideways glance to me as if reading my thoughts. "I don't know what kind of wood this is, but it feels like solid granite." Amazed, she ran her hands along the grain in appreciation.

"Hey! I found something!" Viviane said excitedly, brushing aside some withered, dead vines at the base of one of the stone pillars. An old wooden lever jutted from a small indent in the rock wall, all but begging to be pulled. "I bet this opens it!" She guessed proudly.

"Yeah, and then it lets King Kong out of his pen." I said sarcastically. "Don't touch it." I snarked a bit more sternly than I probably should have.

Hand hovering just above the lever, Viviane stepped back, her eyes downcast like a child who had just been unexpectedly scolded by a favorite Uncle.

"Why not?" Max asked suspiciously, her tone driving away the guilt that I was starting to feel. Moving protectively to the girl's side, I was once again reminded that one, or even both of them might be working against us.

"Because this doesn't feel right." I said sharply before turning to Raegan. "We've been walking a straight line for how long now? What are the chances of just stumbling upon this?"

Raegan said nothing, but frowned as she looked up at the gate. I could tell that she had been thinking the same thing.

"Do you think that it's another trap?" Viviane asked fearfully. "Like in the garden?"

Backing away from the girl, Maxine hunched her shoulders and looked down the corridor in both directions, squaring off as if readying for an attack. "But what if this is what we've been looking for?" She asked with a slow skepticism. "I mean, we have been following

Ray Ray's right hand thing, so it sort of makes sense that we found it, right?."

"Did we though?" I questioned. "When was the last time that we came across an intersection or a turn? Doesn't this seem just a little too easy to you?"

Max lowered her head in examination of her too tight, grime covered clothing before spreading her hands in exasperation and slowly looking back up at me. "Easy?" She echoed.

"He's right Max." Raegan said. "We have no idea what's waiting for us on the other side of that wall."

"So let's find out." She replied, slapping a huge hand against the wooden wall in annoyed emphasis. "I say we pull the lever and we take this thing head on, no more games." There was a noticeable growl in her voice.

"I'm telling you, my spidey senses are really tingling on this." I insisted.

"So we finally find the place, but we're not going to go in?" Max asked angrily. "C'mon J.T." She sighed, softening a bit. "What can this place throw at us that the two of us can't handle? We've got this."

I chuckled at that. I genuinely liked the big gal, and hoped to hell that we were wrong about the whole "traitor in our midst" thing.

"I know." I assured her. "And normally I would have already pulled that thing myself." I gestured to the lever. "But this just feels wrong."

Max sighed in frustration and turned to face the gate, but she didn't press the point.

"So, what do we do?" Raegan asked, looking to me for direction.

Put on the spot, I realized that I didn't have anything that even remotely resembled a plan. I wasn't a leader and had zero interest in the role. It's a shitty, thankless job and I generally regarded those who actively sought it as suckers.

All that I really knew was that I didn't want to ring the doorbell and announce our presence to whatever lurked behind it if we didn't have to.

Spinning in place as I looked around, following the corridor in the direction that we had been heading with my eyes. The walls sloped back down and drew closer in the distance, and from where we stood, I could actually see a break in the hallway where the maze took a ninety degree turn to the right, skirting whatever lay behind the gate.

"Right." I said, trying to sound confident. "This way only goes on for like another hundred feet or so. Let's just walk to the edge and take a little peek around the corner to see what's there. If it's something, we take a vote on what to do next. If it's nothing?" I looked over to Maxine who was listening with barely contained restlessness. "I pull the lever, hop up on Max's back and we go all Master Blaster on this bitch."

At the mere mention of action, a toothy grin split the big woman's face and she nodded in eager agreement.

"How's that sound?" I asked, turning to Raegan.

Exchanging glances with the other two, my Keeper sighed in resignation before reluctantly nodding her agreement.

"Okay." She said apprehensively. "But let's be smart about this. If we wander too far, there's no promise we'll find this place again." She sounded hesitant, but I was already steadily moving down the hall, my pace accelerating to something between "old lady mall walker" and a brisk jog. I felt good; as if I had actually accomplished something. I had a plan that wasn't one hundred percent ridiculous and they had agreed to it.

Maybe being the leader wasn't such a bad gig after all.

"I just want to see what's around the corner." I called out behind me, my voice bold with newfound confidence. "And don't touch that frigging lever." I yelled over to Viviane whom I suspected was still eyeballing it.

Max and Viviane had stepped away from the gate and were talking quietly amongst themselves, their eyes occasionally flickering in my direction. Raegan followed slowly, reluctant to stray too far from any one of us, but helpless to do anything about the growing gap.

I made it to the corner and carefully peered around it, not really knowing what to expect. The new corridor looked like every other; an endless expansion of disappointing grey stone that seemed to stretch on for eternity.

Poised on the edge, I frowned and looked back at my sister who was still gradually drawing near.

"There's nothing." I exhaled dejectedly. "Just more maze." I reported, stealing another look down the endless hall.

Aside from a bunch of dirt, and some fallen rocks where a dense outcropping of ropey vines had pulled them loose from the wall, there was really nothing to-

Vines. Not the leafy blankets of flowery foliage that clung to the walls and housed swarms of tiny pixies, but a thick expansion of growth like the roots of an interloping tree, breaking through the brick.

"Vines." I said triumphantly. Grinning back at Raegan I watched as she tilted her head in question, not understanding my sudden joy. "Vines!" I repeated loudly before sprinting towards them, eager to test my theory.

"John! Wait!" I heard Raegan gasp in horror. Normally that would have been enough to stop me dead in my tracks, but they were barely fifty feet away and I could cover that distance in a few seconds.

Heavy, ropey vines the color of old military canvas draped over the labyrinth wall and clung to every crack and crevice. Several small stones had fallen away, their mortar cracked and crumbled by the ever searching shoots and tendrils of vegetation.

With a quick upward glance I could tell right away that climbing was out of the question. The vines thinned out at the top like tendrils of old webbing, and I strongly doubted that they would hold even Viviane's weight, let alone myself or Maxine. Thicker around and more tightly packed at my chest, I took a few of the ropey coils in my hands and gave an experimental tug.

"What in the hell is wrong with you?!" Raegan's words came out in a blended shout of fear and anger as she slapped me repeatedly on the arms and back.

"Ow! Hey!" I startled, wincing as another flurry of slaps followed.

"You can't just run off like that!" She scolded, punctuating ever other word with another strike.

"Okay! Ow, stop!" I begged, shielding my body and pulling away. "I'm sorry! Jeez." I apologized, my words stemming her attack. "But look! I think I found the vines."

"I don't care." Came her angry reply. "What if you got lost? Or attacked?" She reprimanded, motioning to the floor just beyond where we stood. "Or fell into a fucking pit?" The raw emotion behind her swearing caused me to pause, and I followed her gesture to the maze floor.

Oh yeah, the pointy death pits. I had forgotten about those.

"Okay, those are all very valid and very scary points." I admitted. "But *vines* Ronnie." I said meaningfully.

"You could have gotten killed." The rush of color was beginning to drain from her normally pale cheeks, but the sparks of anger still danced a lively green behind her eyes.

"I know." I acknowledged gently. "And I'll try my best not to get horribly mangled or violently murdered from here on, okay? Scouts honor." I said, holding a peace sign over my heart.

Having never been one, I had no idea what the Scout's sign was, but it was an honest, heartfelt gesture none-the-less.

"You're not funny." She sighed, but her eyes were wandering to the vines that had grabbed my attention. "Just be more careful, okay?" There was a certain amount of resignation in her voice; not exactly defeat, but the tone of child who had finally accepted that goldfish don't live forever.

"I will mom." I promised with a grin. "Now, where's Max?" I asked, tugging at the vines. I had a solid grip, but could barely pull them a few inches from the wall. "I need her to go all Grape Ape on these things."

Raegan touched the plants in quick examination and frowned before nodding her head to the corner of the maze that we had both passed. "Back with Viviane." She sighed, letting a length of loose vine fall back in place. "Come on." She instructed, turning in place and walking towards the corridor of the maze where we had left our companions. "With luck, they have more sense than you do and weren't stupid enough to pull the-"

I put my hand on her shoulder as she rounded the corner and nearly bumped into her as she froze in mid-step.

"Lever."

The others were gone. Or more aptly, the length of hallway were we had left them was gone.

"You know, this place is really starting to piss me off." Raegan growled as we stared at the dead end that loomed over us in the form of a labyrinth wall, eight feet from the corner where we now stood. The stone that barred our path was old and covered in a patchy moss that looked as if it had been there for a thousand years.

Turning on heel and pushing angrily past me, Ronnie stalked back towards the outgrowth of vines, murder in her eyes.

"You think they'll be alright?" I asked nervously, sharing my gaze between the maze wall and my fuming Keeper. A sense of guilt washed over me as I cautiously backed away from the dead end.

"They'll be fine." She snapped. Grabbing a handful of vines, she leaned back and placed one foot on the wall. "Max," She grunted as she gave an angry pull. "Will take care of them."

"Yeah. Unless, you know." I said hesitantly. As riled up as she was, I had to be as delicate as I could in reminding her that there was the very real possibility that her bestie was working for Scrawny McBadlegs.

Letting go with a frustrated sigh, she jerked her head slightly in my direction, but her eyes never left the patch of vines. "Which is why we should get back to them as quickly as possible. Either of them could be in danger."

Raegan's eyes darted over the plants, missing nothing, and I stepped back as she searched in hopes that she would be able work out whatever it was that I was missing.

"What do you think?" I asked quietly after several long seconds.

"Do you see how thick it is?" She responded, pointing to the vines. "Right in the middle there?"

"Yeah?" I questioned, leaning in for a better look.

"Hmm." She bustled in thought. "Give me your gun."

"What's wrong with yours?" I asked, pulling my weapon from its holster as instructed.

"You've already had your jacket off, and I'm all sweaty and gross." She explained, waving an annoyed hand in front of her chest.

I actually chuckled at that.

"You are such a *girl*." I stressed, handing her my weapon.

"Says the man who spends more time on his hair than I do." She shot back as she took it.

"Ouch." I winced. Bringing a hand to my head, I self-consciously ran my fingers over the top of my short dark spikes. It took a lot of care to look like I didn't take a lot of care with my hair.

Widening her stance, Raegan took aim at the center of the cluster of vines and fired the weapon. Shot after shot rang out, the sound rumbling through the nearly enclosed maze like thunder.

"Feel better there, Annie Oakley?" I asked. I stuck a finger in my ear and wiggled it around in an effort to chase away the ringing sound. "You killed the innocent plants."

"Look." She said in quiet victory, or normal victory. I couldn't really be certain given the damage to my eardrums.

Handing me my weapon, she crooked a finger towards the cluster of thick vines.

They were dissolving.

The liquid iron filling that made up the creamy nougat center of our standard ammunition had splattered on impact and was now spreading like a silvery fire across the vegetation. It crackled and spit as it consumed the vines, melting them into a foul smelling brownish glop that hissed and sizzled as it struck the stone floor at our feet.

"Ugh." I made a face and covered my nose as the stench hit me. "It smells like a burning couch." I gagged.

"I suspected as much." Raegan said triumphantly. Crouching, she dipped her finger into a fresh glop of melted vine and brought it closer to her face for inspection.

"Well don't *touch* it!" I groaned, my stomach lurching.

Ignoring me with practiced ease, she continued to study the

melted plant life, rubbing it between her fingers. "The vines react to iron in the same way that most Fae would." She mused scientifically.

"You know what that looks like, right?" I asked.

"Oh." She said suddenly.

"Yeah." I laughed. "Spider fingers have nothing on you now, Poo hands."

"No, not that." Raegan corrected, annoyed by the distraction. "That." She said as she slowly stood and pointed to the still melting vines.

A pinprick of light was shining in the center of the dissolving mass. At first I thought it was merely the glow from the chemical reaction between the fairy vines and the liquid iron, but as it grew, I could see that the light was actually coming from a source on the other side of the wall.

"I think it goes all the way through." She said, glancing to me with a triumphant grin.

Even as the vines were still slowly withering and pulling away from the spreading iron, I could see the growing gap in the wall. As more and more of the plants fell away, dissolving into steaming puddles of brown, it was obvious that the hole they had been covering easily reached down to the maze floor.

And it was wide enough to crawl through.

"So the lever *wasn't* the way into the Keep?" I half-stated, half-asked, unsure of what to make of the dripping passage, but happy to have been right.

"That or we found a secret entrance." Raegan grinned.

"Now what?" I asked as a large section of vine rotted away.

"Now you follow me." She grinned, dropping to her hands and knees. Hesitating briefly at the opening, Ronnie took a deep breath, ducked her head and crawled into the hole.

Prone before me, the perfect roundness of her ass would have once been a naughty treat to ogle; now it made me uneasy and I in-stinctively looked around for someone to punch for staring.

"You coming or not?" Ronnie called from inside the wall, her feet disappearing into the stone.

"Yeah yeah." I assured her, dropping to all fours. "Keep your pants on." I grumbled, focusing heavily on the gooey, muck covered floor and not the view from ahead.

"Be careful of the iron." She said in motherly warning as we started to crawl forward.

"Careful? I plan on rubbing it into my eyes." I muttered to myself as I took a deep breath and followed.

Chapter Seventeen

"Wow." Raegan said, her voice hushed in quiet awe as she exited the tunnel ahead of me.

Sticking close out of the fear of accidental separation, I hoisted myself out of the hole and placed a protective hand upon her shoulder as I stood. Following her gaze, my eyes widened in mute agreement as we took in the lavish courtyard in which we now stood.

"It's beautiful." Ronnie said softly, turning to me as if to confirm that what she was seeing was real.

It was.

Nestled within the surrounding walls of the maze, entering the center of the labyrinth was like discovering a grove of trees untouched by a fire that had consumed the entire forest around it. Lush, peaceful and serene, even the swirling grey haze above us had brightened, smoothing into a soft, soothing blue that gave the entire area the feeling of open sky on a perfect summer's day. Pixies fluttered lazily in the distance, soaring and gliding on a gentle breeze, the shimmer of their wings sparking against the background like tiny silver fireworks.

I took a deep breath and closed my eyes. Lifting my head to the sky, I allowed myself to enjoy the warm fingertips of sunlight as they gently played against my face. I didn't care that this was all an illusion or the result of some long forgotten, insanely powerful faerie magic; it felt amazing, and goddamn it, I was going to enjoy it, if only for a second.

"Aah." I sighed happily, losing myself in the lie.

"What do you think?" Raegan asked, her voice little more than a dreamy whisper.

Opening my eyes, I couldn't help but smile as I watched my sister basking in the false light with an expression of joy that matched my own. Apparently, she had come to the same conclusion and was allowing herself to relish in a sliver of comfort before we dove headfirst into what we both suspected would be a harrowing confrontation.

Looking from side to side, I scanned the massive garden and shook off the sudden urge to lay down in the soft, warm grass. Benches, fountains and masterfully carved statues of every shape and size lined the many walkways that trailed their way prettily past the massive white stone cathedral that rose before us, blocking out part of the sky.

If there was really a magical keep at the center of the labyrinth, this *had* to be it.

Medieval in design, the walls that comprised the building's lengthy exterior were carved in meticulously detailed patterns. It seemed, in a word, expensive; the kind of place that you just knew would be filled to the rafters with awesome things that you'd never be allowed to touch, roped off and on display like pieces in a museum.

But by the same token, the building also looked impossibly secure; a safe haven to take refuge in during an invasion or a protective shelter that would allow you to survive an attack from whatever the hell actually lived down here.

"Meanwhile, at the Halls of Justice." I said, channeling my inner Ted Knight.

A slow grin spread across Raegan's face, washing away some of the exhausted worry that the journey here had caked upon it. I knew that she wouldn't get the reference, and I didn't care; whatever this place was, it had an undeniably calming effect and it was amazing to see her smile again.

"I don't see any windows. Well, at least ones that *we* can reach." I amended, looking upward. Several stained glass windows decorated the top floors of the keep, well out of the way of any invader's sudden impulse to smash. "So how do we get in?" I asked, craning my neck as I searched the building.

"There's probably an entrance closer to the front." Raegan said with a nod in that direction.

"You plan on knocking?" I asked dryly.

Tucking a wayward lock of fiery red hair behind her ear, she looked to the distance and shrugged noncommittally. "Do you have a better idea?"

"No." I admitted reluctantly.

"Well then." She smirked. "I guess we'll play it by ear." Following her lead, I glanced up to the two large towers that protected the keep's anterior and frowned as we started to walk.

"Think we're being watched?" I asked, searching the dark window slits that peppered the tower walls high above us.

"Absolutely." She said quietly, her upward gaze tracing mine. "Just keep your eyes open." She warned. "You never know who or what-"

"Oi!" A thundering voice called out from ahead of us, quickly snapping our now startled gazes back to the garden.

Further down the wall and rounding the building's corner with a speed that belied its incredible size was a creature that would dwarf even Max. Tree trunk sized arms attached to a broad, heavily muscled chest that swelled and rippled with effort as the monster hurried towards us, its slate grey hooves striking sparks against the walkway with every stone shattering step.

"You two! Stay right there!" It commanded angrily, its dark eyes narrowing in as it approached.

The thing was fast. Even if my legs would have obeyed their instinctual urge to run, I knew that we had no chance of outpacing it. There was no way we could beat this thing back to the hole in the labyrinth wall.

"Is that a…" I started to ask, but my mouth went dry.

"Yes." Ronnie confirmed, her voice trembling. "That's a minotaur." She finished as the creature stomped to a sudden halt several feet away, showering us in a deluge of crushed rock and dust.

The minotaur had the head of a man, more or less. With a much broader nose, and blunted, cow-like features, two tiny horns jutted from each temple and curved upward into the creature's hairline, giving it an otherworldly, demonic effect. Its torso was mostly bare, adorned only by a leather harness that undoubtedly housed the massive two-headed battle axe that it clenched in one enormous hand. Wearing little more than a loincloth and a scowl, the minotaur might have been able to pass for human in the dark, were it not for the fact that it was the size of a small house.

"Um. Hi?" I greeted hopefully, giving the creature a little wave to show it that I wasn't a threat.

" 'Ello nuffin'!" The minotaur snorted in a very bovine show of frustration. "Who are you, an' what are ya doin' lurkin' about?" It demanded, its voice the type of thick English cockney that tended to drop the letters "h" and "g" like they were covered in spiders.

Looking around for more intruders but finding none, the monstrous hybrid slowly swung its huge head back towards us and gestured with the business end of the battle axe.

"You ain't supposed ta be here." It growled.

I opened my mouth to speak, but Raegan stepped forward, silencing my words. Glancing around as if she were just as surprised by our sudden appearance as he was, she craned her neck and looked upward with a sort of perplexed innocence.

"We're not?" She asked politely, tilting her head to one side in confusion.

The creature frowned and took a step backwards, thrown off guard by her approach.

"No. Yer not." It said slowly, its deep voice now laced with a quiver of uncertainty. "How'd you get in?" It asked suspiciously.

"How'd we get in?" Raegan repeated, stalling for enough time to formulate an answer.

"Yeah." The minotaur confirmed, looking over his shoulder in distrust before slowly turning back. "It weren't the gate, was it?" It asked, its grip on the axe tightening in a strain of creaking muscle and wood.

"Oh, heavens no!" Raegan quickly assured him. Snapping her gaze back to me, she widened her eyes imploringly and forced an anxious, toothy smile. "It wasn't the gate, was it John?"

"Oh! No!" I stammered in agreement, catching on immediately and offering my best "please don't kill us" smile. "The gate? No way. It definitely wasn't the gate."

The creature snorted again, and cast one last look behind it before focusing its full attention on us.

"Good." It chuffed, relaxing a bit. "'Cause if it were the gate, I'd have ta give ya a smashing." The minotaur warned. Hefting his weapon, he slapped it menacingly against his leathery palm in emphasis.

"Ha. Leather." I said quietly, and mostly to myself when I realized why that thought was particularly funny.

"A smashing?" Raegan asked innocuously as she took a step backward, fiercely jamming an elbow into my ribs as she returned to my side. She was trying to smile and look nonchalant, but even during our brief and painful touch, I could feel her trembling.

"S'right Miss." The minotaur confirmed, his head bobbing into a nod. "A right good one too." It continued, letting the axe drop to its hooved feet in an earthshaking crash of metal on stone. "Trevor they says, anything comes through that gate, anything at all, and you're to give it a proper thumpin'." He explained, absently leaning on the weapon's handle. The letter "f" was replacing most, if not all of the "th" sounds in his words which I would have normally pointed out in some smartass fashion, were I feeling a bit more suicidal.

"We definitely didn't come in through the gate then." I said quickly.

"Yeah." Trevor agreed as he lazily scratched his chin. "Didn't think as much." He admitted. "I woulda heard it."

"You would have heard it?" Reagan asked in that overly polite voice generally reserved for talking to strange dogs while looking for a rock or stick to use as a weapon.

"S'right. Got it all cobbled up an' what not. Sorted it myself." The minotaur said proudly. "Makes a hell of a racket too. Ain't as much as a mouse puff squeakin' its way through there without me hearin' it."

Raegan and I exchanged looks of alarm. If we had come through the front gate, then-

"Of course, that now leaves me with a bit of a dilemma." The creature said, pulling us from our shared thoughts and casting a sly, knowing look down to us.

"Does it?" Raegan asks conversationally. Her body was tensing, and I couldn't tell for sure, but I got the distinct impression that she was getting ready to run.

"It does." He trailed, his voice heavy with thought. "I mean, ifin' you two didn't come in through the gate like ya says ya didn't, then how exactly *did* ya get in?" Fingers flexing, I watched as his knuckles tightened around the handle of the large battle axe at his feet.

It only took a quick glance in my sister's direction to confirm that she was definitely about to bolt. While Trevor was feigning laziness, I had seen how he was moving as he initially approached us and I was certain that there was no way that we could hope to outrun him.

The minotaur had us cornered and what's more, he knew it.

Like a cat playing with a couple of mice, Trevor may have been feigning disinterest, but I could tell that he was coiled, ready to attack. Not knowing what else to do, but knowing that I had to do *something* before Raegan got us both squashed like bugs, I threw a Hail Mary pass and went with the one trick I still had left in my bag, but was never brave enough to use.

Honesty.

"Um…through there." I said. Leaning backwards without making any quick or sudden movements, I pointed towards the hole in the wall from which we had entered.

Keeping one eye on me while still trying to look both casual and trusting, Trevor squinted in the direction I indicated and then blinked in surprise.

"Huh. I didn't know that was there." He admitted, somewhat taken aback. "Bit of a cock up ain't it?" He asked after a moment's pause. "I mean, that's not secure at all, is it?" The air of distrust around him was quickly fading and replaced by amusement as he studied the crawl space at the base of the labyrinth wall. "Sorta makes ya wonder why they got me focusin' on the bloody gate when any bloke and his bird can just stroll on in and have themselves a butcher's."

"Um." I said cleverly, looking to Raegan for instruction. She shrugged helplessly but motioned for me to keep the conversation flowing, as if I were suddenly fluent in huge scary cow-guy.

"But that ain't on me, now is it?" Trevor continued on with a shrug, his hand relaxing and sliding off the shaft of the massive axe.

"No?" I asked hesitantly, unsure of the answer.

"Bet yer arse it's not." He agreed with an emphatic snort. "They said to watch the gate, and that's what I'm doin', am I right? I mean, I ain't got nothin' ta do with any sort of shoddy craftsmanship on their end." He scoffed, gesturing to the hole with the flat of his hand. "I wager if they wanted someone to spackle that up, they would have hired themselves a bloody contractor."

"Exactly." I said in total agreement. Turning to Raegan I shot her a look of genuine disbelief as the creature tilted its head towards the cavern's ceiling and yawned.

"So." Trevor stretched, swinging his arms. "I take it you two are with that other fella then?" He asked casually. Any remaining distrust had vanished as the giant minotaur slipped out of work mode and into a more socially directed conversation.

"Other fellow?" Raegan inquired, finally finding her voice.

I couldn't blame her for being afraid; I knew on some level that it was instinctual, and even though the creature no longer seemed to pose a threat, he was still very much an intimidating, hulking beast. As if to drive that point home, the strong smell of sweat and un-washed cow dripped from him in a barnyard of stench, wafting over us in a lingering assault of its very own.

"Yeah. The fancy lil' toff with the skew-wiff legs." He said off-handedly, gesturing towards the front of the Keep. "Bit of a bender?" He added in quiet confidence.

"Ambrose." Raegan whispered in my direction.

"That's the chap." Trevor nodded, pointing a mammoth finger at Raegan in confirmation.

"Um, yeah." I stalled, weighing my options. "He's expecting us?" The lie was supposed to have been a statement, but I choked at the end, my confidence abandoning me in the wake of the huge monster and his powerful scent.

Sensing my stumble, Raegan leaned in close and put her head next to mine, reinforcing my words with a huge, mouth-splitting smile that I quickly copied.

Trevor stared at us, his brow furrowing in consideration. His dark brown cow-like eyes mirrored our dishonesty as time came to a standstill, and the seconds stretched out before us. I could feel Raegan's nails through my jacket as she tightened her grip, a bead of sweat forming at her temple.

"Right. Off ya go then." Trevor said with a quick shrug.

Ronnie's grip released so quickly, I was afraid that she had fainted.

"'Round the front, mind the steps. They're a bit wonky." He continued with a friendly wave, motioning for us to pass.

"That's it?" I asked in disbelief. Raegan and I traded quick glances, but she looked just as baffled as I was, if not quite a bit whiter.

The minotaur shrugged before looking over his shoulder towards what I assumed was the distant gate.

"Well, don't get me wrong." He hesitated. "I don't exactly get a lot of company down here. I'd love to faff it off a bit an' do some yakkin', but I'm on the job." He said with an apologetic shrug. "I mean, if someone were ta sneak by that gate while I was off gettin' the gen, I'd be made redundant."

"Made redundant." I repeated with what had to be a confused smile.

"Well sure. There ain't exactly a lot of gainful employment to be

had for someone with my particular set of job skills, now is there?"
Trevor frowned. "Sure I could hire on with some invadin' army or another I suppose." He considered, speaking more to himself than to us.
"But it's always Seelie this, Unseelie that, choose your side, blah blah
blah." Looking around as if to ensure that we were truly alone, the
minotaur leaned in and spoke in a voice low with conspiracy. "Me? I
prefer to stay unaffiliated, ifin' we're keeping things just between us,
please and thank you."

"Unaffiliated." I echoed numbly.

"Never had much of a stomach for politics." He shrugged.

"Trevor, is it?" Raegan asked sweetly, drawing him from his
thoughts.

"S'right Miss." The minotaur beamed, brightening at the sound
his name.

"Are you saying that Ambro - our friend Rupert, hired you?" She
cleared her throat as she corrected herself.

Trevor cocked his head to one side and shrugged. "Somethin'
along those lines. Yeah."

"To do what, exactly?" She pressed, offering the heavily muscled
giant her most charming smile.

The minotaur frowned, pursing his lips in renewed suspicion.
"This a test?" He asked, studying my Keeper's face.

Raegan turned her head to me and signaled something that I
didn't quite follow with her eyes. Feigning reluctance she clucked
her tongue, swinging her gaze back towards him. "Oh, I probably
shouldn't be saying anything. There are protocols after all."

"Yes. Protocols." I agreed as I looked to her and screamed the
words "what in the hell are you doing" with my own panicked stare.
Sweet Jesus, I *was* a bad influence.

"Aaaah. Say no more." Trevor grinned. Straightening his back
and puffing out his massive chest, he stood somehow even impossibly
taller and cleared his throat as he began to dutifully recite. "I am to
watch the gate. If anyone comes through, be it friend or foe, I'm ta
give them a proper thumpin' until there ain't nothin' left. Which is

why I wager he had that two of you use the back way in." He added in a shrewd whisper.

"Very good." Raegan praised in a suddenly queasy sounding voice.

"That all Miss?" The minotaur asked, happy to have passed the test.

"Um, yes. That was splendid." She assured him, although the color had further drained from her already pale face. "Thank you Trevor."

"Of course." Trevor nodded. "Anyways, that's enough gabbing." With a reluctant grunt he bent slightly at the waist and picked up the battle axe, slinging it over his broad shoulder. "Entrance is around front, I can show ya the way." He announced. Turning and walking away, the minotaur paused and glanced back just long enough to indicate that we should be following.

Even at a gait slowed for our benefit, Trevor's long legs covered the ground at an astonishing pace and it was a constant struggle to keep up.

The front of the small castle cleared into a large open courtyard dotted with topiaries and framed by the tall stone walls of the surrounding labyrinth. The back of the wooden gate that we encountered earlier and had wisely chosen not to enter was framed in the distance, its heavy door rigged with lengths of rope adorned with bits of armor, shields and metal weapons of all shapes and sizes. Stretched across the entry like a cluttered, abandoned spider's web, I could see that anyone foolishly attempting to open the door would inadvertently set off a clattering cacophony of noise, not unlike a bunch of giant tin cans dancing on a string.

"Just up them steps." The minotaur nodded, gesturing to a set of rock and debris strewn stairs. "Door don't lock, so ya can pop right in."

"Thank you Trevor." Raegan said sweetly. "You've been an absolute dear."

Beaming from ear to ear, or in his case, horn to horn, Trevor dragged his hooved foot in front of him shyly in a shower of sparks and almost blushed. "Aww, weren't nothin' Miss." He grinned.

"Nonsense." She countered. "You've been a tremendous help. I'll be sure to let *Rupert* know that you're doing an excellent job out here." She said, stressing Somnus' name and causing the minotaur's already expansive chest to swell with pride.

"Well, um, it was nice to meet you." I said, turning to follow Ronnie up the rubble covered stone steps. I had no clue how we had managed to get away with any of this, but I wasn't planning on sticking around long enough for our lie to be exposed.

"Wait." Trevor called out in an alarmingly serious voice.

"Shit." I swore under my breath, freezing in place, too frightened to turn around.

This was it. This was how we were going to die.

"Can I ask ya somethin'?" The minotaur continued. His voice was lighter, almost hesitant; like a friend reluctantly asking a favor.

Raegan and I traded perplexed looks as we slowly pivoted to face him.

"Of course." Raegan said brightly, the fear in her eyes masked by her pleasant tone. "Anything."

We were close enough to the castle doors to perceivably make it. Pulling them open would burn a few precious seconds, but if we were quick enough and managed to squeeze inside, I doubted that the lumbering giant could easily follow.

I tensed, but in taking Ronnie's lead I kept a cheerful smile plastered over the fear on my face.

"You wouldn't happen ta know what he's expectin', would ya?" Trevor asked, his voice low with nervousness.

"I'm sorry?" Thrown off by the question, Raegan tilted her head to one side.

"Ya know. To come bangin' through the gate." He explained, stealing a quick glance back at the noisily decorated entryway. "Last time yer mate came poppin' out, he was narked somethin' fierce." Trevor continued. He seemed intrigued, and maybe even a little excited. "What's got him losin' the plot?"

"I'm not sure what you-"

"Is it a proper beasty?" Trevor cut in with another question, not giving her the time to answer as he leaned in, his eyes shimmering with anticipation. "I mean, it got past the Pharoo'zah, and them two zippies ain't never did come back, so I'm guessin' that whatever it is, it's gotta be right big." A worried look flashed across his face. "Not that I'm scared or nothin' mind you. I don't give a sweet fanny adams ifin it's all teeth and claws," He hesitated, a frown crossing his lips. "But I don't fancy them finger wigglers. Not one bit."

"Finger wigglers?" I asked, overwhelmed by the sheer number of words that I didn't understand.

"Ya know. Like yer mate with the spindly legs." Trevor explained as he gestured sourly towards the doors of the Keep.

Magic.

My mind flashed back to my encounter with Somnus, and I felt a pang of sympathy as I empathized with the big guy.

"Only two things really get under my skin." Trevor grumbled, his eyes glancing distrustfully to the doors at the top of the staircase behind us. "And them creepy lil' tossers are standin' at the front of the queue." He said, literally spitting as he spoke. "Ain' no honor in fightin' like that. No honor at all."

"Yeah, I know what you mean." I nodded, his words resonating within me. "I don't care for the bastards much myself."

"So?" He asked expectantly.

"So?" I repeated before catching on. "Oh. Um, no. I don't think it's a magic user." I was aware of a grin tugging at my lips but I did my best to fight it off.

It was me.

This huge, hulking, axe-wielding monster was afraid of *me*. Well, I mean, the idea of me at least. Still, as amusing as the whole situation had become, I just couldn't help myself.

"But I'd keep an eye on that gate if I were you." I warned, much to the shock of my sister. It was her turn to scream unspoken things with her eyes, but I pretended not to notice.

"Yeah?" Trevor grunted, turning to regard the gate.

"Definitely." I said, pressing my luck as I stepped just out of reach of Raegan's incredibly bony elbows. "They say he's a crafty one. Supposed to be damn good looking too." I added, ignoring the sounds of exasperation behind me. "I hear the ladies can't resist him."

"That so?" The minotaur mused with a roll of his eyes. He looked less than impressed by my description of the dashing hero that was coming to slay him. "Well, he ain't gunna be too pretty after I squash his head to jelly." He grinned darkly. "Ain't no one gunna fancy him after that, I'd wager."

The sounds of annoyance squeaking from my sister quickly turned to coughs of suppressed laughter as I felt my stomach do a little flip.

"Trevor?" Ronnie called out sweetly as she stepped to my side, taking my arm.

Pulled from his fantasies of battles and crushed skulls, Trevor blinked a few times and looked up. "Yeah Miss?" He asked politely.

"I just remembered." She paused. "We're expecting two more friends to join us."

"That right?" The minotaur asked, raising a suspicious brow.

"It is." She nodded. "I don't suppose that you could be a dear and show them where we went?" There was a renewed confidence in her voice.

"Yeah. I could do that." Trevor agreed. "Unless they come in through the gate that is. Then ya know." He amended, thumping the head of the battle axe against the flat of his palm. "Gotta follow proper procedure an' all, or I'm liable to get a good bollocking."

"Oh, of course." Raegan acknowledged, although the teasing smile that she wore at my expense was beginning to falter.

"Oh hey, it's been awhile since we've visited." I said, jerking a thumb over my shoulder and taking the focus off my sister. "Where should we go once we get inside?"

The minotaur considered my question for a moment before shrugging halfheartedly.

"Don't rightly know." He admitted. Understanding the look of confusion on my face Trevor continued, his eyes focusing on the door behind me. "I ain't been here all that long. Plus, they says I ain't allowed inside. On account of me hooves, I suspect." He mused. Lifting a mammoth leg, he held up a wicked looking cloven hoof for inspection and gave it a wiggle.

"Oh." I nodded as I tried to ignore the fact that his foot was at least twice the size of my head.

"Yeah, they're pretty good fer kickin' and stompin'. Grindin' bones and all that." He deliberated, as he examined the appendage. "But they're hell on them dear carpets, ya know?"

"I'll bet." I said, unable to look away.

"Thank you for your help, Trevor." Raegan said, pulling on my arm. "But we should really get going."

"My pleasure Miss." Trevor nodded, glancing over his shoulder towards the gate. "I should probably get back to work myself." He sighed. "Real glad ya used that back way in. You seem like right nice totty. Woulda been a shame ta smash yer head in." He added before turning his back to us. "Tarah." With a wave of his free hand, the enormous minotaur began to lumber away.

Raegan's grip tightened on my arm and her face froze in a terrified version of a smile as she stared at the jolly giant's back.

"Hey, Trevor?" I called after him, causing Raegan's already tight hold to go full on death grip. She looked up in alarm, searching my face for explanation.

"Yeah?" He answered, pausing just long enough to look over one massive shoulder.

"What's the second thing?" I asked. I knew that it was foolish, as we were in the clear once again, but god damn it, I had to know.

"Pardon?" He asked, slowly facing us as his forehead wrinkled in confusion.

"You said that there were only two things that really got under your skin. One was the finger wigglers." I explained, waggling my fingers theatrically. "What's the other?"

"Oh." He wavered as he searched his memory. "Uh, penguins."

"Penguins." I repeated, not certain that I had heard him correctly. "Like the birds?" I asked, feeling silly for doing so.

"S'right." He confirmed.

I couldn't help it – I laughed.

"Why?" I demanded incredulously. Sure, it was probably foolish to mock a nine foot tall behemoth about his likes and dislikes, but at the moment I didn't care.

Trevor frowned and adjusted the weight of the battle axe, inadvertently reminding me that it was still very much there.

"Well they're smug lil' bastards ain't they?" He said defensively. " Waddlin' around all high an' mighty, like they're somethin' special 'cause they got themselves them built in suits." Trevor grumbled. "Who are they to make me self-conscious about the style in which I choose to dress?"

I had absolutely no answer for that.

Sensing my lack of rebuttal, Trevor turned away once more and with what I took to be a bit of added annoyance to his step, walked away.

"You know, I really, really like him." I chuckled, switching arms with Raegan as we too turned and headed towards the Keep.

"For someone who was ordered to murder us, he was actually very sweet." She agreed, glancing back as if to ensure that the minotaur had truly gone.

"Yeah, well, we've pushed our luck far enough. Let's get inside before he realizes something's not right and changes his mind." I suggested.

"Agreed." She breathed with a shake of her head.

Leading her up the remaining steps, I gave the doors to the Keep a quick inspection before slowly pulling them open. When no alarm sounded or attack came, I gestured for Ronnie to enter as I held onto the dark wooden edge of the door.

Ducking under my arm, she slowly stepped through, her footsteps quiet on the thick red carpet lining the sparsely lit hallway that stretched before us.

"Penguins." I chortled to myself.

Taking one last look behind me, I followed her in.

Chapter Eighteen

The air shifted and went still as the doors of the keep closed behind us, moaning against our ears like a dying gasp.

Exchanging nervous glances, as if we were each reassuring ourselves that the other was still there, we moved away from the entrance and into the long hall that opened up before us. Soft, expensive looking carpet the color of fresh blood covered the hard marble floors beneath our feet, muffling the sound of our careful steps as we cautiously explored our surroundings.

The interior of the Keep was comprised of the same greyish stone that made up the building's external walls, although here in the soft light of the many magical sconces that illuminated the corridor, they seemed much less weathered; even well maintained. A dozen suits of metal armor stood at full attention on each side of the carpet, their empty helmets and wicked looking weapons glinting dangerously as Raegan began to creep slowly past.

"I know what you're thinking." She said in hushed tones, her eyes dancing over the many halberds, swords and axes lining our way. "But don't touch any-" An explosion of metal echoed around us

237

like a car crash, interrupting her words and sending her into a startled leap as she spun backward, her firearm drawn.

Eyes wild and frantic with fear, her gun trembled as she searched for the source of the attack, only to find me standing sheepishly at the base of where one of the imposing suits of armor once stood.

"Wow." I breathed in honest surprise. "That was frigging loud." I had known before I had even acted that knocking over the metal display would probably make a bit of a racket, but the stones themselves seemed to hum and vibrate as my ears pulsed with the fading clatter of the now tumbled armor.

"Are you out of your bloody mind?!" Raegan hissed through clenched teeth. Disbelief and rage battled across her face as she slowly spun in place, her head twitching to every corner of the long hall in anticipation of attack.

"Um, no?" I frowned in resentment. "I passed the psyche test with flying colors." Stepping away from the now empty base, I sidled up to the next closest suit of armor, my eyes locked on hers. "McKenna disputed the results for like two weeks straight, remember?" Then, with a playful grin, I slowly and deliberately pushed over the display.

The shaped metal pieces rang out like a chorus of church bells as they bounced across the floor, the rich carpeting doing little, if nothing to muffle the sound.

Panic overtook confusion as Raegan leapt forward and grabbed me by the arm, halting me in mid step as I moved towards yet another armored stand. Eyes wild, she searched my face nervously, her worried gaze darting frantically to the space just above my head.

"What in the hell are you doing?" She demanded. The horror in her voice was magnified by her bewilderment. "He'll know we're here!" She added imploringly as she tugged at my arm.

"Gee, ya think?" I chuckled as I looked back at the scattered pieces strewn across the hall. Placing my hand atop hers, I looked down at my sister and gave her my most reassuring smile.

"I know, and you're probably right." I admitted halfheartedly. "But I figure this; our boy Somnus seems to be pretty up to snuff on where we've been and what we've been doing just about every step of the way. Right?" I asked, not giving her time to answer. "I mean he sent Mickey and Malory to nab us, but not until *after* Max went all Juggernaut and got us past that locked gate." I explained. "Which means that he knew exactly where we were in the maze."

With the fear fading from the vibrant green of her eyes, Raegan looked back at the mess that I had made and pursed her lips in thought.

"You think that he's watching us." She said in understanding.

"Oh, I have no clue." I admitted. "But Trevor's big ass is squatting with that axe out front like a beefy lumberjack, just waiting for someone to pull the lever - a lever that the maze, despite *being* a maze, seems to have brought us directly to." I shook my head. "I'm guessing that ol' Rupert can either see us, or at the very least, knows the roundabouts of where we are."

Tipping her head to one side with a frown of deliberation, Raegan considered my words for a moment before shrugging in agreement. "That's not unsound logic." She conceded. "If he's tied himself to this place, and the magic that surrounds it, it would stand to reason that he would be able to sense any spikes or sudden changes in the flow of energy."

"Exactly." I beamed, hoping that my confident smile would hide the fact that I had been thinking more along the lines of a security system and cameras than any sort of crystal ball.

"Still." She sighed. "That doesn't mean that we have to announce our arrival by making a mess, does it?" There was a sort of tired irritation in her voice as she gestured behind us.

That made me laugh.

"Yeah, well I'd rather ring the doorbell and let him know that we're here than have these goddamn things sneaking up on us when we're halfway down the hall." I chuckled as I made my way to the next expensive looking display stand.

Raegan froze in place and her eyes went wide. Slowly she turned, nervously crooking a thumb in the direction of the armored statue towering beside her.

"Do you sense something?" She whispered, her voice cracking with both fear and wonder.

"Newp." I said, drawing out the word as I toppled yet another one, kicking an empty bucket helm away from the hollow shell of its torso for good measure. "But I've seen way too many episodes of Scooby Doo to not know what happens with an empty suit of armor as soon as you turn your back on them. Better safe than sorry."

"Scooby Doo." Ronnie repeated, her voice flat with disbelief.

"Yup."

"The cartoon dog with the speech impediment." She continued as if double checking the math on an answer she didn't understand.

"That's the one." I confirmed. "I've sculpted my life around his teachings." I added in reverent tones just to screw with her.

Conflict clouded her face, but quickly parted as she shrugged in resignation and with a half-hearted shove, turned and knocked over the armored statue that she had been standing in front of.

"That's my girl." I grinned.

We made quick work of the rest of them, the long hall rumbling with the metallic thunder of our now combined efforts. Meeting no resistance, the once pristine walkway was littered with crumpled chainmail shirts, empty gauntlets, and discarded weapons skittering to a halt as they ripped their way through the fibers of the expensive looking carpet.

The noise was nothing short of incredible.

While there may not have been any actual battle, it certainly sounded as if there were one, and the ceiling above us vibrated with little showers of dust for our efforts. If Somnus didn't know that we were coming before, there was no way in hell that he didn't know now.

With the last of the suits of armor falling into a harmless heap of dents and broken clasps, we walked the remaining few feet of the now cluttered hall, slowing in step as it emptied into a large, well lit, oval shaped room.

A grand staircase, the kind you'd see in old black and white movies where the hero would carry the woman up, whisking her away to some hidden bedroom for implied sex if he was lucky enough not to have thrown out his back, took up the majority of the space, climbing upward in a series of walkways as it connected to the two floors looming above us.

To each side of the stairwell lay twin hallways that branched out into this level of the Keep, and a small, recessed door at the bottom of a few marbled steps.

We stood in silence, each gauging our choices. In the vast openness of the room with our ears still ringing with the ghosts of broken metal, it felt unnaturally still and eerily quiet.

"We go down." Raegan said quietly, staring at the few short steps and the doorway sunken into the wall at their base.

"How do you know?" I said, staring at the door myself. I knew in my heart that she right, but that didn't mean that I wanted her to be. I glanced left, then right, trying to gauge the connecting halls, but they seemed peaceful in their emptiness, apparently abandoned by anything that would live above ground.

"If he were above us he would have already shown himself, especially after that commotion." Her lips turned downward in an annoyed grumble. "Besides, it's always downward, isn't it?" She chuffed.

"I know, right?" I asked emphatically, my voice driven high by my absolute agreement. "Why doesn't the bad guy ever have a lofty apartment, or a really nice bachelor pad with a wet bar? Noooo, it's always dungeons, or caves, or frickin' castles in the middle of a magical mazes." I complained, letting her annoyance fuel my own.

Raegan laughed softly, my ranting somehow allaying her mood. Flickering her gaze upward and tracing the staircase with her eyes, she pursed her lips in thought and hummed quietly under her breath.

"Still." She mused. I could tell by the darting of her eyes, and the way that her lips twitched with half spoken words that she was trying to convince herself of her decision's validity.

"Where do these stairs go?" I asked, wondering if she had noticed something that I had missed.

Turning her face to me, but keeping her eyes locked upon the landing, she paused in consideration before lifting a slender shoulder in the barest of shrugs. "They go up." She said simply.

I blinked and shook my head. "Did you just make a Ghostbusters ref-"

"We should do a quick check of this floor and the ones above us before we head down. Just in case." She said, cutting me off as she explained. "There's probably nothing more than a handful of servants quarters and hosting rooms, but," She hesitated, her eyes catching mine. "If the girls are up there and we don't check…"

She let her words hang.

I looked up.

"Do you think they're really up there?" I asked doubtfully. Even with the two of us standing at its middle, the place just *felt* empty.

"No." She admitted with a sigh. "He'd want to keep them close. Together. We're probably looking for a central chamber that he can easily keep an eye on and that would allow him to better focus the energies of this place. But," She paused, looking over her shoulder to the scattered hall of broken armor behind us. "Better safe than sorry, right?"

"I don't think that applies to stairs." I bemoaned, mentally counting steps as I followed their path upward.

"Let's clear this floor first." Raegan said quietly, her gaze following mine. As far as we had come, and as tired as we were, neither one of us was looking forward to a climb, no matter how slight.

The bottom floor of the Keep was mostly empty and contained little more than an abandoned kitchen, dining hall, and several small rooms filled with moldy couches and chairs that had most likely been used for entertaining. The upper levels provided even less to discover as most of the rooms were missing doors, furnishings, and were largely unfinished. The entire place, at least the above ground portions, was deserted.

After several minutes of slinking nervously around, our steps became heavier and more relaxed. We toppled a few more suits of armor, ripped down a painting just to ensure that its eyes weren't following us, and Ronnie even took an uncharacteristic amount of joy in the destruction of a particularly creepy looking Satyr statue.

And through it all, we were met only with silence.

Finding ourselves once again at the bottom of the grand staircase, we slowly approached the recessed door at its base and cautiously moved down the few steps of the landing.

"So." I said hesitantly.

Raegan's eyes narrowed in concentration as she took in every crevice and crack of the wooden door. Through the three barred window in its center, we could see little more than the sloping ceiling of what had to be yet another set of stairs.

"This feel like a trap to you?" I asked rhetorically as the hairs on the back of my neck prickled and stood on end.

"Without a doubt." She confirmed. Then, with a resigned exhalation of breath, my Keeper stepped forward and outstretched her arm, reaching for the black metal handle and thumb plate that would open the door.

"Wait." I cautioned as I gently placed my hand over hers, pulling it back.

"What?" She asked her eyes flashing with alarm as she looked up at me. "Do you see something?"

"No." I said, trying to ease her concern with a soft smile. "But none of this fairy shit ever seems to really hurt me." I explained. "If you open the door and get turned into a frog or something, I'm going to feel like shit every time I have to clean your tank."

"You'd get me a tank?" She gasped, placing a hand on her chest in mock appreciation. There was humor in her voice, but I could see the true gratitude behind her eyes as she allowed me to take her place in front of the door.

"Well, not a *big* one." I teased. "Those damn things are expensive." Holding my breath, I reached forward and grabbed the handle firmly before pressing my thumb down on the latch.

A familiar dull click of metal vibrated against my hand as the thumb plate went slack and I froze in place.

"Are you alright?" Raegan asked worriedly.

"Yeah." I confirmed, not moving a muscle.

"Magic?" She squeaked.

"Worse." I pulled on the handle and the door slammed against its frame. "Locked." I announced giving it an irritated, yet still vicious jiggle.

Gently nudging me out of the way, Raegan stepped forward and tested the door herself. "Well shit." She swore grumpily.

"No worries. I've got this." I said, rolling my shoulders and cracking my neck. Shifting my weight to my back leg, I dropped my stance and exploded forward, slamming my shoulder into the wooden surface of the door.

I knew the moment that I hit it that there was no way I could ever hope to break it down. Made of the same thick, dense timber that made up the outside gates, it felt more like steel than wood.

It didn't so much as creak as I bounced harmlessly off it.

"Ow." I winced, rubbing my arm. "Okay. I don't got this." I frowned, ignoring Raegan's barely concealed looks of amusement. "Shut up." I grumbled. "Max made it look easy."

"We could try the lock." She suggested.

"Hang on!" I said, fishing around the inside pocket of my jacket. "I have a paperclip and a pen. Think that you can use them to go all MacGyver on it?" I asked hopefully.

I might have been teasing a bit, but it was actually a pretty impressive talent. Raegan had a knack for locks, gears, and anything mechanical designed to keep people out. And while I had never thought to ask exactly *how* she had acquired these skills, I had sworn on several occasions to have her teach me.

Dropping to a crouch in front of the door, Raegan narrowed her eyes in concentration and squinted at the lock.

"Maybe." She said, her tongue poking at the corner of her mouth. "But there's something not quite...yeah. I thought so." She said with a bit of satisfaction, nodding her head in agreement with herself.

Removing the pen's cap as she looked up at me I thrust it toward her, pairing it with a badly bent but still fully intact paperclip.

"Oh. You're simply adorable." She said with a patient, but incredibly sarcastic smile.

From the depths of her suit coat, Raegan produced a thick fold of black cloth and immediately began to unravel the leather cords that held it closed. Gently unfurling the bundle, her fingertips danced over a dozen small metal picks of various shapes and sizes, each nestled lovingly in its own special pocket.

Careful in her selection, she finally retrieved a bumpy, oddly curved length of steel and an L-shaped bar from her kit. Looking back to the lock that she had been studying in confirmation, Raegan gently placed the tools at the keyhole and cautiously prodded the lock's inner workings.

"Oh. Oh yeah." She whistled low before sliding her hands to the side of the mechanism in an odd splaying of slender fingers. "That's quite nasty." There was a quiet appreciation lacing the words as she looked up at me and grinned.

"Watch this." She instructed, twisting the pick sharply. There was a soft metallic clicking sound, and for a moment I thought that she was simply showcasing her prowess at picking locks.

"Yeah yeah." I rolled my eyes, trying not to show how impressed I really was. "You're amaz-" Before I could finish my words, a large, wicked looking needle sprang from the center of the lock and stabbed violently into the air where her fingers should have been.

"Holy shit." I swore in surprise. The hollow length of rusty metal was easily half an inch long and dripping with a dark blue liquid that hissed in angry little puddles as it fell to the floor.

The lock was trapped.

Smiling smugly, Raegan leaned in and gingerly sniffed at the needle, her nose wrinkling in instant disagreement with the smell.

"Ugh. Imp blood." She announced, touching the back of her hand to her nose in an attempt to drive away the scent.

"How in the hell could you know that?" I asked, both dubious and impressed at the same time.

My Keeper beamed up at me, mischief crackling behind her eyes.

"It's blue." She grinned, but continued before I could roll my eyes again. "And it's one of the few Fae poisons that I've actually come across in my studies. Hob goblins are said to dip their darts in it. Plus, it has a very distinct odor." She explained, still making a face. "Like fish and feet."

"Is it like, super deadly?" I asked as she turned back towards the lock and resumed her studies, taking obvious care in avoiding the still bubbling needle.

"Not really." Raegan shrugged, her focus now more on the lock than me. "It's more of a strong psychedelic than actual poison. Not unlike the secretions of the cane toads of South America, really." She added absently.

"So it what, gets you high?" I scoffed. "What kind of deterrent is that?" I'd heard of licking toads to get stoned in my youth, but had never really met anyone who had done it and largely regarded it as an urban legend.

"Well, it's incredibly fast acting, extremely potent, and the effects can last several hours." She explained, still jabbing at the lock. "I'll wager that it's rather hard to focus on robbing someone when you're tripping balls." She grunted, twisting the L-shaped bar that she had inserted at the base of the keyhole.

Before I could ask her exactly where she had heard that particular expression, the lock gave a loud, defeated click and the thumb plate went limp, falling to the top of the handle under its own weight.

"There we go." Raegan grinned. Grabbing the door handle, she stood and stepped back, pulling it open as she did. Unlocked, the door swung effortlessly open, propelled by both the tug and its own considerable weight.

Shoulder to shoulder, we leaned forward as one, each of us trying to get a view through the now unobscured doorway. The carved rock walls were adorned every few feet with small, indented alcoves that each held a single burning candle. Impossibly bright, they burned with a heatless flame that damaged neither the wick nor the wax and left no oily soot upon the wall. A spiral stairwell that seemed to be formed from the stone itself dropped quickly out of view, its true depth masked by the flickering of candles and its own curving effect as it wound downward and out of sight.

"Maaaaan." I lamented, placing a foot on the first step and leaning heavily to the right as I tried in vain to get a better view of what lay beyond the descending stairs.

"Quiet and careful." Raegan whispered behind me, as she gently nudged me forward.

"Why do I always have to go first?" I grumbled, pulling my weapon from its holster as I obeyed.

The stairwell itself was suspiciously clean, surprisingly spacious, and lasted only a dozen or so feet before connecting to the floor below. Rectangular in shape and well lit by the same magical candles as the stairwell, the room that we now found ourselves stepping into was largely empty, save for the distraction of its far wall.

Three evenly spaced door handles, similar to the one that we had just bypassed, but containing no locks gleamed in the flickering light.

The first two were flush with the wall, as if they were to mark the place where a doorway should be. The third, furthest to the right, was attached to an actual wooden door and was seemingly the only way to exit the odd room. Above them, centered over the middle door handle, hung a golden plaque written in the same familiar gibberish language as the one that had decorated the gate Maxine had bulldozed her way through.

"Someone must have gotten a bulk discount on those things." I remarked, tilting my head towards my sister, no longer impressed by the wealth of this place.

Raegan's lips moved silently as her eyes flashed over the script. Taking a step forward she let out an annoyed breath and slowly shook her head.

"Well, how bad is it?" I asked, mirroring her exasperated tones. I had no idea what the sign actually said, but it was already working my very last nerve. Mimicking my Keeper's stance, I took in the newest barrier before us and tried to work out what she was seeing.

The first handle was embedded in the wall next to a series of small, round holes that peppered the entire surface of where a door would be. It would be next to impossible to the reach the handgrip without centering yourself directly in front of at least a dozen of them.

The second, similar in design, was set in the middle of a grid of deep cut slits that crisscrossed the rock in a series of chaotic patterns. Scratches and deep gouges marred the edges of each line, giving the impression that something sharp, or incredibly fast moving could pop out without warning at any time.

And then there was the door.

Made up of a dark, old looking wood, it was unmistakably heavy, and undoubtedly solid. Windowless and fit snuggly into the surrounding frame, it was impossible to tell what lay behind it.

But it was definitely a door, and as far as I could see, our only way out.

"Well, they kind of make that an easy choice, don't they?" I asked wryly, wondering who would be foolish enough to touch the first two handles, but still suspecting that the third was the real trick.

"It's a puzzle." Raegan explained in a tired voice.

"Ahhh." I nodded, pretending to understand.

"Blessing, blade and bullet." She explained, darting her hand over each of the handles as she spoke.

"Yeah. Not following." I admitted. If it was some sort of a trick, then it was the one where you asked your younger cousin to select a card, but held out the one you wanted him to pick in a super obvious way.

Heh. Kids are dumb.

Raegan turned to me, her face calm but deadly serious. "Two of these doors are trapped." She said solemnly. "If we open the wrong one, we'll most likely be very badly injured, or even killed."

"Okay?" I said, still not following as I looked past her to the door handle adorned wall.

"The third door, should we find it, will lead us deeper into the keep. That is the blessing of passage, I suspect." She continued. "We just have to figure out which is which."

"So two of them are built to kill us, and one of them just lets us through?" I asked, looking to the actual door in confusion.

"That's what it says." She nodded.

"Do you mean, like, the handles?" I asked, still failing to comprehend. I was starting to feel stupid for not understanding and the back of my neck pricked with an uncomfortable warmth.

Raegan shrugged in frustration. "It could be anything. The

handles, the door itself, or maybe the floor collapses or the ceiling caves in." She explained, looking upward. "There's really no way to tell until we try one."

I looked to the door in confusion, and then back to Raegan who was now creeping forward as she studied the section of wall pocked with holes. Leaning in, she furrowed her brow and brought a single finger a bit too close to one of the openings for my liking.

"Are you actually *trying* to get yourself killed?" I asked in disbelief, slapping at her hand.

"Relax." She grumbled. "I'm just looking." She added defensively, but retracted the wounded hand nonetheless.

"For what?" I asked sarcastically. "A face full of lead, or iron, or whatever it is that these psychopaths use for bullets? Seriously, who in the hell builds this stuff?" I lamented as I took her by the shoulder and pulled her back. "Just, don't touch anything until we figure this out, okay?" I said, scolding her out of frustration, wondering if this is how she always felt around me.

Raegan smiled, probably noting the uncharacteristic role reversal herself. "I'm just looking for some sort of hint or clue that might give us direction. There's got to be something." She mused. "We just need to eliminate one of the choices." Her voice trailed in thought.

"*What* choices?" I asked, my voice going shriller than intended with exasperation.

Thrusting out my arm, I crooked a finger at the first door.

"Bullet." I said, pointing to the place she had been prodding only a moment before. "Blade" I continued, gesturing to the wall that held the grid-like slices. I could easily imagine thin, razor sharp swords protruding from them and then tried to quickly push the thought of my impaled, dying sister away. "And door." I finished, pointing to the actual frigging door.

Raegan gave a motherly sigh and shook her head. "I appreciate the help, but it's just not that simple John." She explained as if she were thanking a child for making a well-intended mess.

"Um, yeah. Yeah it is." I argued, insulted at the tone. "Bullet holes, slicey blade slit thingies, actual frigging door." I said pointing again, this time using my entire hand for emphasis. "Not exactly rocket surgery from where I'm standing."

Raegan looked back at the wall and frowned, her brow creasing at my continued argument. "How can you be so certain?" She asked, tilting her head as she turned to me.

"Are you messing with me?" I asked skeptically. "You didn't get pricked up there did you?" I asked pointing to the ceiling. "So help me if you're stoned right now."

A light went on behind her eyes, and looking over her shoulder at the wall of certain death, Raegan smirked.

"Tell me what you see." She said quietly.

I followed her eyes, suddenly doubting my own. "A handle in a bunch of holes that look like they could fire bullets or darts or something, one in a bunch of crisscrossing slits, and an actual doorknob in an actual, real door." I said hesitantly. "Why, what do you see?"

Ronnie's face split into a smile as she turned to face me, her eyes sparkling.

"A door, a door, and a door." She explained without looking, still grinning widely. "Three wooden doors, identical in every single way."

I looked past her in confusion, completely lost.

"It's an illusion." She explained, her voice brimming with happiness. "And a powerful one too, if I had to guess." She sounded almost proud.

"But I only see the one door." I said uncertainly. I squinted my eyes, and tried to blur my vision, but nothing changed for me.

"Exactly." Raegan beamed. Standing on her tiptoes she kissed the tip of my nose. "You, my dear brother are simply amazing." She said happily.

"Don't be weird." I blushed, pulling back as I lamely rubbed the kiss from my skin.

"So this one then?" She asked, turning from me and all but skipping to the actual door.

"Yeah." I confirmed, still wiping. "Be careful."

Raegan examined the handle for a moment before taking it into her hand. Looking over her shoulder to me, she took a deep breath and gently applied pressure to the hard metal lever. It clicked harmlessly in her grasp and with a clanking of steel against steel, the door cracked open a fraction of an inch.

"You know, sometimes," Ronnie beamed, pulling against the handle. "You're pretty damn handy to have around." She laughed as she happily swung open the door.

And then, she screamed.

Chapter Nineteen

Psychically staggered by Raegan's surprised shrieking, a suddenly appearing Viviane stumbled out of the now open doorway and into my Keeper's arms. Barely able to catch the girl in time, she wilted under the abrupt weight of another body, but somehow managed to get them both safely to the floor in a tangled, awkward hug.

"John!" Raegan called out to me in alarm.

The kid was a mess.

Her clothing was ripped and filthy. One entire sleeve of her blouse was completely gone, leaving her arm bare save for a bracelet and several dark, angry looking bruises. Her hair was a tangled mat of snarls and snags that only aided in lending to the impression that she had just been dragged through an open sewer.

But it was her face that broke my heart and sent pings of anger and fear rippling through my thoughts.

The entire left side was swallowed by a raw looking purple bruise that yellowed at its edges and went almost black at the center. Her eye, still open despite the fact that she looked like a prize fighter after a bad round, was red from crying, and her entire body wracked with sobs as she held Raegan in a tight, clawing embrace. There didn't seem to be any serious swelling, but the color in contrast to her normally pretty features was unsettling.

"Jesus." I swore under my breath. Moving to the tangle knot of petite limbs, I braced Raegan as she shifted into a more comfortable position in which to hold the sobbing girl.

My sister looked up at me, her face awash with worry as she cradled Viviane, gently rocking the battered teen as she wept.

"What in the hell happened to her?" I asked as quietly as my fear would allow.

Raegan shushed and comforted Viviane before slowly pushing her away, pulling back just enough to catch her eye but not daring to break the embrace. The non-purple side of girl's face was slick with tears that both cleaned away and accentuated the dirt and filth staining her skin.

"Viviane?" Raegan called out gently, trying to get the girls attention. "Viviane?" She repeated the name until the girl finally gave a loud, steadying sniff and attempted to stifle a still growing sob.

"What happened?" She asked, searching her eyes.

Viviane looked at her blankly and then slowly to me as if surprised to see us. Understanding and relief wracked her slender frame as she broke down into a fresh bout of anguished tears.

"Where were you?" She wailed. "You...you just disappeared! Why did you leave us?" She cried, the pain of the accusation choking out her words.

"The maze shifted." Raegan tried to explain, consoling the girl as she rubbed at her bare arm. "We would never leave you on purpose." She swore, fighting back tears of her own.

"We tried looking for you, but it got dark so fast." Viviane continued, her wide eyes darting between us.

"Dark?" I echoed. It was still light barely an hour ago when we entered the Keep. "How long have you been down here?"

"I don't know." Viviane blinked in sudden realization as she wiped at her face. "It feels like forever." She added numbly.

Raegan and I exchanged worried glances.

"How'd you even get in here?" I continued, trying to make some sense of the situation. "You didn't go through the ga-" I started to ask, but then a sudden, horrible thought raced through my mind. "Where's Max?" Jumping to the open doorway I scanned the long corridor for signs of life, but saw no one else.

At the mention of the large woman's name, Viviane's eyes began to well with new tears. "We tried to follow you, but you were just *gone*." She said, and I could hear the blame in her voice. "When we went back to where we started, the maze was different. Miss Stonebridge was different." The girl sniffed loudly and tried to remain calm. "She changed."

"Changed how?" Raegan's face darkened with a knowing anger.

"She wasn't as fun anymore. She seemed mad." Viviane explained. "I stared to get scared, but she told me not to worry. She said that she knew another way in." She added quietly.

"How in the hell would Max know another way in?" I asked under my breath, directing my words close to Raegan's ear.

Ronnie set her jaw, but said nothing.

"It got dark, but we kept walking." Viviane continued. "Finally, we found this big pile of stones and Miss Stonebridge seemed happier. She said we had to move them because they marked a secret way into the Keep." Her voice wavered with uncertainty, like a child who was expecting to be reprimanded for tattling. "I didn't know how she knew, but she was right. There was a metal door beneath."

"It's okay." Raegan reassured her. "Keep going." She pushed, trying to keep the information flowing.

"There was a room down there." Viviane turned back towards the still open door and to the corridor that lay behind it. "There were books and tables and...and...that's when, when she..." Unable to continue, she broke down at the memory and buried her face into Raegan's shoulder once again.

"That's when she what?" I asked, growing impatient.

Raegan gave me a soft, imploring look as she cradled the crying girl.

Viviane looked up, her eyes locking on mine in a storm of fear and resentment. "She hit me!" Tears streamed her face, darkening her already bruised skin.

My heart sank.

"When I woke up she had one of those *things*." Viviane coughed out between sobs. "Like the ones that attacked Agent Young."

A latrodenzian. It had been Max all along.

"She tried to put it on me." Viviane laughed humorlessly. "She thought that I was still knocked out." Her eyes flashed with fury. "So I laid still, and when she got close, I kicked her in the knee as hard as I could."

"And?" I asked, my heart pounding as my mouth went dry.

"I ran." She said quietly, eyes downcast. "I ran forever, until I couldn't breathe." She sniffled, indicating to the open door with the barest twitch of her head. "Then I heard your voices."

I caught Raegan's eye as she stroked the girl's back, still entangled in the collapsed hug. Nodding to the staircase I gave her a worried look and stepped towards it, wringing my hands as I paced.

My sister gently freed herself from Viviane's embrace, shushing the girl and assuring her that we weren't going as far as she did. Reluctant to give up the physical comfort, Viviane finally nodded in understanding and instinctively brought her knees to her chest, hugging them tightly to her.

"How in the hell could all that have happened?" I asked in an agitated whisper, wringing my hands when Raegan finally drew near.

Ronnie didn't respond, but her face flushed with concern as she glanced back at the girl who was now slowly rocking back and forth, her head buried in fetal attempts of self-comfort.

"Walked for hours? Ran forever?" I recapped, my voice straining in its quiet. "How in the hell is that possible? We *just* left them." I stressed.

Raegan took a deep breath and ran her hands over her face before slapping them down to her sides. "I don't know." She sighed. "It might be you."

"Me?" I flinched. "How in the hell is this my fault?"

"You could be affecting the magic of this place. Time itself."

She explained, her voice wrought with frustration. "Like with the Quicklings. It might have only been a couple of hours for us, but for them, away from your abilities? There's no real way to tell."

"Okay." I said, readily accepting that. I might not always be the brightest bulb in the knife drawer, but even I could see that this place affected me differently than it did everyone else. "I'll buy that I'm to blame for this." I admitted. "But Max working for Somnus? Slapping the kid around?" I nodded with my head to Viviane. "Really?"

Ronnie followed my gaze, her own eyes glistening with the promise of tears. "It makes perfect sense." She said with a soft quiver. "Max has unrestricted access to every corner of the school. No one would even think to question her presence. It would have been easy for her to bring in mirrors, or misdirect the police during the search for the first missing girl."

My face fell. I knew she was right, but what hurt me more was the knowledge that *she* knew that she was right, and it was destroying her.

"Do you really believe all that?" I asked, my heart falling.

Raegan's eyes widened slightly and went ice cold as she stared, the already startling green cracking and igniting with a fury that I never imagined possible.

"Not for a fucking second." She growled. Her sudden change in demeanor took me by surprise, and for a long fearful moment, I thought that her ire might be directed at me.

Looking back and forth between the two women in a panicked confusion, it took me a few seconds to realize what I wasn't seeing; Ronnie's eyes weren't actually focused on the girl, but on the space a few inches above her head.

"She's lying?!" I asked incredulously.

Raegan said nothing, but nodded once, her gaze never wavering.

And just like that, my doubt was gone. The pity and the fear that I had felt for Viviane dropped from me like a discarded robe, replaced in an instant by the absolute trust that I held in my sister.

"So what's the plan?" I knew that she had one, and goddamn it, I was going to follow it to the letter.

"We find Max." She answered, her eyes all but glowing with barely contained rage. Cracking her neck in a gesture not just unconsciously borrowed, but ripped from my everyday routine, Raegan took a deep breath and called out to the grieving teen.

"Viviane?"

The girl's name was wrapped in a blanket of silk. The darkness, the wrath, the literally *everything* was gone from Raegan's voice, replaced by a genuine sweetness that crawled my skin and stopped my heart.

Viviane looked up as my sister slowly approached.

"Can you show us?" Raegan asked gently, kneeling as she placed a hand on the girl's bare arm.

The teen's eyes went wide with fright. Panicking, she snapped her head back towards the still open doorway.

"No!" She protested. Lurching forward she grabbed Raegan in a frantic, tearing hug and buried her head fiercely into my sister's shoulder. A fresh storm of fearful wailing shook them both as Viviane begged us to stay.

If the kid was acting, she deserved a goddamn Emmy.

Are you sure? I mouthed uneasily. Kirk Lazarus couldn't stay in character this long.

Raegan's eyes flashed hard. Nodding her certainty she brought her hand reassuringly to Viviane's back and rubbed it in a motherly fashion. The last remaining tendrils of doubt faded from my mind. I trusted Ronnie more than I had ever trusted any other human being in my life, and with that final reassurance I went from uneasy, to pissed off.

"Shhh, shhh. It's okay." Raegan soothed as she pulled herself an arm's length away. "I need you to be strong." She smiled compassionately, taking the girl by the shoulder and searching her eyes. "Listen to me. We're going to get out of this. I promise." She said calmingly. "But right now, we need you to be strong. Can you do that for me? Can you be strong?"

Viviane nodded quickly, her eyes downcast as she wiped at the undamaged side of her face. "Yeah." She coughed before bracing her shoulders in a show of promised strength.

"Can you take us to where you last saw Max?" Raegan asked tentatively.

Viviane pushed away her tears and breathed in deeply. Looking back at the door as if willing herself to be brave she nodded slowly. "I think so." She trembled. Glancing to me she started to smile but hesitated, her face twitching in a moment of honest worry.

My temper had gotten the best of me and I realized that I was scowling.

"We're going to get that bitch." I swore, pulling my gun from its holster and moving towards the door. Holding my breath I stomped in angry emphasis and prayed that my blustering was enough to cover the mistake.

As I clomped theatrically past, I caught the hint of a relieved smile spanning Viviane's broken features and sighed in relief, mentally kicking myself for the slip. Pausing at the doorway, I peered down the long hallway and narrowed my eyes to the distance. More of a tunnel than actual hall, the corridor walls were smooth and glassy, as if something incredibly hot had bored its way through the hard, slate colored rock.

"Are you sure that we should be going after her?" Viviane asked from behind me. I didn't dare look back in fear of tipping my hand again. I might not be much of an actor, but if the kid deserved an Emmy, Ronnie was going for a goddamn Oscar.

"We have to put an end to this." Raegan replied gently, but I could hear the telltale snaps of her holster as she drew her weapon. "Before anyone else gets hurt." She added, and I had a feeling that her words were meant for me.

"Right." I said, nodding my agreement as I stepped through the doorway and into the connecting hall. Although cooler, the air was thicker and layered with a musty, earthy smell that reminded me of the forest after a heavy rain.

"Don't worry." I heard Raegan say softly as Viviane hesitantly followed. "I'll be right behind you." Pulling up the rear under the guise of the protector, I knew damn well that underneath that milk pale skin and nurturing voice smoldered a fire so intense that the devil himself would take pause and reach for the air conditioner.

Which was actually sort of comforting, in a scary kind of way. My back might have been exposed, but whatever game the kid was playing at was going to be a hell of a lot harder to win with a red-headed Tasmanian Devil breathing down her neck.

The hallway, although long and oddly hewn, seemed to be just that; a hallway. We passed a couple of small rooms lined with barrels and dusty crates, a few empty alcoves, and a foul smelling herb closet covered in a vibrant orange mold that clung to the remnants of what-ever it was that once hung there, but beyond those exceptions, there was really only one direction in which to go.

So we walked, the solemn silence broken only by the occasional sniffle or nervous whimper squeaked out by Viviane. I knew without a doubt that it was an act; a show designed to throw us off or keep us sympathetic and unsuspecting of her true intent, but goddamn if it wasn't getting to me. My brain knew the facts, but my heart was telling me to stop, turn around and just hug the living shit out of the poor kid.

Luckily, the hallway ended before my soft heart could turn com-pletely into sucker mush.

Widening towards the exit, the corridor expanded into a large, roughly carved chamber. Bookcases lined every wall, breaking only in the middle as the hallway continued beyond, gently curving out of sight. Brightly lit and warmed by a wrought iron chandler that housed countless candles, each glowing intensely behind a small shield of burnt orange glass, the room would have almost felt welcoming, were it not for the many obvious signs of a fight.

At the stony library's center, amidst a small countertop bar still adorned with a number of toppled beakers and oddly colored contain-ers, lay the remains of what I would have guessed to be a wooden table of some sort, and two broken, rather flattened chairs.

Glass and shards of debris littered the area, pooling behind an overturned, kicked-up throw rug like water being blocked by a damn. Books, their pages bent and curled, lay at the base of one of the book-cases. Every shelf below the highest was broken or cracked, forcing it to spill its precious tomes to hard stone floor.

"She's gone!" Viviane exclaimed in surprise as she rushed past me, skirting the sharper edges of the scattered wreckage. Moving to the base of the damaged bookshelf in confusion, she looked around the room before glancing to the tunnel that continued down the opposite wall.

Brushing my arm as she slid beside me, Raegan and I exchanged frowns before returning our focus on the still searching girl.

"She was laying right here!" Viviane said earnestly, pointing towards the small pile of crushed books at her feet. "I swear." She added in a small voice, her eyes wide with innocence and fear.

"Why would she still be laying on the floor?" Raegan asked, her voice hard.

"And why wouldn't she have chased you?" I added, nodding to the hallway behind us with a twitch of my head. "That wasn't exactly a million mile hike. I thought you said that you ran for hours?"

Viviane's eyes flashed with worry. "What? No. I mean, it felt like…it must have changed like the maze did." She stammered as we raised our weapons. "What are you doing?" Tears began to fill her eyes as she took a step backward, stumbling over the broken shelving.

"Where is Max?" Raegan demanded.

"I told you! She attacked me and e-" The girl panicked.

"I'm not asking again." There was no mistaking the threat behind the statement, and I braced to follow whatever lead my Keeper took.

Viviane's expression melted in an instant, her quivering lip and terrified eyes turning upwards in an annoyed, self-defeated smile. Throwing a hand in the air with an exasperated sigh, she looked at us and shrugged in lazy concession.

"What gave it away?" She asked, obviously disappointed with herself as she scratched at the back of her head. "Were the tears too over-the-top?"

I quickly shook my head. "No, not at all! You were *incredible*." I admitted breathlessly as I lowered my weapon. Ronnie had earned my trust a thousand times over, and because of that I knew that this very confrontation and reveal had to be coming…

…but the kid had definitely missed her calling.

"I mean, you were good. Like really, *really* good. Have you had any formal training?" I asked, absently wondering where she would have found the time. She was like sixteen, at best. If she had been enrolled at the school for the last-

"Where. Is. Max." Raegan asked again, her voice reaching those dangerous levels of irritation that snapped me back to the reality of the situation and inspired me to raise my gun once more.

Viviane broke from our little sidebar on the arts and smiled. Shifting her weight to one leg, she made a show of idly inspecting her fingernails before looking up through the tops of her eyes in a bored fashion. "She put up one hell of a fight, if that matters at all." She teased, lightly touching the bruise at her cheek. "Max was actually a hell of a lot stronger than she looked." She chuckled, glancing to me. "If you can believe it."

"Not re-"

"Really going to need you to focus here, John." Raegan snapped, her finger twitching against the trigger as she stared down the teen.

Viviane stopped smiling, her face twisting into a contemptuous look of disdain.

"Oh don't worry, *Ray Ray*." She sneered Max's nickname for my sister. "You'll be joining her soon enough." She looked over her shoulder, across the room to another doorway. "And think about how happy Daddy will be when I bring him you." She added, glancing to me as her lips curled into a cruel parody of a smile.

"Daddy? Ew." I blanched. "Come on kid, he's like three times your age." I pointed out, wrinkling my nose in disgust.

"Don't be gross." Viviane scolded, surprisingly taken aback.

"Ambrose is her father." Raegan explained, her eyes never leaving the girl.

I blinked in disbelief, lowering my weapon once more.

"You really are the smart one." Viviane rolled her eyes mockingly before turning her gaze to me. "What's wrong Agent Talik? Can't you see the family resemblance?"

Cocking my head to one side, I turned to Raegan and frowned.

"His papers say anything about him having a kid?" I asked in a low voice.

"No." She replied without looking.

"Oh, there's no official record." Viviane explained. "I was something of a surprise." She admitted. "My mother never told him that she was pregnant. They were young, it was a fling, and she ended up marrying someone else." She shrugged in acceptance. "It happens."

"So what sparked the Manson Family reunion?" I asked. The kid's demeanor was almost cocky, and she was anything but scared. The back of my neck began to prickle as I glanced around the room. In a place where nothing ever felt right, something really wasn't feeling right.

"She got sick." Raegan said flatly, answering for her. Viviane raised an eyebrow in surprise before touching her nose and pointing at my Keeper.

"Hereditary bone and muscle disease." She confirmed, impressed. "It usually doesn't become a problem until much later in life, but..." Viviane shrugged. "I was always an early bloomer."

"You look pretty healthy to me." I frowned. I had seen what the disease had done to Ambrose, and she showed none of the signs of the condition.

"Why thank you." She said with mock shyness as she pretended to blush with compliment. "Actually, I should be thanking Kara, Sammy and Gabby. Oh, and definitely Miss Stonebridge." She flexed her hand into a fist in thought.

Grinning wickedly, Viviane gave me a nasty, sideways glance.

"Lydia."

The name left her lips like a dagger and my face began to burn as I saw red. Snapping my weapon to a ready stance, I slid my finger from the side of the frame to the trigger.

The teenager's smile widened, seemingly unimpressed by the fact that I she was about to be shot. "She really likes you, you know." Viviane continued mockingly. "And not just because of all of the hot freaky sex you two are having." She waggled her eyebrows meaningfully.

Everything suddenly snapped into place. The first girl had been her roommate. The next two her classmates. If she was the one controlling the latrodenzian, then the little bitch had access to everything; their abilities, their training, and their memories.

"How are you doing it without the crown?" I growled between clenched teeth.

"What crown?" Viviane laughed. She might have been toying with us, but there was an honest confusion behind the question.

"Enough." Raegan said sternly, drawing the girl's attention back to her.

Viviane's eyes darkened, and her smile dissolved into a sneer of contempt as she turned to Raegan.

"And you." She chuffed in disdain. "I'm still..." She paused, throwing a hand into the air as if she were swatting away a bothersome fly. "...sorting through everything from Max. I mean, I haven't had time to really understand it all, but c'mon. You don't write? You don't call?" Viviane shook her head. "You really have no idea how lonely she is, do you? Do you even care?"

I saw, no - I *felt* Raegan's heart sink in her chest as the words hit home. Guilt, shame, and sadness rushed past her anger, flushing her pale skin in a tidal wave of embarrassment and remorse.

It was one thing to go after me, but my little sister was off limits.

"Hey. You sick of this shit yet?" I asked Raegan with a dry, derisive laugh.

"Yeah." She answered, her eyes growing wet. And with that confirmation, we both shot her.

Twice.

All four shots caught the diminutive teen squarely in the chest. At barely ninety pounds, her tiny frame should have been lifted from the ground and thrown backwards into a groaning pile of ouchies and hurt. Instead, Viviane simply stood there unharmed before slowly looking down at her now grey and silver spackled shirt.

Looking up, she waved her hand in a questioning gesture as she pointed to the bruised side of her face.

"Did you really think that was going to hurt, after this?" She asked sarcastically. Moving with a speed that shouldn't have been possible, the small girl closed the gap between us in the time between heartbeats and lashed out, kicking Reagan square in the chest.

Ronnie flew back as if she had been pulled by invisible wires, dropping her gun as she bounced off the far wall and crumpled to the floor in a broken heap.

"Wow." Viviane exhaled in breathless wonder, apparently as thrown off by the sudden feat of strength as I was. "Did you see that?" She asked me excitedly as I stood stunned and gaping, my own weapon still extended in front of me in a firing position.

If she wanted an answer, I didn't have time to supply one.

Balling up her slender hand into a delicate little fist, she extended her arm and backhanded me with force of a sledgehammer. The world around me exploded into a kaleidoscope of bright lights and bursting stars.

For the briefest of moments I was vaguely aware of a flying sensation, and then I struck something hard and unyielding. Surprisingly, there was no pain at first; only a ripple of shock and the detached feeling of impact as I collided with a bookcase, its contents pouring around me in an avalanche of heavy thumps and fluttering pages.

Satisfied that we were properly incapacitated, or at the very least no longer threats, Viviane strolled the room at a leisurely pace, casually kicking our forcibly abandoned weapons well out of any possibility of reach as she glanced around the room.

"I can't believe this is what she feels like every day." She laughed to herself as she furled and unfurled her small, but incredibly powerful fists. "This strength is unbelievable."

My tongue rolled out of my mouth as I tried to form a fitting, yet still incredibly witty comment, but all that I could squeak out was a half-mumbled moan and a bucketful of drool mixed with fresh blood.

The room spun like a carnival ride as Viviane paused and pivoted at the waist. Her lips pursing in thought, she folded her hands and tapped at her mouth with a pair of steepled fingers.

"Now where did I leave those last two– aha!" She grinned. Moving to the cluttered counter space she carefully cleared away a few of the larger shards of broken glass. "There you are." She cooed playfully.

Retrieving whatever it was that she was looking for, Viviane cradled them to her chest in a childlike fashion and skipped back towards the center of the room.

Struggling to all fours, I wobbled unsteadily and resisted the urge to throw up as I concentrated on the stone in front of my face. Raegan was barely lifting her head and fighting to get her arms out from beneath her as Viviane approached.

"One for you." She said sweetly as she set a silver, egg-like object on the floor a few feet from Raegan's head. Her legs blocking it from view as she turned and skipped towards me, I was helpless to do anything but blink slowly as I fought through the fog of pain clouding my thoughts.

"And one for you." She grinned, setting another of the metal ovals in front of me.

Numbly, I tried to focus on the object as it began to shift, and my heart began to pound as it slowly unfurled in an all too familiar fashion.

"You know," She said conversationally, still bent at the waist, her face mere inches from my own. "So far, everyone I've been connected to has been a woman." She mused. "This could be really *interesting*." I swung my head to Raegan who had collapsed back to the floor, and then to the small metal spider that was coming to life in front of her.

Giggling to herself, Viviane backed up a few feet as the latrodenzian in front of me righted itself, slowly rising up onto its many metal feet.

Fear inspiring movement, I scrambled backwards and slammed into the wall, instinctively snatching a heavy book from the pile around me as I did.

"Oooh, sorry." Viviane grinned, absently running her hand over the bracelet at her wrist as she watched my reaction. "But you're too late. Once they open like up that, they lock onto their target's brainwaves. Nothing can stop them."

Raising the book as a weapon, I cocked back my arm as I slid up the wall and into an unsteady standing position. Viviane laughed lightly and shook her head as she read my intent.

"Go ahead." She shrugged. "You won't hit it. It's already synced to you." She said, somehow managing to sound bored. "It'll know where you're going to throw that before it even leaves your hand."

I ignored her as I pulled back my arm, my eyes on the spider as it clacked a single step towards me, its claw-like mechanical leg hovering above the ground as it slowly swayed from side to side.

She rolled her eyes. "Seriously, stop. You can't hit it, and it's only a matter of time before-"

With a war cry that may have sounded suspiciously like a high pitched girlish shriek, I threw the book with all of my might; not at the latrodenzian in front of me, but at the one poised to spring upon my still dazed sister.

Viviane realized my true target a fraction of a second too late, and even propelled by her enhanced speed missed her chance to stop the throw, the hard leather cover brushing past her fingertips as she leapt to intercept it.

The heavy volume spun like a weighted Frisbee, hitting the floor a few inches in front of the mechanical spider and skipping into it like a stone across the surface of a still pond. The book and latrodenzian collided, its momentum carrying them across the room where they hit the stone wall with a satisfying crunch of twisted metal.

"JOHN TALIK!" I roared in victory as I stomped forward, bringing my foot down upon the robotic spider in front of me. If the little bastard could read my thoughts, it didn't, because in a perfect imitation of the first one I ever fought, it crunched under the heel of my shoe and went still as I ground it ferociously into the stone.

Thrown off balance by her attempt to catch the book, Viviane staggered and regained her balance, turning to me with fire in her eyes.

"You're going to pay for that." She growled, clutching her hands into small, menacing fists.

"Easy now Rowdy." I said nervously as I raised my own hands

and held them out flat, palms towards her. "I don't want to have to hurt you." I bluffed as I began to defensively circle.

Viviane's eyes widened excitedly, and she grinned dangerously at the challenge. Countering my circle, she followed my movements with the grace of a stalking cat, nonchalantly kicking the heavy work bench that I was hoping to keep between us out of her path like it weighed next to nothing.

"Wait!" I cried out as she jumped forward in a clumsy attempted to punch me in the face.

Viviane might have stolen Max's strength, but she didn't seem to have downloaded any actual fighting experience or training, so the blow went wide and I was easily able to dodge out of the path. Still, I could feel the wind as her fist soared past my face, and the frigging *breeze* from it made my jaw hurt. I had no doubt that if she would have connected, I would have ended up at least a foot shorter.

"You don't have to do this." I asserted as she feigned to the left, cutting off my escape. Leaping backwards I stumbled and nearly tripped over a small pile of fallen books.

"I know." She smiled, her eyes glinting with malice. "But I want to." She lunged forward again in an attempt to close the distance between us.

Taking her by surprise, I did the unexpected and stepped towards her, swinging my fist in what should have been a devastating right cross. Except, she didn't fall back. Instead, Viviane set her jaw and rolled with the punch, her eyes closing in an attempt to control the rage that now seethed within her.

"I'm sorry." I offered in a little voice.

"You hit like a girl." Viviane spat, opening her eyes and turning her head to face me.

"The bracelet." Raegan moaned from a prone position. She had managed to push herself up onto her forearms and was watching the fight through clenched teeth. She looked as miserable as I felt, and I could see the pain in her eyes as she took a labored breath.

"Shut up bitch." The teen snarled, stealing a quick glance at my sister as she calculated the threat.

The bracelet.

There *was* no pretty princess tiara; the goddamn thing had been fashioned into a bracelet. I stared at Viviane's wrist. Sure, the gems were smaller, and a lot less gaudy, but there were still eight of them lining the loose silver band that circled her wrist.

I knew what I had to do.

"Hey." I called out in an attempt to steal back the girl's full attention. It worked because with a slow, predatory turn of her eyes, Viviane locked her gaze on mine.

"That bitch is my sister." I said suavely. With a slow, deliberate motion, I pulled my arm straight back until my fist was almost level with my head. Lashing out, I aimed for the exact center of her face as I perfectly telegraphed the move.

This time however, the punch didn't connect. Instead she caught my fist in her small hand with almost comical ease.

"That was dumb." She sneered, squeezing my hand in hers. The pain was incredible, far greater than I could have ever anticipated, and it dropped me to my knees in agony.

"What kind of stupid punch was that?" Viviane asked mockingly. Laughing down at my gasps of pain, she effortlessly held me in place as I tried to pull back my arm.

"The smart stupid kind." I hissed between my teeth, my witty banter admittedly lacking in the moment. But in my defense, it's kind of hard to be clever when one of the Power Puff Girls is trying to crush your hand to a pulp.

Relying on her strength to keep my balance, I shifted my weight and grabbed her wrist with my free hand, pulling the bracelet over our interlocked fists, and fully onto my wrist. Viviane screamed in comprehension, but she was too late. Her nails raked over the back of my hand in angry, bloody scores of curling flesh, but there was no longer the force of supernatural strength behind her attack.

Standing as quickly as I could, I pulled back my head and slammed my forehead into the bridge of her little button nose in what was easily the strongest and most well-executed head-butt of my entire life.

No longer powered by the lives stolen by the bracelet, Viviane rocketed backwards, her eyes rolling white as she toppled to the hard stone floor.

"YEAH BITCH!" I screamed, jumping into the air and punching it in victory. "Next time, you might wanna try..." I looked down at her tiny, battered frame, and sighed, my perfect one-liner dying in the light of realization. "...not being a ninety pound girl."

"Goddamnit." I swore, bringing my still throbbing hand to my face. "I don't suppose we can tell people that she was a killer robot from the future?" I asked hopefully as I looked over to Raegan who was now pulling herself to her feet with a pained groan.

Her hand moving to her stomach, she cradled her ribcage and limped towards me, wincing with each step as she did.

"I'm pretty sure you took the bracelet *after* you knocked her on her ass." She said, offering me something between a grimace and a smile.

"I love you." I chuckled, moving to her and catching her in a hug.

"Ow, ow. Easy, easy." She implored, but returned the embrace with more than a hint of vigor. "I love you too."

"You okay?" I asked, pulling away and giving her a quick once over. She wasn't exactly a solid mass of muscle and had taken a blow that probably would have killed me.

"Yeah." She nodded. "Ribs are sore, but I don't think anything is broken. You?"

"I'll have to eat nothing but pudding for the rest of my life, but I'll live." I said, rubbing the side of my face. "How'd you know it was the bracelet?" I asked.

"If she was using Max's strength, she had to have a conduit." Raegan explained. "And the gems were the right color." A sudden frown creased her face as she darted her eyes to the space just over my head. "How are you feeling?" She asked suspiciously.

"Like I just had my ass kicked by Street Fighter Barbie, but past that, fine. Why are you asking again?" I tilted my head, worried that she might be the one with a concussion.

"But nothing else?" She pressed, this time with a meaningful look to the bracelet that I now wore around my wrist.

"Oh. You mean like super strength, speed, or the urge to giggle about boys and start a fandom blog on Tumblr?" It dawned on me that I was now wearing the lives of five other people as a fashion accessory. Raising my arm in front of me, I gave it a quick inspection. It slid down my wrist a bit, but no memories or magical abilities came flooding in. "No more than usual." I shrugged.

"Good." Raegan let out a relieved sigh. "I was hoping that it wouldn't work on you." She nodded to herself.

"You want it?" I asked, knowing that she'd probably be more responsible with it than I would. Hell, I had only been wearing it for a couple of minutes and I was surprised that I hadn't lost it yet. Sliding it across my wrist in offering, I started to take it off, but Ronnie put her hand over the back of mine.

"No, don't." She shook her head quickly. "Magic like that always comes with a steep price." Motioning with her eyes, I followed her gaze to the body of the still unconscious Viviane.

No longer imbued by the bracelet, the unconscious teen was beginning to slowly revert to what I guessed to be her true form. The healthy, perfect sheen faded from her skin, leaving her face sunken and gaunt. Her limbs contracted at odd, painful angles and her right hand was steadily curling into a palsied fist.

"Now what?" I asked guiltily turning my eyes away from Viviane's now frail body.

"I'll stay here with her." Raegan said firmly as she scanned the room. "I'm guessing that this place was his lab. Finding Max and the girls won't be enough. We need to know how to free them without causing them any harm. If there's a key to that, it has to be here."

I shook my head. "I'm not leaving you alone with her."

"Yes, you are." She countered. Retrieving our weapons, she checked them for signs of damage before offering them to me.

"Ronnie." I tried to argue.

"Go. End this." She ordered in a soft voice as she look past me to the open doorway opposite of where we had entered.

"Will these even work on him?" I asked, taking the guns from her and turning them over in my hands.

Raegan laughed. "Probably not." She looked up at me. "But…"

"Better safe than sorry?" I supplied.

She brightened considerably and pushed up onto her toes, kissing me on the nose. "Just be careful. Please?" There were a thousand words spoken in those four, with a lump in my throat I nodded.

"Careful is my middle name." I said, trying to drown the seriousness of the moment in humor.

"I thought it was Danger?" She teased, but I could see the worry in her eyes.

Shaking my head I turned towards the doorway and the corridor that lay beyond. With a little bit of luck there would be nothing standing in the way that would stop me from finding Somnus. With a lot a bit of luck, he'd see the error in his ways, repent and help us out of this godforsaken labyrinth, but I wasn't holding my breath.

Hesitating at the hallway's mouth, I paused and looked over my shoulder back to my sister who looked as if she were sending her only son to war.

"If I'm not back in five minutes," I trailed, my eyes downcast.

Fear washed over her face, as if she had never considered that failure might be an option.

"Wait longer." I grinned.

Turning in place without looking back, I took off down the smoothly hewn corridor in a fast jog.

Chapter Twenty

The stone passageway began to narrow considerably the further I jogged, its glassy walls gently fading into the muddy, earthy tones and crumbling rock of a natural tunnel. Dark roots and patches of muted moss dotted the soil, illuminated by the only plant life that I could positively identify, fairy or otherwise, with any real certainty.

Pixie dust.

Radiating a soft, yet still somewhat unsettling green, the flooring beneath my feet gave way to the familiar crunch of dirt, and a cool breeze carrying the unmistakable smell of water upon it wafted around me. Slowing my steps, I cautiously inched forward as I reached the corridor's end.

While infinitely smaller than the labyrinth itself, the cavern was still enormous by any standard. Domed like an overturned soup bowl, its ceiling was coated in the same glowing fungus as the entryway, providing a reliable if not dim source of light. Unimpeded by the magical haze that acted as a day and night cycle in the maze above us, it twinkled and glimmered gently across the nearly undetectable waves of the lake that lay beneath it giving the illusion of dusk under open sky.

"Well, that explains the breeze." I said under my breath as I stepped onto the rocky beach.

Curving as if purposely following the contours of the room, the shoreline spanned for several hundred feet in both directions before disappearing into the cavern walls. A causeway of wet stones glistened just above the waves, neatly bisecting the lake as it provided a path across the dark waters to the opposite shore. The orange fluttering of firelight danced in the distance, and narrowing my eyes I could just make out the mouth of a well-lit cave on the other side.

"Because that's certainly not a trap." I said humorlessly.

The sand, if you could call it that, shifted underfoot and rolled with every step leaving deep impressions that marred the ground behind me. Wrinkling my nose at the strong scent of seaweed and dead fish, I gingerly approached the water's edge, kneeling just to the side of the stone path.

It was narrow, but wide enough to walk without the need of any sort of balancing act. The stones were nearly flush with the water, barely breaking the surface tension in spots. While I couldn't see the lake's bottom more than a few feet in front of me, I suspected that it grew a lot deeper a lot quicker than I'd wish to discover.

"Oh, yeah. This looks totally safe." I said out loud, nervously looking over my shoulder for any sign of sneaky life. When no threat came, I turned back to the water and sighed, my mind bursting with images of kraken-like tentacles and all of the horrible things that they usually did to unsuspecting Japanese cartoon characters.

Scooping a handful of the gritty pebbles at my feet, I stood and backed up several yards, hopefully robbing the Watcher of an easy snack, should he come too close in search of dwarven prey. With an underhand toss, I pitched the stones into the lake, across from where I had been standing at the shoreline and watched as they peppered its surface in a rainstorm of rock and sand.

The ripples shimmered in the reflection of false moonlight and quickly went still, spreading and fading as if they had never been.

"Okay." I considered, nodding my head from side to side. "So there's no-"

Twenty feet out, something *large* stirred beneath the surface. The water lifted and rolled as whatever it was drew nearer, creating curves of blackness in its wake. My heart fluttered in my chest and my mouth went dry as several more waves appeared, converging on the first and causing the water to crash against the shore in small, breaking peaks.

I caught a quick glimpse of something pale, like the underbelly of a fish as it flashed beside the causeway. Then, without a hint of sound or even the faintest splashing the top of the creature's head slowly emerged from the surface of the lake, and I found myself staring into two very human, very attractive eyes.

Even with three quarters of her face submerged, I ached with the woman's beauty as she stared at me in alluring wonder. Several more of the strange females joined her, and although hidden by the darkness of the water, I knew without a doubt what I was staring at.

"Mermaids." I whispered to myself in awe.

Real, honest to goodness mermaids.

There were a dozen or so that I could see, and within that small sampling eyes belonging to every race and color regarded me with curious amusement. They said nothing, and did nothing beyond stare, each rapt in their focus as they bobbed in stunning silence. Although not one of them had come out of the water beyond their eyes and the near darkness of the lake concealed what lay beneath, the teenage boy in me knew that each and every one of them was completely naked.

"They're water nymphs, actually." A voice from behind me corrected.

Spinning in place, I stumbled slightly as I tried to distance myself from both the voice and the water, inwardly kicking myself for falling into a literal booby-trap as I did.

Somnus stood a short distance down the rocky beach, passively watching my interaction with the gaggle of nymphs. Although his eyes were focused on the creatures in the lake and shone with academic appreciation, his body was turned towards me, no doubt poised and ready for an attack; or so I would guess.

To be honest, it was a little hard to tell given the fact that he was coated in a layer of the same small stones that made up the beach on which we both now stood. His upper half, free of the pebbles and sand was wrapped in the kind of soft, dark robes one would expect an evil wizard to wear, and I found my mind briefly wandering to the thoughts of what a specialty clothing store for bad guys would actually look like.

But it was his lower half that snapped me out of my musings.

From the waist down, the caster was covered in tiny rocks that shifted and moved seemingly on their own accord, obscuring his legs as they melted into the beach in a thick column where his feet should have been. Blinking several times with passing thought, Somnus turned to me and smiled before moving forward in perfect silence, his stony wheelchair gliding effortlessly across the shore.

"Oh shit." I swore, fumbling for my holster. I know that I should have had my guns at the ready, but the jog had taken more out of me than I had anticipated while holding them, and they were heavier than they looked. Returning mine to my shoulder, I had tucked Raegan's behind my back in "gangsta" style, and at the time had felt quite badass for doing it.

Now I just felt stupid.

Rolling his eyes, Somnus snapped his wrist in a bored, backhanding gesture and the weapon was ripped from my fingers. Tumbling through the air, it landed in the lake with a soft splash, the water instantly churning and frothing white at the spot.

Pausing in place, the magician frowned as he glanced to the water, his lips pursed in annoyance as he turned back to me.

"That was supposed to be both you and your weapon." Somnus admitted with a tired sigh. "Still immune to my magic I see." He added before brightening considerably. "I cannot wait to dissect you and find out why." The sheen of true anticipation in his eyes made my skin crawl.

Knowing that I could now be easily disarmed, I didn't bother reaching for my second pistol, hoping to keep it in place as a last ditch hail Mary play. Backing up slowly I raised my hands in an obedient fashion and shook my head.

"Why in the hell does everyone want to cut me open?" I lamented, mostly to myself.

The stone covered wizard grinned in honest amusement and smiled, spreading his arms in a sweeping gesture. "Because you are an absolutely amazing specimen, Agent Talik." He explained conversationally. "Think of all that I could do with the power that you take for granted."

Good. I got him monologuing. Bad guys love to do that.

Admittedly, I didn't have a plan, exactly, but if he was going to go all Bond villain, it might buy me enough time to figure out what to do next. With his lower half encased in stone and eliminating his reliance on the metal arm braces, I doubted heavily that he'd be so easy to knock out with a panicked punch this time around.

"You may be a bumbling moron, but you possess a magic like nothing I've ever seen." Somnus continued, raising his hands to the air. Weird greenish-white electricity crackled and played between his fingers, arching and snapping with crisp little pops of energy that danced down his palms and disappeared into the sleeves of his robes. "I can actually feel it flowing around you."

"You're not so bad with the hocus pocus there either, Palpatine." I pointed out, my eyes focused on the magical bursts of light still sliding across his skin.

Lowering his arms and ending the display of power, the dark wizard smiled smugly and bowed his head in a showing of thanks. Sliding forward once again, he moved soundlessly across the beach on a wave of stone, closing the distance between us.

"Which is really weird because I thought that you Merlin worshippers were a bunch of wannabe hacks." I stalled, desperately hoping that an insult tossed in the direction of his LARPing buddies would buy me a few more seconds to figure a way out of this.

It worked, because Somnus hesitated mid-pebbly glide and tilted his head to one side, regarding me with interest.

"You've heard of the brotherhood?" He asked, outwardly impressed. It might have been my imagination, but he seemed to puff up a little at the mention of his order.

"I've heard enough to know that they're a group of bathrobe wearing role players who like to dress like Hot Topic had a sale on cheesy jewelry." I jabbed before pausing in genuine curiosity. "So how is it that you're able to use real magic?" I asked.

He grinned at that and offered a haughty shrug. "It would seem that some of us are more worthy of our father's gifts than others." He explained with an arrogance born of pride.

I wasn't sure if he was catching on to the fact that I was trying to stall him, or if he was simply eager to poke my insides around with a stick, but the rocks at the base of his column began to shift and once again Somnus began to ooze towards me.

"What about our daughters?" I asked meaningfully, holding my ground and doing my best to resist the overwhelming urge to run.

He hesitated and slowed to a silent stop, but this time he raised a questioning brow as he studied my face.

"Viviane revealed herself, did she?" Somnus asked with a tight, humorless smile. "She informed me that your group had been separated by the maze." The rocks cascaded around him, but he remained rooted in place. "I wasn't thrilled of course." He shrugged, his false smile slowly growing into one of actual pride. "Although I do have to admit, I didn't think that the latrodenzian would work on the security guard. I'm quite pleased with her on that front; it was a very well thought out plan."

"Yeah, she's a real teacher's pet." I said drolly

"Indeed." Somnus mused, looking past me to the cavern's entrance. "Agent Talik," He began conversationally, but his voice hit a dangerous pitch. "Where is my daughter?" He asked, turning his eyes back to mine.

"Someone was being naughty." I said, raising my arm and dangling the stolen bracelet for him to see. "So I had to give her a time out."

Ambrose's eyes flashed wild with a panic. The rocks around him exploded upward, drawing from the beach to cover his arms and chest. Doubling in size, he towered above me as he threw his head back in an anguished cry.

"YOU IDIOT!" He roared, the column that had made up his waist splitting off into a mammoth, rock-coated leg. Lifting it from the shore, he stomped a single ground shaking step forward, and the beach vibrated beneath me. "You have no idea what you've done!" A raw, primal, parental anger quivered his words, but behind that fury I could hear a note of genuine fear.

"WHOA!" I leapt back, flicking my wrist and gripping the edge of the bracelet with my palm. Cocking my arm behind I me, I looked towards the water and twitched my hand in a menacing promise. "Unless this thing can float, I'd be backing the hell up Ben Grimm." I warned, hoping in the back of my mind that it actually couldn't.

"You don't understand." Somnus shrunk slightly, his voice straining with worry as a few buckets worth of stone fell away. "She needs that, or else she-"

"Goes all Stephen Hawking." I cut him off. "Yeah, we saw."

Grinding his teeth into a set jaw, Somnus took another thundering step forward. The stones at his chest and arms flattened, pulling together to form an armor-like plating that obscured the robes beneath from sight.

"You have no idea what you've done." He repeated, but took a deep breath in an effort to push away his frustration. "But that doesn't matter. I can fix this." He insisted. Smiling through his barely restrained hatred, he looked me in the eyes and sneered. "Go ahead. Throw it."

I pulled my arm even further back, my shoulder straining as I held the pose. "I'm not dicking around here Balboa." I warned. "Look, I'm sorry about your kid, I really am. But you take another step towards me and we're going to see if Ariel and her friends over there have a thing for jewelry."

Somnus laughed ruefully as he began to spin his hands in an odd, jerking motion, his fingers twisting into deft, fleeting shapes. "Those pitiful creatures have no desire for bobbles or gems." He spat. "They lack the intelligence needed to understand the mere concept of material possessions."

"I'll do it." I insisted, but my threat was starting to feel hollow, even to my own ears.

"Tell me Agent Talik." He started, closing his eyes as he concentrated on his motions. "What do you actually know of water nymphs?" It was as if he were conducting a small orchestra, but if he was casting a spell, nothing was happening.

The truth was, I knew absolutely nothing about water nymphs. Hell, until a few moments ago, I didn't even know that there *were* water nymphs. The only nymphs I had ever encountered lived in forests and want to do nothing but…

Somnus smiled as I my eyes widened in realization.

"Ahh, so you have a passing familiarity with them I see." Finishing his weird finger waggling, he seemed quite satisfied as he regarded me with a level gaze. "Then as you undoubtedly know, nymphs are only interested in the more base of the instincts."

"Then I guess we're lucky that there aren't any trees down here." I said suspiciously. I didn't like the change in his demeanor, and I knew that his elaborate hand motions couldn't mean anything good for me.

"Trees? Ah. No. I'm afraid that water nymphs don't do *that*." He corrected with the air of a disapproving teacher. "You see, while they do crave a man's, shall we say, affections?" He hesitated, carefully choosing the word. "When they are finished with mating, they don't absorb him into their forest. No. They devour him." Somnus finished, his voice going hard as the corner of his lip twitched with the seething hatred I had witnessed before.

I swallowed hard and stole another glance to the water.

A small group of nymphs had come closer and were hovering just off shore. Several of them had risen out of the water far enough to reveal the swell of their full, plentiful breasts.

They were breathtaking.

Their skin shined with a moistened glow as the light from the cavern's ceiling glinted off every shade of perfect, pale flesh. Aware that she had caught my eye, one of the creatures swam even closer, arching her back in an effort to better display her mind-numbing attributes. Hair the color of blue, tropical waters, she lifted herself out of the lake to her navel and smiled, beckoning me closer with a playful curl of her webbed finger.

It was that smile that broke her spell and jolted me back to my senses. Her teeth, far too numerous for her small, pouty mouth were jagged and serrated like that of a shark.

"It's said that they've been known to eat their prey alive before copulation has even finished." He shrugged in an offhanded manner. "But by all means, don't take my word for it. I found that experience is often the best teacher in matters such as these."

Swinging his open hand in a backwards slapping motion, I barely had time to react as something heavy attacked me from behind. Instinctively rolling forward into what I considered a rather impressive somersault, I was met with a spray of hard sand. Stumbling to my feet I turned in an effort to keep my new attacker in the same line of site as the mage. Much to my surprise, instead of an accomplice, I came face to, well, palm with an enormous hand. Made completely out of sand, the phantom limb straightened and flexed in time with Somnus' movements.

The gestures. The spell. The bastard had made himself a dirt arm.

"Oh, come on!" I whined, motioning to the arm as it lurched forward for another strike. Leaping back I managed to sidestep the construct, and turned to face the still waving mage. "How is that fair?" I objected.

"Fair?" He scoffed, his face going red with concentration. "How is it fair that an unworthy simpleton such as yourself-" Grunting he took a labored swing at the air, but by focusing on his movements I was able to easily avoid the blow. "-is gifted with a healthy body and the power of the Gods-" He lashed out again, but the added layers of rock, while granting the ability to move and protection from attack, robbed him of his speed and the slap went wide. "-while those of us deserving of them-" Breathing heavily he brought his arm down in a crushing motion and the ground beside me exploded in a hailstorm of rocks and gritty sand. '-are cursed to live like this!"

For all my Shatner inspired Kirk-rolls and action film star levels of heroic dodging, I was getting pretty winded, and I could feel my muscles burning with the effort. Trying to keep one eye on the arm and the other on Somnus in order to gauge the direction of his next attack was beginning to take its toll, and I knew that I was growing sluggish.

Bellowing in frustration, the mage pulled back and slammed his fist downward. The magical arm, in response to the motion, pounded itself into the shoreline and quickly vanished from site.

"Well." I panted, using what little breath I had left in me to further antagonize the man. "Maybe you just need-"

The sand at my feet pitched wildly as Somnus curled his fist and pumped his arm in a vicious pantomime of an uppercut. Rocketed by the suddenly reappearing hand, I was thrown through the air, my clever retort ending in a startled yelp of surprise as I flew over the beach and into the inky black waters of the underground lake.

In that quiet, serene split-second of impact when you're plunged into an icy pool, the world went still and time itself seemed to slow to a stop.

Then the cold hit me.

I wanted to scream but I couldn't because my breath had frozen in my chest. Instinctively I righted myself and kicked, propelling my body upward, but dozens of strong hands seized my flailing limbs and held me helpless in their grasp.

The water nymphs. Panic induced terror powered my legs as I kicked harder and tried to lash out against them, but in their element they were far stronger than I was. Lungs burning, I opened my eyes only to find myself face to face with the blue haired creature that I had beckoned to me before.

Even underwater and obscured by motion and darkness, there was no denying her beauty. Her eyes were now a solid black, like those of the very shark her toothy maw embodied. Smiling that horrible chainsaw of a smile, the creature leaned forward and kissed me gently on the forehead. Then, much to my surprise, she and her sisters brought me swiftly to the surface, dragging me from the depths back to the shallower waters, where the safety of the lake's bottom shifted and crunched beneath my weight.

Coughing and sputtering, I staggered to my feet as waves created by my own panicked floundering, lapped at my thighs. Stumbling and nearly falling as I fought for balance, I spun in place as I cast my terrified eyes back upon my saviors.

Each and every one of them was hanging their head in a show of respect as they bent at the waist in a reverent bow. Confused, I looked back to the shoreline where Somnus and his big dumb dirt hand still stood, the rock-strewn limb as frozen as its master in its mimicking of his extended fist.

If I was dazed by the sudden turn of events, Somnus was nothing less than stunned.

"How?" He asked in a small, defeated voice. "How is this possible?" Flopping his arms to his side in a baffled shrug, he looked to me with imploring eyes as if begging to know my secret.

The blue-haired nymph was the first among us to move. Straightening her head, she offered a knowing, thankfully closed lipped smile, and swam closer. Cupping her hands in the water, she lifted them, the water within shimmering and twisting itself in her palms like molding clay as it formed a solid, unmistakable shape.

An acorn.

And then it dawned on me why I had been spared. Once, not that long ago, I had returned a stolen seed, the "heart of the forest" to one of them. Well, not to one of them actually; I had returned it to a wood nymph, or more succinctly, *the* wood nymph as she was their Matron. They might be primal, primitive creatures born of nature and instinct, but they still were capable of showing gratitude and thanks.

That single deed must have marked me somehow, to the point where others of their kind could sense it upon me. I knew then and there that no matter their behaviors and predispositions towards other men, these creatures were bound never to harm me.

Gently extending my hand, I curled my finger under the water nymph's chin and raised her averted eyes to mine as I nodded my appreciation. Smiling in an unspoken understanding, the nymph leapt backwards and dove into the lake, the water acorn disappearing back into the depths without a ripple.

Newfound allies in hand, I turned back to the shore as I waded deeper into the water, splashing playfully as I did.

"Come on in FDR." I taunted, not daring to approach the shore-line and the still awaiting magical arm. "The water's fine."

To his credit, Somnus seemed to take my sudden advantage in stride, smiling as he bowed his head in the briefest nods of respect.

"It would seem that I've underestimated you." He admitted.

"Yeah, you assholes just love to do that." I grinned, taking in a mouthful of the cold water and spitting it towards the shore.

Somnus accepted the jab with a tight lipped sneer as he moved to the water's edge.

"You circumvented the key guardian." He started. "Somehow managed to *corrupt* my Quicklings," The way he emphasized the word "corrupt" spoke volumes of his unhappiness. "Navigated the maze, and got past my minotaur."

"You mean Trevor?" I asked innocently, unable to resist the urge to rub it in. I wasn't sure how I was going to actually get out of the water, but I knew damn well that he wasn't about to get in, so I took a certain amount of joy in the gloating.

"Yes. Trevor." Somnus answered shortly. "It would appear that the rules of magic and the creatures born of it do not seem to apply to you, Agent Talik."

"I've never been really good at following the rules." I admitted it, making a show of enjoying my leisurely pool time.

"Indeed." He said coolly, before stepping into the lake.

Nearly choking on the mouthful of water that I was slurping up to spit at him, I slapped spastically at the lake's surface as I fought to regain my footing.

"But, I can't help but notice that you appear to have no such im-munity to more *physical* manifestations." He smiled shrewdly as he waded further in.

Whether bound by his magic, or some unspoken agreement, the nymphs made no attempts to either seduce or devour the smiling wiz-ard. If anything, they seemed repulsed by him and would disappear into the water, only to reappear several yards further away.

Matching my depth, Somnus began to spin his hands, twisting his fingers in the now-familiar arm movements that had spawned the sand hand that still lingered at the shore, its rocky fingers copying their owner's gestures with an eerie precision. The water at my waist pulled away, and I could feel the current at my back growing stronger as he continued.

"You're making a giant water hand, like right behind me, aren't you?" I asked humorlessly.

Not daring to turn around to verify my suspicions, I flickered my gaze to the small, tightly clustered group of nymphs in hopes of finding an ally. Instead I found them all staring; not at me, but at Somnus as he continued to cast whatever spell he and his dirt hand were weaving. They nymphs weren't looking at him in wanting, or even fear, but disgust.

"You're probably wondering why they're not attacking me." The wizard said in conversational tones, motioning to the group with his eyes as he continued his elaborate hand gestures.

He was stalling; probably so that he could finish his next spell or summon some nightmarish sea creature to pull me screaming into the briny deep. I glanced to the shore and weighed my choices, but the magical hand was still standing guard, and knew that it would take a swipe at me as the second my foot touched the shore.

"Is it because you're a dick?" I asked, turning back to fully face him. Maybe if I could make him mad enough, it would throw off his magic and give me a window of opportunity.

"It's because they can smell it on me." He said, deftly ignoring the insult.

"The cheap cologne?" I poked again. "Because I didn't want to say anything, but since you're mentioning it, goddamn."

"The sickness." He sighed with a tired roll of his eyes. "The death." The last word stalled him as it left his lips and he paused long enough to give the group of nymphs a contemptuous glare. "They may be stupid, feral animals, but their nature still drives them." He explained. "They want only strong, healthy men to mate with." There was a loathing in his voice; whether it was aimed at himself or them, I couldn't be certain. "And because of that, they will never desire me."

Desire.

My mind began to race and my pulse quickened. Sure, they might have had smiles ripped right from the nightmares of a British dentist, but they were still nymphs, right? Slowly reaching into my jacket, my fingers brushed against the small glass vial that Alistair had given me.

It was still there.

"Awww. Are the hot cheerleaders mean because they won't go to the prom with the creepy kid?" I mocked. "Personally, I don't think it has anything to do with you being sick." I countered, wading a bit closer to the shore. Somnus paused in his casting and the sand hand went rigid before matching my trajectory. "I mean, I've only met you twice and I can't stand you." I said, sliding back into the deeper waters, mentally removing that escape route from my plan. "Maybe they can just tell that you're an asshole." I shrugged.

Somnus sneered dangerously. "Tell me, will you be so glib when the life is being crushed from your body and your lungs fill with water?"

I could feel myself paling at the thought. I might be a smartass until the bitter end, but drowning didn't seem like a pleasant way to go. Hell, if it came to that, I'd make a dash for it and take my chances with the nymphs.

"Give me the bracelet and I promise to make your death swift and painless." He offered, grinning in self-satisfaction at my visible blanching.

I looked to the bracelet that I still clutched around my hand.

"And then what?" I asked. "You and your daughter get to live happily ever after?" I scoffed. "I don't think so. Face it Pebbles, even if you kill me, the Agency knows all about you and your dastardly deeds." I reminded him, hopefully using the word dastardly in its proper context. "No way this ends well for you."

Somnus stopped, his eyes going momentarily soft. "Do you honestly think that this has anything to do with me?" He asked, his voice tinged with sadness. "Do you have children, Agent Talik?"

"Not that I'm aware of." I answered with slow suspicion. "Although there were a few times in the heat of the moment where I was all "Hey, why not?", and I didn't use a-"

"Then you do not know love." He said with certainty, cutting me off. It wasn't a harsh statement, or one crafted to throw me off, but a simple, honest truth. Glancing down at the water, he gave a forlorn smile before looking up at me through the tops of his eyes. "Oh, I have no doubt that you know sex. Lust. Maybe even actual fondness for someone besides yourself." He clarified.

"Hey." I protested.

"But until you have a child, the true meaning of the word is lost to you." He continued, ignoring my objection. "It's like trying to explain fire to a dog. The animal might appreciate the warmth, but it lacks the capacity to actually understand what drives the flame." Somnus sighed and slowly shook his head as if chiding himself for even trying to explain his motives. "The bracelet will only work for her Agent Talik, that was the deal. I may be dying, but my daughter will live a long, full and healthy life."

Whatever compassion or humanity that he had fueling his words, left with that final statement, and his eyes went hard. "Now, give me the fucking bracelet." He hissed.

Looking to my hand, I stared at the modified controller before turning back to Somnus, his words resonating with a meaning that I was on the edge of grasping.

"Wait a minute." I said, suddenly understanding. "Deal? What deal?" I asked, but he didn't have to answer.

It was the magic; his unprecedented control over its forces and this place! The brotherhood of Merlin *were* a bunch of wannabes. There was no real power there, its claim to a bloodline was meaningless. Which meant that...

"Someone told you about me!" I blurted out. "They're the ones who gave you all of this." I gestured around the cavern with a closed fist. "And they sent you after me that night in the parking lot."

It was all finally making some weird sort of sense.

Somnus bobbed his head in acknowledgement. "It would seem you're not as stupid as I initially thought. Pity." He lifted his hand far above his head and the water strained behind me, rushing past my legs. "Goodbye Agent Talik." He said, drawing his fingers into a tight fist.

"Wait wait wait!" I yelled, the vial that I had removed from my coat pocket now hidden in my closed hand.

The wizard paused with his arm above his head in a striking motion and arched a curious eyebrow.

"You said that the nymphs don't desire you, right?" I asked shakily.

Rolling his eyes, Somnus pulled back his arm and focused his spell.

"How about we fix that?" I asked as I threw the small glass vial with all of my might, aiming for the center of the magician's stone covered chest.

With his concentration broken by the unexpected attack, Somnus brought his arm down in a quick sweeping motion and deftly snatched the missile out of the air with one stone-gloved hand. Shattering on impact, the mage smiled victoriously as a light, creamy brown liquid began to ooze out from between his closed fingers.

"And what did you expe-" He started to ask before he was overcome by a sudden, powerful stench.

Chocolate. Pure, raw, concentrated chocolate.

It wafted through the air like an invisible fog, its sickly sweet scent potent to the point of nauseating. I turned my head and held my breath, but it was overwhelming and I soon found myself growing dizzy with its intensity.

Gagging, Somnus flung the remains of the vial away in disgust, rubbing his hand down the front of his magical armor in a vain attempt to push away the smell.

"Chocolate?" He retched in disbelief. "You thought to defeat me with *chocolate*?" Despite his dry heaving, he seemed almost amused by the very idea. "What were you hoping that this would to do me?"

"Not you." I gasped. Fighting for breath, I pressed the back of my hand against my nose and tried to focus on anything but the smell as I looked to the water nymphs. "Them."

I had always heard that sharks were capable of smelling a single drop of blood in a million drops of water, and I was praying that the same could be said about the sharp toothed nymphs. While I was never exactly a quick study, one of the few facts that I knew from experience was that the shapely creatures went absolutely bonkers for chocolate. It was like catnip to them; an honest-to-god aphrodisiac, unlike those empty promises in the back of the discount porno magazines that I never read as a kid.

What I did read however, in one of the countless books that Raegan was constantly forcing upon me, was the fact that the Swiss had absolutely nothing on the Elves. Elven chocolate was a rare and prized commodity, and considered the undisputed best of either world. Its concentrated essence was enough to bring even the Queen of the Fae shaking to her knees with desire, and well...

...with Lydia being of nymph blood and all, let's just say that it promised to make our nightly sessions even more memorable than they already were.

So, cashing in a few favors, I had managed to acquire a single vial of the stuff from Alistair, in what he swore to be its purest form. And while it pained me to waste it, especially after witnessing my girlfriend's piqued interest in the creamy liquid, I was praying that it just might save my skin.

Somnus' eyes widened in understanding as he followed my gaze to the small group of aquatic fairies.

The nymphs were motionless.

Eerily still like pale, half submerged statues marking the ruins of a forgotten city, their eyes had expanded to impossible proportions and their collective pupils dilated to the point of pain. Slowly, one by one, they sank into the water without a trace.

The wizard let out a sigh of relief and smiled triumphantly. "It would seem that your little plan has fail-"

There was an explosion of water as a nymph leapt from the depths in front of him, throwing the man off balance as he scarcely managed to avoid being tackled by the creature. Another burst from the shallow waters behind him, leaping upon his back and wrapping her shapely arms and legs around him. Somnus cried out in surprise as the others joined in, launching themselves out of the lake in a desperate, frantic display of unquenchable lust.

D. H. Irving

"GET THEM OMMFPH!" He screamed, only to have his words muffled by a deep, frenzied kiss from one of the nymphs. Fresh blood trickled from the corners of their joined mouths as the frail mage faltered under their weight. Tumbling backwards in a tangled knot of writhing bodies and supple limbs, Somnus was quickly pulled into the deeper waters which began to froth and churn with their feverous thrashing.

At the shore, the magically conjured hand twitched and shuttered before dissolving with a crash into a collapsed pile of coarse sand and rock. Taking that as my cue that open swim was now done for the day, I quickly and awkwardly ran-waded to the beach, throwing myself out of the water as I scrambled to put some distance between myself and the lust induced carnage.

The nymphs may have honored me, or marked me in some fashion for having saved one of them, but I doubted that even the Matron's boon would hold up in the wake of a freaky chocolate sex frenzy.

The water bubbled and stewed at the spot, the white lather of activity darkening to a telling crimson before finally going still, leaving only a spreading pool of blood and the sweet scent of cocoa to mark the place where Somnus the Wizard had once stood.

Pulling myself to my feet, I glanced around the now quiet cavern and blinked rapidly as I tried to process everything that I had just witnessed.

Chapter Twenty-One

For a full minute, I did nothing more than stand there, dripping in uncertain silence.

Dying waves lapped weakly at the shore as the lake's waters once again grew still, marred only by the occasional soft splash or gentle ripple stirred by the still lurking nymphs. With their feeding frenzy finished as abruptly as it had started, they had retreated to deeper waters, the scent of chocolate still lingering in the air.

There were only a few of them now. The others, their lust presumably sated by whatever fate befell Somnus, were gone, leaving only a handful of younger looking nymphs bobbing in the distance. While they kept a respectful distance, their eyes were still black with longing, and it gave them a frightening, almost alien appearance in the dim light.

One of the creatures started to swim closer, only to be pulled back to the fold by several of her less hungry sisters. Smiling seductively, her eyes never left mine as she was restrained. Her tongue darted pink against her pale skin and she chewed at the corner of her lip in wanton desire.

Luckily for me, that coy little lip bite is a lot harder to sell when your mouth looks like the inside of a blender.

Knowing that the longer I stayed, the more danger I was putting myself in, I moved to the edge of the stony path that divided the dark waters, leading to the opposite shore. Testing a rock with the toe of my shoe, I put a bit of tentative weight on it and was relieved to feel no play or give. I didn't know how quickly I would need to pick my way across the jutting rocks, but with the whole place reeking of fairy Spanish Fly, I really didn't want to find myself surrounded and stranded at the middle.

With one eye on the nymphs and the other on the slippery path, I took a deep, determined breath and stepped off the beach. Focusing on the cave at the opposite shore I moved at a steady pace, taking care to not show signs of slowing or hesitation as I crossed. There was a ripple of excitement in the direction of the nymphs, and the water lapped more forcefully at the soles of my feet, but nothing attempted to bar my way as I made my hurried journey.

Shifting underfoot, the gravelly sand gave a satisfying crunch as I all but leapt from the walkway to the beach. Spinning as I landed, I shot a panicked glance to the water, but the lake was now empty. The nymphs were gone, and I was once again alone.

The mouth of the cave was far from a natural occurrence, its opening carved into the cavern's rock wall with the same familiar craftsmanship and precision that I had noted in the Keep. Lit by two brightly burning torches that served as a beacon in the surrounding darkness, even at this distance I could see the scattering of rock and dirt as it gave way to steady flooring. A soft, steady light radiated from the room's interior, its glow pushing back against the flicker of flame that illuminated the beach.

Be careful. I could almost hear Raegan's voice in my head as I drew near, mothering me in her absence.

While the outside of the cave may have seemed like the entrance to a medieval dungeon, the interior was anything but archaic. Clean, smooth marble floors connected to pristine white tiled walls that climbed to a domed, finished ceiling. Fogged globes of frosted glass bobbed in the air far above, bathing all that lay beneath in a perfect imitation of florescent light.

Besides a pair of out of place work stations dotted with laboratory equipment and stacks of old books, the room appeared to have been furnished into a small, makeshift hospital. Several small beds, nearly hidden behind the corners of their cloth privacy screens, lay tucked neatly into a series of indented alcoves, their occupants unmoving as I approached.

The missing girls.

Dressed in white gowns, their hair had been carefully brushed and their bodies positioned in a mimicry of sleep. Moving to the side of the nearest girl I nudged her gently, but there was no response. Lifting her wrist, I felt for a pulse, and panicked for a moment when I could find none.

"Please don't be dead." I pleaded, dropping her arm as I reached up and pried open her eyelid, uncertain of exactly what I was looking for.

Still clear and not clouded with finality of death, there was no movement to her eye, and her pupil showed no signs of dilation. Placing my hand on her forehead, I softly touched the girl's skin which felt warm and flushed against my own. Heart racing, I tried to remember the basics of CPR when a thought, still echoing in Raegan's voice, rang faintly in my ears.

The latrodenzian induced a trance-like state; maybe she wasn't dead, but in some sort of stasis.

Carefully turning her head to the side, I ran my fingers through the soft hair at the base of her skull as I searched for any hint of the small mechanical spider. Something smooth and metallic twitched as I probed, and letting out a soft groan of discomfort, the girl's face wrinkled in a display of distant pain.

She was alive.

I let out a breath of relief and scanned the room. There had to be something that I could use, some sort of device that would let me turn off or remove the creature without hurting its host. Stepping from her side, I started to head back towards the pair of lab benches when

I noticed a large shape slumped on the floor at the base of an empty bed.

Either too large to fit or too heavy to be lifted, Maxine had been dumped unceremoniously at the foot of an alcove, her face flush with the hard marble that she now laid upon. Checking her as I did the first girl, I was happy to note that while in the same unconscious condition, she seemed no worse for wear. Raising her head, I carefully turned it to the side before lowering it back to the cold surface of the floor.

"Sorry Max." I apologized, grabbing the comforter from the bed and dragging it off to cover her. "You didn't deser-"

Wincing, I brought my hand to my forehead and pressed my thumb and index finger into my temples in an effort to keep an old familiar pain at bay. The headache was incredible, and for a moment it was all that I could focus on. I hadn't slept, hadn't eaten, and had been walking for what felt like years. I was tired, hungry and growing sicker and sicker of this place by the minute, so I guess I really shouldn't have been surprised when one of my migraines of old showed up to poop out a cherry for the top of the shit-sundae that this little adventure had become.

The throbbing in my head vanished without warning and left me woozy with remembered pain. My ears rang with phantom silence and I looked around the room in a disconnected, almost dreamlike state. Everything seemed too still, too quiet; like the first few moments after sleep where you're not one hundred percent sure that you're really awake. Shaking my head I took a breath and felt the world begin to move again as I glanced around the improvised infirmary, a new sensation replacing the pain of old.

I was being watched.

Spinning in place, I could feel eyes on me where there were none and my skin began to crawl. Turning to one of the dimmer corners of the room, I narrowed my eyes but found no one. It wasn't brightly lit, but there was more than enough ambient light to foil any intruder's attempt to blend in with the shadows.

"Who's there?" I called out, putting a bit of bass in my voice for effect.

Only silence answered.

Frowning, I slowly canvased the room with my eyes, and although I found nothing, I refused to dismiss the feeling as mere foolishness. My gut had served me well in the past, often snatching the role of compass out of the hands of reason or sensibility. And while I was definitely beginning to doubt myself, I wasn't ready to give up quite yet as I could still feel an invisible gaze weighing upon me.

A sliver of pain, almost gentle in its prodding sent a ripple of electricity through my brain, as if a memory was fighting for life somewhere in the deep recesses of my mind. I tried to focus on the shock, but no thoughts or sudden epiphanies came bursting forth, just that old familiar feeling I used to get back when…

"It's Fenrus, right?" I asked, suddenly sure of the source behind my headache.

There was no response.

"I don't think that we were ever properly introduced." I continued, looking around for any signs of life.

Still only silence answered.

"Look, I know you're there." I bluffed. I was starting to feel rather silly and the tendrils of doubt were creeping back in, but still I pressed. "And judging from that crappy dye job on your beard that you're fooling absolutely no one with, I'm guessing that we're both way too old for all of this hide and seek bullshit." I said, turning to the darkest of the room's corners and crossing my arms.

I was trying my best to seem blasé, but my resolve was starting to fade as that sneaking doubt began to devour the last of my suspicions. Lifting my head and sighing heavily, I rolled my eyes in exasperation, both at the situation and myself, and was starting to turn away when the shadows began to swirl and darken. Clouding the purest of black, they stormed and raged and then evaporated, leaving a small, black clad leprechaun in their wake.

Stepping forward he locked his dull green eyes on mine and pursed his lips in an irritated show of concession.

"How?" He asked, cocking an eyebrow. The single word asked a thousand questions, and even hinted at a grain of begrudging respect.

"Easy." I shrugged, trying to keep up the air of confidence despite the fact that I was facing not only a powerful Fae, but one that apparently didn't like me very much. "You were the dramatically introduced but quickly forgotten secondary character."

My explanation was met with only a deepening of annoyance and a cold, stony gaze.

"Am I the only one in the world who still watches Scooby Doo?" I asked rhetorically as we began to slowly circle one another. He wore the demeanor of a closing shark, wherein I suspected that I looked very much like something that the shark wanted to punch repeatedly.

"My brother's coin." Fenrus said with a look of understanding as he glanced to the top of my head.

"Never leave home without it." I confirmed, lightly tapping my temple.

The dark leprechaun stopped his predatory pacing and frowned. "Well." He said, somewhat deflated. "This is a rather awkward situation, isn't it?" Fenrus spoke with a practiced cadence, as if his every word had been carefully rehearsed. Unlike my poker buddies, his accent was barely noticeable, if there at all.

"So now what?" I asked. I didn't really know what to say or do, but something told me that I should try to stay on his good side.

Fenrus shrugged somewhat dismissively. "To be perfectly honest, I was really hoping that the wizard would have taken care of you." He admitted. "This would have been so much simpler." He sighed regretfully. "All that effort and energy, wasted."

"Yeah well, promising to fix his kid was kind of a shitty move." I said dryly. Part of me couldn't help but sympathize with Somnus' plight. He might have been a first class, grade-A dick, but in the end the guy was still just trying to save his daughter.

Unused to being spoken to so candidly, the dark Fae raised a single eyebrow and regarded me with a dangerous sort of contempt. The gesture while slight, was pant-shittingly intimidating as I immediately remembered the incredible power that his kind could wield without breaking a sweat.

"I merely granted a wish." He explained, spreading his hands in feigned innocence. "After all, he did manage to capture me, and those are the rules."

"Yeah, I bet it was quite the chase." I said sarcastically.

Fenrus forced himself to smile, scorn dripping from the corners of his upturned mouth. "Still." He said meeting my eye. "As much as it pains me to do so, it appears that I'm going to have to handle this little situation, myself." He sighed, looking down at his hands. "I do despise getting my fingers dirty, but desperate times and all of that."

The evil leprechaun took a single step forward and I yelped, throwing my hands up into the short space that separated us.

"Whoooa. Whoooa. Easy there Edward Teach." I panicked, trying to stay the creature. "You're not allowed to touch me, remember?" I cautioned as I continued to back up nonetheless.

"Oh, I'm not am I?" He paused, amused.

"The Norn-"I started.

"Isn't here." He finished for me. Looking around the small cave he spread his hands again in that same blameless gesture. "And with your unprecedented, and frankly unpredictable nature," He said innocently. "Who is to say what really happened to you in a nasty place such as this?"

Eyes glinting with cruelty, the leprechaun's lips curled into an angry snarl as he took another step towards me.

I swallowed hard and closed my eyes. After all the beard jokes, I had no doubt that this was going to sting just a little.

"That would be us." A familiar voice announced.

Materializing in mid-step, Seamus and the boys stepped out of thin air and moved in front of me forming a short, but protective barrier between Fenrus and I.

The black Fae not only halted in his stalking advance, but backpedaled several feet, his eyes opening in alarm.

"Hey there Johnny." Padraig greeted with a quick jerk of his head, barely glancing back at me.

"Hey there Paddy." I grinned, my pulse slowing to a mere thousand beats per second at the sudden appearance of my friends.

"You okay?" Beircheart asked.

"Never better." I lied.

"This…this is impossible." Fenrus stammered as he tried to regain his composure. Like a thief trapped in a police spotlight, the color had drained from his already pale face, as he was caught completely off guard.

Michail snorted a sharp bark of a laugh and spit at the ground between them. "That word don't apply to us. Even you should know that by now, ya black little snake."

His spine stiffening at the insult, Fenrus sneered, but his eyes were still flickering with fear as he tried to figure out how he had been out maneuvered. "How? How then? Not even the Norn can see him!" He protested, crooking a shaking finger in my direction.

"Aye, she can't." Beircheart agreed. "But we weren't keepin' an eye on *him*, now were we?" He asked, slowing his words and punctuating them with meaning.

Fenrus stared in silent confusion.

"Oh fer the love of - we were watching you, ya dunderhead." Michail explained with a roll of his eyes.

The dark leprechaun's look of confusion melted into that of insult and rage. "How dare ya!" He hissed, his true accent breaking through his practiced façade for the briefest of seconds. Calming himself with a short, angry breath he sneered through clenched teeth. "Spying on one of your own? That goes against every-"

"And it seems like we had a good cause for doin' it too, don't it?" Padraig chided, cutting him off.

Fenrus soured considerably and crossed his arms in stubborn indignation. "I have done nothing to warrant your suspicions." He insisted. "You had no right to violate-"

"No right?" Seamus asked incredulously. "So yer tellin' me tha' you had no hand in tha targetin' of our boy here? Is that what yer sayin'?" He scoffed, his voice lilting high. "So we're jus' supposed ta believe that yer pet wizard jus' happened to go an' figure all of this out with no help at all from you or yours?"

Fenrus cracked a dark, arrogant smile. "Where's your evidence?"

He asked. "We both know that you can't prove anything Seamus." He taunted.

"Oh. Oh no." Padraig laughed waving a hand. "I think yer misunderstandin' our intentions here." He chuckled. "We don't *need* ta prove anything." He explained.

"Aye." Michail agreed. "We would only need evidence if we were actually plannin' on taking you in." He smiled with dangerous meaning. Balling up a meaty fist he took a menacing step towards his dark counterpart.

Scrambling backwards, Fenrus raised a hand in defense of a blow that never came. "You wouldn't!" He yelped, his frightened gaze on Seamus who stayed Michail with a motion of his hand.

"I'm gunna say this one time, darkling." Seamus said to Fenrus, his voice deep with warning. "Walk away." He ordered, his fingers going flat as he reaffirmed his command to Michail who seemed all too eager to initiate an attack. "Walk away now and leave our boy be. Give us yer Oath and this is the end of it." There was a gentleness to the words that I didn't expect, a soft pleading from one leprechaun to another.

If the words were meant to mollify, they had the exact opposite effect as Fenrus bristled and put on a cocky air. "Who do you think you are to make demands of me?" He scoffed. "You have no authority over-"

"We have every authority!" Seamus thundered. "He's our ward, under our care and he sits at our goddamn table!"

Fenrus stepped forward, ignoring Michail as he defiantly met Seamus's eye. "And you make a mockery of our ways! This, this *abomination* has no right to walk among us! Your pet has-"

Seamus moved faster than my eye could follow, blurring forward at a speed that would have impressed even the Quicklings as he struck Fenrus across the face with the back of his hand. The slap, while loud and startling, was more for show than injury and the dark leprechaun stumbled in place.

"You speak to me of rights?" Seamus asked in a low growl. "Our boy here has earned more rights by us than a twisted lil' Unseelie bastard such as yerself will know!"

"You can't-" Fenrus whimpered, holding his hand to his reddening cheek.

"I can't?" Seamus repeated, raising his hand in the promise of another blow and causing Fenrus to flinch. "I can't? No ya devious lil' bastard, I *shouldn't*." He grumbled in disgust as he tried to calm his own temper. "I shouldn't, but I damn well can. There's a universe of meanin' that dances in the space between those two words and it would serve ya well to learn tha difference."

Fenrus fell silent, but backed away, refusing to meet Seamus's angry glare.

"Ya went against the Norn." Mike said, breaking the brief silence.

"That don't sit too lightly." Padraig added, singing his words.

"I did nothing." Fenrus insisted defiantly.

"Oh páiste," Bierchart chided. "Ya did enough."

Seamus nodded his agreement and pointed a finger at the dark leprechaun. "I'm not repeatin' my offer, Fenrus." He promised. "Swear it. Swear on yer blood that ya will leave Johnny be, and you walk away from this no worse for wear, if not a lil' wiser. Don't and..." He shrugged, letting his words hang.

Fenrus' eyes went wild with insult. "And what?" He jeered. "You'll threaten me? Mebbe slap me aroun' some more? And why? Because you'd choose that feckin' human, over yer own kin?" He roared in outrage, his true accent slipping through his frustration.

"Careful who yer callin' kin." Mike spat.

"Aye. And tha' human there is more family to us than you'll ever be." Beircheart agreed.

"Family." Fenrus scoffed. "When I take my rightful place-"

"No." Padraig said cutting him off with a sad shake of his head. "You have no place. Not at our table, nor in our company."

"And ya never will." Beircheart said simply.

Fenrus' body went limp with shock, his arms slowly falling to his sides as if the full implication behind their words were hitting him for the first time. Fear, insult, and honest sorrow brimmed his eyes as he looked between them.

"Ya can't." He said in a small voice.

"There's that word again." Seamus cautioned.

"Seamus." Fenrus stepped closer, his words soft with loss. "Listen ta reason, surely this pathetic creature isn't-"

"You dishonor your brother's memory." Seamus said sternly, meeting the man mid-stride. "A memory not only kept alive, but made right by that pathetic creature." He echoed the term scornfully. "Fergus chose a stranger's help; a human's help, over that of his own brother." His voice went low. "That speaks volumes."

"Fergus was a fool." Fenrus grumbled, casting an angry eye in my direction. "As are you Seamus, if you think that I honestly believe that the council would ever take that shaved ape's voice, over mine."

"You have no voice." Seamus said icily. "And on my blood and on my oath, you never will."

While the true meaning of those words were lost on me, they struck Fenrus like a physical blow and he stumbled backwards, anguish and a knowing dread washing over his features. The others said nothing, watching in somber agreement as the dark leprechauns eyes welled with anger and rage induced tears.

"You think that means anythin'?" His voice cracked. "That yer words hold any power over me? You think that yer pet is safe?" With a desperate, maniacal laugh, the evil Fae backed further away, stumbling into one of the work benches. "I don't need you!" He insisted, scrambling against the table. "I don't need any of you!"

The leprechaun council simply stared in somber silence, each of them now standing side by side; a wall of solidarity forged by Seamus' decision.

"And I don't need him!" Fenrus declared, pointing a shaking finger in my direction. "So ya wish to join them, do ya? Rob me of my rightful place?" He sneered, his eyes frantic as they danced over me. "Well then, wish granted!" He laughed, reaching into the folds of his black coat.

The barrier of protective leprechauns exchanged a quick set of worried glances before returning their now uneasy focus back to Fenrus.

"Lemme be tha first of many ta welcome ya into the fold!" Pulling his hand from the inside of his jacket, he held up a small, metallic globe of shimmering gold. Crushing it in his hand with an audible pop, he threw a handful of iridescent powder into the air, where it formed a brightly glowing symbol that hissed and popped before falling to the ground in a twinkling of swirling glitter.

"Let every creature, dark or light know what you truly are!" Fenrus' voice boomed as it reverberated throughout the small chamber. "I call upon our brothers and sisters to reclaim what is rightfully ours, and if we cannot, may the Collector himself come forth to retrieve it!"

An audible gasp rippled down the line of leprechauns as Fenrus' words died in his throat, his eyes crazed with triumph as the room fell eerily silent.

"What have ya done?" Seamus asked numbly as he looked at the dark Fae, following his fevered gaze to me.

"What have I done?" Fenrus asked with an insane, scornful laugh. "I've returned order to this mockery!" He grinned as he backed towards the corner from which he had first appeared. "It will be mine Seamus, eventually." He considered. "Even you can't stop what's coming. None of you can!" He shouted with demented glee.

Before the others could react, the darkness behind him deepened and swirled as the shadows swallowed the dark leprechaun, leaving only the ghosts of his mocking laughter to mark the spot where he once stood.

The others looked between themselves, their faces solemn in their exchange of worried frowns.

"Well, that can't be good." I said, not understanding what had just happened, but knowing that it probably wasn't all kittens and kisses. "One of you want to explain what that was, or why I have the sudden, overwhelming urge to piss myself?" I asked.

"Paddy?" Seamus inquired quietly, with a nod of his head.

Moving to the still settling film of golden dust, Padraig knelt and careful dragged his pinkie over its glimmering surface. Lifting it to his mouth, he touched his finger to his tongue before spitting in disgust.

Looking up to Seamus, he slowly shook his head and sighed. "It's done."

Seamus cursed under his breath, and lifted a hand to his forehead. Michail, in response to his companion's swearing let out a new and amazing vulgarity that would have normally impressed the hell out of me, were I not confused and for some reason, extremely nervous.

"Guys?" I prodded, my groin tingling with that sinking feeling usually reserved for rollercoasters and pregnancy scares.

"He did it." Seamus said in soft disbelief. "The little ponce really did it."

"Did what?" I pressed.

Turning to me, Seamus put on a false but bright smile that did nothing but strengthen my fear. "It's nothin' lad." He assured me. "No worries. It ain't nothin' we can't fix, eh boys?" He asked, looking to the others to back him up.

"Bullshit." I challenged. I had played poker with them long enough to know when one of them was lying, and right now Seamus was laying it on with a trowel. "What did he do Seamus?" I demanded.

"He announced it lad." Beircheart said quietly. "He announced it to tha world."

"Announced what?" I asked, still not understanding.

"You." Seamus sighed.

"I don't follow." I said, growing frustrated.

"He announced you, ya idjit." Mike said, his normally gruff voice tinged with sadness. "What ya are, an' what you've got goin' on in that big misshapen melon of yours." He teased, but there was no real humor behind the words.

"Wait. What?" I blinked in alarm. "Um, I thought you guys said he would never, ever do that?" I reminded them.

"Yeah, well, he's a nutter now ain't he?" Mike countered.

"That's well an' good." Padraig said, standing as he moved to Seamus' side. "But what about the Collector?" He asked in not-so hushed tones.

Seamus looked troubled at the mention of the name, and darkened in thought.

"Yeah, what about the Collector?" I parroted. "Or better yet, what in the hell is a Collector?" I asked, not knowing what the creature was, but fearing it none-the-less.

Seamus shook his head and threw out his arms in focus. "That don't matter." He said certainly. "We've got plenty of time, so we'll worry about that mess when we need to. Right now," He looked to me, and I could see the concern in his eye. "We need to get you out of here before-"

The room began to shake.

Rumbling beneath our feet like a very real, very non-magical earthquake, the walls cracked and groaned and dust rained from the ceiling. Several beakers and test tubes rolled from their overturned spots upon the work benches and shattered as they fell to the floor.

"That happens." Seamus finished wryly as the room shivered to a still vibrating standstill.

"I'm guessing that's bad." I said, pointing to the ceiling where a large crack had appeared.

Michail actually laughed at that, and gave me an appreciative smile. "Yer a genius, you are." He grinned before turning to Seamus. "I think it's time for us to be goi-"

And just like that, they were gone.

All of them.

No flash of light, no swirling mists, not even a snap of magic as they vanished from sight. Michail's words still hung in the air, severed from their speaker. The ground shook again, and this time one of the empty beds moved several feet, the privacy screen beside it tipping over it and clattering to the ground.

"Okay guys." I swallowed hard. "You got me. Ha ha." I said, refusing to believe that they were really gone. "Veeerrry funny." I drew out the words as I sarcastically waved my hands in the air. "OoOh. Let's pretend that the cave is going to collapse and then disappear so that John thinks we left him to die." As if to punctuate the joke, the room quivered in an aftershock before falling deadly silent.

I closed my eyes and focused, but there was nothing. I couldn't sense them, or feel their presence in any way. They were really gone.

"Well shit." I swore, cursing my luck.

Scanning the room, I looked to the three girls and Max and weighed my options.

I could carry one, hell, maybe even two of the girls if I could manage to sling them over each shoulder, but that would mean leaving one of them behind. And Max; there was no way in hell that I was going to lift her. Even if she didn't weigh a ton, she was at least two feet taller than I was and made up almost entirely of long, heavily muscled limbs.

"Goddamnit." I cursed again. If only they were awake; we'd at least have a chance.

And then I remembered the bracelet.

Lifting my arm I narrowed my eyes in examination of the jewelry. Thin metal bands, almost like strands of spider's web encircled my wrist, weaving in and out of small silver beads that melted seamlessly into the blood colored gems adorning its face. There was no hook or clasp, just a continuous loop of metal; but it was pretty thin and appeared to be incredibly delicate.

"Well." I considered as I slipped it off my wrist. "This is either going to kill them instantly," I clenched my teeth as the room gave another short, but violent shake. "Or it'll wake them up just in time to be buried alive under a ton of dirt and rock." I grumbled, grasping the bracelet in both hands.

Pulling it in each direction, I tested the jewelry's strength and although surprisingly strong, I felt the metal give a little as it straightened against my tugging. Taking a deep breath, I heaved with all of the strength I could muster, hunkering down with a grunt as I did. Popping and twinging it in my grasp, I could feel the gems shifting as they began to break loose from their webbed settings, the tearing sensation only spurring me on as I pulled with all of my might.

My fingers went numb as the metal cut into my flesh, but I could feel the bracelet stretching in my grasp. With one last jerk and a scream of pain, I was rewarded with loud snap that was immediately followed by a burst of hot, blinding red light.

Lifted from my feet by a blast of magical energy, my ears rang as I closed my eyes and prayed for a quick death, my body going limp as I was flung out of the room and back into the cavern.

Chapter Twenty-Two

"Is he dead?" A quiet voice asked in worried tones. It sounded young, female, and more than a little disgusted by the possibilities of the question it had just posed. "He looks like he's dead."

"Oh! I think I saw his hand move." A second female voice exclaimed enthusiastically.

"Touch him." Suggested a third.

"You touch him!"

"Ew, no. You!"

A moment later I was vaguely aware of something hard and pointy prodding me roughly in the ribs. Moaning in agony, I tried to lift my arm to swat away the unwelcomed poking, but it felt as if it weighed a thousand pounds. Whether or not I connected with anything, I wasn't sure, but the gesture brought a chorus of startled screams that ripped through my head like a referee's whistle.

"Miss Stonebridge!" One of the voices cried out in alarm.

Fighting through a ruby red cloud of pain, I pushed myself clumsily to a sitting position and tried to focus my vision past the blurring shapes that whirled around me in a haze of shrill voices. Something large and solid blotted out the ambient light and forced its way into the foreground of my sight. Squinting my eyes, it took me a few seconds to recognize the meaty object for what it was.

"You okay?" Maxine looked down at me, her offered hand still bobbing in front of my face like an oversized catcher's mitt.

"I think so." I groaned, clasping her by the wrist. With a powerful but steady pull, she hoisted me effortlessly to my feet. Tipping a bit, I wobbled and swayed unsteadily as I tried to regain control of my legs. Clearing the cobwebs with a shake of my head, I groggily took in my surroundings and the small group of girls nervously hiding behind the enormous security guard.

The missing students.

"Oh thank god." I sighed, wiping at my eyes. "It worked." I smiled weakly before noting that one of them, a short, olive complexioned girl, was holding a long gnarled branch of wood in her small hands. "And, ow, by the way." I grumbled, frowning at her in disapproval. "Where in the hell did you even *find* a stick?" I asked, rubbing my side.

Before the girl could answer, the rocky beach rumbled and shook, and I was sent stumbling into Max who easily caught me in her massive arms, and kept me from falling back to the ground that she had just pulled me from.

"That your doing?" She asked perceptively.

"Sort of, yeah." I admitted as I pulled away. She looked, well, smaller. Don't get me wrong, the woman was still an amazon by any definition of the word, but her clothes no longer strained and stretched to contain her impressive form. Whatever it was that had affected her, was gone.

"Where's Raegan?" She asked solemnly as if fearing the response.

I jerked my thumb over my shoulder towards the opposite shore of the lake. "I left her with Vivi-"

"What?!" Max cried out, her head snapping to the distance as she followed my gesture. "We have to get her, now!" She insisted, stomping across the beach and to the water's edge.

"Max, wait." I called to her weakly as I turned and tried my best not to slip on the rocky sand.

"You don't understand!" She shook, her voice full of dread. "It was Viviane! She's his daughter!"

"I know, I know." I nodded, closing my eyes with a dismissive wave of my hand. "We took care of it." I explained. The temperature by the lake was noticeably cooler, and I felt some of my strength returning as I took a deep breath and drew in the damp, soothing air.

"How?" Max asked, regarding me with noticeable suspicion. I couldn't blame her really; if Viviane was able to take her down, it only stood to reason that I should have been an even easier target.

Holding up the remains of the broken bracelet that I still clutched in my hand, I tossed it across the beach. It landed at her feet with a metallic clang as it bounced across the rocks. The gems, no longer powered by whatever dark magic Somnus had used were dull and lifeless, several of them showing large chips and cracks across their once smooth faces.

"It was what was keeping her from going all rubber-legged like dear old dad." I explained. The disorientation from the blast was finally fading and I was starting to feel more like my normal battered, beaten, and rudely poked self. "So I guess breaking it actually worked." I added in afterthought, thankful for the fact that I hadn't killed them all, and myself in the process.

"Okay, so what's the play?" Max asked, stepping away from the lake. "And, where in the hell are we?" With her fear for Raegan's safety abating, the enormity of the underground cavern was finally grabbing her attention.

"Somnus' secret hideout, I think." I guessed, meeting her halfway. "And the play is to find Raegan." I said, pointing across the dark waters to the opposite shore. "She should still be back at the library guarding the kid."

"John!" Ronnie's voice echoed throughout the chamber.

"Or you know, right over there." I amended. "Jesus, how long was I out?" The sudden realization that my next cat-scan was going to have more colors than a fractal painting quickened my pulse as Max and I stared over the water.

"You three stay here." Max instructed, nodding her head to the close cluster of girls. "C'mon J.T." She ordered, and following her lead we took off at a careful jog across the narrow path of wet stones. The cavern shook as we ran and we were peppered by falling rocks and debris that bounced painfully off our skin and disrupted the mirror-like sheen of the lake. I scanned the ripples for signs of life as we quickened our pace, but no nymphs appeared.

I hit the shoreline a good ten strides behind Maxine, just as Raegan exited the tunnel and stepped out onto the beach. Her head was tucked under the arm of a mostly unconscious Viviane who was being more dragged by the Keeper than actually walking on her own.

The girl looked horrible. Pale and sickly, her free arm was bent at an odd angle and her hands were twisted painfully as they formed gnarled fists. Viviane's eyes lolled freely in their sockets and her breath came in sharp, rasping bursts.

"You okay?" I asked, checking my sister for signs of injury. Other than the wounds sustained by the once super-powered teenager, she looked largely unharmed.

"Yeah, you?" She nodded, giving me the same once over.

"A little frazzled, but alive." I smiled in relief. "Plus, I found the girls. And Max." I nodded my head needlessly in the direction of the large woman.

"Jesus Ray Ray, what did you to do her?" Max breathed, easily taking the small girl from Raegan's arms and lifting her into a cradled position.

Raegan frowned and shook her head. Despite all that had happened, her eyes still darkened with worry as they fell upon Viviane's unconscious form. "Removing the bracelet must have triggered something." She said guiltily. "And now-"

The world shook around us as something large fell into the lake with a loud splash that showered us in a spray of cold water.

"That." She frowned. "Where's Ambrose? And why does it smell like someone murdered Count Chocula in here?" She asked, raising the back of her hand to her nose as she winced at the smell.

"Gone, and long story." I said quickly as I looked across the lake to where the three girls stood anxiously watching. "I promise to explain everything if we don't die." I said with a sideways glance as I waved my arms, motioning for the teens to join us on this side of the cavern. "But this place feels like it's about to come down around us, so I'm guessing we should make like a hockey stick and leave."

"Not back that way." Raegan shook her head, guessing my plan for exit.

"Why not?" I paused, turning to her. "If we can get to the maze, we might have a chance." I said hopefully.

"The Pharoo'zah." She answered, looking over her shoulder. "Well, I think it was the Pharoo'zah. It was dark. All I saw were teeth."

"Shit." I swore.

"Yeah." She agreed.

"Okay, new plan." I said, clapping my hands and pointing back to the direction from which Max and I had just come. "Everybody back into the evil lair!"

Running across the stones, we met the girls near the lake's middle and I motioned for them to turn around. Slowing to a confused halt, the last in line slammed into her friends and sent the first girl tumbling into the lake.

My heart leapt into my throat as the teen disappeared beneath the surface, only to emerge a second later frantically slapping at the water as she clawed at the rocks and pulled herself from the murky depths.

"You okay?" I asked, looking to the lake. She nodded an embarrassed yes and moved back to the safety of her friends.

"Head back." I instructed, pointing past them. "That way is blocked." I explained, flickering another glance to the water. The nymphs were gone, or at the very least had no interest in being anywhere near our ragtag little group.

Following my gesture the girls turned in step and rushed back towards the beach. Leaping onto the sand, I ushered them all back into the tiled room, stopping Raegan just past the entrance as Max roughly deposited Viviane onto the nearest bed.

"What in the hell is happening to this place?" I asked quietly.

"I'm not sure." She admitted, her eyes searching the room. "But I think the magic that was keeping this pocket of Fae space open is fading. Fast."

"Meaning?" I asked, not liking the sound of that.

"Meaning everything not of our world is getting pulled back into its own." She added as another strong tremor shook the room.

"Okay." I said, following her fully into the room. "So what happens to us?" I asked as her eyes darted around the now cluttered chamber. Something large roared in the distance, its guttural screams echoing weirdly throughout the small room, as if one voice was coming from several mouths at the same time.

"Bad things." Max said as she pushed past me. Grabbing the top of the entry way's frame, she swung her body partially out of the room as she scanned the darkness for the source of the noise.

"Ronnie?" I prodded, ignoring Max's answer and praying that she wasn't right.

"Everything of the Fae realm, returns there." Raegan repeated. "Everything not born of this place…"

"Gets buried alive?" I supplied as more dust and several small stones rained down upon us.

"If we're extremely lucky." She answered sarcastically.

"Awesome." I sighed. "Any ideas on how we can avoid that?"

Nodding her head in quick determination, Raegan looked around the room and motioned to the girls. "You three. Look around for anything that seems out of place. Move the beds and the screens and search the alcoves; there has to be another way out of here." Turning to the doorway, she pointed to the hulking security guard. "Max, you and John take the walls. Focus on tiles, hooks, rocks, anything that might activate a secret door or passage way. I'll grab Ambrose's notes, maybe there's something in there."

Splitting off, we followed her orders without question. The girls, still maintaining their own small group ran to the nearest alcove as Max and I started slapping spastically at the walls of the room. Where I found only cold tile and hard stone, Max was leaving a series of fresh cracks and broken marble in her wake.

"Um, hey. Red haired lady?" One of the girls called to Raegan. "I think we found something." With the book that she had been flipping through still in hand, Raegan moved to the girls, her eyes flashing to a large object hidden beneath a bed sheet. Lifting the edge, she snapped her head to me and cried out in excitement.

"John! Here! Look at this!" She exclaimed as she ripped the protective covering off the object. My hands stinging from the beating that I had been giving the wall, I broke off from my own task and joined them at a far alcove.

Silver metal carved with delicate runes framed a large antique mirror. Full length in size, it was big enough that even Max would have been able to see most of her reflection, if she was careful not to flex.

"A mirror." I said unenthusiastically. "We're saved." With a dry look, Raegan ignored my sarcasm as she glanced over to giantess as she slowly approached, her head bent in curiosity.

"Max did we ever find the mirror the Doppelganger was using to enter the school?" She asked, focusing her attention back on the silvery frame as she carefully traced an oddly carved rune with her finger.

"Never really had time to look." She admitted with an apologetic shrug.

"Look at the writing on the frame." Raegan instructed, her fingers brushing over the smooth glass. "This has to be Fae made." She whispered in awe before snapping her eyes to mine. "If this is the same mirror that the doppelganger was using, it might still be linked to the one inside the school."

"Yeah, but if that thing is some kind of evil fairy portal, how do we know what's waiting on the other side?" Max asked, stepping closer to the large mirror.

There was a loud grinding of stone as a section of the domed ceiling above us broke free and fell with a loud crunch, completely crushing one of the empty beds several alcoves down.

"We're running pretty low on options." I pointed out.

Nodding in quick agreement, Raegan held her breath and reached out, thrusting her hands into the center of the mirror. Her fingers curled as they connected with the reflective surface but didn't push through.

"Damn it." She swore under her breath. Grabbing the side of the mirror she looked behind it before frantically searching the runes. "There has to be a trigger. A button, a word or some sort of a switch." She insisted as she danced before the glass.

"Maybe you just have to-" I extended my hand to steady the mirror as it rocked beneath her searching. The moment I made contact with the silvery frame the carved runes began to glow with a soft, pulsing green light. "Whoa." I exhaled as the center of the portal came to life.

Placing her finger on the glass once more, the mirrored surface rippled like water under Raegan's delicate touch. Grinning in understanding she turned to me, her eyes brimmed with joy.

"Let go." She instructed, and as I did the glowing runes faded and the portal went still.

Tapping her finger over the now solid glass, she grasped the frame in the spot that I where my hand had been and frowned as the mirror failed to respond.

"Touch it again." She ordered.

Nervously I placed a single finger on the very edge of the mirror's silver frame, and once more the writing etched upon it began to faintly glow.

"Shit." Raegan cursed again.

"What?" I asked. Startled by her continued swearing I withdrew my finger and the green light slowly faded from the mirror's edge.

"This place is dying." She answered with an angry sigh. "So the mirror won't stay active unless it's being powered by magic."

"So?" I scoffed, not understanding her frustration. "I'll hold it open, and you guys jump through. When you're on the other side I'll..." My words died in my throat as I realized that I wouldn't be able to keep the device active and walk through at the same time.

"Well shit." I griped, stealing her words.

"There's got to be another way out." Reagan frowned. Looking around the room she chewed her lip in conflicted thought as she darted her eyes to me.

"I'm not seeing one. Are you?" I asked, gently touching her arm.

"We don't even know if it is safe." She argued.

Max moved closer and nodded. "So let's find out." She offered, dropping her gaze expectantly to me. "J.T?"

Grabbing the side of the mirror, I could feel the hum of magic as the portal began to brightly shine. Ducking her head Maxine stepped through the shimmering glass without hesitation, passing through its center as easily as if she were walking through an open doorway and vanishing in the blink of an eye.

The moment she entered the mirror, the giantess' bowed head broke the surface and she stepped back out, a pleased look beaming across her features.

"Storage closet at the back of the library." She said proudly. "It was covered with a tarp and facing the wall, which is probably why nobody saw it." She grinned. "Almost broke the damn thing when I stepped through, but I propped it up good and steady. We should be able to walk right through."

"Line up girls." I ordered, dropping my grip on the frame as I gestured to the scared teenagers.

"John, wait." Raegan said imploring, but a fierce tremor shot through the room, and water began to trickle in through the entrance, pooling at our feet.

The lake was rising.

"We don't have time to argue." I said angrily. "Get them through, and get to safety. I'll think of something." I promised, offering a brave smile. "I always do, right?"

Raegan said nothing, but turned away from me, hiding her face.

"Max?" I asked, looking to the large woman as I grabbed the side of the mirror with both hands, bringing it back to life.

Nodding in understanding she motioned for the girls to come

closer, and as they did she guided them one at a time, gently pushing them through the now active mirror.

"You going to be okay?" She asked as the last of the students disappeared from sight.

"I've got a few tricks up my sleeve." I said gruffly, hoping that she couldn't tell that I was bluffing.

Brightening considerably at that, Max moved to the bed and hoisted the still unconscious Viviane as if she weighed nothing at all and tossed her into the portal with far less care than she probably should have.

As if objecting to the girl's hasty departure, the mirror flickered brightly, and the lights that ignited the runes began to dim.

"I think my batteries are starting to run out." I grunted, holding onto the frame even tighter in hopes that a stronger grip would some-how increase its power. "You better hurry up."

"John." Raegan said softly, her eyes wet as she turned back to me.

"Stop." I said with a forced laugh. "Do you think that the boys would allow me to be crushed, or killed or eaten by monsters?" I grinned, trying to push the thought of their sudden disappearance out of my mind. If the magic of the place was leaving, it would make sense that they would be the first to go. They hadn't abandoned me; they were kicked out. "They have plans for me, remember?"

"I'm not leaving you." She asserted. Stubbornly crossing her arms as she wiped her eye on the fabric of her shoulder she planted her feet firmly in a cementing of her resolve.

"I know." I confessed. "Max?"

Wrapping her arms around me in an awkward, but surprisingly soft hug, Maxine kissed the top of my head and laughed.

"Try to make it out alive, okay?" She requested.

"I will." I lied.

With a sad grin, the kindly amazon shook her head in a pained gesture of defeat. "You better." She chuckled. "Because if you don't, she's going to friggin' kill me."

Grabbing my sister roughly by the shoulders, Max tossed Raegan through the flickering portal before the stubborn redhead had time to react and quickly dove through the mirror behind her. Releasing my grip on the frame I let out a tired breath and shook my hands, wringing my fingers as they suddenly began to ache.

I felt literally drained.

"Okay Johnny." I said to myself as I breathed in deeply, trying in vain to find my second wind. "There's gotta be another way out, right?" I asked, looking around the room in the foolish hope that some magical doorway would appear and that I would be miraculously rescued.

When no salvation came, I looked back to the mirror with a feeling of deepening dread and frowned.

"Maybe if I hold onto it, like this, and step through," I said positioning my hand at an odd angle. "I'll just get Skywalkered." I deluded myself, trying to sound chipper. I knew it was my only real option, but how do you go about deciding which limb you want to have chopped off.

"Screw it." I sighed, grabbing onto the mirror's edge. "Maybe I'll wind up with a cool robot hand, with like lasers and I shit." Bracing myself, I waited for the portal to flicker to life.

But it didn't.

Sputtering softly, the runes barely even glimmered before going completely dark. Shaking my hands I took a determined breath and gripped it once again, concentrating on the mirror with all of my might, but there was no reaction.

"Maaaaaan." I lamented in a whining voice as the room began to shake.

A large rock about the size of my fist broke free from the ceiling and fell beside me, slowing in the air as it tumbled before stopping altogether. Hovering inches from my face, it hung there, suspended by nothing.

"What the?" I blinked in confusion as I narrowed my eyes and examined the rock. A trail of dust and debris still clung to it like the tail of a passing comet, marking its halted journey to the floor.

"So brave." A woman's voice cooed from behind me.

"So alone." A deeper voice added in amused tones.

The world slowed for a second time as tendrils of creeping dread slithered over my skin. I didn't need to see the source behind the statements to know that that I was dealing with the strange Quickling duo that we had encountered in the garden.

"Um. Hi?" I said uncertainly as I turned to face them.

If the pocket of Fae space was truly collapsing and all things fairy were being pulled back into their realm, nobody had bothered to tell the Quicklings. Still clad in the shocking blue Victorian garb that they had been wearing when we first met, the odd couple hovered in the doorway, blocking any hope I had of escaping from the room.

Although they were standing eerily still, the water at their feet shimmered and twitched like droplets dancing over the surface of a blaring speaker. Stalking forward with the slow, purposeful gait of a prowling cat, the woman's eyes began to crackle as bolts of blue lightning blazed across her unstable gaze, which was now locked upon me.

"We know now." She said, each word in perfect sync with the hypnotic sway of her hips as she moved closer.

"Um, we know what?" I swallowed hard.

"It is not kin." She answered in a throaty whisper as her hands clenched and unclenched at her sides.

"Or cousin." The male added helpfully from his place at the doorway. Unlike his sister, he seemed to be entertained by the whole situation, the smile at his lips brimming with mischief and joy.

"Or cousin." She echoed sharply, stopping well within the boundaries of whatever personal space I may have wanted to keep.

Fergus. I realized. If the black little bastard had really announced my condition to the entire realm of Fae, it made sense that those closest to the broadcast would have heard the news first.

"And if not cousin?" The male asked, prodding his sister. It might have been my imagination, or merely the slightest of involuntary twitches, but in saying that I could have sworn that the Quickling ended his words with a reassuring wink in my direction.

"Then it lied." She answered, the startling blue of her eye flashing with homicidal rage. Stretching out her slender hand, the unstable Fae reached for my throat and smiled, her lips parting in cruel anticipation.

"Did it?" Her brother asked, leaning against the door frame as he examined his finger nails in a bored fashion.

The female stopped and blinked before pulling back just far enough to turn her head inquisitively to the other Quickling.

"Didn't it?" She asked, her fury now replaced by the uncertainty of her question.

"Does it matter?" He asked, looking up from his hand with the question.

Clenching the hand still poised at my throat into a small fist, she pouted but turned her attention fully to him. "But it lied." She asserted.

"*We* lie." He grinned with a chiding cluck of his tongue.

The act of murdering me in cold blood apparently forgotten, the woman brought her hands to her face and covered her mouth in an impish giggle. "We do lie." She agreed.

"Everybody lies." I said, forcing a nervous laugh. "Am I right?"

The female Quickling snapped her attention back to me so quickly, I'm not even sure that I saw her move. One moment she was laughing with her brother, the next, her forehead was pressed against mine as she stared into my eyes with psychotic intensity.

"Oh, it trembles." She drooled. Like a wolf with a cornered deer, her body was tense with anticipation as her every predatory movement begged for me to run.

I did not.

"As does this place." The male pointed out as he examined a suspended rock with disinterest, rubbing the dirt between his fingers as he did.

Lowering from her tip toes, the woman backed away, her bottom lip jutting out in disappointment as she spun on her heel, turning to face her brother. "We liked this place." She whined.

He gave her a patient smile and brushed a strand of white-blonde hair from her face. "There will be others." He promised as she closed her eyes and purred beneath his touch. Slowly opening them, she leaned heavily into her companion and looked back to me in obvious annoyance.

"And the liar?" She asked moodily.

"Hmmm." He hummed his response. Twitching his head in surprise, his eyes widened in time with his growing smile as he pushed past her, and carefully approached. Stumbling with the sudden lack of support the female Quickling stared at her counterpart in disbelief, a brief flash of concern darkening her brow.

"Brother?" She asked uneasily as she approached from the side, her focus split between the two of us.

"Sister?" He responded, his electric blue eyes searching my face.

"What do we see?" She asked, her voice quiet, yet quivering with anticipation.

"We see fun." He promised.

She clapped her hands excitedly, the sound causing my pulse to race and my knees to go weak, but I didn't dare to move. "Oh, we like fun!" She squealed hopping in place.

I didn't like the sound of that, at all.

Fun to them could be a silly prank, a dirty joke, or simply pulling off my arms before I could move. While I realized that when I was around them, I was somehow in sync and able to move at their natural pace, I had no doubt that if challenged that they would be infinitely quicker than me, as I had witnessed that incredible speed before.

So while I wasn't sure if they had a good side, due to the fact that they were both squirrelier than nut shit, I was going to do my absolute damnedest to get on it, and stay on it.

"I like fun too." I announced in a tiny, tiny voice. "Yaaay. Fun." I cheered, carefully waving my fist in the air in a show of solidarity.

Tilting their heads towards each other in perfect unison, they looked at me as if I were speaking in tongues before turning away from my panicky interruption.

"We could keep it." She suggested coyly.

He raised an eyebrow in amused disbelief. "Keep it?"

Grabbing her brother by the arm she jumped up and down in place like a child begging for a puppy. "It could be ours!" She tittered.

"Or." He waggled his eyebrows suggestively.

"Or?" She paused mid-bounce.

"We put it back."

At first she looked at him in confusion, but a slow wave of dawning comprehension washed over her and her eyes grew in wonder. "Put it back?"

His grin deepened, and upon seeing the confirmation to her question in his smile she gasped, bobbing in the air with the force of her surprise.

"There will be anger." She said with mock aghast.

"There will be trouble." He promised in a sing-song voice.

She brought her hands to her mouth, covering it briefly before pulling them away in scandal. "There will be chasing!"

"There will be fun." He countered, causing her to squeal in delight as she rapidly clapped her hands in a delighted fashion.

"Guys?" I asked, drawing their attention back to me. I was pretty sure that my fate had been decided favorably, and that I was no longer in danger of being disarmed, literally, but I was also too tired to tell them that I had no clue what they were talking about.

I doubt they would have understood me anyhow.

Flickering forward like a horror movie ghost, the female Fae paused in front of me and met my gaze. Bending slightly at the waist she clenched her hands into tight fists, her eyes twitching wildly as she tried to focus her words on me.

"It. Must. Go. Through." She said, as if under a great strain. Lifting a slender arm, she pointed to the mirror behind me and gritted her teeth through a tight smile.

Looking over my shoulder, I shook my head. "Yeah. Not happening." I explained, grabbing the frame in one hand. "Look." I instructed as the runes sputtered dimly before dying out. I tapped the glass with a fingernail to show that the portal was solid.

With an imploring look of pain, she turned to her brother who quickly approached.

"It must step through." He clarified, his voice as stressed as hers.

"No go Denim Dan." I shrugged, taking the few seconds that I probably had left to live to mock his wardrobe. "It's dead. No power. No juice. Batteries not included. Get it?" I asked grasping the mirror and releasing it in rapid succession.

With an exchange of puzzled looks the siblings rattled something between them so quickly, their voices merged into one high-pitched helium nightmare. Then, blurring past me like pale bolts of lightning, they materialized on each side of the mirror. Grasping their respective section of frame, the runes exploded with a bright green light a thousand times brighter than anything that I had managed.

"Go." The male ordered through clenched teeth, the effort of holding still that long causing him visible distress.

"Quickly." She urged, matching his discomfort.

They were helping me. Knowing that time was of the essence, and not one to look a gift Quickling in the crazy mouth, I rushed the mirror, pausing only long enough to offer them each a sincere bow of my head.

"Thank you." I said, unsure as to why they were helping me escape. They probably had a thousand reasons, each more bizarre than the next, and I doubt that I would ever truly understand...

...but something told me that it was more about the mischief my escape would cause, than any aid that their helping me would actually bring.

Holding my breath, I offered them one last appreciative nod of my head, and leapt forward into the portal.

Chapter Twenty-Three

Once, while chasing down a fleeing Redcap, I had thrown myself through a portal. Not a mirror, or magical doorway, but an honest-to-god, ripped right out of a sci-fi movie, shimmering-in-midair, portal.

And it was a nightmare.

After tumbling through an endless series of badly shaken lava lamps, I had landed in a pile of rotting trash at the bottom of a filth strewn alley and spent the next solid hour of my life puking my guts out. Ripped apart and reassembled a thousand times in a fraction of a second, it was easily one of the worst experiences of my adult life, and I swore that I'd never do it again.

This portal however, was nothing like that. Stepping through the doppelganger's mirror was literally as easy as walking through an open door. One second I'm in the collapsing pocket of Fae space fearing for my life, and the next, I'm slamming head first into Max's firm, yet still unmistakably feminine backside.

Standing protectively in front of the mirror in an effort to keep Raegan from trying to reenter, the muscular security guard let out a startled yelp as I goosed her quite forcefully with my face. Spinning in hasty response to our unplanned contact, her body tensed in anticipation of an attack, but quickly relaxed as I regained my footing.

"You made it!" She laughed happily, scooping me into a bone crushing bear hug that would have put most Kodiaks to shame. Dropping me to my feet, she watched in joy as the air rushed back into my now useless lungs; or it would have had Raegan not immediately rushed in, tackling me in a much smaller but in no way less enthusiastic version of the embrace.

"How?" She asked, her eyes overflowing with happiness as she searched my face.

"I had some help." I said truthfully.

"Seamus?" She asked in surprise.

"The Grady Twins." I said, still not believing it myself.

Raegan looked confused for a moment before a flash of sudden understanding lifted her eyebrows in astonishment. "The Quicklings?"

"Yeah." I confirmed.

"How? Why?" She asked.

I shrugged my shoulders. "I have absolutely no idea." I admitted with a tired laugh. Trying to keep up with the leprechauns had become a full time job, and they were mostly sane. Attempting to unravel the thought patterns of those two would be like trying to follow the flight path of a drunken bat. It might have only been a few steps from the Fae space to our world, but in those brief few seconds I had already given up on ever hoping to understand the motivation behind their help.

I was alive, and I was grateful, and that was enough for me.

Peering over the top of Raegan's head as she wrapped her arms around me in another constricting hug, I glanced around the room and tried to get my bearings in the faint light. The three girls were now hovering protectively over the body of a very pitiful looking Viviane, who lay upon the floor in a broken, twisted heap. They had no clue what she had done, and now a growing concern for their suddenly sick schoolmate brought them even closer together as one of them stroked her hair and looked to us expectantly.

The room smelled of musty books and stale ink. Wrinkling my

nose at the familiar but not exactly unpleasant smell, I scanned the cramped area as Raegan released me from her death grip and turned to Max.

"Where are we?" I asked, not recognizing the place.

"Storage room at the back of the library." Max answered. Flipping a switch at the wall, she brought an old yellowing light bulb weakly to life.

There was a soft plink of crystal from behind me, like two glasses meeting in a muffled toast. Turning back to the antique mirror I watched as a large, wicked looking fracture appeared and spread like a web of lightning down the front of its reflective surface, marring but not shattering the glass.

"The other mirror must have broken." Raegan explained with a sigh of relief. Nothing monstrous was going to be reaching through in a last ditch effort to fulfill its horror story obligations.

"How are the kids doing?" I asked, glancing from the cracked mirror to where the frightened looking teenagers stood guard over their fallen friend.

"They're a bit disoriented and confused, but no one seems to be hurt." She said under her breath as not to alert them to the conversation. "They have no idea that any real amount of time has passed. For them, it's only been a few hours." Her eyes fell as she sighed. "Plus, they keep asking about Viviane. It's breaking my heart."

Surrounded by her young, healthy, and extremely well rested classmates, Viviane looked like she had been chewed up and spit out by Death a dozen times over. Still comatose, her body was curled in sleep, with her wrists and feet bent at painful looking angles. Moaning in an agony that seemed to transcend her unconscious state, there was no way that I could feel anything but pity for her.

"She going to be okay?" I asked, the awareness that I was partially to blame for her current condition settling in.

Anger flashed behind Raegan's eyes, but it was quickly lost to the same compassion and remorse that I was feeling. "I'm not sure. I know nothing of the magic that was used to connect her to the latrodenzian, or even how you managed to sever it." She admitted, with a sideways glance to me. "But she seems to be degenerating rapidly. I'm guessing that her symptoms are much worse now than they were when she first put the bracelet on. I told you, that kind of magic comes with a horrible price."

"Anything we can do?" I asked guiltily.

Raegan shook her head. "No. They're awake now, but she's not. It's almost as if she's being thrown into the slumber that she had forced upon them.

"They're awake." I said, a single, joyous thought filling my heart. "Lydia." I grinned, rushing to the door.

Bursting out of the storage room and into the library, I navigated the area behind the service desk with renewed vigor, jumping over and sliding across the smooth countertop with practiced ease. Picking my way through the rows of bookshelves and reading tables, I hit the front doors like a charging rhino and exploded into the hallway.

And had absolutely no idea where I was.

Spinning in place I peered down both lengths of hall, completely lost. "It's the goddamn labyrinth all over again." I cursed under my breath.

Catching up rather quickly, Raegan stepped out of the library and pointed down the long hallway. "This way." She smirked, taking the lead. I looked back to the still open door as Max and the girls emerged, Viviane cradled once again in the gentle giant's arms.

"Go." Max nodded, noting my hesitation. "I got this." She assured me, gesturing back to the teenagers with a quick bob of her head.

Grinning widely, I nodded my thanks and took off after Raegan, the halls of the school blurring by in a series of quick turns and close-knit lockers. The nurse's office wasn't as far from the library as I had feared and we arrived before I even had a chance to lose my breath.

Throwing open the door, I was greeted by the sight of the nurse, McKenna, and Headmistress Merry standing at the bedside of my very confused, but very awake girlfriend. Sprinting the short distance, I crossed the room and slid to her side. Grabbing her face in both hands, I kissed her without thought or care as to who was watching.

Caught off guard by the sudden lip lock, Lydia melted into the kiss, but tapped me several times on the shoulder in an effort to redirect my attention to the rest of the room. Reluctantly pulling away, I searched her face, my eye focusing on hers as my heart felt ready to burst. "Are you okay?" I asked, my eyes growing warm. "How are you feeling?" I pushed, not giving her a chance to answer as I looked up at the nurse. "How long has she been awake? Is everything okay?"

Lydia smiled and weakly hugged my head to her chest.

"I'm fine." She soothed. "Just, tired."

I let her cradle me for a few greedy seconds before breaking the embrace and looking back to the nurse for confirmation. The woman kindly looked on, nodding her silent agreement.

"You look amazing." I promised Lydia as I refocused my attentions on her and lovingly stroked her cheek with one hand.

"You look like hell." She replied, smirking weakly. "Rough day at the office?" She teased.

"Well yeah." I laughed, wiping at my eye. "I mean, someone had to do all the work while you just laid in bed doing nothing."

Hugging me to her again, I felt the weakness in her arm suddenly strengthen as she pulled me closer and buried her nose in my hair. "Oh my god." She purred, her skin flushing warm against me. "You smell incredible."

The essence of Elven chocolate.

Wasted.

Every. Single. Drop.

Maaaaaaaann.

The door to the Nurse's Office exploded open with a loud bang, snapping me from my bout of perverted self-pity as Max kicked her way in, her arms still occupied by Viviane's lifeless body. The missing students followed closely on her heels like kittens too afraid to be far from their mother's side.

The nurse, seeing the obviously injured girl cradled by Max hurried from Lydia's side to meet them, directing the giantess and her cargo to an empty bed.

"What happened?" Headmistresses Merry asked in a panic as she too rushed over to the fallen girl.

Laying Viviane down with a careful motion infinitely more gentle than I would have expected after her unceremonious portal tossing, Max stepped away and shrugged as she looked down at the worrying school head. "I think she's supposed to be like this." She said, looking to me for support.

Standing slowly, I reluctantly pulled myself from Lydia's side, her hand lingering in mine as I stepped away. I could feel my temperature rising as I approached, and I focused my anger on the Headmistress.

Luckily, Raegan stepped in front of me, cutting me off en route as she spoke to the nurse, her eyes never leaving Merry for a second.

"She has an illness inherited from her father. It should be on file." She explained, slowly closing the gap between the head of the school and herself. "In the staff records."

Headmistress Merry took a step backwards, her eyes expanding in fear. Confused and confronted by my sister's rage, she had no place to run as Raegan coolly approached.

"Did you know?" She asked, her green eyes going cold.

"I beg your pardon?" The Headmistress stammered with nervous insult.

"Did. You. Know?" Raegan repeated, dangerously emphasizing each word.

Placing my hand on my sister's arm, I moved beside her, hoping to defuse the situation. With her anger putting mine to shame, I was able to reflect on the situation and take in the woman's response. My gut told me that Merry had no clue what was going on, but I knew that Ronnie needed to hear the words for herself.

I just hoped that she spoke them quickly.

"Know, what?" She asked, more to me than Raegan as she was no longer willing to meet my Keeper's furious gaze.

"That your boy Doctor Evil had himself a mini-me." I explained, motioning to the bed where Viviane now lay. The nurse danced around the girl in a flutter of activity, but I doubted that there was anything that she could do beyond make the poor kid comfortable.

Merry paled considerably, her eyes widening with the news as she lifted a hand to her mouth to hide her shock.

"Yeah. I didn't think so." I confirmed. Tugging gently on Raegan's arm, I gained her attention almost immediately and tried not to flinch beneath the remains of her still burning rage. "Hey, it's okay." I soothed. "She might be a scary old battle axe, but she's not a monster."

Still horrified by her newfound knowledge, Merry turned to the girl and whispered quietly to herself, no longer looking in our direction. "What did you do to her?" She asked, her voice fearful.

"Wasn't us." I shrugged, but she missed the gesture as she was now staring in horror at the twisted remains of the child that she had placed in our care.

"She's sick, like Ambrose." Raegan explained. The anger was gone from her eyes, but her voice was distant and still sharply edged with blame.

"But..." Headmistress Merry trailed, pointing to the girl with a shaking hand.

"They were using the other girls to keep her healthy." I answered before she could ask the question I knew she was forming. "That's why he was taking them, to keep her from becoming that."

Merry nodded in slow acceptance, her eyes unblinking as she stared at the bed. Turning to me, I was surprised to see tears welling as she spoke in a soft, worried voice. "What are you going to do with her?"

That was a really good question.

"Yeah, what are we going to do with her?" I asked, looking to Raegan for direction. "I mean I know that she's evil and delusional and kind of a psychotic bitch and all, but she's still just a kid." I pointed out.

Raegan's face fell as she considered the girl's fate. "She's still a danger, John. Even like this."

"To who?" I balked, not exactly sure why I was defending her. She kicked my sister, stole my girlfriend's memories and tried to kill us both, yet those things seemed a thousand miles away. All I could see was a bedridden, dying child.

Raegan turned to me and took my hand with a sad smile. "To all of us." She said patiently. "She was in their heads. In Max's head. In…" She didn't finish the thought but instead looked to Lydia who appeared to be as conflicted as I was.

"But she's a kid, Ronnie. A *sick* kid." I pointed out.

"And we'll see that she gets the best medical care possible." She agreed. "But with what she could know, what she could do-"

"Tartarus." McKenna said darkly, leaving her cousin's bed for the first time. Her icy blue eyes locked onto Viviane with a frigid loathing.

That blew me away, and I threw my arms up in defeat. "If you guys are telling me that Doctor Who is real and that we have a Tardis, I'm done. Out." I swore, crossing my hands in a strike motion in front of me.

"Fairy Alcatraz." Reagan supplied, throwing my old words back to me in an effort to hasten my understanding.

"Yeah, but she's not a fairy." I pointed out hesitantly. "Is she?"

My Keeper shook her head rapidly. "No, but she's involved with this world." She clarified. "They have special accommodations there for those among us who would be a risk on the outside."

"She'll be treated well there." McKenna said frostily. "Which is far better than she deserves." She added as if the girl's health and care were the last thing she wanted to provide.

They were mad, and they had every right to be, but I didn't want that anger to taint their decision, or influence mine. I slowly turned to one of the only people that I felt had an actual right to decide Viviane's fate, and put my faith in her answer.

"Lids?"

Lydia was still staring at the girl, her eyes flashing from anger to sadness as we spoke. There was no doubt that she had heard everything, and as much as it enraged her, her eyes softened as they met mine.

"It's for the best." She assured me. "It's not personal John, I promise."

I nodding, accepting her answer as law as I turned back to

McKenna and Raegan, my heart sinking as I considered the shitty hand the kid had been dealt.

"What of the school?" Headmistress spoke softly, reluctant to interrupt, but desperate in her need to know the institute's destiny. The three students had been listening in as well, and were distancing themselves from Viviane upon learning that she was the shadowy figure behind their recent abductions.

"The school will remain open." Raegan announced as both student and staff alike breathed in relief. "But, there will be a *full* investigation." She continued, her voice sharpening in warning as she spoke. "And I promise that it will end poorly for anyone we find that has had any involvement."

"Full school sweep too." Max agreed, moving to Raegan's side and addressing Merry directly. "Top to bottom. Every room, every office, and every mirror. No exceptions."

Headmistress Merry seemed taken aback by the directive, but she said nothing. Instead she nodded her silent acquiescence to the heavily muscled security guard.

"But first." The tone of command left Raegan's voice as she looked to the girls. "We should probably call your parents." She said with a smile.

The tallest girl, a pretty blonde that could have easily been McKenna's younger clone looked suddenly alarmed as her hand shot into the air, requesting permission to speak. "Are we in trouble?" She asked, the question echoing through the emphatic nodding of her friends.

"No sweety, you've just been asleep for a very long time." Raegan gently explained.

Headmistress Merry stepped forward, clearing her throat.

"I'll take care of it." She announced, finally meeting my Keeper's eye. "You Agents have done more than enough." She explained, stressing the title with a newfound respect. "This school...I owe you a debt of gratitude that can never be repaid."

McKenna and Raegan exchanged looks of pleasant surprise before nodding their silent thanks.

"The rest of you should come with us back to the Agency as well, just to be safe." Raegan proclaimed, drawing nervous, questioning looks from the majority of the room. "There were artifacts and magics involved here that we have little to no working knowledge of." She explained. "I'd feel a lot better if every single one of you was given a clean bill of health."

"I can get the proper paperwork in order." Max offered. "Arrange transportation, call parents and get the proper permissions and what not."

"Agent Wallace might be able to assist you with that." Raegan suggested, looking to McKenna. "Max was under the latrodenzian's effects as well. I want you with her just in case there's an aftershock or a side effect that we're unaware of."

Nodding in agreement McKenna turned her eyes to Lydia. "You as well." She said, leaving no room for argument. "I'm worried." She said, the normal layer of frost off her voice softening with concern. "While I'm not as well versed as Agent Connelly in how these things work, you seem to have been more adversely affected than the others."

Lydia weakly agreed as McKenna approached and put her hand on her shoulder. "If anything, we should have your head examined thoroughly, given your recent taste in men." She whispered, glancing to me teasingly.

Oh yeah. I had forgotten about that.

Approaching the opposite side of Lydia's bed, I smiled sheepishly as I knelt beside her. "Well, no more sneaking around at least." I said, blushing slightly. "And don't worry. I'll be there every step of the way." I assured her, kissing her forehead lightly.

"I'm glad you agree." Raegan said, joining us at the bed. "Because you're getting a full physical as well."

"Me?" I balked.

"Yes you." She said sternly. "You were exposed to more magic than every one of us combined. And while you were seemingly insusceptible to the bracelet's effects, you were still wearing it."

"Yeah, but I'm immune to this stuff, remember?" I scoffed.

Raegan darkened considerably as she crossed her arms angrily under her chest. "No, seriously Ronnie – I'm fine. The one ring doesn't affect me at all. There was no connection to the rest of them. No magic, no memories-"

"I felt you." Lydia said quietly, her voice barely a whisper.

"What?" I asked as I turned to her in startled surprise.

"It was like a dream, but I think I was there. With you." She continued weakly. "I can't explain it, but I knew that you were coming for me."

I shook my head in disbelief and looked to Raegan for some sort of an explanation. "I thought they were in stasis? No brain activity, no dreams, no nothing?" I accused.

"She should have been." Raegan said apologetically before hardening in her stance. "Which is why you're both getting the all clear before you even think about coming back to work."

Oh gods, the paperwork.

If there was one thing the Agency truly loved, it was mountains of mind-numbing paperwork. There was no hippy-dippy "go green" incentive for us. Hell, even the briefest encounter or verified Fae sighting was enough to wipe out an entire rainforest of trees. This was going to be...

"Hmmm." I considered, taking Lydia's hand. "You know, maybe a few days stuck in our own private quarantine isn't that bad of an idea." I said, kissing it gently. "We can think of it like a day spa with painful, probably invasive testing."

Lydia offered a tired smile for my lame attempt at humor, but there was something else lingering behind her eyes. Something almost sad.

Pushing that new fear to the back of my mind and chalking it up to exhaustion, I looked to Raegan as another thought struck me. "Someone should probably let Assistant Director Blair know that everything is back to, well, whatever passes for normal around here." I suggested. "You know, before she nukes this place from orbit and all."

Taking the incentive, McKenna pulled her cellphone from her

jacket pocket. "Agreed." She said as she snapped her fingers to Max. "I take it that you have a complete list of contacts in your office?"

Max shrugged. "Yeah, of course."

"Good. Let's go." The tall blonde said crisply. Moving to the doorway, she slowed as Max stepped through in front of her, pausing briefly as she turned her attention back to me. "Take care of her." She said almost sweetly.

"I will." I replied, surprised by the rare show of emotion.

"Or else." She added, her eyes flashing with the threat as she exited the room.

Yawning loudly, Lydia gave a tired, but rather impressive stretch and snuggled into the pillow that she was resting on. Kissing her forehead lightly I released her hand and stepped away, watching as her chest began to rise and fall with the quick onset of exhausted sleep.

Moving to Raegan's side, we watched the nurse as she busied herself at Viviane's bed, unsure as to what more she could do for the girl as she covered her with a blanket.

"I'll make sure she gets the best care." Ronnie said quietly as she flickered her gaze back to my sleeping girlfriend.

"I know." I assured her. "But…what do you think is going on with her?" I asked nervously.

Raegan took my hand and rubbed my arm in a soothing fashion. "We won't know until we get her home." She sighed. "But I promise, she's going to be fine."

"Yeah, unless the Doctor's new assistant turns out to be a murderous dragon, or blood-crazed midget ogre." I forced a chuckle, but I was only really half joking.

"Climate's too warm for dragons." She teased, laughing lightly as I looked to her in alarm.

"You suck." I chuckled, realizing the jest.

"Still getting bored with the job?" Raegan asked, turning to fully face me.

"I was actually thinking that we might need to dial it down a notch or two." I confessed. "I'm getting too old for this shit." I added gruffly.

"You did good John." Raegan beamed, and I could see the pride in her eyes which just made everything awkward.

"Good?" I scoffed, using humor as a defense against the discomfort her compliment brought. "Everything we've gone through and all you can say is "good"?" I asked, trying to sound offended. "There better be promotions and medals after all of this shit. And not just cake this time – I'm feeling….parade." I said, splaying my hands in front of me in a dramatic fashion.

"I'm serious." She laughed, punching me in the arm. "You've come a long way, I'm proud of you."

Proud of me.

Her words echoed through me and suddenly I wanted to tell her everything; my run in with Somnus, how they boys saved me from Fenrus, the threat of the Collector; the works. But I was exhausted and we were both overwhelmed. Ronnie looked as if she was finally relaxing, and I knew that if spilled my guts she would burn herself out with worry, so I held my tongue.

It could wait.

"And we've got a long drive." I responded, fishing the keys to our car out of my pocket and dangling them out to her.

"Really?" She blinked in honest surprise. "You're giving up the keys?"

I waved a dismissing hand. "I'm exhausted and you drive like a zillion times faster than I do." I yawned. "Plus, I figure the sooner we get home, the sooner I get my ticker-tape and substantial cash reward for saving the day, again." I stressed the last word, earning me another playful punch to the arm.

"So you're just in it for the money eh?" She grinned, turning to the door.

I looked over my shoulder to where Lydia lay sleeping. The nurse was tucking a blanket around her and gently adjusting her pillow.

She was beautiful, she was safe, and she was mine.

"And the fame." I said half-heartedly, slowly moving to the door but reluctant to turn away. "Don't forget the fame."

I felt Raegan slip her hand in mine as she guided me to the exit.

"That's the most important part, right?" She asked squeezing my hand lightly.

"Well yeah. You think I'm doing all of this just because I'm a nice guy?" I asked, facing her as we stepped out of the nurse's office, and closed the door behind us. "C'mon Ronnie, you know me better than that." I scoffed.

Like I said, I never considered myself a hero.